REVELATION

THE SAGA OF VENOM AND FLAME

REVELATION

VICTOR ACQUISTA

LIVONIA, MICHIGAN

Edited by Tori Ladd
Proofread by Samantha Stenzel

REVELATION

Published by BHC Press

Library of Congress Control Number: 2020937632

ISBN: 978-1-64397-230-5 (Hardcover)
ISBN: 978-1-64397-231-2 (Softcover)
ISBN: 978-1-64397-232-9 (Ebook)

For information, write:
BHC Press
885 Penniman #5505
Plymouth, MI 48170

Visit the publisher:
www.bhcpress.com

To all who illuminate with the light of truth

REVELATION

PART ONE

FANGS

1

"Thank you, Servant Van Duyn for an illuminating presentation. Do any of the Brothers have questions?" A single hand raised, waiting to be acknowledged. "Servant Freeman, you may speak."

"Thank you, Consular. Brother Van Duyn, when will this government program be ready for deployment?"

"Our best estimates are four to six months."

"If there are no further questions, our final presentation is from Servant Li." Consular Rothschild paused to scan each of the twelve family heads. In the absence of questions, he continued. "You may proceed."

Li despised the chairman. His adherence to this self-gratifying meeting protocol, Luciferian service, and banal presentations strained Kenseiko's patience. Van Duyn's secret mind-control black op offered little advance to what they already employed. *He's a fool! They're both fools!*

"Thank you, Consular!" Li looked at his two video screens showing the other twelve family heads. He wanted to see their expressions as he ran through the presentation.

"This is drone footage of a remote village in New Guinea taken six months ago. Population estimated at 124 inhabitants." Unremarkable scenes of active villagers followed. Men, women, and children went about their routines. Evident poverty and rudimentary technology stood out as the only notable features.

"This is the same village one month ago."

As the gasps and somewhat shocked faces of the others flashed across his screens, Li felt a sense of pleasure. The footage revealed only a single dark-skinned woman running from body to bloody body. There was no sound, but her silent screams of anguish didn't require audio. Dogs licked at puddles of blood; chickens and crows sampled the carrion, ambivalent to the death surrounding them and evidently unaffected. Li gave the members a chance to absorb the scene before continuing.

"The pathogen is a modified Hendra virus, one of several agents causing viral hemorrhagic fevers or VHFs. Our engineering significantly enhanced the pathogenicity and eliminated the animal vector." The drone zoomed onto a horse meandering about a feeding trough. "Typically, this type of VHF is spread by contact with horses. As you can see, this animal is unaffected. Our agent solely infects humans, including children and adults."

Recorded images of pigs, cats, and rats complemented additional footage of the dogs and birds previously shown. Gruesome, bloody pictures of children, men, and women flashed—the same villagers viewed previously. Some, recognizable by the same bright clothing worn months earlier, now lay bloodied and lifeless.

Li continued his narration as the drone revealed three different corpses, all showing obviously pregnant women. The single living woman, face obscured by a rag, centered into the recording as the drone panned down and showed a small baby bump. "You are no doubt wondering about this single survivor." He watched as the other family heads leaned in to study the woman.

The scene shifted to a larger village, perhaps a small city. There were cars, power lines, and evidence of more development. A small building nestled among several clustered shops came into focus. A sign written in a foreign language filled the screen. "For those of you who are not familiar with Hiri Motu, the sign reads 'Health Clinic.' Outreach workers from our clinic had traveled to the survivor's village to do a pregnancy check and to administer a prenatal shot. The deceased pregnant villagers you previously viewed were too far along in their terms to be vaccinated. We must give our injection in the latter part of the first trimester."

The drone footage returned to the woman. "The prenatal shot contains a truly elegant strand of DNA that incorporates into the fetal genome; it is combined with an antiserum to the VHF we deployed. Insertion into the fetus is within twenty-four hours. The antiserum gives temporary immunity to the modified Hendra virus. I won't bore you with all the details, but as you can see," the drone panned back, "the agent is 100 percent lethal unless antiserum neutralizes it. What you can't see," the drone zoomed in to the woman's abdomen, bulged by the baby beneath her ragged clothes, "is the effect upon the fetus."

Consular Rothschild interrupted. "A better human being."

"I like to think so." Li hid his annoyance at the chairman's comment. "I have previously presented on Advanced Bionics' successful genetic reprogramming efforts. This infant will have all the latest improvements. Noteworthy about this brief presentation is that it is our first trial combining these two different research efforts. It represents an important step forward in achieving the master plan." The video darkened, leaving Li's stoic face filling the screens for all the remaining family members to look at.

Rothschild spoke. "Servant Li, thank you for another excellent update. We are ever closer." Applause followed. "Do any Brothers have questions?" He paused as two hands raised. "Servant DuPont, you first, then Servant Freeman."

"Thank you, Consular, and thank you, Brother Li. How was the agent deployed?"

"We introduced the targeted biologic into the water supply, the village's only well."

DuPont followed up. "That is effective if there is a single source and no methods of filtering or decontamination. That would be a difficult method to use for most municipal water systems."

"Agreed. That is why we are developing a microdroplet dispersion system that can seed the clouds." Li smiled. "That method would be particularly lethal during monsoon season." Impressed murmurs of agreement followed.

"Servant Freeman, your question?"

"Thank you, Brother Li, for your exemplary work. What about the vaccine that you administered? Have you concluded trials?"

"Trials are ongoing, but we are confident in the results."

The chairman resumed. "As there are no further questions, I remind you that our next meeting will be together in fellowship under the Hill. I ask Servant Li to bind us in prayer."

"Thank you, Consular Rothschild. Prior to the blessing, I almost forgot... next meeting I am planning a surprise."

"All rise." The thirteen men stood, raised their left hands, and placed them over their hearts.

Li spoke. "We, the chosen, pledge to serve the light Lucifer has brought to us..."

"To illuminate," they said in unison and touched their foreheads.

Li continued. "May he guide us..."—they each touched their left shoulders—"and bless us..."—they touched their right shoulders—"until his light shines upon all." All thirteen rested their hands back upon their hearts.

In unison they recited, "May the light shine upon us in glory."

2

"Are you listening to this?" Bryson sat on the clay floor. Sunlight shone through the hogan's central opening.

Serena eased down from her tortuous asana and sat next to him. Sweat glistened on her toned body. "I usually block everything out when I'm focused on my yoga. What's up?"

He raised the volume. "There are food riots in Sudan. Listen. It's bad, and they're saying it's getting worse."

Scenes flashed. "It's horrible, Bry! People are starving." Anger replaced the calm from moments before as graphic pictures of violence highlighted the magnitude of suffering.

The CNN foreign correspondent continued his report; images of police in full riot gear, Molotov cocktails, demonstrators clashing with authorities flashed in rapid succession. *"The government has declared a state of emergency and is appealing to the United Nations for assistance. A 7 p.m. curfew has been announced."*

They looked at each other with grim realization. Serena voiced what they both were thinking. "It's just the beginning."

"It's one of the tactics Uncle Pete mentioned as possibilities. I think you're right; it is just the beginning. People fight and kill one another, and the population shrinks. A militarized government has free reign to do anything it pleases. Scary!"

"What are we going to do, Bry? I'm so fed up with waiting to hear about the next disaster." As frustration mounted, her sound-sight accentuated. Bursts of red predominated.

Bryson felt it. "Calm down, PTG." Gentle neck massages loosened the tension.

Serena composed herself. "I'm a Candelaria. What good is all the Circle training if I don't know what to do with it? I'm supposed to be a Lightbringer, to combat falsehood with truth. At the rate I'm going, there won't be anyone left to save."

Since they had returned from Peru two months ago, Bryson witnessed a growing pessimism. "We've had this discussion a dozen times, Serena. I know you're frustrated, but negativity solves nothing. Speaking of circles, that's what we're doing—going round and round and getting nowhere. BB's supposed to arrive in Chicago next week. We should drive out there. It will be good for you, for both of us."

"You're right. At least it's something. Who knows, maybe Gurumarra has been communicating with Ooljee. I desperately need guidance, Bry."

"I'm looking forward to meeting Beangagarrie. It will be good to see Claus and Uncle Pete too." He stood up.

But the CNN reporter's closing comments neutralized Bryson's attempts to calm Serena. *"Official estimates are twelve thousand dead. Unofficial counts place that number at five to six times official estimates and growing daily… This is Jonathan Skiles for CNN."*

They looked at each other, sharing the same unspoken thoughts: *How many more dead? How much more bloodshed? How many more lives lost?*

3

At times, Serena grew dark and sullen. She complained about centuries of mind control and manipulation, lies and distortions, the rich and powerful exploiting the masses. Bryson let her rant. After purging, during moments when calm returned to his travel companion, Serena showed excitement about reconnecting with BB and taking steps toward combatting the Illuminati agenda of establishing a New World Order.

They both had strange dreams. Bryson relived his dream hallucinations from when he was in a coma following his snakebite. Serena dreamt about dark caves with unnamed, dark creatures. Bryson tried his best to keep an upbeat attitude. They got all talked out and drove long stretches in silence. The endless flat landscapes in the heartland provided no scenic distractions; the miles ground on.

NPR updated them on the crisis in Sudan and other world events. The Sudanese government had shut down internet access. Isolated reports from humanitarian relief workers put the death toll at over 230,000… Climate scientists projected the warmest year on record to date… The World Health Organization had discovered a new strain of Viral Hemorrhagic Fever…

At a rest stop near Topeka, they broke to freshen up. A disheveled man sat on a curb with a sign and a plastic drink cup containing a few bills and coins. "DISABLED VET. HUNGRY. CAN YOU HELP?"

Bryson reached for his wallet and winced as Serena gripped his arm.

"No!" She tightened her grip.

"What do you mean, 'No'? What's wrong with you?"

"He's lying. I see the deceit. Don't ask me how. I just know it."

"What, he's not hungry?"

"He's not a vet, and he's not disabled."

The man looked on, his eyes hollow in defeat.

"So, what? The guy's down on his luck, and twenty bucks isn't going to break the bank." He withdrew two twenties and put them in the cup. "Hey, buddy, I hope this helps." As Bryson bent forward, body odor assaulted his nose.

The nameless man wiped a tear with a grimy shirt sleeve. "Thank you… Thank you!"

"What's wrong with you, Serena? Are you so focused on the big picture that you forget about the little guy? One small, good deed at a time, and we build a better world." Her stubby nails had broken his skin. He rubbed his arm leaving a smear of blood.

"It's just…just that there are lies everywhere, Bry. I can't take it anymore. Everyone's lying, everything screams lies at me." She sobbed. "At the hogan, I'm protected. It's like I'm in a cocoon. But out here, in the real world, I see it all so clearly. It's all around me, and it's all a fat, gigantic lie."

Bryson turned toward her and locked eyes. "Don't you also see that he's a victim, just like everyone else? If lying is what you need to do to survive, that's what it comes down to. We're all dancing to the piper's tune, but most people don't even know it."

"You're right, Bry. I don't know what came over me." She fetched a bill from her belt wallet, jumped over to the panhandler, and put it in his cup. "Sorry!"

They bought a few snacks and exited. By then, the man had left his spot on the curb. Serena hugged Bryson. "Thanks for reminding me. I feel better."

Damiaan Van Duyn looked out his office window at the expansive view of Manhattan and rubbed his hands. *So many people. Too many! I should call Li and congratulate him.*

Half a world away, Dr. Li's private phone rang. "Kenseiko, I am calling to congratulate you…actually, both of us."

"Damiaan? It's 2:30 in the morning in Singapore."

"Right… Sorry, but this is worth waking up to. We sold our first order of the 24-K11s. The Sudanese Government has purchased five hundred units. I thought you would like to know. All the families should celebrate. I hope your soldiers are ready."

"I am aware. You may remember that your system helps to outfit the soldiers that we supply. Sudan is paying handsomely. The depot in the Himalayas will furnish, and we'll restock. You should ship the 24-K11s hardware there. I planned to call you later to coordinate."

"I see you already have the good news. Sorry to disturb you, Kenseiko. I'm sure the outfitted soldiers will be more than up to the task. Live in the light, Brother."

The connection clicked. *Li sounded annoyed. He is a difficult man who thinks the world revolves around him.* Damiaan watched the ant-sized traffic hurrying along the streets and sidewalks. *It will all be so much easier when we cull their numbers. They are clueless, a herd of mindless sheep.*

4

S erena raced to greet him. Standing a head taller than anyone else, the Australian geneticist was hard to miss. Their hug at the baggage claim carousel lasted a full minute. "How was the flight?"

"Long!" BB's musical laugh followed. "Ah, Galinawa, much has happened in your journey since we last embraced. And look at you—you look like a fierce Tasmanian devil." He rubbed her head. "And your hair has grown back thick and full, like a wombat. Can this be the same girl?" He turned. "This, no doubt, is Bryson Reynolds." BB extended his hand. Even Bryson's height did not match the Australian's.

"It's a pleasure to finally meet you, Dr. Brindabella. Serena has told us so much about you and your adventures over land and sea." Clasped hands pulled forward to a hug. "Thank you for taking such good care of her!"

"Same to you, Bryson. It's a group effort." He looked serious for a moment. "We need to get something straight right off, mate. We can't be on the same team unless you call me BB." His enormous teeth flashed in the biggest smile Bryson had ever seen; another deep laugh rumbled.

"Righto."

Serena missed that genuine smile and sweet, baritone laughter. She gave BB another hug. "And this is Claus. He's another member of the team."

The two men shook hands, and Claus lifted both suitcases. "The car is right this way. I'm hoping that once you're settled, you can introduce me to a proper shout. I'm meaning the authentic real-deal Australian kind of serious drinking. First round is on me."

There was so much to catch up on. Bryson and Claus listened from the front seats as Serena and BB relived some of the excitement of the past few months. He showed Serena a note from DJ reminding her of her pledge to do a walkabout with him in the Aussie outback. He promised to cook up some nice witchetty worms. Serena laughed recalling her wilderness escapades together with DJ. In no time, they arrived at the Reynolds' estate.

Peter's staff prepared a wonderful meal. By unanimous consent, tonight precluded talk of business. BB entertained them all with many stories about

Gurumarra, the Wanderer. With food, wine, and friendship, external threats of world domination and resistance seemed remote. That all changed the following morning.

Much like any high-level corporate meeting, Peter Reynolds set and followed an agenda. "All your previously requested items required to set up a covert cutting-edge genetics lab are at the secure site. BB, you only need to get there and organize the equipment. When you are ready, Claus will take you there."

"I'm ready to start today. My assistant, Tarni, will arrive next week to help. That corresponds to a break in the academic calendar. Kenseiko Li, despite his tentacles throughout the world of genetics research, should have no way to trace my assistant or this new laboratory."

Peter expressed his pleasure. "Excellent." He looked tired. "I shall be away all of next week. Unexpected requirements for some military procurements have me working and traveling for Baxter Consolidated. As I'm sure you're all aware, some of this is Illuminati business."

"What are they planning, Uncle?"

"I don't know, Bryson. Whatever it is, I venture it's big. The family heads have been conferring. There's something brewing with DARPA and the US Government, but the lid on information is drawn tight. If I begin asking questions, you can be sure that will draw scrutiny. Best I can say is, the sooner we get started the better."

"What's the plan?" Serena's quiet voice asked the obvious. She had the restlessness of a caged animal, anxious and ready to be set loose upon some prey.

The details were sketchy, but Peter spelled it out. "Beangagarrie and his assistant will pick up where his research left off years ago."

BB held up a stack of floppy discs. "I assume someone here can organize this into a more readily searchable database. These have all my published research and unpublished notes."

Bryson raised his hand. "I'll handle that. I've already reviewed your published work, at least what I could find, and I already have some questions. I'm happy to help you however I can. I'm a quick learner."

"Boss, I've been giving this a little thought," Claus said. "You know, we make some of the hardware used in many private and commercial jets. I think we can upgrade the software that supports our components and manage to track the family heads as they travel. It will be limited, but it's a start toward keeping an eye on their whereabouts. Bryson, I'm relying on you to write some code."

"I'm on it, Claus. Just get me the source code, programming language, chip designs, and hardware specs. I'm sure I can hack something."

BB added, "Tarni is also trained in virology. We may need additional supplies. I'll know next week."

Peter answered, "Yes, whatever you need. I've set up different accounts to expense things; Claus can show you how to access the system. The file is labeled 'Christmas Party'; I've budgeted 1.5 million dollars, more if you need it. It requires an encrypted password to gain entry. Again, Claus will take you through it."

Claus let out a soft whistle. "That's gonna be some holiday party, boss."

"I've covered our short-range plans. So, is that a wrap for now?"

"Not really," Serena said. Her throat tingled. "Where do I fit in? Sounds as if everyone on this team is on a project except me. What's my job, get coffee?"

Peter ignored the sarcasm. "I thought you knew." He looked at Bryson with a puzzled expression. "I thought you and my nephew had already figured this out."

Now it was Serena's turn to look puzzled. "Not so. I may be a light bearer, but I'm totally in the dark." She glared at Bryson. "No one's discussed anything with me."

Peter began to speak, but Bryson interrupted. "PTG, you're going to Egypt."

"I am?"

"Yes, it's the only thing that makes sense. You need to be trained in how to use your voice, and I'm not talking about singing lessons. You're the secret weapon, Candelaria warrior woman. Problem is, your secret is even secret to you. That's gotta change. That means Egypt."

Peter, BB, Claus, and Bryson all looked at her expectantly, waiting for her answer.

"Who's coming with me?"

No one spoke. "How am I going to get there?"

Bryson replied, "I'm working on that; I'm still working on that."

"Well then, that's settled—Egypt it is." She stood up. "Who wants coffee?"

5

Kenseiko Li flew on his private jet from Singapore to Kathmandu, then by helicopter to the remote mountain cave complex. He had made this trip many times. Li enjoyed every visit to the several hive sites, but this one in the Himalayas remained as his personal favorite. It had produced the most successful large-scale projects. Genetic manipulation and hybridization had some peculiarities. He couldn't say for sure, perhaps the altitude, Earth's geomagnetics, or lack of EM interference led to better results. For this initial order, he wanted to showcase the best of the best. The Himalayan Clone Twelves, HC-12s for short, were the cream of the crop from experiments Li had started twenty years earlier. These soldiers were the first generation of elite combatants engineered from a mix of genes into human chimeras.

Combined with the 24-K11 hardware, they formed a superior fighting unit. Strong, agile, intelligent, and resourceful, the engineered humans could outperform any elite soldiers from any country, including Russia, China, and the United States. With further manipulation using epigenetic techniques, Li had nearly eliminated their response to pain and significantly enhanced their endurance and reflexes. Some militaries used drugs to achieve these results, but the drugs wore off; his improvements were built in.

Li almost couldn't wait to see them in action. *The Sudanese Government doesn't realize what they are purchasing, but soon the world will find out.* Only Li really understood why these soldiers were so effective. The genetic enhancements were only half the reason. The biometric sensors on the weapons they carried, whether knives or guns, paired to the headsets' display and processor, giving the combatants superior information and response times. The weapons Li programed to the soldiers didn't require triggers; they were neurally activated. The headsets linked the soldiers together as a cohesive group in constant communication at the level of the brain—a thinking, reacting, fighting collective. Superior parts operating as a superior unit—nothing in history matched this achievement in coordination.

A quote from Genghis Khan bubbled to his consciousness as Li hobbled into the hive complex. *"There is no good in anything until it is finished."* Now I *finish what I started fifty years ago. This is just one piece of something much, much larger. When I am done overseeing the programming, I'll check on another piece.* A hint of a smile crossed his features.

"Dr. Li, per your instructions, I have the first group of HC-12s seated in the programming booths."

"Thank you, Dr. Zhāng. You've made no changes to the protocols since the last time I was here?"

"No, sir, only the implantation specs requested by the Sudanese on control panel Delta. There are no other changes."

"Are you as anxious as I am to see how our efforts are rewarded?"

"Yes, Dr. Li. I am both curious and confident to see how they perform."

"Good, let's proceed."

Twenty separate programming stations consisted of black booths and comfortable armchairs. Once the doors closed, light and sound were blocked. Each soldier wore the programming goggles and a headset with the optogenic inputs centered over their eyes. The soldiers' lids were retracted. A clever automatic dropper administered a surface anesthetic and lubricant. This phase of the programming took about ninety minutes. Audio suggestions could be implanted during this phase. For this unit, specifications listed on control panel D would be incorporated. Sudan could always request a new set of guidelines be optogenically downloaded in the future. Of course, this would be at additional cost.

Ninety minutes later, the goggles and headsets were replaced by the 24-K11 military gear; the biogenetic tactile sensors linking weapons to the ocular display in the headpieces were activated. This required only thirty minutes. Every two hours, the group of twenty cycled; thus, the entire effort to prepare five hundred soldiers required a little over two days.

Li supervised the first two cycles and observed the first forty soldiers in simulated combat drills. Satisfied, he left the remainder to Dr. Zhāng.

Biologically, the HC-12s were nineteen years old; although, they were fully mature. Li entered a lower cave level and faced six identical females. Though three years younger than the soldiers, they had already crossed the threshold of maturity. Compact, well-developed lean musculature, neither attractive nor unattractive—they appeared as healthy young Asian women who could blend in almost anywhere in the world. These six were the other reason for his visit, something of a more personal nature.

He rarely smiled, but an almost paternal grin broke Kenseiko's stoicism. "My little Ninjas: N1, 2, 3, 4, 5, 6." He tapped each one as he counted down the line. They stood there motionless. "Who wants to go first?" As a group, they each stepped forward. He closed his eyes walking back and forth several times before stopping in front of N4. "Come, come with bàba."

The Ninja chimeras had a disproportionate amount of Kenseiko Li's own DNA. He believed that with Dr. Zhāng and the scientists here in Tibet, he had engineered a hybrid-clone with superior intelligence—a superhuman. Now he wanted to test his creations, his progeny.

N4 followed him to a different programming station with two booths. A moment after they arrived, a technician brought a Himalayan Clone Twelve. Li selected the software, prepared both subjects himself, then downloaded identical instructions. Ninety minutes later, the three were outdoors in a training ring. The overcast daylight did not bother Kenseiko at all. An idea occurred to him, and a different expression broke out, a twisted grin of sorts. Another technician arrived with a laptop and satellite hookup.

"Brother Damiaan…"

"Kenseiko? It's 3:15 a.m. Where are you? Why are you calling me?"

"I'm at the hive in the Himalayas. I wanted to show you some of the fully functional soldiers in action. Get to a computer and dial this secure IP address." He rattled a series of numbers.

Moments later, a robed Damiaan Van Duyn appeared on the laptop screen. Li replayed the training results he had recorded earlier.

"Very impressive! It's very impressive, Kenseiko, but I think you could have waited a few hours to show me. I'm sure you are still programming other units. You won't finish for at least another day."

"That's true, Brother. I woke you for a different reason. I want to make a wager with you."

"A wager, what are you talking about, Kenseiko?"

Li panned around to the training arena. The two hybrids stood facing one another, each studying their opponent.

"This is my supersoldier." He zoomed on the female, then panned over to the male. "This is one of my other supersoldiers. I designed them both. They are both superior humans. I give the physical edge to the HC-12, but the intelligence edge to my little Ninja. In hand-to-hand combat, who do you think will win?"

"You're joking, right? Brains over brawn? It isn't a fair fight, Kenseiko."

"They both have received the same set of programming instructions—fight to the death. One winner, one loser. I'll wager ten million US dollars that the girl wins."

"Are you sure the high altitude hasn't oxygen-starved your brain? It's your money, Kenseiko. I don't mind taking it from you."

"Begin."

The two combatants bowed first to Dr. Li, then to one another.

6

At least she had focus for the near term. On the surface, going to Egypt looked straightforward, but getting there and coordinating with the Black Serpent Sisters required finesse. Serena had to admit the plan Claus and Bryson devised, and Peter Reynolds approved, was nothing less than brilliant. One thing for sure about Claus, the man had a talent for strategy and tactics.

Claus jokingly called it the Martian Plan. "You'll be traveling as Alice Mars. She works for Baxter Consolidated as part of the flight crew for cargo transports. We deliver equipment and components worldwide and have a scheduled delivery for an Egyptian operational and training base located at Ras el Tin; that's near Alexandria."

"How will I impersonate her?"

"We got that covered, PTG. Alice is going out on pregnancy leave. Uncle Peter has instructed HR to collect all passports for personnel traveling abroad on company business so that a location chip can be attached. This way, if a passport is lost or stolen, the company may be able to find it with minimal disruption. It's not a bad idea and totally plausible. Her passport is stamped from plenty of overseas trips, so you should pass through without any trouble. She won't be needing it for at least eight weeks."

"Sounds good. What does the Martian girl look like—green skin, elongated skull, antennae?"

"Hey, that's pretty funny, Serena. In truth, we don't have to photoshop the image at all. She's a little taller than you, and you'll need to wear blue contacts. Otherwise, you could be sisters. Here, see for yourself." Claus held out a US passport.

Serena studied her new identity's image. Apart from the blonde hair, blue eyes, and a few years in age, the resemblance was passable.

"You should get familiar with some of the locations Alice has been to in case you get asked. I've hand selected the crew you'll be traveling with. They're trustworthy and won't get nosey. Do you have any questions?" Claus took back the passport.

"What about my return? What's my cover story?" She was beginning to think this was an espionage novel or movie with her impersonation as Alice Mars casted as a covert operative.

Bryson said, "Easy, once you've coordinated with Moon 2, the story is that you are staying in Egypt to visit the pyramids with friends. So, you'll be splitting off from the military cargo transport crew. We'll book a commercial return flight for you in Alice's name, and you'll have the ticket with you."

"It looks like you two have figured it all out. What could go wrong?"

Bryson and Claus looked at each other and both said, "There's a lot that can go wrong."

The two hybrids cautiously circled and evaluated. Then an explosion erupted—lunge, parry, kick, advance, retreat. N4 leaped over the HC-12; he somersaulted, reversed, and charged. As Li watched, the hybrids put on a clinic of martial-art techniques. Another leap by N4 to evade a flurry of arms and legs. For a moment, he seemed to have her, but their combined center of gravity shifted with her twist, and then both tumbled. He rose to his feet first; she jumped high to evade. As the soldier watched her movement through the air, the Ninja's foot shot forward, crushing her opponent's trachea. He staggered backward to the ground, wheezing gasps that sounded like an asthmatic struggling for air.

Without hesitation, he forcibly thrust his thumb below his collapsed windpipe, opening a crude hole while sucking a lungful of air and blood. The N4's eyebrows raised in surprise, then she coolly placed her foot over the crude tracheostomy. He writhed, twisted, clawed, and struggled to remove her foot to no avail. Moments later, she stepped off the still body and bowed gracefully to Dr. Li.

"Looks like I win, Brother Damiaan."

"I want one. How much for the Ninja model?"

"Sorry, private stock, not for sale." He motioned to the young female. "Come closer and explain your strategy to me and my Snake Brother."

There was nothing emotional in her explanation. No apparent gloating or evident sense of pride in overcoming a physically stronger adversary.

"Prior to beginning our battle, I reasoned we both were conditioned to block pain. With a normal assailant," she pointed to her groin, "a strike to the genitals might be effective in disabling a foe, but not likely with this attacker. So, my strategy was to deliver a death blow to the soldier's greatest weakness—his neck. A well-placed hit over the trachea had a high probability of success. I have the same vulnerability, but his height made attack to my neck more difficult. After our initial testing of one another, my aerial maneuvers were primarily to observe how he tracked my movements and exposed himself. When the opportunity came, I made my strike." She rubbed over her windpipe. "This area has little protection with the chin up; the blow did not require much force, only that it be properly delivered."

"Did you hear that, Damiaan? I think the 24-K11 headgear needs protection extending down to the anterior neck. Is that something you can pass on to your designers?"

"I'll notify our military engineers. I think you should show this one-on-one battle to the unit before they deploy. A weakness has been exposed thanks to your little girl-soldier. We'll discuss this again after I've reviewed the match a few times. I don't like wagering with you, Kenseiko. Where should I send the money?"

"Keep your money. Her victory is all the reward I need. Live in the light, Brother."

The screen went blank. *As Genghis Khan stated: "It is not sufficient that I succeed; all others must fail."*

7

Although infrequent, when sleep eluded him, he gravitated to the trophy room. Almost inaudible footsteps on the plush Persian went unnoticed as he pondered his unease.

"Your Lordship." One of the manservants held an intricate silver platter with a decanter, snifter, and several glass vials. "I took the liberty of delivering something to help settle you."

His head nodded.

"Cognac from your private reserve and an assortment of tinctures."

He watched as the servant unstoppered the Hungarian crystal, poured the libation, and placed it upon a gold coaster inlaid in ivory with the Rothschild family crest. White gloves hid the manservant's missing distal portions of several digits, the mistakes of youth. Despite this, the platter moved from fingertips to desktop without the small glass vials shifting even slightly.

Edward selected one of the hematinics, removed the top, added it to the amber liquid, and palmed the snifter with gentle swirls. The red tincture spiraled and disappeared, but he could smell the shift in the cognac's aroma.

"Will that be all, your Lordship? Shall I summon one of the young ladies, or perhaps one of the boys?"

"No. You may take your leave."

With silent footsteps, the manservant exited, and Edward moved about the room, idly sipping while admiring some of his prized possessions. It settled him, helped him to decipher his underlying disquiet.

He picked up a medal from the World Council of Economic Justice, smiled in recall of receiving the distinctive award, and placed it reverently back in its display. *It's Li. He's getting into my head.*

Another sip. "Camauro and Mitre of Pope Gregory IX"—Edward felt especially proud of acquiring this from the Vatican collection. He almost removed the conical headpiece to place upon his head. *Time to order a new Inquisition?*

His upper lip curled to smile. *I should be pleased at how our plans are proceeding. The virus, the soldiers…* His lips turned downward. *Li has his fingers on everything. He's insolent, arrogant. He needs to be taught a lesson.*

He retrieved St. Edward's Staff—the original, not the copy included among the British Crown Jewels. *Glory days for the monarchy and for our Brotherhood. Soon…soon I shall help shepherd a new order.* He held the staff in one hand and his glass in another as the stroll continued past his collection of Renaissance art: Caravaggio, Brunelleschi, Jan van Eyck. He felt better as he swirled and drained the last of his cognac.

Edward stopped in front of a pedestal with an empty display case, marked only by an engraved gold faceplate: "Candelaria Necklace." Anger swelled, lips snarled, nostrils flared. *Witch! Li never mentioned the witch. What is he hiding? Does he have the girl? Does he have the necklace? What is the surprise he promised for next meeting? Conniving dog-muncher!* Edward almost brought the staff down upon the case; instead, he threw the snifter and watched it bounce along the carpet without shattering.

A leather armchair beckoned. He sat and bathed in the soft glow of a salt lamp. Snarling first at Li's insolence and evasiveness, then at something else. *What? What is it? Li… He looked so energized in his Asian boy face. That's it! He rejuvenated! He's been to The Womb, and he did it without my authorization.* First a sneer, then a smug look of satisfaction, the kind that follows finally figuring out some emotional niggle. *Shrem, you old würm.*

8

Bryson kept his thoughts to himself after watching Serena go off alone. He told himself it had to be this way. He should have explained it to her, but he didn't. Maybe he wasn't sure himself. In his heart, he felt he was holding Serena back. As long as they were together, she relied on him to figure things out. He was the brains, the genius, and she deferred to him. But he couldn't do this for her. In Egypt, he would just be a distraction, someone holding her back. Who could he even talk to about this? Neither Claus nor his uncle would understand. He took a chance.

"BB, I know you're super busy setting up the lab, and you know I want to help you as much as I can…but I'm hoping you can help me with some advice."

"Sure, always time for a mate who's askin'. What's on your mind, son?"

"I'm conflicted. I feel as though I pushed Serena into going to Egypt. It would be okay if I went with her, but I feel as though I would only be an obstacle. Still, it's dangerous there, especially with what's been happening in Sudan."

Beangagarrie motioned to the lab bench, and the two sat. "Why did you push her? I point out that it didn't look to me as though she required much prodding."

"It's confusing. We're both still processing everything that's happened in the past few months—the Illuminati, this war between serpents, Candelaria destiny, my father, her great aunt. When I step back, it's overwhelming for me; I can't imagine how it is for her."

"I have observed her moods vacillate. At times she is… What's that word you Americans like? Snarky. I believe that's the word."

"Well, she's always been a little snarky, especially if she needs coffee. But it's more like she's preoccupied by the need to do something; she just doesn't know what to do."

"So, that's why you pushed her to go to Egypt?"

"Yes, but it's also that I don't want to get in her way."

"In her way… How so?

"I'm holding her back."

The scientist thought about Bryson's answer before responding slowly. "It's because you love her."

"That obvious?" He grinned.

"I am not so old that I do not remember what love looks like." BB shut his eyes for a moment, appearing lost in a memory.

"It's true; I do love her and care about her, about her safety."

"Naturally. And when you love someone, you both want to allow them the chance to develop fully as a person and to protect them. Here is your conflict, Bryson. When you love someone, you must set them free, free to be all that they are. At the same time, you want to keep the people you love safe." Unexpectedly, tears welled. "I could not keep my love safe. We both paid dearly for that." He recovered. "But these are old matters now past."

"I'm sorry, BB. Serena told me about your wife."

"Serena is a special person, and she is in danger, much less because of this trip and much more because of who she is. Be assured, Bryson, there is much more you can do for her here than in Egypt. She will be fine." He stood. "Break time over."

"How can you be certain?"

"Trust. No dramas, mate. Things will work out."

Bryson smiled. "Yeah, I've told myself that same answer. I haven't quite convinced myself yet."

"Have you seen her in action? Convincing enough for me. Pity the bloke that stands in her way. She'll be okay; stop worrying. It distracts from the important work we need to do."

Fist bumps ended their conversation.

The flight uniform for Baxter had her name stitched in the upper right. *At least it doesn't scratch like that Kevlar Moon insisted I wear.* Serena looked forward to reconnecting with the instructress and hearing the latest about Pyramid Communications' efforts to expose the lies and conspiracies being propagated by the controlling cabal. The long and uncomfortable flight to Alexandria acted as a marker. *I'm now leaving the normal world to head back down the rabbit hole.* It gave her time to think.

Bryson had been acting weird lately; at least that's the way it seemed to her. Keep in touch; text me at least once a day; be careful. *What's wrong with him? I can take care of myself.* On the other hand, she missed him. She didn't like feeling so alone and on her own. Serena tried to sort it all out. Normally, it was easy for her to get to the bottom of things and see the underlying truth. But her emotions got in the way. She heard the aircraft wheels move to landing position. *Heads up, girlfriend. I'm not in Kansas anymore, and Bry's not here to watch my back.*

Nothing prepared her for stepping foot onto an Egyptian military base. An ant colony of armed personnel, Ras el Tin buzzed with check points, escorts, and activities. A palpable heightened-awareness and anxiety throbbed. *Everything here is coiled like an over-wound spring getting ready to snap.* She put a piece of gum in her mouth to look casual.

A corporal interrogated her. "Why are you not returning with the rest of your crew?"

"I have a lot of unused vacation. I'm meeting friends to visit the pyramids." She had done her homework, knew Egypt had a well-developed tourist industry. "Have you been to the Valley of Kings? We're trying to decide if we should go there."

The corporal remained stone-faced as he examined her papers, including passport and return-flight documents. He asked some questions about countries stamped on her passport. "How did you like your trip to South Africa? I've never been there; is it nice?"

Trick question. "I wasn't there long enough to do anything fun." Every time Serena told a lie, she cringed inside. She ignored the pricking pain in her throat. Chewing gum helped.

He meticulously unpacked and went through every item in her bag. He studied her snake cuff bracelet. "Interesting piece of jewelry. Where did you get it?"

"At a bazaar in Istanbul during a layover." She snapped her gum and swallowed to relieve the discomfort in her throat.

Satisfied, the corporal finally passed her through. "Enjoy your stay in Egypt, Ms. Mars. Yes, you should go to the Valley of Kings."

She made her way to a nonrestricted part of the base where civilians were permitted. Per instructions, she took a taxi to a street address in Alexandria, paid the driver, and waited until he left. She dialed a secure number on a burner phone, entered an alphanumeric code, and waited.

A moment later, the phone rang. A male voice said, "I'll be right there."

She took a deep breath. *Everything will be fine. I can take care of myself.*

9

Once a month, Kenseiko Li did an inspection/tour of the main research lab. This small division of Advanced Bionics, known as the "Imaginarium," housed the newest and best developments the company pioneered. Antiaging, viral insertions, and advanced gene splicing and combining all started at the Imaginarium. All the hive sites incorporated enhancements developed in this division.

Dr. Yuri Koslov, a prodigy from Kazakhstan, updated the director.

"We are behind in our progress on the new vaccine–the one to deliver some additional messenger RNA. I am sorry to report this delay, Dr. Li. We are working to correct it."

"What is the reason for the delay?"

"The molecular cloning reagents we use supplied by NBio Diagnostics are on back order. We are unable to complete the site-specific mutagenesis assembly without the Q-reagent. There are other solutions in short supply, but that is the main one."

"We own NBio. Instruct them to make your orders top priority."

"I've already done that, sir."

"What is their explanation?"

"I didn't ask, sir."

"Let's go to your office and call them, Yuri. The situation is most unusual."

A brief phone call with a very apologetic Kim Chul-su, the CEO of NBio Diagnostics, yielded some curious information. Apparently, a large order for many reagents, as well as equipment, caused the shortage. Kim Chul-su assured Dr. Li it was only temporary.

"Where were these supplies shipped to?"

"The order details show delivery to a location in the port of Vancouver."

"Send me the address and any other information you have. If a subsequent order is placed from the same customer ID, notify me prior to shipping out anything."

"Yes, Dr. Li. I'll call you myself."

After berating Yuri for not notifying him sooner, Kenseiko left the Imaginarium. *Someone is setting up a new genetics research lab. Who might that be?*

"I'll pass it through to Baxter Solutions, and they can send it out as a patch. You're sure it will work?" Claus had no reason to doubt Bryson's code.

"Positive. We've already tested it on the Reynolds' private fleet. It will take a while to weed out the jets we're not interested in monitoring, but it should be a start in tracking activity." He added, "But it will be a lot easier than monitoring flight logs. Besides, that could draw attention."

"Exactly." Claus muttered, "Attack where the enemy does not defend."

"What? What was that you just said?"

"*The Art of War.* You haven't read it? It's not an exact quote, but it says what I mean. It remains as the greatest book on military strategy ever written. Here, our surveillance strategy zeros in on something undefended. Why would the enemy, an enemy that controls just about everything, think to prevent surveillance of their leadership? We're small, but we're not stupid. That's why I give *us* the edge. They don't even know we're going to bring them down."

Bryson wasn't sure what to say. "I don't have the same degree of certainty, Claus. Probability favors the big and powerful."

"Bullshit. Arrogance breeds complacency, and complacency breeds failure."

"Another quote?"

"Yeah, Claus Gorman. It's original. Let's get this software patch out for distribution. It's just a start. We should brainstorm our vulnerabilities. I don't want to get caught with our pants down."

"Good point. How am I going to manage while you're away?"

"It's just a week. Boss says he needs me on another project. Don't forget—garbage goes out on Tuesday."

"Shoot. I've got to pick up BB and get to the airport. Tarni's flight arrives at five o'clock. You're sure it's okay that he stays here?"

"Makes no difference to me. When Serena gets back, we'll have to figure out something else. BB is sleeping in the small room in the lab. I don't see how his assistant can stay there too. Remember, Tuesday—garbage."

"You told me. I've got a good memory."

Bryson drove with BB as a passenger. The more time he spent with the Australian scientist, the more he liked him. They discussed the genetic research BB had done years ago. A portion of reptilian DNA BB had sequenced appeared dormant. But there was a similar sequence in human DNA that appeared active.

"How are you going to pick up where you left off? Genetics research has changed drastically since they expunged your published papers."

"True, but the tools are so much more sophisticated now. The new sequencers give us results in days that used to take weeks. And epigenetics opens up new avenues. I finally have the tools to hopefully unravel the mystery. For starters, I want to look at your DNA, and my own, and Serena's too. I'm sure Tarni will have ideas as well. Plus, her knowledge of viral techniques to add and subtract codons far exceeds mine. She really is quite brilliant."

Bryson looked confused. "She? You mean Tarni is a woman?"

"Of course. And she is very smart, certainly smarter than me and maybe even smarter than you."

"And you know her how?" The two of them waited at baggage claim.

"She follows Gurumarra. She is quite beautiful as well. Our Chieftain says if he was younger, he would like to dance with her. He says she is very colorful."

A hand shot up and waved. Beangagarrie's height made him hard to miss. "Yoo-hoo, BB, over here."

Attached to the hand stood a statuesque woman straight from the pages of a pop fashion magazine. She had Kool-Aid-pink hair and heart-shaped designer sunglasses.

A distinct Australian accent left little doubt. "Hurry, mate, I've got to pee."

"Dunny is right over there." BB pointed to a nearby restroom.

Bryson swallowed. *Oh my!*

10

A black SUV pulled to the curb where Serena waited. The mirrored glass window on the driver's side retracted slightly, and a voice ordered, "Get in."

She knew that voice. "Youssef?"

"Get in. Hurry, we do not have a lot of time." The front passenger door opened, and she sat down, placing her bag on her lap. She leaned to the side and held his arm. "Youssef, it's so good to see you!"

"Yes, it is good to see that you are safe. This time we shall make sure you stay safe, Serena Mendez. Or is it Chanda Patel? Or is it Alice Mars?" The SUV entered traffic, and he grinned. "You are hard to keep track of, child. Let us hope the enemy does not follow your trail." A moment later, he spoke over his Blue-tooth. "I'm stopping at the market to get some fish, what kind do you want?"

A voice crackled. "Whatever is on sale."

Password exchange for today, Serena thought.

"I'll be home soon." Youssef Mourad, security head for Pyramid Communications, seemed pleased. This part of the operation had apparently gone smoothly.

Ten minutes later, they pulled into a driveway. Youssef looked directly into the surveillance camera and spoke a string of numbers. The door to the safe house opened.

A woman in a gray burqa stood there. It concealed much of her face, but the scars left no doubt.

"Moon!" She hugged her Serpent Sister and felt Moon's prosthetic arm in the firm embrace.

"You are safe, that's what's important. Here"—she extended her good arm—"put these on."

Serena slipped out of her flight uniform with no misgivings about the security guard's presence. He turned to look aside, and she handed her clothes to Moon.

She in turn gave them to Youssef. "Burn these. Alice Mars was never here." Then she gathered a couple of woven sacks and pointed to a traditional Egyptian basket. "These are our provisions and supplies. Come, we are on a tight schedule. We'll have plenty of time to talk in the car and afterwards."

"Where are we going?"

"To see our Mother. To learn what you can do."

Serena updated Moon on all the events since her hasty departure from Cairo to Lisbon, then off to Mexico, Peru, and finally back to the Navajo reservation. When the young Candelaria finished the story of her chakra openings, Moon reached into her sleeve and produced another serpent arm cuff.

"Remember, I told you that when your sixth is opened, you use the power of the eye to amplify the fifth. Now we will learn what your voice can do. In our tradition, you get the right-arm serpent after the eye is opened. We'll ask Mother to bless both your bracelets, to imbue them with her spirit force."

"She sounds very powerful."

"You cannot begin to understand until you see for yourself."

Moon refused to give further details, explaining that such information is protected; something permitted not even to Youssef. Instead, she relayed all that had occurred at Pyramid Communications in the time since Serena's last visit.

"It is bad, much worse than when you left. The government has cracked down, and they have imprisoned many journalists. We are careful not to criticize the authorities for fear they will shut us down. You know as well as I what is happening in the world. The food shortages are worsening. Sudan is in crisis though it seems to have stabilized of late. Riots have started in Gaza. Of course, the Israeli Government does not like the world to know what is really going on there. We are free to report on that, and we do." She went into detail about the truth of the oppression in Gaza.

When she finished, she said, "You see how all of this is orchestrated? They have contrived the food shortages. Many have died already. If war erupts, many, many more will die. I fear it is only the beginning of the enemy's great plan to reduce the population. 10 percent, 20 percent—some say as much as 80 percent. These are very dangerous times."

Two hours later, they stopped. Moon directed Serena to give all her belongings to Youssef; he would bring them to their headquarters in Cairo. Serena balked; she didn't want to be out of communication with Bryson, but Moon insisted.

"One text to your people in the US. Youssef will send it from our base, where we can prevent the signal from being intercepted. There is no coverage where we are going, anyway." She turned to the security guard. "Pick me up from this same spot at 11 a.m. the day after tomorrow."

The two watched the vehicle's dust trail as it traveled north. Serena looked around; they stood in the middle of a small village, little more than a cluster of homes and a crude marketplace—very rural. Moon stopped at a nondescript building and spoke in Arabic to the owner, who returned from an outbuilding leading two donkeys on ropes. Moon examined the animals, nodding her approval. Money exchanged hands. They placed provisions on the beasts, mounted, and walked south. Fifteen minutes later, Moon turned the animals sharply to the west. There was no road, only desert in all directions. To any onlooker, they looked like natives dressed in conservative garb, perhaps a mother and daughter going about their business.

To the north, she could see pyramids. Serena guessed that maybe they were the ancient Pyramids of Giza, but she wasn't sure. "Where are we going?"

Moon pointed west to a different, but much smaller, group of pyramid mounds. "Abusir. It is about seven miles. We arrive at night, which is as desired."

Her donkey had a smooth rhythm and even pace. As twilight eased into darkness, the stars overhead erupted into something Serena missed. Back at the hogan in Arizona, far from the light pollution, she and Bryson would stare for hours at the Milky Way.

Moon pointed overhead. "It's seldom that I get out from the city, from the lights and the noise, to travel beneath the quiet beauty of the night sky. It reminds me of my youth." She described her childhood growing up in a rural town. "Our lives were simple. We toiled, we toiled hard to work the land, but life seemed uncomplicated. We struggled, but not like now. Life should not be so hard."

Serena shared her own stories of growing up in New Mexico. After age eleven, after her failed initiation in the cave, her life had been hard, but in a different way. The austere desert served to bond the two women. All around showed evidence of survival, proof of perseverance and determination against adversity.

"The desert is a harsh mistress, child. You and I share that though our lives are a world apart."

"It's the same world we all share, Sister. Most people have forgotten this truth. We are more similar than different."

A sliver of moon peaked over the horizon. Shimmering bits of light stretched for miles over barren sand. The donkeys clopped along.

"Did you ever marry? Do you have children?"

"I had an arranged marriage. He was a good man. We never had children." She laughed in a mournful way. "Not for lack of trying, I assure you."

"What happened? Did he pass away, or did you grow apart? What was his name?"

"Jamel. He was a journalist." Her voice quavered. "He died in an Egyptian prison."

Serena felt her Sister's pain and found herself first wanting to cry, but she quickly grew angry. *How many have died standing up to the powerful? How many more shall die? What can I do to stop it?* "The struggle to serve truth has too many martyrs along the way," she said.

The elder woman halted her animal and sat erect. "Jamel used to say the same thing. He also said that we can never allow the torch of truth to go dark. We must pass the torch to the next light bearer and believe our death is in the service of something much greater than one single life."

"He sounds like a very beautiful and very brave man—a man with a big heart, and an even bigger soul."

"You are wise beyond your years, Serena. He would have been a wonderful father. Thirty years and I still miss him…"

"The World Health Organization reports another outbreak of hemorrhagic fever, this time on an island in the South Pacific." Video footage of a WHO team in full hazmat suits and gear moved in and out of tents. Shrouds covered bodies, but the pools of blood left little to the imagination. *"Again, some pregnant women survived. Epidemiologists are puzzled by the sporadic outbreaks occurring so far from one another without an apparent vector. Birds are suspected, but scientists are still trying to unravel this new virus. Officials at the CDC have already begun work on a vaccine."*

"In other news, the unrest in the Sudan has reportedly subsided though the country remains in relative blackout. Demonstrations in nearby Gaza have intensified." Video footage of chanting demonstrators throwing rocks at Israeli security forces filled the screen as the police fired tear gas cannisters and beat protestors with batons. *"Israel denies the claims of a death toll in the thousands but has refused to allow international monitors access to confirm or deny these reports."*

"We turn now to our economics correspondent in London."

"Thank you, Michael. World markets are reeling…"

A voice shouted from across the room, "That's enough… Turn it off, or switch the station, or something." Tarni sounded adamant, and Bryson was in no mood to argue.

"What's the problem? Aren't you interested in what's happening in the world?"

"Of course, I am, but I can do without the earbashing. I don't need a steady diet of bad news. I've known you two days, and you're consuming too much of that negativity. It messes with your head, mate. Besides, most of it is a load of bloody bullshit. Furphies, like most of the news. Smart boy like you should know that." She toweled dry her pink, curly locks.

"Furphies?"

"False, erroneous. Stuff people take as factual that's widely believed, but not true. People think the news is reputable. Big mistake."

"Here we call it 'fake news,' but politicians twist it so people don't know what's real and what isn't. I like to know what's going on and to sort out the propaganda myself."

"Pollies in Australia do the same thing. Suit yourself. I like chocolate ice cream, but I don't eat a whopping portion every day. Consuming too much fake news will cause a mental technicolor yawn." She stuck two fingers in her throat to mimic forced vomiting. "If you receive my meaning."

She spun around, showing off her very attractive figure. "C'mon Bryson, lighten up a little. If we're going to be roomies, I need you to be upbeat."

Tarni was bossy, but not in a bad way; it was more playful. "Okay, you're right. Besides, BB is probably wondering why we aren't with him at the lab yet."

"He'll have to wait; it's not even 8 a.m. I always work my best when I look my best, and I'm not there yet." She spun around again. Her flirtatious smile had Bryson spinning, but in a much different way.

Whoa, slow down. Take a cold shower or something. Fortunately, his phone ringtone broke through the testosterone surge—text from PTG:

In Egypt with Moon. Everything ok but will be unable to communicate for at least a week. Too long and too rushed to explain. Miss you. A heart emoji completed the brief message. Bryson stood there holding his phone.

"I'm ready, mate." Bryson didn't move. "What's wrong? Is everything okay?" Tarni's sincere concern came through.

"I'm not sure."

11

Dr. Li picked N4's brain, questioning her on a variety of topics. Her answers pleased the scientist. Finding the right combination of genes and gene edits was the easy part; combining them into a viable chimeric hybrid, that's where his years of development had finally achieved the results he desired.

"Tell me, how do you think I can improve on your genetic profile?"

"Bàba, I believe the male soldier you had me fight was very skilled. Perhaps our male and female genes can be combined to achieve an even more capable human being."

"It is a good answer, my little Ninja, but you each have the maximum edits I know how to accomplish. Your joined DNA would be unstable. It is unfortunate that neither of you can reproduce on your own; however, sometimes nature, in her wisdom, overcomes what man cannot."

A secure phone rang; he replied in Chinese and put it on speaker. He wanted the N4 to listen. "Dr. Zhāng, I need you here in Singapore to program the supplemental order requested by the Sudanese Government."

"How many additional soldiers?"

"Two hundred."

"I've not been there in some time. Are there still only six programming booths?"

"Yes, that is correct. I do not have time to prepare them myself. I am called to a meeting. Use the same protocols as before. Van Duyn is delivering the 24-K11s here."

"Very good, sir. I'll leave today. I will not let you down."

"Thank you, Dr. Zhāng."

"Live in the light, Dr. Li."

He turned to the girl. "My plans for the perfection of humanity are moving forward nicely. Do you know why we often close by saying, 'Live in the light'?"

"No, bàba. Please explain why you use this expression."

"Better yet, I will show you. Remove your clothes and step by the window."

They each removed their clothes, and Kenseiko pressed the remote controlling the blinds. As sunlight streamed through even the building's mirrored glass, after a few moments, Dr. Li's skin began to become gray, and he held his head in obvious pain. The girl stood next to him, completely unaffected. He stepped away from the sunlight and quickly dressed. He stared at the girl and admired her perfection. Eventually, he shut the blinds; his skin returned to normal.

"All the chosen families are sensitive to light; some more so than others. It results from light sensors in the pineal gland." He pointed to his forehead. "Sunlight in particular triggers our pineal and also reduces our ability to mask some of our surface pigmentation. This capability is much like a color-shifting chameleon. We consume certain blood elements to mitigate the sun effect, but the benefits are temporary. Get dressed."

He continued. "When I was young, my father, seeing my clubfoot and my extreme light sensitivity, concluded that my genes were flawed. He wanted to put me out in the sun and leave me to die. That was the way he handled such imperfections. That was a long time ago. My mother convinced him to let me live."

"Thank you, bàba, for this explanation, but I still do not understand. Why tell your brethren to 'Live in the light'? It seems this only encourages pain and unmasks weakness; it makes no sense to me."

Li nodded in agreement and smiled. "Yes, this is true. But the perfection of our genes means that one day we shall live in the light without harm. Father was right; my genes are flawed. Genetic imperfection is true for not only the chosen, but of all humanity. But you, you have the best selected genes that I could combine, and you stand bathed in sunlight without discomfort."

He limped to where she stood, placed his hands upon her shoulders, and tenderly kissed her forehead. "You are flawless. Today I name you Wán shàn— perfection!"

The rhythmic cadence of the donkeys' hooves entranced them both into meditative silence, yearning for pasts that never were. Memories of what might have been filled Serena's mind. She wondered how her life would be different if Ooljee successfully began the Candelaria training as planned. *No. You can't change the past. Focus on the now. What can I do now to change the future? I'm ready… I'm ready to take the next step.*

They arrived at a group of buildings, more rubble than actual structures. In the moonlight, Serena could see that none had roofs, but one had a door of sorts with a lock. Moon produced a key, and they entered, dismounting and setting out hay and grain for the animals. Moon uncovered a cistern, cupped some water, and moved aside to allow the donkeys to drink. "This is sacred water. It flows from an aquifer beneath."

Serena looked around, seeing only a crude firepit, a basin, a kettle, and a pot. Moon unpacked the sacks while calling out their supplies. "Lentils, flour, oil, salt, dried apricots—everything is getting so expensive with all the shortages."

"That's it? I'm sorry if I sound annoyed, but I imagined our visit to the head of the order would include something a little more upscale. This is less than a hovel. Where exactly are we?"

"We are at the edge of the Abusir Necropolis."

"I'm sorry. I could use a bath. I smell like ass. Literally." One of the donkeys snorted. "And I need coffee."

Moon said nothing, waited until Serena's pout disappeared, then reached into the basket. "It isn't as strong as the Turkish coffee you seemed to enjoy when first we met, but I think you will like it. We sisters must look after each other."

Serena's tone softened. "I'm sorry; I'm tired too."

Moon unrolled two blankets. She filled the kettle and placed it on the floor, concentrated, and spoke, or rather sang, some words Serena didn't comprehend. A moment later, the water was boiling.

"Wait a minute, how did you do that?"

"Brew some coffee then rest, child. Mother is strongest at 3 a.m., so there is not much time until you meet her. Tomorrow, if my suspicions are true, you will boil your own water."

12

Dr. Beangagarrie Brindabella inhaled to steady himself as he read the printout. A tremor shook the quality control run report. Without Tarni, he wasn't sure he could be anywhere near this point. It had been nearly thirty years since he had last calibrated the equipment–thirty years and a sea change in genetics research since he last struggled with unlocking the mysteries in man's DNA.

She peered over his shoulder. "Looks good." He doubted she could see the tears in his eyes.

He exhaled. "Amazing! It used to take us three days to do a control run. The good news is human DNA hasn't changed in thirty years, a mere speck of time in our evolution. Come, now the fun begins." Unspoken, BB thought, *What secrets have been hiding all these years? It's long past time to unravel some mysteries haunting my past.* "Who wants to go first?"

Bryson volunteered. BB handed him a collection tube and swab. "That's it, just some saliva and a cheek swab?"

"Where have you been hiding, geek boy? Spit-a-bit and swab-a-gob as we like to say in my lab down under." Tarni paused long enough to gather her own sample. "You mean you haven't already done this for Ancestry or 23andMe, or one of the other commercial labs?"

She handed her kit to BB. "When we've run this, I'll check it against the profile I already did in Ancestry. It will be another way for us to verify accuracy."

"No," Bryson said, "I've been opposed to having my DNA results in a commercial company's database. In case you haven't noticed, I have privacy issues. Who knows who else gets the information—government, law enforcement, big pharma, insurance companies? If you're not concerned about that, you should be."

"Fair enough, Bryson. I hear you. Now I've got to get to work. Watch and learn."

"Yes, enough chatter. We need to concen—" But BB never finished the sentence as Bryson sped toward the door. "Where are you going?"

"Makeup class tomorrow, Professor. I just got an idea and need to do a little cyber-sleuthing." Smile creases erupted, and he chuckled. "Get packing and start hacking as we used to say back at the Farm."

Serena and Moon stood facing the back wall. She instructed Serena to feel the wall.

"What do you see? What do you feel?"

"It looks and feels like stone made of earth, almost like adobe back home."

The elder woman began to hum, then she spoke words Serena did not comprehend. "Now what do you see?"

"Nothing… It looks the same."

"Look harder. Focus like when you do your kundalini yoga exercises."

The humming and foreign words continued. "Now do you see the difference?"

"Not really. If there's something I'm supposed to see, I'm missing it. It's dark." The early morning hour, the lengthy travel, and donkey ride accounted for the annoyance in her reply.

Moon studied her younger Snake Sister. "I see it in your auric field. You are suppressing your third eye. Open your eye and look."

Something about the power in Moon's voice, in her commanding tone, caused Serena's sound-sight to explode in light patterns. Moon repeated her incantation. As she did, Serena saw shifting colors as words and sounds illuminated her being. The wall shifted into a pattern of scintillating sparkles.

"Yes, I see it now. Everything is sparkling. The wall is transparent and shimmering."

"Good... Follow me."

They stepped through the back wall. Serena felt nothing, no resistance, nothing. They stood in a dark passageway. More words, and the rock walls began to emit a soft glow. In twenty yards, the passage ended at a stairway down.

"All those who possess the power of the voice can use the commands of illumination, provided they know the words and the sounds."

Each time Moon spoke, colors danced in ever-shifting patterns of sight and sound.

"How do you do it?"

"Light is in everything, child. You just need to know how to call it out. This is one of many things that our Mother teaches. You have the gift of the voice; Isis herself opened your fifth. What good is the power unless you can learn to use it? You are a Candelaria. You and Mother will have much to discuss."

13

Wán shàn looked out the private jet's window. She sat far from her bàba, who insisted the craft's window shades be drawn. Now, she watched as the tiny fields and cars enlarged and the world below approached normal. The jolt from landing startled her but just for a moment. She read the terminal's letters.

"Why are we stopping in Chongqing Jiangbei International Airport? I thought our destination was Dublin Airport."

"That is our final destination. We must first pick up some passengers."

Shortly, the craft's front door opened, the stairway descended, and a line of children queued to board. They all looked younger than she and all wore the same uniforms that displayed "Humanix School for the Gifted."

They numbered twelve—eight girls and four boys. She detected an easy pattern: two were blonde with fair skin and blue eyes, two had dark hair and skin, two had brown skin, two looked Asian, two looked Mediterranean, and the remaining two fit no clear category. She grouped these two as "exotic."

"Who are these children? What is the purpose of the Humanix School?"

"I shall answer your questions but first answer mine. What do you notice about them?"

"Ten are grouped in twos according to anthropomorphic characteristics. Two defy ready classification. All appear unusually attractive and healthy. Shall I go on?"

"Excellent. You make your father proud. They are your cousins. The in vitro lab at the Imaginarium conducted the joinings, the same as for you. We then transferred the viable embryos to Humanix to complete growth, receive special programming, and be prepared for service."

"Service?"

"Yes. There are many wealthy patrons who pay large sums for hybrids. We produce only the best-bred hybrids, and they are completely loyal to their new owners." The crew sealed the aircraft's door; all passengers strapped in, and the plane began to taxi. "This group represents our finest effort to date. They are a gift for my Illuminati Brothers. What do you think?"

"They are excellent specimens, bàba." In her mind, she couldn't help but think, *My cousins do not look very happy.*

"Come, sit next to me. I want to show you something and get your opinion."

Wán shàn listened as Dr. Li showed her a travel route starting at the NBio Diagnostics' plant, then to Vancouver, Canada, followed by destinations in the United States: Denver, St. Louis, and Chicago. At each location were routing numbers and addresses for shipping depots as well as date stamps. At the final location, a note read: *"All packages picked up by Jones Shipping and Storage, signed by company representative Austin Markle. NO SUCH COMPANY OR PERSON IDENTIFIED."*

"Given this information, what conclusions can you draw?"

"One: someone made the shipping of these items difficult to track. Two: someone has gone through great trouble obtaining these data points. Three: the unknown identity of the final known pickup makes it difficult to determine the final destination."

"Good. Any questions?"

"Is there surveillance footage from the last known depot in Chicago? If available, such footage may reveal vehicle information such as a license number or provide a video of Austin Markle."

"Excellent! I asked the same questions. Unfortunately, the man wore a hat and a bandage on his face, making identification impossible, and there is no useful vehicle information. Now, what if I told you another package for delivery to the same customer was ready to be shipped?"

"I would place some type of hidden tracking device among the contents being shipped."

Dr. Li scrolled on his phone to a text message he exchanged while they were on the tarmac at Chongqing Airport:

Kim Chul-su: *The delivery is ready to be shipped per your instructions, Dr. Li. Do you now want me to authorize the shipment to go? I remind you that the customer requested expedited delivery.*

Advanced Bionics: *Yes, you may proceed.*

Li turned to Wán shàn. "Exactly. Your strategic analysis is everything I expected. I hope you like flying. I expect you will make another trip soon."

Bryson strode into the lab. The Cheshire-cat look matched his swagger. Neither of the geneticists even looked up from their work. Now he appeared a little foolish with the I-know-something-you-don't-know look on his face and no one paying attention.

"Anyone up for a break?"

BB answered, "Tarni and I are just finishing up with the results from yesterday."

"Tarni? You mean the girl with the Robertsonian translocation on chromosome twenty-one? Where do you think her seven percent Scandinavian heritage comes from? I'm guessing some distant Viking cousin living in Britain and sent to Australia as one of those penal colony volunteers. She does have a kind of Viking attitude, don't you think?"

"What! Where did you get that information?" The intense look on Tarni's face was more than fierce. She barked, "Belt up! You don't want to see me madder than I already am."

"Calm down. I told you that having your information in a company's database is not a good idea."

"You stole it! You hacked into a secure site and stole my genetic profile. That's outrageous, Bryson! You spill my private info and act like Bob's your uncle. I tell you straight out, mate, that's not all right. Nick off!"

"Okay…okay. I'm a jerk and shouldn't have stolen your private data. In the trade, we call it 'ethical hacking,' but I can understand the hacked person doesn't see it that way. I'm sorry…really! But I wanted to make a point. I'm sure there is a ton of information we can mine, and this is just the first one I cracked. Yesterday kept me busy; they had a lot of firewalls and encryption to decipher, but I did get through. Sorry, I shouldn't have looked at your private information. All of it is damn interesting. All that haplogroup data and the migration patterns and the gene-specific single nucleotide polymorphisms. It's fascinating, and I'm sure we can use it."

"Yeah, well you weren't the only busy person yesterday. You've got some interesting SNPs of your own." She still looked steamed. Bryson figured it was best if he kept quiet.

"Tarni is right, Bryson, about both things. I think the ethics of breaking into such a database are questionable. Still, I understand your motive, and you've made a good point about security. She's also right about your DNA. For one thing, you have a disproportionately high amount of Denisovan genes—a very interesting genetic profile."

"Denisovan, you mean the early hominids before Neanderthals?

Tarni smirked. "Primitive humans, probably lacking in any decency judging by descendants like you."

"Stop it, the two of you. More interesting is the section of DNA I am most concerned about. The one that overlaps with a DNA section in reptiles. Yours is different; it's more active, turned on by influences I must study more. I'm already isolating some messenger RNA and transcriptase proteins to begin to unravel the significance. It may be nothing, but neither Tarni nor I show this pattern."

"What does it mean?"

BB shrugged just as the door opened.

"I thought you all were hard at work, not sitting around talking." Claus had yet to visit the final lab setup; he did a quick survey. "Impressive!" He turned to Bryson. "Looks like someone forgot to hook up the security camera at the front entrance."

"G'day, Claus, I'm Tarni. Thanks for letting me crash. I may be looking for a new roommate soon; this one"—she thumbed at Bryson—"is too ethical. And I don't mean that in a good way."

Claus looked at Bryson, then back at Tarni. "Okay then. Maybe we can discuss your housing situation over a cold beer. It's nice to finally meet the woman with two shelves of cosmetics and beauty products in the guest bathroom." He inhaled. "Nice perfume. Cacharel Anaïs Anaïs, I didn't think they made that anymore. Smells better on you than in the bottle; goes well with the hair."

"I like you, mate. We'll down a schooner later. Just the two of us." She made a petulant face, then broke into a laugh. "Just messin'. We should all lighten up and have some fun together after work. First shout on me."

BB approached Claus with a specimen kit. "What's this?"

Bryson explained, "BB's running samples for DNA analysis. He needs some saliva and cells from inside your mouth along your cheek."

"A spitty-bitty and a swabie-jobbie—got it." Claus took the tube. "Piece a pie. Oh, almost forgot"—he handed the sample to BB—"Bryson, the corporate jets are on the move. There's an unusual number headed to the same destination. Looks like something is going on in Ireland."

14

A strange group of men. Wán shàn studied each of them carefully while making mental notes. She recognized Van Duyn from her battle with the soldier. Her training included detailed information about the Illuminati Order, the thirteen families, many historical elements. Bàba had told her additional facts about each of the heads of the thirteen families: they met once a year as the Council. He didn't know if anyone would bring a second-in-command. He said they would all present on progress with the plan. His instructions were clear. "Say nothing. Just observe. Trust no one. Reveal nothing about your five sisters. Eventually, you will all be my eyes and ears."

Her day held many surprises thus far. They left Dublin in a small bus with all the impeccably behaved schoolchildren. They traveled to the Irish countryside to a place called "The Hill of Slane," a megalithic structure with a ruined castle, an old monastery, and hidden passages deep beneath. They entered a cairn then into a ring barrow and descended. Bàba pointed to a tunnel headed upward, to the motte in the center of the castle; they continued deep below. Several side chambers flanked a central subterranean meeting room. The room resembled any modern meeting venue. Conference table and chairs seemed out of place deep within the bowels of Slane's burial mound.

The Pindar, Rothschild, loved to meet under the Hill. St. Patrick, dispatched by the Vatican to rid this soil of the Druids, was of his bloodline. The Merovingian family had deep roots here as well; someone named Dagobert was exiled to the Monastery at Slane. These bits and pieces of bàba's history lesson percolated in Wán shàn's mind as she studied the Illuminati brethren. She was the only female and the only one with pale skin. *They do not shield their gray when gathered together. In secret, they show their true colors.* They all had a unique scent. With her eyes closed, she could identify each one. She even smelled Bundy's arousal when he looked at her. She made a note. *Trust no one.*

Rothschild opened with a blessing from Lucifer. He passed out vials.

"A special tincture to celebrate our progress. This comes from a Peruvian tribe—very pure, very invigorating."

"To the light!" They drank, then sat.

From her location in a shadowed spot to the side, Wán shàn could view both the presentations and all the attendees.

Van Duyn presented on the performance of the soldiers, Sudan's secondary order, and some additional orders for more soldier units. He acknowledged the help of Servant Li in the programming and development.

Rockefeller and Rothschild copresented on the initial economic panic in monetary markets and systems. They were coordinating with central banks.

A lengthy and elaborate presentation by DuPont included work done by her bàba and by Servant Van Duyn. Coordinating with DARPA and agribusiness, a horde of insect allies had been released in India. Genetically modified food crops there were susceptible to a transgenic virus that the insects harbored. Targeting India first would maximize the population at risk and the consequent death toll.

There was a presentation on geoengineered climate change. Russell went through detailed population statistics and how the cull was likely to proceed. That's how they referred to it—the great cull. Kennedy overlaid the several different strategies being employed and then sketched out the timelines for phase one and then phase two—the onset of the New World Order. Graphs and charts of countries and regions, highlighted the current and future population statistics projected on a timeline from one to fifty years. Best projections were five to ten years for the population to stabilize, but only two generations until the majority of the world's population had genomes without humanity's flaws. The central flaw or defect engineered to extinction was man's desire to evolve spiritually, to ascend to mythical union with God at higher levels of consciousness.

Kennedy joined his thumbs and index fingers to form a triangle as he spoke. "The light of truth that Lucifer himself revealed, perfection of the earthly form of man, the ascent to Godhead, is something we are now on the threshold of achieving. We shall all still be here to witness this triumph." Kennedy blessed himself and sat down.

Wán shàn's strategic mind assembled the various pieces. Most of the efforts were indirect. Cause hardship, fear, war, and let people slaughter one another. Some efforts were direct, such as the new hemorrhagic virus and the vaccines that Li and DuPont had prepared. She concluded it was all well thought out and very elegant.

At last, her bàba's turn came. That was her signal. She got up, left the room, and returned moments later leading the schoolchildren. They no longer wore uniforms; instead, they had on loose-fitting, colorful robes in different styles. They stood in submissive silence.

"Before I update our Council of Thirteen, I ask the Pindar's permission to present a gift to all my Brothers."

Rothschild signaled his agreement. Wán shàn saw his momentary flash of disdain.

"These servant hybrids are among the best genetic combinations we have produced from our efforts at the Imaginarium. Completely without desire to ascend spiritually, they are fine physical specimens and programmed for loyalty. Observe." Li called to a blonde female and a brown-skinned male and whispered to each.

As the Council members watched, the two children removed their robes and began to stroke their genitals. Wán shàn caught wind of arousal within the room. The other children stood there. Bàba whispered again, and the demonstration concluded. The two dressed and joined their schoolmates.

"I can teach you many command code words that they respond to." He held up a cord and a small trocar with a bulb on the end. He whispered to one of the exotic children, a redhead with long braids. They all watched as she drew the cord around her arm and inserted the needle into her vein. A moment later, Li unscrewed the trocar's top and showed the blood neatly in a bulb-shaped cup. He presented the offering to the Pindar. "Much neater than snipping, your Lordship." No one laughed. Rothschild declined.

After placing the blood-filled cup on the table, Li continued. "You can all draw lots and claim your gift at the end of the day's session. I have prepared a command list for each child." With that, he dismissed the children. They exited on their own.

Wán shàn observed it all—the Council of Thirteen, especially Rothschild, the children and their reactions, and, most of all, her bàba. *What is his strategy here? What game does he play? Are these gift children spies? How else has he programmed them?*

"But these children are only a sample of the improved humans we have engineered. Throughout our hives, we stand ready with over two million workers and a smaller number of overseers and caretakers. They will help to control the masses that remain until new, more compliant generations repopulate." Li fielded questions, but he wasn't finished.

He asked Wán shàn to stand. "This is my masterpiece. This is Wán shàn; in Chinese, the word means 'perfection,' and she is indeed genetic perfection. She is a chimera of the best of our combined and engineered DNAs. In some ways, she is the child of us all." Amid heads nodding in approval, Van Duyn attested to her battle prowess and tactical genius.

Servant Li concluded. "Her presence here tells you that she is now my second. This specimen of perfection"—he stood behind Wán shàn and placed a hand on each shoulder—"is immune to sunlight. She is the first of us who truly lives in the light."

The Council members stood and shook Li's hand, and they touched and poked and admired Wán shàn. She made mental notes. All the while, she wondered, *What commands has bàba placed in my head and the heads of my sisters? He will use us? Use us to show that he is present in many places at the same time? Use us as his eyes and his ears? That is very clever. I did not know there were so many hive sites. I will ask to visit some, to see for myself what the new and improved humans are like. These men are smart, but not as smart as bàba; he is very strategic.*

15

The stairway down ended after less than twenty steps. They entered a room with upward-sloping walls. Serena could hear water running.

"The walls are quartz." Moon pointed to the black polished floor. "Basalt. The room itself is a small pyramid. Telluric currents generated by the earth and flowing water power the crystalline structure.

Mother can explain better than I. She has told me of the time when the Pyramid at Abusir was still intact. She could be both here and there at the same time. This all must seem strange to you. I'm sorry, Serena. I should have prepared you better."

Serena looked around. The walls emitted a soft light. She couldn't describe it, but she felt a potent energy. It vibrated and pulsated. Her kundalini sang in harmony. The sense of being aware, alive, awake, and activated in all her chakras took her breath away. Moments later Serena spoke. "What's the story with the pedestal? Where is Mother?" Every word she uttered had a corresponding explosion of mental color.

In the center of the pyramid stood a pedestal with a green tablet. It glowed!

Moon approached and pointed. "This is an Emerald Tablet, fashioned by Thoth himself."

"We had a presentation on the tablets in my conspiracy group back home; I wasn't sure they even existed. Is this one of the twelve? Does this contain the ancient wisdom of Atlantis before its destruction?"

"The White Snakes promoted the lie that there are only twelve. The Pyramid Priests, the sun worshippers whose progeny are the Illuminati, collected only twelve. There are others, and this is one of them." She placed her hand upon the tablet. "And this is our Mother; she is bound to this tablet."

Energy crackled, and a shimmering form appeared, at first translucent then gradually coalescing into substance, taking the form of a woman. She appeared middle-aged, dressed in a simple white robe.

"Sarah, have you returned for more training?"

"No, Mother. I have brought a new pupil. Though she is not of the Black Snake Sisters or the Isis Mystery School, she desires testing and training. Isis herself opened her voice."

The Mother image said nothing for a moment as she placed her own hand over Moon's. "Yes, I absorb this knowledge. A Candelaria? An ancient scion, one I have never instructed. Come, child, place your hand upon the tablet."

Upon joining hands in contact with the emerald carving, waves of pulsating energy burned intensely up and down her spine. Her throat felt scorched by fire, and bolts of light streamed in and out through her head. She couldn't move. Time stopped as she relived every moment of her life in a brilliant flash. When the sensation passed, she felt clean, pure, as though all the lies of her past had been expunged. The veil obscuring reality had been stripped away, and she stood naked and strong.

"I see all in the memories of your cells, back to your first incarnation in Atlantis, to before the time of breaking, before the unjoining, when matter and spirit danced in harmony as one, when darkness and light, male and female, sun and moon all sang together."

Serena couldn't say for sure, but the Mother apparition sounded sad as she spoke.

"Who are you? What are you?" Serena asked Mother.

Moon answered, "Mother is subtle energy, the spirit energy of a temple priestess of the great Giza complex that Thoth himself built. Her etheric embodiment is bound to this place and to this tablet."

"So, Sarah, can I call you that instead of Moon? Are you saying that Mother is a ghost?"

"For now, you may think of her as such. In time you will understand how soul energies can manifest here into the material plane and the true nature of her being."

"I chose freely to be the teacher of Thoth's wisdom, to guide and share with those who came after. I have taught many hundreds in the mysteries available in this tablet. You have much to learn, Serena Mendez."

One of the few things he insisted upon when he agreed to work on the project was a place to sleep at the lab. Peter Reynolds had been more than obliging. BB had a small kitchenette and an oversized bed to sleep in. They all assumed that the long work hours BB logged made commuting to and from a waste of time, a luxury they couldn't afford. They were all wrong. BB knew that eventually he would need to tell them. Tomorrow would be the first day he stepped outside since arriving in Chicago. A trip to the zoo to collect some reptilian DNA. The weather forecast called for clouds. *Good. The bright lights sometimes trigger a migraine. The specialist said that might happen. He gave me five to six months. Gurumarra thought even less. We've made good progress. One step at a time… One step at a time.*

Thankfully, the zoo collection concluded without incident; although, it had fatigued him. Now past 10 p.m., BB felt beyond exhausted. Tarni left three hours ago. He still smelled her perfume mixed in with the residual paint odor that permeated the space: a converted auto body repair shop in this industrial part of town. Obscure, out of the way, windowless, without even a sign on the front. *I'll tell Tarni first. She'll understand. She'll know what to do.* BB looked at the small wooden crate with the virology supplies she had ordered. *That's got to be our second priority. Li, he's my first concern.* As the geneticist looked heavenward, he didn't focus on the dropped acoustic panels or the flickering fluorescent lights. *Kalinda, I will find out why, why they took you and our child, why they did this. I just need some more time. Give me more time, I beseech you, my love. Give me more time.* His arm shook, and, before he realized what was happening, BB fell to the tiled floor. His whole body writhed in spasms. A puddle of urine gathered beneath his unconscious body.

16

"You still haven't heard from Serena? Isn't your contact that Moon lady at Pyramid Communications? I gotta say, for a communications company they seem to be doing a great job at not staying in touch."

"I'm worried, Claus. I haven't heard squat, and the whole Middle East is turning into a powder keg. It's ready to explode. Worst part is I feel powerless."

"Whoa, Bryson, that's where you got it wrong. We knew this whole Martian plan we devised had some holes. We can't assume anything bad has happened, but in the meantime, we also can't assume everything is going okay. We need to be thinking about contingencies. And we also need to be thinking about attack and defense, tactics and strategy. Have you read *The Art of War* yet?"

"Since you mentioned it the other day, I sped through it. Good stuff! Attack where the enemy does not defend; defend where the enemy does not attack. That's the basic idea."

"Right. So, what have you been doing for the five days I've been away besides reading? I tell you, you are not thinking straight, man. You missed the security cam on the fritz at BB's lab. You didn't tie into the private jet program to link to your mobile. You're smarter than that, Bryson. What gives?"

"I don't know, I guess I'm just worried about Serena. Alone, by herself... I should have gone with her."

Claus put his arm around Bryson, a big brother sharing advice. "That's only half of it. Let me help you on this." He extended his hand, palm down, at the height of Bryson's nose. "About this tall, gorgeous body, perfect skin, perfect teeth, *pink curls*, and wicked smart. She smells damn good too."

Bryson looked down at his shoes, saying nothing.

"There's no shame in that, man. Or 'mate,' as she would probably say. She's got all the curves in all the right places. Why do you think I'm planning to go off on another gig? Hanging around in my own house addles my brain."

"It's just that I can't," he stammered, "I can't sort out what the hell I think."

"Bryson, I heard you took the trouble of researching her DNA, but do you even know what her name means?"

"Yeah, I looked it up. It means wave or surf. What's so special about that?"

Claus snickered. "Wrong dictionary. Check the urban dictionary usage. I'll wait."

Bryson thumbed a quick entry on his secure search engine. Claus watched as Bryson's Adam's apple stopped midswallow, and his eyebrows arched. "OMG… GODDESS! How do you defend against that?"

"You want to come with me?"

"Where are you going?"

"I don't know. Anywhere that's not here. There's always the hogan."

She could overhear snippets of conversation—Council of Foreign Relations, K68, Rhodes-Milner something, the Tavistock Institute. She made a mental list of questions to ask bàba. All the family heads wore identical white cloaks with black cowls except for the Pindar's. His golden hood set him apart, but she had no trouble recognizing any of them, partly from their stature, mostly from their scents. Wán shàn had her own garment, a shorter cloak, but the hood obscured her peripheral vision, an annoyance for sure. Observation. She excelled at this task. Scantily clad men and women served food and drink. She ate sparingly and avoided conversation.

Much about the rituals was familiar to her from her studies. Still, reading and learning differed from attendance and experience. The Humanix students, many naked or with torn garments, roamed throughout the ceremonial halls. One of the girls was missing part of a finger. She recalled her bàba's comment earlier to the Pindar. Another matter she would ask about. She saw Freeman and Bundy whisper into their gift children's ears, and the group of four moved to a side alcove. The four engaged in sexual activities. For a brief moment, Wán shàn made eye contact with a brown-skinned boy bent over a small table while a Council member thrust his genitals forward. The boy's eyes pleaded for relief, but he remained stoic. Vacant stares characterized the servant children's faces as though they had been drugged or hypnotized. *Mind control—powerful and potent, but these are only children.*

A central fountain bubbled with blood. *Some additive must prevent coagulation.* One of the family heads approached her from behind. She felt the presence beyond where her vision remained obscured by her cowl. *Bundy.* She smelled his desire but did not react; instead, she allowed it, allowed his hands to probe her tiny breasts. She could have broken his arm or his neck, but his behavior provided another lesson. She turned to face him, saw the blood around his mouth and on his robe. Up close, his gray skin looked old and wrinkled. She did not feel anger; she did not feel disgust; she did not feel desire. Curiosity. While Wán shàn could sense his lust, there was something else. She catalogued this to review later; if she could not understand, she would ask bàba. Done with her observations, she began to walk away when Bundy grabbed her arm.

"Li says you are perfection. Let me judge that for myself." He pulled her forward.

"Aaron, I don't think that's a good idea," Freeman said.

"Do you want to join us, Chester? Aren't you curious to see what Kenseiko's idea of perfect is?"

Wán shàn stood there. She said nothing, showed no emotion. She was certain she could break both their legs if she chose to.

"You're blood drunk, Aaron. You don't want to get Li mad at you. He'll inject you with something and turn you into a Komodo dragon or something worse." Freeman pulled his Illuminati Brother away, and the two walked toward the fountain.

Rothschild and her bàba stood facing each other in a side alcove. They were discussing, no, arguing. Even with her excellent hearing, Wán shàn could only discern bits and pieces. She inched over. Something about Shrem. *Why are they talking about him?* Something about a candle necklace, some girl, where is she, what have you done with her? Bàba looked angry. She would ask about this exchange later.

As the festivities closed with a ceremonial chant about light and Lucifer, she made her way to the sleeping quarter. She encountered one of the children, the redhead, the exotic-looking one that her bàba had displayed earlier. The girl had blood on her face and chest; she sobbed quietly. For a moment, Wán shàn stopped to study the child, only two or three years younger than she. Again, there was a feeling of observing something she did not fully comprehend, feeling something she had never felt before, something she needed to catalogue for future review. Wán shàn felt dirty.

17

I t didn't take Serena long to figure out Mother's approach to starting a new pupil on the "Path of Wisdom," as she kept calling it, and to learn to be the "Mouthpiece of Thoth," in order to speak truth with power. Mother's teaching method was frustratingly tedious, an agonizingly slow combination of part history lesson, part demonstration.

"The creator beings who fashioned mankind twisted matter and spirit, joining them in bondage to the material plane. The journey to unbinding is the journey to enlightenment. The body is the vessel during this sojourn. When the body passes to dust, the spirit rejoins the eternal flame until the next cycle of incarnation."

Yes, yes, I already know all this. Serena's thoughts drifted back to being in class and feeling bored out of her skull. *Let's get on with it. She must not have much opportunity to speak to someone new. I could use a cup of coffee. No, a pot of coffee.*

"Thoth's teachings arise from the wisdom accumulated by the great race of Atlantis. Prior to its destruction, it represented the pinnacle of man's development. Central to these teachings is the role of the mind, for the mind represents the link between the physical and the eternal dimensions of existence. It is through man's intellect that one can transcend the material plane and fully embrace the spirit plane while still being alive. Thus, mastering the great cosmic dance between duality and nonduality requires the discipline of the mind."

The student's hand shot up. "Question." Before Mother could acknowledge, Serena blurted, "Then why is it so difficult for people to become enlightened? Why can't we think it through, mental discipline, that sort of thing?"

Mother looked at Moon with a quizzical expression, then turned to Serena. "This is a consequence of the great corruption. The corruptors altered the creators' instructions governing man's ascent. The mind, instead of being the tool to walk the Path of Wisdom, has been poisoned and manipulated to enslave man to the physical plane. Are you not aware of the War of the Two Serpents? This is the reason Thoth established the mystery schools."

"Um, I know about some of this."

She continued. "In order to use the power of voice, the sound energy and vibration vocally projected, an adept must first learn to see the play of energy that underlies all manifest forms. Thus, the third eye must be open, and the mind must interpret what is seen correctly. Upon seeing the patterns of vibrations and knowing both the words and the tones to project, you can change those patterns and alter the forms."

"That makes sense. It's like the alchemists turning lead into gold. If you can see the elemental construction energetically, and you understood how to manipulate that energy, you could do it."

"Sarah, has this child been prepared?" Mother's voice, unmistakably irritated and stern, conveyed her annoyance. "She cannot train to be an adept without the proper formation."

"Mother, her studies were undertaken in India, with the Naga Sisters, a distant order allied with us. Their ways differ from ours." She added, "The war is upon us now. The child comes during a time of great need, a time when those shining the light and speaking the truth are few in number against a potent enemy."

The apparition flickered and grew translucent. "I am weary. Return tomorrow." She vanished.

"There's definitely something on this image, Uncle Pete." Seated across from Peter Reynolds, Bryson and Claus waited for a response.

"Where are these satellite images from again? When were they taken? How did you acquire them?"

"I'm a little limited in what I can do remotely. If I was back home in Taos, I could get much better resolution and a shitload more pictures. These are from Dublin International Airport, near where the private corporate jets are serviced. This is one of the planes we've been tracking."

Claus pointed to a grainy figure. "We think that's Li."

"Could be; can you sharpen the picture?"

"No, Uncle Pete. Even with filters and image enhancement, that's as clear as I can get it. So, do you think that's him? The plane started in Singapore, then stopped off in China at Chongqing Jiangbei Airport. We're pretty sure that's where the kids were picked up. Scroll to the next picture and you'll see what I mean."

Peter studied the image of thirteen children, they looked to be in their teens, and they all were dressed in the same uniform except for one girl. She looked a little older and stood next to the man, presumably Li. "Do you know what the uniform says?"

"Yes, we successfully reconstructed the words from composite elements taken off different children, but we can't find any reference in any database to the words. They spell out, 'Humanix School for the Gifted.' Does that mean anything to you, Uncle Pete?"

Peter placed his elbows on his desk, drew his hands up, and leaned his face into his palms. He shook his head. "It's true then." He removed his right hand and pinched the bridge of his nose with his left thumb and index finger. His head was down, and his eyes were closed. "It's true, and I didn't want to believe him." A long sigh followed.

"I'm sure that's Kenseiko Li." Peter opened his eyes and looked directly at Bryson. When he spoke, his voice quavered, and his skin had noticeably paled. He looked weary. "The only other time I ever heard of 'Humanix School' was from my brother George, your father. He had overheard whispers during a meeting break. It was a side conversation between Li and Rockefeller that made little sense to him until he pieced some of it back together in his mind. The two of them were discussing a program Li had already started. George knew it had something to do with human cloning. Everyone that's high enough in the Illuminati knew that Li was experimenting with altering human DNA. The whole reason your father went to Singapore was to confront Dr. Li about his intentions regarding the clones or hybrids or whatever Li was up to and what would happen to these clones. My brother suspected this school had something to do with it. The whole idea of growing people in labs and secretly training them for who knows what reasons really bothered your father. It cost him and your mother their lives." Peter shook his head with a deep sigh.

Bryson didn't respond immediately; instead, he asked a question. "So, what are they all doing in Dublin?"

"Probably the annual gathering. The Council of Thirteen meets once a year under Snake Hill. I don't know where that is, but it's somewhere in Ireland. Thirteen children and thirteen family heads. They could be gifts—Li showing off. Or worse." He pinched the bridge of his nose again, shutting his eyes. "Could be a sacrifice."

Claus and Bryson looked at each other, saying in unison, "Attack where the enemy does not defend." Claus continued. "Maybe we can throw a surprise party the next time they meet together."

"Wait, there're more…rumors, but I think we have to assume they are true." Peter leaned into his palms again, almost covering his face as he spoke. "People, conspiracy-theory types, crazies according to some, have been saying there are these huge underground farms where the Illuminati are raising thousands or even millions of these hybrids. George had suspicions, but he could never get any proof. Just as he could never get any proof about that school. He called them hives." Peter shuddered. "It's probably all true; I just never wanted to believe it."

"Do you know where they are? Maybe we can gather some intel."

"I've only heard of two: Denver, under the airport in a series of caves, and someplace in New Mexico. A small town with a military base called Dulce. George thought there was a big one in Tibet somewhere. I don't know. I'm sure there's more."

Bryson grabbed his laptop and typed furiously. "Claus, do you think it's safe for me to go back to my house?"

Claus shrugged. "Probably, you're most likely off NSA's radar. We can sweep for any new surveillance bugs since I zapped your property with the EM pulsar. Why do you ask?"

"Dulce Base is only about two and a half hours from home. Besides, I need to clear my head, if you get what I'm sayin', mate." He winked and saw Claus's grin of understanding.

"Uncle Pete, I'm going to find out what Dad was on to. But I'm not going to get myself killed. The bad guys will never see me coming."

18

The perfect opportunity for Dr. Li to further test his creation occurred during the return flight to Singapore. He asked Wán shàn to synthesize her observations about the other family heads. Her astute and insightful analyses pleased him, even exceeded his expectations.

"What you learn by experience complements what you have learned in the relative isolation of the hive where you and your other Ninja sisters were raised. There is much more to learn; you have done well thus far. Your time in Singapore will be brief. The package I am tracking has been delivered, and I want you to go and learn who is secretly doing work on genetic research. Find out who and why. Do you have questions for me, daughter?"

"Why did you and the Pindar argue about Shrem? What is his role?"

"Put simply, Shrem is involved in everything the Council of Thirteen and the entire Illuminati Order does. Rothschild does not like that Shrem and I have a special relationship. In fact, Rothschild does not like me, and the feeling is mutual. The Pindar is the Council head; that position has remained as a Rothschild for centuries. They are more concerned about money and power than anything else. Even Shrem has grown weary of Rothschild's stewardship. My efforts, along with some of the other Council members, have taken us to the final steps to create not just a New World Order, but a race of superior humans. That culmination will be despite Rothschild's leadership, not because of it."

"Are you saying Edward Rothschild should be replaced?"

"Not at all. He serves a purpose. I may be angry at him, but Genghis Khan says, 'An action committed in anger is an action doomed to failure.' As long as he does not impede our progress, he is useful."

Wán shàn seemed to think for a moment. "Genghis Khan also says, 'Man's greatest joy is to slay his enemy, plunder his riches, ride his steeds, see the tears of his loved ones, and embrace his women.' It is reported that he also hated aristocratic privilege. Perhaps you share such sentiment with the Mongolian general. Still, I still do not fully grasp what it means to be angry, to exhibit hatred, or to shed tears over a loved one."

"That, Wán shàn, is the most beautiful thing you have told me."

"Explain, please."

"Never. To explain this to you only creates a burden that I do not wish for you to carry, my daughter."

Wán shàn paused for a moment, then changed the subject. "What about the candle necklace? You and Rothschild discussed a girl. What is her significance?"

"You ask many good questions. I will give you the short answer. The Candelaria oppose our plans to perfect humanity. They were defeated long ago though one has somehow risen again. The girl is nothing but a pebble in our shoe. I don't need her because I have something better. I have her genes."

"And the necklace?"

"An item of jewelry the girl possesses that the Pindar desires. A testament to what he deems important."

Mother blessed the matching serpent cuff bracelets in a binding ritual. The blessing itself voiced strange harmonics, foreign yet somehow familiar. As Mother sang, Serena felt a strengthening of her own kundalini energy, almost as if part of her sang along, almost as though the words came from a distant shared past, a dream recalled of ceremonies in song and light. She sensed an effervescent tingling sensation in her throat. Colors coalesced and shifted. In her mind's eye, the matched serpents sparked with hues of green that seemed to emanate from the Emerald Tablet that her hands embraced. Now, when Serena wore the bracelets, she felt somehow closer to Mother and clearer in her thoughts.

Today, she practiced opening the back-wall entrance. Sarah had taught her the words and sounds. So too, Sarah instructed Serena in the sounds of illumination, to light the passageway. With the bracelets on, it was easy for her to hear vibrations, to see the light energy everywhere, and to see what happened when she used her voice to rearrange the patterns. Sarah explained it in more detail than Mother.

"We base our perception of reality upon recognizing how energetic vibrations organize into coherent systems. To see the truth requires effort. One must dispel the false beliefs that cloud normal perception. What you normally see is illusion; useful, but not a true representation."

Directing her kundalini energy through the chakras and up her spine required effort and concentration. With practiced discipline, Serena had become quite skilled. She could enter the "zone," as she called it, at will. The effort Sarah described seemed like the opposite. She called it a polarity.

"To channel *sekhem*, you must unfocus your mind and let the energy flow unimpeded by mental chatter. Conversely, what Mother instructs requires an extreme focus of the mind. Only then can you see through the illusion and direct the energies that surround us. You first see reality through your mind's eye and then project out through your voice. It requires great concentration."

For the young Candelaria, this new recognition, literally a re-cognition of the energetic structure of reality, was nothing less than astonishing. Finally, she began to understand what it meant to see the truth. She was only beginning to understand and appreciate how speaking truth with power had the potential to reorder reality.

"It's hard. It gives me a headache."

Serena watched as Sarah boiled water, saw the elder woman act as a conduit of energy from above and below.

"The real adepts are much more skilled than I. I have some strength with air and a little with fire, but the true masters could manipulate earth, air, fire, and water. Lead into gold is easy, I am told, though I lack the vision to see the material world as required to do this. Stones into bread—that is true mastery. Yeshua achieved this level of proficiency; he also mastered air and water and could thus calm the Sea of Galilee. I'm sure you've heard the stories. Moses mastered earth, air, and water, striking a stone to produce a stream, parting the Red Sea. As I have told you previously, we still teach these ancient alchemies of Horus in our Isis Mystery School. To some, these are stories, but to those familiar with Thoth and such teachings, they are but examples of applying the voice. Though not of our Isis School, those who project through the fourth chakra can perform great acts of healing. These are not miracles, Serena, as some might say. These are capabilities we all possess, capabilities that have been twisted to make them difficult to realize."

"What do you mean?" Sarah had been giving Serena a crash course, covering a lot of knowledge gaps in order to enable the Candelaria to best utilize her time with Mother.

"When perception and expression align, there is truth. Anything that is either misrepresented in its expression or presentation, or is incorrectly perceived, is false. The Brotherhood of the Sun promotes lies and deceptions to distort truth, to create an alternate reality. Most of humanity has been conditioned to not question these lies. They live in a grand illusion, a result of the distortion of how mankind was actually created to be."

"I learned of this both when I was in India and in Australia. Somehow, our DNA was corrupted. It blocked man's spiritual ascent. Is this the distortion you mean?"

Sarah smiled. "Yes. The genetic code itself was altered. The 'spawn of another star,' as Mother puts it, made changes to the blueprint. This happened before Thoth and before the destruction of Atlantis. The result was a human susceptible to fear and emotions that clouded the mind. When the mind is clouded thus, it blocks progression to spiritual union of the physical with the infinite."

"But why? Why prevent man from achieving enlightenment?"

"Child, don't be dense. It is for control. Enough history for today. We should eat and rest until your next session with Mother. I will leave you with her in order to rejoin with Youssef. I shall return the animals. When I am gone, do not venture from this structure. Our presence here must remain secret. I'll see you in six days."

"Understood. Answer me one last thing, Sarah; I'm curious, what are the most potent things you can do using your voice?"

"You are permitted to call me by my birth name here, but never in public. To answer your question, I can conjure a summer breeze…and I can boil water."

"That's it? How long have you been studying here?"

"Ten years. But do not be dismayed by this. Mother says you hold much promise. And you are a Candelaria. We shall find out what capabilities are in your DNA. I'll return in six days."

19

On Sundays, BB allowed himself the luxury of reading the newspaper. It wasn't fashionable with all the new technology, but he rarely listened to news reports as he worked, and he rarely stopped working. He couldn't afford the distraction. He had another seizure last night, and he knew that a morning off might be what his body was trying to tell him it needed. The headline was not good:

> CROP FAILURES IN INDIA…Massive and unprecedented crop failures of both rice and wheat have devastated the Indian economy and sent prices skyrocketing. India is the world's second largest producer of both rice and wheat. An insect-born mosaic virus is the culprit. Scientists have never seen both crops affected simultaneously, and never as widespread. Local farmers blame a government-sponsored plan that employed biologic control measures using presumed beneficial insects combined with mandated use of genetically modified seed stock. These genetically modified crops are uniquely sensitive to the mosaic virus. The Indian government denies these claims. Thousands of Indian farmers, unable to provide for their families, have committed suicide [see related story page 6: Farming in India, a Social and Cultural Crisis].

He turned to the lifestyle section to mitigate the growing dread he felt inside. No use. The story of mounting worldwide food shortage had "Illuminati Plan" written all over it. The lifestyle section gave the impression that everything in the world was just fine. He shook his head and tossed the paper into the trash. *I shall do what I can for as long as I can to stop this madness.* He returned to the latest run of specimens, trying to unravel what proteins this gene segment turned on or turned off, trying to understand why he was shut down so many years ago. *I need more time. I need DNA from the family heads, to see how it differs. And I need some of Serena's DNA to see why she is special.* Then it hit him.

He called Bryson. They hadn't left for Taos yet. No, he hadn't heard from Serena in Egypt; he was naturally worried. BB asked for something with Serena's cells—a comb, a brush, her toothbrush. He would look. Bryson felt certain he could find something. He'd bring over whatever he could find today since tomorrow he and Claus planned to leave.

Two hours later, Tarni came to work.

"Bryson's busy with a load of things. I wasn't doing anything, and I figured the drive here would be good for me. Those two gents are driving me crazy with all their surveillance talk." She held up a bag, put gloves on, and placed a comb, brush, lip gloss, and stuffed kangaroo on the counter. "Bryson says she likes to hold the stuffed 'roo by her face. Personally, I think it's a wallaby."

BB let out a much-needed laugh. "You are a delight, young lady, and indispensable."

"I figured it would go faster if I helped. You're supposed to be taking a day off. Would it be asking too much to learn what exactly you're looking for? What's so important about this girl? I don't even know what she's doing in Egypt." Tarni put on a lab coat. "Why is everything so secretive?"

Should I tell her? It's better that she doesn't know...safer. But she deserves to know. She's sacrificed a lot to be here, on nothing more than Gurumarra's insistence.

"It's time I tell you. There is much you will find hard to believe, not just about Serena Mendez, not just about Beangagarrie Brindabella, but about the world as a whole, about the War of the Two Serpents." He retrieved the paper pointing to the headline from India. "There is more to this story than you realize."

"Spiffy! 'Bout time someone clued me in on things. Go ahead. I'm listening." Tarni sat down.

"Are you familiar with the Aboriginal word 'Galinawa'?"

Four hours and a frozen pizza later, after incredulous revelations about the trip from India, surgery at the Royal Hospital and pursuit, Serena's chakra opening in Australia with Gurumarra reaching in to grab the snake in her belly, BB's personal revelations about the suppression of his research, his pregnant wife's death, and suspicions about Dr. Kenseiko Li, he finished with an overview of his best understanding of the Illuminati plans for a New World Order.

"So, what's happening in India, what's going on in the Middle East, world markets, you're saying it's all connected?" Tarni blinked. BB had given her a lot of information to process.

"Yes."

"I had no idea. I don't ordinarily see myself as a clueless drongo, but if what you say is true, most of the world is swimming up to their nostrils in Kool-Aid."

BB sighed. "There's more, and I'm afraid the inevitability of what I now say will both surprise and alarm you. Last night I had a seizure, one of several recent episodes. Please share this with no one. I have an advanced brain tumor. It's inoperable. I have forgone other treatments such as radiation or chemotherapy; these therapies would not be curative and would only impede my work."

Tarni stood immobile then reached forward to grab BB's hand. Tears welled. "I don't know what to say, Beangagarrie. I'm gobsmacked by everything you just told me... Now you throw this last piece in." She sniffled and clutched a tissue. "How...how long?"

"Three, maybe four months. I doubt I'll be able to continue that long. I assure you there is no pain. I am hoping you will continue the fight after I am gone."

She had smeared mascara and tears running down her face. "We don't have a lot of time."

20

Serious business. Once Mother got down to instructing, she didn't mess around. Serena imagined it to be like stories she'd heard from her own mother about nuns and Catholic schools. Strict didn't capture Mother's approach to training the voice of her pupil.

"Your first trial is with earth energy. Study the two coins on the table; one is gold, the other is silver. See the energetic structure giving rise to their composition. Can you see the difference with your focused mind?"

"Yes."

"Now repeat the words and tones I speak. Hold the image of the silver and imagine it transformed to gold as you speak."

Mother said, "*Pentubir alost.*" Each syllable had a different pitch.

Serena repeated the words *Pentubir alost* using the exact same sounds. She waited.

"Try again. Focus your mind."

Again nothing happened. "I'm doing it like you instructed. Nothing's happening."

"Perhaps over time you will learn. Transmutation powers can be fickle. When Isis released your voice, such power may have been omitted. The Candelaria blood may not possess this skill. We shall return to this lesson at a future date."

"I don't see how this helps in the fight against the Illuminati, anyway. They are tearing the world apart. More gold will not help."

"Your impatience, Serena, does not serve the cause you fight for. Be still. Learn to still your mind."

Easy for you to say.

"Air surrounds us. Learning to manipulate this requires deep knowledge of the ways in which air moves. I will test you today, but few initiates demonstrate skill with air at their first testing. A feather rests upon the table. Use your mind to lift it. Repeat, '*collinear epu sanghest.*'" The words sounded musical.

"How? What am I supposed to do?"

"Use your mind…and your voice!"

She stared at the feather, saw the ridges connecting each section, imagined it floating on a gentle current. Saw herself blowing out candles on a cake. "*Collinear epu sanghest.*" Nothing. "*Collinear epu sanghest.*" Still nothing. *This is bullshit!*

"As I said, few initiates pass the first trial with air. Study the wind, see with your mind how it moves and swirls. Observe the clouds overhead. A cough, sweat leaving your skin lifted by the air, a breeze, a gale—all can teach you the movement of this elemental. When you understand these movements, and can clearly see them in your mind's eye, I shall teach you the words. Until then, study and learn what your eyes see but do not see."

Serena could not help but feel a failure. *All this time, all this work, for what? I'm nothing—a warrior without a weapon.*

Through the Emerald Tablet connecting them, Mother could read Serena's thoughts. "You think you are the first to feel discouragement? The first to doubt? If you do not believe in yourself, how will you convince others to believe in you? Speak truth. You cannot deceive me though you can deceive yourself."

Mother's gaze withered any resistance.

Serena bristled with defiance. "I always tell the truth! I never asked for this! I never claimed to be someone special. Other people seem to feel that I am, that I have some great destiny. Everything seems so hard. I've accomplished nothing except managing to stay alive. I can't be responsible for doing something I'm not equipped to do."

"Perhaps, perhaps not. Is the final piece of straw any different from all the others piled on before the camel collapses? Is it all that different from the last one, the one that seemed also to fail? Does that piece have a destiny lesser or greater than the final stalk?"

"Why should I care? Part of me doesn't care about Snake Brotherhoods and Sisterhoods, or the Illuminati, or this great war I'm supposed to be a warrior for. But I will tell you what I do care about. I care about the truth. Because ever since I was a little kid, I've been lied to. I'm sick of lies and deceit. I'm sick of it enough that if there's something I can do to put an end to all the falsehood I will. And here's another bit of truth: that makes me pretty dangerous."

"Good. I think you needed to say that, not for me but for yourself. A life lived in the pursuit of truth is a life lived with honor."

Serena said nothing. Her tirade had loosened something, opened something inside she'd been holding back.

"The soul incarnates and chooses how to live and sometimes how to die. There is no destiny; there is only choice. So, Serena Mendez, shall I continue the testing, or are you too burdened to try? Is your spirit now broken like the camel's back? Do you choose defeat prior to battle? Some would label this cowardice; it is your choice, your soul. I give you naked truth and do not parse my words. Do we continue, or do we end your training now?"

Whatever had just loosened, tightened, and she shut down. Serena wanted to cry. She felt like a confused little girl searching for a way to escape. *I'm lost.*

Lost and alone. Running away from my life, running into some destiny, or not. Running in circles and getting nowhere. Don't know what to do. Don't know what I'm supposed to do... "SHUT UP!"

Her own voice startled her, but insight erupted in speaking those words. *STILL YOUR MIND! That's what Mother told me—BE STILL!*

"Did you just order me to be quiet?"

"Um, no. I, er...was talking to myself... I think I'm ready now. No, I know I'm ready now. Let's do it. Don't hold back, Mother. I'm a little screwed up sometimes, but I'm not ready to give up."

Whatever equates to a ghost taking a deep breath, Serena watched Mother's shimmering apparition pause.

"Fire. Consider ice, water, and steam. All are the same composition, energetically differing by the pattern of movement. All elements are in motion within themselves and among one another. When you see these movements and add energy by harnessing *sekhem* through your voice, you create heat. The great adepts can even master the removal of heat. To understand fire, to control fire, you must understand movement. Study the piece of cloth on the table. When you are ready, say this word. It is the easiest as it is a single syllable and sound—*ghrest*."

Serena nodded. She saw the cloth, the threads, the fibers, the strands that made the fibers. The closer she looked, the more she saw. Chaos! Like seeing a school of fish and trying to watch each animal move, or a giant murmuration of starlings, each beating their wings, each influenced by the movement of the other birds.

Something shifted. "I see it." It all made sense. A pattern emerged from the chaos of movements in the cloth. She allowed kundalini to flow upward and downward, projecting out through her vocal cords. *"Ghrest!"*

The cloth ignited then curled into gray ash, completely consumed. Smokey satisfaction filled her nostrils.

"You see, everything is in motion, you only need to speed it up. Now, study the bowl. Imagine how the clay moved when in the kiln, heated by the furnace that formed it. See the clay and speed it beyond the heat of the kiln."

No encouragement needed. At the word, *'ghrest,'* the bowl began to glow red. Serena continued to watch, repeating the word only louder and with more force. The table beneath the clay bowl caught fire.

"Enough!" Mother's voice broke Serena's concentration.

"What does the word mean? In the old language of Atlantis, what does '*ghrest*' mean?"

"The simplest translation is 'burn.' What was it like to use your voice in this manner?"

"I like it! It came easy to me, not like the other two."

"There are seventy-two commands in this tablet that govern the fire elemental forces. How many would you like to learn?"

"All of them."

21

Edward slammed the decanter, nearly pushing it off the cart. Nothing among his trophies and treasuries relieved the agitation. Swirling his goblet helped even if the cognac and blood mixture didn't. He got up and retrieved his guillotine cutter; he kept it inside the humidor. He didn't know why, probably because that's where his father had kept it. Not that he wanted to smoke a fine cigar. No, he reserved that indulgence for relaxed pleasure, when a fine Cuban enhanced an already good mood. He held the jeweled cutter. He had others, including a priceless tabletop, but this was his favorite. This one had a certain elegance—dual blades with a stop. *The stop is a handy feature, but I like this one because it was father's and because of the sound.* He nestled his fingers into either end and gently squeezed until barely past a tiny resistance within the mechanism. Click! He smiled and did it again. Click. Something about that sound, not an insect chirp, more like a pleasant snap. Click. It settled him.

As he depressed the blades several more times, a thought gestated and gelled. *It never occurred to me before, but the sound reminds me of the hounds. Like when Moxy grabbed that hare and cracked its leg.* A vision memory of that fine afternoon in the Scottish countryside, of Moxy wagging her tail, blood dripping from her jowls, accompanied a momentary easing of Edward's disquiet. Click. Edward Rothschild salivated. *Yes, that will be a nice start. Sorry, Kenseiko, I couldn't resist.* He rang his manservant.

"Fetch me the new girl." He sneered. "The gift from Dr. Li, the one I returned with from the meeting." Click.

I don't like the way he challenged me, insulted me even. He needs to be put in his place, taken down off his perch. Edward had returned to his chair and goblet. He swirled and put his legs up on the ottoman. *He can deny it all he wants, but he must have rejuvenated. He was hardly limping. I'm sure he went to see Shrem. Unless…unless…* New thoughts began to percolate and coalesce. *He could have a new blood source, something more powerful, purer, more potent. The girl! Could he have her? Li stopped talking about her, stopped pursuing her. Why?*

Edward glanced over to the pedestal and empty Candelaria case. *He doesn't have the necklace or the girl. Or does he? He can't. That beady-eyed dog muncher! There's no way he could know. Father said only the Rothschilds knew about the real purpose.* He felt his agitation growing. He didn't even notice the manservant's return with the girl. *Still, I should notify that cousin in Tenerife. What's his name? The one with all the defects.* He shuddered drawing his lips back in disgust. *Something Spanish, what is it? Rafael? No, no, Riccardo? Yes, that's it. I'll call Riccardo and tell him to be on the watch. If Li or the girl should show up, I need to know.*

Now, who else can I get to help me? No one in the Council but still someone in the family. Someone I can trust. An ally…someone who hates Li. Edward grinned. *Of course. Why didn't I think of this sooner?* He strode across the room taking big steps, confident steps. He picked up the desk phone. "Connect me overseas to the US to Peter Reynolds. Ring me back when he's on the line… No, I don't care what time it is." Only then did he notice his servant and the girl. Only then did he realize that he still held the guillotine cutter.

He looked at the girl. Click. He put the instrument on his desk. "Never mind. You're both dismissed." With a hand wave, they vanished. He tapped his fingers, waiting for the phone to light and then smiled.

"Peter."

"To what do I owe this honor, Consular Rothschild?"

"I have a proposal for you. I want to solicit your help. It involves an old friend of yours…"

Despite her initial resistance, Serena enthusiastically embraced her training time with Mother. When Mother's energy grew weak, usually around 9 a.m., Serena returned to the dwelling, slept, cooked, washed, and practiced. Scorched walls, a melted kettle, and charred hay gave evidence to her skill, or lack of skill. She found releasing fire energy to be easier than controlling it. She had already learned four commands and still had another two days before Sarah returned. 3 a.m., time to join Mother in the pyramid chamber.

"I am weak today, child. Our session may be short. When the nearby Pyramid at Abusir was still intact, the power it resonated charged my own etheric energies. Today, with the moon still dark and the pyramid crumbling, I am tired."

Mother retested Serena for power of the voice over earth and air, but nothing happened. She trialed the water element, but the young Candelaria lacked this skill.

"Water, too, is everywhere, but you must be cautious not to call water forth from living creatures, plants, or even yourself. Water is both the giver and the taker of life."

"Fire language, Mother. Teach me new words."

"Quite a different student from a short while ago now speaks to me, hungry for new knowledge, hungry for more words of power. Be on your guard, Serena. The voice must be wielded with care and with caution. Practice the four words and sounds that you know. Tomorrow we shall work on others."

Serena battled back impatience. "Tell me, Mother, even with the weapon of my voice, how can I use this to fight against the sun worshipers? They are powerful. How do we of the Luminarian blood fight against them?"

"The truth is more powerful than lies. Even when lies masquerade as truth, even when lies twist and distort such truth. As is written within this tablet, 'The truth shall set you free.' Still, most do not understand what this fully means. Even you, Serena, you who value truth so highly, do not comprehend the depth of meaning."

"I'm listening. I want to be free."

"When the corruptors altered the strands of life, it was only a physical alteration. All creation, including all of life, is composed of both spirit and matter. Such is Thoth's wisdom to see that the physical alteration only imprisoned man's spirit energy. With the correct words, spoken with power, the binding could be undone, to free or release the spirit held captive. He understood that the true words could remove the distortion and restore the strands of life to their original pattern. These spoken words of truth have the power to set free that which is in the core of each of us. Perhaps you sense this in your Candelaria blood. Now I have revealed this deepest of truth as Thoth himself revealed it to me."

It made sense. Mother's words resonated throughout Serena's spine and head. Pulsating energy vibrated as she absorbed this deep truth. Like ore being refined in the crucible of her mind, the words Mother spoke burned away all the impurities and mental misconstructions leaving only the distilled essence. Truth!

"What are these words? Where can I learn them?"

"These are not known to me and are not in this Emerald Tablet. Some say they are lost. Others say they are with stones held by the Twins, the wisdom keepers from the time before Atlantis sunk. The Twins hold the first and the last tablets. The first stone includes the language of the creator beings; the words guarding the seven seals that bind spirit to matter would be written there."

Serena nearly choked at the lump forming in her throat. She managed to whisper, "Say that again… Wait…" She found a dusty spot on the polished black floor and wrote:

ETIEPESEPMERI

LPVRINENIPEPNEIFANT

EAFM IPNINI FMEAREI

NARMPRLMOTARE

OLM INRANFR TAEBNPEM Reven NVINAPIMLIFINIPI NIPIAN

EVPMIRNA ENVPMTI EPNMPIR VRVIVINRN APVI MERI PIVNIAN NTRHN

NBIMEI ANNEIPERFMIVIFVE

"Are these the words?"

"I don't know, child. I do not speak the language of the creators. Where do these words come from?"

Serena relayed what she knew of the apparition of the Virgin Mary to the Guanches in the Canary Islands. "The seven words written upon the hem of her robe—" She never finished. Mother interrupted.

"The one you call Mary was of the Isis School. It takes great power to manifest, but if there was a pyramid chamber such as this, it could be done. These might be the words of unbinding, but even if you found this location, even if this was in old Atlantis at the place of the Twin wisdom keepers, you still could not enter without the rainbow key."

"Explain."

"The six colors of the rainbow activate the key. I can teach you the words, but they are useless without the key."

"Last I checked, there were seven colors to the rainbow."

"These are the six known to me." Mother repeated the words and sounds.

Hearing the sounds, a vibrant succession of colors starting with red and ending with blue filled Serena's inner vision.

"Amazing! I see a clear burst of color with each word. The harmonic progression sounds familiar too. Tell me about the key. What does it look like?"

"Thoth fashioned it as a snake coiled around a candle. The candle glows with a halo of golden light." A faint rumbling could be heard in the distance.

"You mean like this?" Serena hurriedly drew a sketch of the Candelaria necklace. The rumbling grew closer. *What is that noise?*

"I have never seen the rainbow key, but what you draw matches the description."

Now it was loud, almost like a truck approaching with a broken muffler. Pop, pop, pop, POP…BANG! *Gunshot? Could be a backfire.* Silence. Moments later she heard footsteps. Serena prepared a fire command when suddenly Sarah burst into the room.

"Hurry! We must leave."

"What! What's going on?" She followed behind the older woman, leaving the pyramid room, entering the passageway and then the dwelling.

Sarah looked about, saw the charred remains, the scorched walls. "I see you've been practicing."

"STOP!" Serena hadn't intended to yell, but the command carried power. Sarah froze just for a second.

"Egypt has closed all but it's western border. If we don't leave now, I cannot say when you will be able to leave."

Sarah pointed to a motorcycle and handed Serena a pair of goggles. "Put these on." She drew in the kickstand, pumped the starter, and throttled the engine. "War surrounds us."

"War? What happened? When? Who?"

22

Claus worked the joystick on the copter-drone while flying the unit through different rooms of the house. The control pad had an integrated screen; he watched the drone's surveillance video in real time. He opened the front door, sent his eyes-in-the-sky flying overhead, and looked at Bryson's home through the camera embedded in the drone.

"Hey, looks like you got a broken roof tile." He snapped a photo. "You can show this to the roofer."

"Would you shut the front door; you're letting the bugs out."

"This baby is smooth, Bryson. I can't wait to test it tonight. It's got the latest IR tech for low light; that's where the real money is gonna be."

"Looks like somebody has a new toy. You're like a kid at Christmas."

"How about your new toys? Looks to me that you geeked out big time."

"It's a bitch, really. No fun at all thanks to the NSA. Install is going well enough; I've got a lot of data to move over to the new servers. The raid set me back with syncing everything, but I expect to be up to full speed in a couple of days. We should know what Serena's status is then."

Claus landed the drone. "It's getting messy over there. I'm sure you saw the latest. Sudan did a raid into Libya. It was some military op; they used elite soldiers. But all they hit was a food depot. They must be desperate. I did service time in Libya; even when times are good, it's still tough on the citizens there."

"I heard. We should probably see if there are any updates." Bryson used a remote to light a TV screen; he scrolled through some stations. None showed any new developments.

"Did you see the satellite images I pirated? I'll get my own once I hook up all my hardware."

"They're terrible. I saw them. They stink, but they beat that old stuff on the internet. I mostly need night images. For this op, that's where the real money is."

"Okay, that's the second time you said that. Why night?"

"Easy. Less guards out on patrol, fewer people up and about, and most importantly, way slower response time. This is gonna be a hit and run. Hit them hard and get the hell out."

"Sounds like you have it figured out already."

"You're not the only one who's been busy. You saw those banks of fans. That's gotta be a big underground installation in Dulce. Who knows how many levels and how far under the mesa?"

"Weird, considering how close by it is. I was clueless about this place but have been doing my homework. From all those conspiracy theory sites I stayed up late looking at, there are at least seven levels and maybe more. If only a fraction of what I looked at is true, there is some messed-up stuff going on there."

"The size isn't so important as the ventilation system. It looks unprotected. For a military base, they don't look prepared for an attack. That's to our advantage. I'm thinking this will probably be a gas-n-go. The fans suck in the gas, and we go in to get whatever we can get. We're gone before they even realize they've been caught with their pants down."

"Sounds good to me. I'll leave the planning up to you, Claus."

"You're good with gas, Bryson. Did I tell you I laughed so hard I almost fell out of my high hide in the tree when you dropped those cannisters on NSA and the marshals?"

"Only about a dozen times. This one won't be so easy."

"We'll see. First order of business is to test this copter out at night. If it works per specs, I'll deliver it tomorrow. I've already identified possible sites from the satellite maps."

Bryson waved his hand. "Sh, sh...quiet!" A TV special report interrupted normal programming.

"Turn up the volume."

As the two men watched, the reporter updated viewers on the crisis in the Middle East. War had been declared between Libya and Sudan. Israel had closed all its borders. Saudi Arabia invaded Yemen. Refugees were pouring into Egypt. The UN General Assembly had called an emergency meeting.

They looked at one another. Bryson swallowed. "We gotta get her out!"

Slow and methodical, my usual approach, is not suitable. So much has changed. Where can I cut corners? He placed his glasses on the counter and rubbed his eyes to reduce the strain. Beangagarrie scanned the lab; a series of sequencers hummed quietly. The thermal cycler stood idle, and blocks of tubes with a sophisticated PCR mixture waited for a sample to amplify and copy. *If I only had some DNA from the heads of the families, I could make some real progress. If their bloodlines have been the most well-preserved over the centuries, that might help me to understand. Just a small sample is all it would take.*

Despite hours of studying this reptilian segment under the electron microscope, the snippet of DNA he began researching years ago, he felt stymied.

"Tarni, can you fashion a viral probe to attach to this segment? I think that if we turn off or turn on whatever this part of the genome is doing, we can study the proteins produced in our cell cultures and see how they differ from the controls."

"I've been wondering about that too. Maybe use a messenger RNA-viral-encoded probe to attach to this portion specifically. Better to try and turn it on. That way we could tag some ribosomal RNA to see what proteins are formed. It would be tricky."

"What viral carrier would you use?"

"That's a problem. I've worked with influenza virus, but without an approved research protocol, I don't know where we could get a strain I can use." Tarni shook her head. "I'll try and work through other possibilities."

"No. Work on the computer models. I'll have the base pairs for this segment and the geometry of this portion of the strand finished today. You can model using those parameters. Get me the specifics of what you need for viral cultures, reagents, anything you require. I'll pass it up the chain. I'm meeting with Mr. Reynolds this evening to give him an update on our progress."

Tarni looked almost as tired as BB. World news had everyone on edge. "I'm going to crack a fruity if I don't take a break. I'm stepping outside for some fresh air to clear my head."

"That's an excellent idea. I've not been out in two days. I'll join you in a moment."

When he stepped outside, it surprised BB to see Tarni talking with a young woman, a teenager. The bright sun hurt his eyes, and he went back inside. Tarni returned ten minutes later.

"How do we review the security camera video? Did Bryson or Claus leave instructions about that?" She fumbled over a monitor.

"Slow down. What happened?"

"I may look like a floozy, but I'm no dummy. Something off about that girl, for sure. Foreign exchange student—my ass!" She looked up sheepishly. "I mean, my backside. Pig's bum. That girl's not ridgie didge."

"You need to slow down and tell me about this girl."

Tarni bought none of the teen's story about someone from a dating app giving her this address to meet up. She refused the girl's request to use the bathroom, saying they were waiting for a plumber to fix it. The small talk the girl attempted seemed awkward and out of place.

"Girl had a lot of questions about what kind of work we did here. Why wasn't there a sign? How long we'd been at this location? Why did I wear a lab coat? She started off okay, commented on my nails and hair. I put on my dumb-girl hat and fed her some nonsense about the type of work we're doing. Good thing you went back in. I saw her looking right at you for the ten seconds you were outside."

"So, what are you saying, she was spying on us? A foreign teenager?" BB looked concerned and a little confused.

They tried to reach Bryson or Claus to have one of them walk through the lab's digitally stored surveillance files and how to access them. No response to voice mail or text messages. Eventually, the two researchers figured it out.

The girl had been in different parts of the building's parking lot on several feeds. She had even come straight to their door and tried the handle, but found it was locked. They saw her using her phone to take pictures.

"This is not good, Tarni." He shook his head. "I don't know what this means, but it cannot be good."

"Maybe, but maybe not." Tarni grabbed swabs, a solution off a shelf, and a couple of specimen tubes. "Be right back."

Moments later, a broad grin exposed her perfect teeth. She held up three tubes, each with a swab and some liquid.

"The door handle. Snoop girl grabbed it right around minute sixteen. Big mistake. Better fire up the thermal cycler. Once I separate out our DNA, we should have something to work with."

"Brilliant! You are nothing less than incredible. How did you think of that?"

"*CSI: Australia.* They have that here in the states, don't they? I almost went into forensics, but I fancied genetics as way sexier." Tarni beat her long lashes. *Can't wait to show off my stuff to genius boy. He's not the only one who can play detective.*

23

At high speed, the cycle's exhaust noise was barely tolerable. As Moon slowed, the tapping and backfire when she stopped blasted Serena with explosions of color. The stops were frequent. Military check points slowed their progress. Journalist IDs allowed them to continue to the border, to the Salloum crossing into Libya. Their cover story—Pyramid Communications was covering the flight of Egyptian citizens living in Libya now escaping the war zones.

During the ride, Serena watched the wind. She remembered riding a motorcycle when she dated some loser back in New Mexico. Then, the feeling of wind in her hair and against her face was pure escapism. Now, with her full faculties, she saw the air as it streamed across the bike, around Moon seated in front of her, in the sky overhead. Like colored gas revealing patterns in a wind tunnel, Serena could see it all in her focused mind.

She leaned forward and yelled into Moon's ear, "It's beautiful!"

Moon simply nodded her head. At the next break, she explained seeing as the first step to directing air energies. She also explained the crisis surrounding them.

"After Sudan conducted the raid to gather food, Libya declared war. They thought Sudan had little military capacity, but they were wrong. The Sudanese must have been hiding a covert training and arms program."

"So, you're saying Libya is losing?"

"Badly. Libyan refugees are already heading to Egypt, Algeria, Niger, even Chad, and that country has been a hell spot for years."

"What will the Egyptian Government do?"

"I don't know. The Saudis closed their borders after invading Yemen. Egypt wants to stay out of that conflict. Israel has its hands full with the uprising in Gaza. No one wants to deal with Syria; they just launched another chemical attack against their citizens."

"Everything is a mess! The world is coming apart." Serena got no response.

With good conditions, traveling the 720 kilometers to the border crossing would take no more than eight hours. Broken-down cars, caravans of vans and busses, most heading away from the border and toward Cairo, slowed their progress. Yet, despite a clear stretch and having refueled less than an hour before, Moon pulled over at a rest stop.

"Why are we stopping?"

Moon pointed northwestward. "Sandstorm. Can you see it?"

Serena scanned the horizon. "No."

"Look harder." The scars on Moon's face stood out, and Serena saw the movements of her breath as the older woman spoke.

Looking again, she saw the disturbance—a massive movement of raw power and energy. "Yes. I see it now. It's beautiful."

"You won't think so in ten minutes. Keep your goggles on."

As Serena watched, visibility plummeted. She huddled inside the meager shelter joined by a few dozen other stranded travelers. She gathered many were Libyan refugees. Most spoke in Arabic. Over the intense wind and swirling dust, she heard the fear in their voices.

"If you wish to make a call, I will allow it, if you are able. A haboob such as this often topples the cell towers." Moon returned Serena's cell phone.

Too late. Serena had no signal. "How long do these haboobs last?"

"A few hours if we are lucky. Rest. We are trapped here."

In New Mexico, she would see a dust devil and feel amused. The swirling dust and debris looked almost comical, like something in a cartoon. Sand and dirt used to get into everything during the bigger sandstorms she'd experienced. Those disturbances paled to the force pummeling them from all directions. Even inside the rest area, dust and sand infiltrated her hair, her mouth, her nose. Through it all, she focused on the movement of the energies engulfing them. Power immersed them in a display of nature unleashed. Serena could not rest. The storm invigorated her, energized her. She felt alive with power and wanted to sing. *I must implore Mother to teach me the words and sounds to move the air element.*

The two women looked around; they appeared every bit as worn and beleaguered as everyone else caught in this nexus. Strangers prayed together, not for shelter from the storm, not for food to fill their bellies, or a place to sleep. They prayed for their lives and the lives of those they loved. They prayed for their sons and daughters and brothers and sisters who carried the guns and grenades, flew the planes, drove the jeeps and the tanks. They prayed for their children, that Allah or God or whoever they worshiped would protect them. They wept for their dead.

Three hours of dark howling, sometimes screaming sand, and then it passed. The stragglers rolled their prayer rugs, gathered their belongings, and continued their journeys. Fearful for what might lie in the road ahead for these people, innocent victims caught in the conflict, Serena silently mouthed a blessing. She followed with a silent curse upon the powerful elites, the ones pulling the strings drawing so many to their deaths.

The two Black Snake Sisters mounted the motorcycle, and Moon pumped the starter. The engine turned over, coughed, and sputtered. After the third failure, Moon swore; at least Serena thought it sounded like a swear word.

"The filter must be clogged. I'll try and clean it."

Serena knew nothing about combustion engines beyond where you fill the gas tank. Moon disassembled parts of the engine. Using her prosthetic hand made it difficult; Serena assisted as best as she could. An Egyptian man in his mid-thirties offered to help. He seemed to know what he was doing. He retrieved tools from his truck, cleaned some parts, reassembled things, and tried to start the engine. Again, it coughed and died. After six or seven tries, he shrugged his

shoulders, spoke rapidly in Arabic to Moon, then turned to Serena. "No fix...
broken." He left.

She looked at Moon and checked her own name badge: "Chanda Patel—
Pyramid Communications." It was the same photo they used as before except
they had changed the eye color to match the passport ID for Alice Mars. She
needed one ID for the military checkpoints and the other for the border crossing. "How did he know to address me in English?"

"Because you didn't react when he asked me where your husband was."

"What did you tell him?"

"I said he was in the United States, that he worked for the government and
couldn't fly back because of the war."

"We're stuck here, aren't we? No phone, no motorcycle...stuck! Any ideas?"

Moon didn't buckle under pressure, but Serena couldn't mistake the sound
of sand grinding between the older woman's teeth. "None."

24

"Commercial air travel is out of the question. The Egyptian Air Force
has declared a no-fly zone over their airspace, and we've got no
military equipment they want at the moment. That last shipment when Serena
landed in Ras el Tin stocked 'em full. They must have smelled something getting
ready to happen. I still have some contacts in Libya. I'm sure they would like any
military hardware we can send. They are getting their asses kicked."

"I don't know what we should do, Claus. Did you speak to Uncle Pete?
Does he have any ideas?"

"Boss is all messed up about something. Says he has to go to London."

"How about the State Department? Is there anything they can do?"

"Your uncle did say he put a few calls and feelers out, but nothing so far.
I'm thinking the border between Egypt and Libya is pretty porous. I'm sure
armies on both sides are scurrying like roaches in a kitchen. With some luck and
paying off the right people, we might be able to sneak through. We'll need official cover, something from the CIA that we're undercover on assignment. Can
you hack something official looking?"

"I can work on it. I'm sure I can come up with something."

"I'll tell you right now, Bryson. We could easily get shot."

"So, let's not get shot."

"If we get caught, we still might get shot." Claus stroked his chin. "They'd probably torture us first and then kill us."

"We can't help Serena if we're dead."

"Right about that. Between you and me, I don't like this plan, but I'll let the boss make the final call."

Kenseiko sat back in his chair, idly rolling the glass globe and chatting with Wán shàn. They had just teleconferenced together with the family heads, but Li had little new to report. Much of the meeting focused on the media and propaganda efforts to stoke fear—which news organizations spread hyperbole, and which were promoting a more measured and sober accounting of world events. If it were possible to take the temperature of the world, not as a measure of climate change but as a measure of mounting social anxiety, the world clearly had a fever.

"So, what do you think, daughter?"

"I think the disinformation efforts are skillfully played. Social media manipulation is an effective tool. The techniques are old, but the application opportunities are magnified by the communication tools people employ."

"Good. I agree."

She added, "I still have a difficult time understanding why there is so much fear. I understand this from research but not from my own experience."

"Fear is a mind killer. That's all you need to know. Now go prepare for your trip back to the hive. You need to bring your sisters up to date on your observations."

After she bowed and left, Kenseiko reflected on what had occurred in Chicago. The picture of the woman with the pink hair was no one he recognized. The tall man Wán shàn described from their brief encounter sounded like Brindabella.

He rescued the girl from India, sheltered her in Australia, and now he reappears in Chicago. Beangagarrie, will you never give up and go away? Peter Reynolds, this

*smells like your involvement. Chicago is your home. Your nephew, George Reynolds'
son, was last reported in Peru with the girl. Coincidence? I think not. Peter, Peter,
Peter, what are you up to?*

Still, Kenseiko didn't see any real threat. This seemed more of an irritation.
He placed the globe back on his desk, having settled upon a course of action.
Nothing. He would wait and see how big of an annoyance Peter became. If this
nuisance grew too troublesome—he ground his clubbed foot on the floor in
mocking fashion—*I'll squash that pesky inferior. Nothing can interfere with my
plans.*

Time for some tea.

25

The truck bed wobbled; Moon and Serena sat amid straw, chickens,
and eggs. The smell nauseated Serena. Moon didn't seem to mind;
she said it reminded her of the chickens her family raised when she was just a
girl. Each time they hit one of the many potholes, a bird squawked, and Serena
felt as though she would gag. The money that Moon exchanged accounted for
the farmer's kindness. His eyes read shrewd more so than kind. No matter; they
were fortunate he stopped at the rest area, fortunate that he had the means to
get them to Salloum.

With an array of ropes, he had managed to fix their motorcycle to a tow
hitch and rack. When the truck swerved, Serena half expected the tethers would
let loose; she imagined the cycle left roadside in a heap. Following the storm,
road traffic had slowed in both directions.

At last, they had cell service again. Moon called her people. They would
send out a truck to pick up Moon and the bike, and Serena if she didn't pass
through the border guards.

Moon looked somehow conflicted but still resolute. "I spoke with Youssef.
He does not think it wise for an American girl to be alone in Libya. On the Libyan side, at the Emsaed Gateway, there are thousands of refugees trying to escape.
Egypt has stopped allowing access. The refugees stretch all the way back to Musaid,
which is full of soldiers and terrorists. He says you are crazy to go there."

"I can take care of myself."

"Yes, Serena, but it is unwise to use your powers in public. No one there would hesitate to call you *sahira*, a witch. If not shot, you would be stoned. I agree with Youssef. This is a fool's errand. Still, the decision is yours."

Serena didn't answer. A debate raged in her mind. *I've got to get out of here as soon as possible. Mother said I need to find the Twins. I need Bryson to help me connect all the dots. Home. Got to get home. Can't wait here. The longer I wait, the worse things get. But it's not safe over the border. At least I have Moon here with me. Do I really want to go over on my own? Maybe in a few days, Egypt will allow flights out.*

She tried to reach Bryson. No answer on his voice mail. She sent a text: *Delayed getting out of Egypt due to circumstances and a sandstorm. Headed to Salloum Crossing to try and get into Libya. I'm okay. Moon is with me.* She waited for his reply. Nothing.

What to do, what to do? Think, girl. Yes! She scrolled through her saved numbers and called the lab. *BB lives there, sleeps there. He should answer.* The phone rang eight times before he picked up. A sleepy Australian accent greeted her.

"Hello? Who's calling?"

"BB, it's me, Serena. I tried to reach Bryson; he hasn't responded. I'm okay, but I'm stuck in Egypt."

"Slow down, girl. I can only hear so fast."

Apart from his total relief at learning she was okay—they had all been so worried—BB reported some good news. She could not reach Bryson or Claus; they were flying to the Al Jufrah Airbase. He didn't know where that was exactly, but it was somewhere in Libya.

"Wait, stay on the line." Serena turned to Moon. "How far is Al Jufrah Airbase from Musaid?"

"That is far. I don't know for sure. At least a thousand kilometers."

"How long? How long to go that far?"

Moon thought for a moment. "With all the turmoil, a minimum of fifteen hours. I don't know, Serena, I can ask Youssef to estimate."

"BB, when did they leave?"

"About six hours ago. They left from Denver but were going somewhere east to board a military flight. Mr. Reynolds would know. Do you want me to find out?"

"Thanks. Yes, text me any information you learn about their departure from the United States. If you hear from them, tell them I'll meet them somewhere in Libya. We'll figure it out."

"Be careful, Serena. It is very dangerous. Be careful."

Bryson hated the flight. Their military cargo transport had no creature comforts. The handful of soldiers, in uniform with weapons currently stored but still close at hand, made him nervous. He frequently used the bathroom. At least there was good news. When they landed in Maryland, he had messages from Serena and from BB.

PTG is trying to get into Libya. If she's able to, the State Department will assist to get her to the Embassy. We really lucked out. It turned out Peter Reynolds had serious connections at the State Department. When they learned that there was a US citizen seeking passage into Libya from Egypt, and that Alice Mars worked for a Reynolds' company affiliate, they agreed to help. According to Uncle Pete, when they heard it was George Reynolds' son's fiancé—a little white lie Peter thought would put more urgency to the matter—some higher-up at State must have gotten involved.

Claus looked over their documents. He explained that getting them wasn't that difficult and all the paperwork was absolutely legit. He already had a prior government security clearance, and that qualified him to work for the State Department as a Foreign Service Security Technical Specialist. Similar situation for Bryson's title as an Intelligence Operations Specialist.

"The tricky one was getting something for Alice. Turns out she had a marijuana-related arrest six years ago, and they wouldn't clear her through State. But boss made a deal with a private company the government contracts with, Safe-T-Con, Security Systems; your new fiancé is a Diplomatic Security Operations Assistant."

"Fiancé? Very funny. Her last text to me said her phone battery was almost dead. Do you think I should tell her?"

"Nah. Let it be a surprise."

As the fifteen-hour flight from Andrews AFB flew on, Bryson dozed. He had weird dreams. His old "hallucinations" with Ooljee chanting and singing emerged unwelcomed. Memories of his mother and his father, their family trip to Maine, their plane crash, and the graveside ceremony made appearances. In between his waking trips to the restroom, PTG showed up in several of his dreams; so did Tarni.

Claus poked him. "Wheels down in twenty minutes. Better put your tray table up and check that everything is secure." He winked.

Bryson looked one last time at his diplomatic passport and at the hand-written note someone from State had tucked inside. *"Your father was a good man. Congrats on the wedding!"*

26

Bad news awaited the two women upon arrival at the Salloum Gateway; authorities had suspended travel through the crossing from either direction. Moon spoke to a soldier, tried to use her press credentials, offered a bribe, and translated the guard's response: "The border is sealed."

"When will it reopen?" Serena asked.

"He said maybe tomorrow, maybe next week."

"I can't wait that long. I've got to find those tablets the Twins guard, and they're nowhere near here."

"Where are they, Serena? Do you think you will find them if you are taken as a hostage? What ransom will be set on your head? A terrorist, a smuggler, an officer—anyone would be happy to use you to their advantage." Moon continued to implore her sister to remain in Egypt until it was safe to leave.

"I know I walk into the lion's mouth, but I've made up my mind. A day becomes a week, a week becomes a month. The war has not reached this far north yet. I'll be okay."

"Are you sure, Serena? Youssef said someone would be here in about six hours. I cannot pass through to Libya with you. We can go back to Cairo, figure out how to get you home. If you choose to go now, you will be on your own."

Serena surveyed the Salloum border crossing. "I'm sure." Moon gave her some Egyptian pounds, explaining they would be good in Libya. She reviewed the exchange rate to dinars and said Serena should go to Tobruk and find lodging. There would be more than enough money.

Never had the Candelaria seen so clearly what lay beneath the faces of those surrounding her. She saw it in their eyes—fear, desperation, fatigue, hopelessness. They looked upon one another for answers; they looked to the army or police patrolling in force. No one had answers. And to the children wailing from hunger and fright, their parents tried to provide comfort, drawing from a well within that offered no refreshment. Many sat with their bags and packs, doing nothing—defeated by burdens they could no longer shoulder.

"Look around, Sister. I cannot remain."

They hugged. "When you have cell coverage, text me that you are safe. May Isis protect you."

The energy boost from the sandstorm had long since dissipated. Serena ran on fumes and dust. No one entered from the Libyan side. As she approached the plaza, armed guards in riot gear stood stationed to hold the border against the mob gathered on the other side. It could get ugly if they stormed the gate. She saw the fear on the soldiers' faces too—afraid what might happen if the caravan of people seeking refuge broke through, afraid for the lives of the innocent men, women, and children who only sought protection, afraid what they might be ordered to do. Military vehicles and tents stood against a background of barren desert. Fencing and razor wire marked the territory separating the two countries like an unnatural line in the sand.

Everyone is afraid. They fear the person next to them almost as much as the person on the other side. Strangely, she had no fears. Calmly, she showed her passport. The agent asked her questions, and she answered, but he shook his head.

"The border is closed." His statement left no room for argument or dissuasion. It didn't matter that she was an American citizen. He added that it was lunacy to cross into Libya without an escort. His English was quite good. He pointed and insisted she return past the line of soldiers. Reluctantly, she withdrew then watched. And watched. Until she saw what used to be invisible to her.

Behind the veil covering her face, no one heard the strange words she sang. A small fire erupted in the guard station. Amid the chaos and confusion as the guards scrambled to find a fire extinguisher, no one heard her words, but an unoccupied army jeep mysteriously burst into flames. Commands were shouted, soldiers on the Egyptian side ran, an alarm sounded. In the bedlam that followed, the refugees on the Libyan side yelled and stirred and banged against the gate.

When the tear gas exploded among the Egyptian forces, the desperate crowd yearning for refuge could see the commotion, the coughing, and the choking. As the gate fell and they poured across the border, Serena walked to the edge, away from the column of soldiers readying an advance to repel the mob, away from the mayhem. She walked against the human current, against the onslaught of asylum seekers. She walked into the lion's den.

She kept on walking until the screams and uproar of the riot at the border crossing faded behind her. She didn't look back. Serena focused on the path in front of her, single-minded in what she needed to do next—get to Tobruk, get her cell phone charged, get the hell away from this madness. She stopped looking at the faces of despair. Other than curls of smoke and occasional gunfire, the disturbance was far enough away that the people she brushed up against either didn't know or didn't care.

Serena stopped only to buy a bottle of water from a roadside vendor. As she took a sip, shielding her eyes from the late afternoon sun, someone reached from behind and grabbed her arm. She froze.

Tarni pulled the blanket to just below BB's chin. Why was it that the men she most respected and cared about didn't seem to make it to a nice old age, holding grandchildren on their knees or telling them stories while camping in the outback? Her dad didn't make it, succumbing to lymphoma at age forty-five. *Damn, all the things I never got to learn from him. Life's not bloody fair.* It could explain the fondness she held for the senior geneticist on their two-person team. It could be why she soaked up everything the man said. Not about genetics— they both knew she had training that exceeded his—but about life, about what's important and what isn't, and how to live life with integrity. No surprise there, given all the advances BB had been sidelined for. She loved her father as much as any daughter might. But losing him at age twelve, she never got the chance to appreciate her father's wisdom. Knowing that soon she would lose this remarkably wise and gentle man, who lay resting on his bed, gave her the determination to continue.

She leaned forward and whispered, "Rest. You had another seizure. I'll take it from here."

Tarni doubted that BB heard her as she left the spartan bedroom in the back of the lab to resume their work. The results didn't make sense. She would run them through a third time.

Two hours later, BB surprised her as he touched her on the shoulder. He still had the blanket draped on his shoulders; his big smile greeted her.

"I don't think Mr. Reynolds pays you to sleep here. You know we have work to do, Fuchsia."

That was his nickname for her. She figured it was because of her pink hair, but BB explained that *Eremophila decipiens,* a flower native to Australia and also known as slender fuchsia, was his wife's favorite. The two of them would travel every spring to see the blossoms and to inhale their fragrance. He told Tarni the delicate flowers were every bit as beautiful as she. That was classic Beangagarrie—he knew so much about so many things. Genteel, erudite, and refined, BB came across to Tarni as a Renaissance man with the character of a saint. She loved just being around him.

"What do you mean 'sleeping'? I was just reading." Her broad smile matched his own. "You know, the backs of my eyelids."

Amusement flashed and faded. He sighed. "Time for us to get serious again, Tarni. Did you run another analysis?"

"I did. I still can't believe it."

The DNA analysis from the hair and cells belonging to Serena surprised both researchers. The reptilian gene segment, the focus of all their attention, showed a lot of activity, and the cell cultures tagged distinctly greater protein synthesis. Something about Serena's DNA was clearly different, but neither was prepared for what the samples from the teenager snooping in the parking lot revealed.

"The same results as before?"

Tarni nodded. "Do you even think she's human?"

BB's answer surprised her. "What characteristics determine humanity? Is it DNA? We share ninety-nine percent of the same genetic material with a bonobo chimpanzee. Is it our cognitive capacity? Self-awareness? A soul? These are questions for philosophers. As a geneticist, I would say I don't know."

But Tarni knew the answer to the question. That girl's DNA revealed the most sophisticated and elegant masterpiece of combining genomic elements that she had ever seen or ever read about. The combination of genes and how they had been assembled surpassed everything achieved at the cutting edge of genetics research.

Tarni shared the results of her analysis. "She's a hybrid clone. Genetically human, I think; although, that reptilian segment we've been focused on is absent. She doesn't even have it."

"She's a chimera, likely a mosaic. Genetically distinct cell populations living harmoniously together in the same body. As you know, this can occur in nature on a limited scale. What we see here are orders of magnitude more sophisticated. And I guarantee it is not natural." Tarni watched him shudder.

"What does it mean, BB? Is an engineered person even a person?"

He rubbed his temples. "In mythology, the chimera is a monster. They are beasts that breath fire from a lion's head attached to a goat's body with the tail of a serpent."

Tarni looked at the sadness behind Beangagarrie's large brown eyes. She looked back at him, searching for answers.

"Yes, Fuchsia, I'd say we are dealing with a monster, but it is not the girl." BB's eyes now glared cold and angry. "His name is Kenseiko Li."

27

Too many thoughts raced through Bryson's head, making it impossible to sleep. The flight over to Al Jufrah Airbase had been fairly miserable. He didn't enjoy flying; he didn't like soldiers in uniforms with guns. The State Department van now transporting them had bulletproof glass, armor, and came equipped with four rapid response operatives—fully armed—with vests, night-vision goggles, the works. *At least they're American soldiers. Claus says most likely ex-Marines, maybe Seals. He's pretty sure Baxter makes the goggles. Geez, this vehicle is more of a tank than a van.*

Bryson had to admit to himself that he didn't feel safe. At the airbase, along the road, the pervasive military presence couldn't be ignored. When he looked out the window as they drove along the coastal road, what little he could see looked scary, somehow threatening. Even Claus had commented things looked noticeably worse since he had last been to Libya a dozen years ago. He talked about his prior job here as a military communications expert. He talked about the debacle in Benghazi at the US Consulate that had been so much in the news. He mentioned there would probably be a heavy security presence at the Embassy. He was right about that.

"It only recently reopened; they had closed it in 2014…" Claus droned on.

Bryson wasn't listening. Less than two days since he had left US soil, and he already couldn't wait to get home. He kept thinking about Serena, wondering if she was okay. The diplomatic assistant traveling with them in the van told them what she knew about the riot at the Salloum border crossing. It didn't sound good.

Now he lay in bed, all showered and fed and "protected" in what amounted to a bunker. His cell was useless, jammed by the equipment at the Embassy. He didn't even know if Serena had gotten his last message to meet in Tripoli at the US Embassy. Worried sick, feeling utterly powerless, he waited for news and jumped at the knock on the door.

"Bryson, you still awake?"

"Claus, you got some news?"

"Nothin' on Serena, but I do have something interesting. Wondering what you think?"

"Come on in. I could use something different to think about."

Claus had run into an old buddy, Frank Spagho. They had been out of touch for a dozen years and had gone their separate ways—Claus into the private sector and his friend into the State Department.

"FSM—that's what we used to call him, stands for Franco Spaghetti Man—says the Libyans captured one of the Sudanese soldiers and were interrogating him. The guy was one tough son of a bitch and wouldn't talk. They said he was some sort of supersoldier, had advanced high-tech headgear and an assault weapon biometrically synced somehow."

"Do they have the hardware? I'd like to have a look at it."

"No. State doesn't have it. The Libyans asked for State to run through some audio from the headgear."

"What kind of audio?"

"Bryson, hold the questions and let me finish. FSM says this head unit kept repeating the same message every fifteen seconds. It was in Chinese, and they had to translate it. Basically, the message said, 'Failure,' then it counted down, 'three, two, one.' They asked the prisoner what the significance was, but he wouldn't crack. Said he didn't know. What do you make of that?"

"Dunno." Bryson shrugged. "I would like to get a copy of the audio, run it through some filters, that sort of thing."

"Yeah, that's what I'm thinking too. But here's the bizarre part. Someone had the bright idea of putting the headgear on the guy to let him listen. Bad idea! Ten seconds later, the guy's eyes roll back, and he starts convulsing in some epileptic fit. By the time he stops, the poor bastard's dead."

"Holy shit. I didn't know we could do that type of stuff."

"Apparently somebody's figured it out. State doesn't know either, but there are a lot of black ops they're not in on. FSM figured that with my background in comms and private military contracting, maybe I knew something they didn't."

"We really need a copy of that audio."

Claus displayed a thumb drive and a broad grin. "Piece-a-pie, my man. Piece-a-pie."

She didn't turn around. "Let go of my arm."

Rapid Arabic followed; the only word Serena understood: "…American…"

Another voice spoke, this time in English. "My cousin wants to know where you are going."

"Tell your cousin to let go of my arm."

More rapid Arabic exchanged between the two voices. The grip tightened. "He wants to know whether you like it in the front or in the back. He thinks American pigs probably like it from behind. He says he will let you choose. After he finishes, we'll flip you to the other side and it will be my turn."

"Ask your cousin which he prefers, to have his arm broken or his nose? The choice is his."

After translating, Serena heard their laughter. "My cousin's nose is already ugly, but if—"

He never finished. Neither of the two men followed the blur of motion: the twist, the leap, the crushing blow to the face, or the back flip that pulled her assailant's arm from his shoulder socket.

With one down on the ground, good hand probing, the blood dripping from his smashed nose, and the other man suddenly looking fearful, Serena faced him.

He looked to be late teens, maybe early twenties, and had unslung a semi-automatic. It pointed at Serena.

She studied him, studied his posture, his weapon. All the while, she looked as calm as a pedestrian waiting for a light to turn green to cross the street.

"Your cousin took too long to make up his mind, so I broke them both."

The young Libyan brandished his weapon; a crowd had gathered at the standoff. Some pointed to the wounded man still moaning on the ground. Someone offered a rag to stop the blood. Serena understood nothing of what they were saying. Then she added, "You wanted to know where I am going? I am going to Tobruk. Do you have a car?"

To the small crowd of bystanders, Serena knew they didn't understand why her assailant suddenly dropped his weapon to the ground and left it there. The conversation between the man and the American girl no longer seemed tense. The crowd likely wondered if this was just a fight between two cousins over a woman. The man held up keys for Serena to see. He ignored his cousin still moaning on the ground and stared intently at Serena. The crowd dispersed.

She watched as he jingled the keys, not reclaiming his weapon. "Good. I am going to Tobruk, and you are going to drive me there."

In the car, he asked how she had made the gun so hot. Why did she need to go to Tobruk? His name was Hassan. She introduced herself as Alice. He had a lot of questions. He had never met an actual *sahira*. In the stories Hassan heard as a boy, they were always ugly. But he did see an American show on television where the witches were all very beautiful.

"Are American witches all as beautiful as you, Alice?"

But Serena was only half listening. Fortunately, Hassan had a charger that worked for her phone. As she powered it up, she got Bryson's last message.

"In America there is an old movie where the bad witches are ugly, and the good witches are pretty. Tell me, Hassan, how far is Tripoli?"

"Oh, that is far. At least fifteen hours."

"Change in plans. I need to go to Tripoli. I will pay you for your gas and your time and even buy you dinner. If you get us there in less than fifteen hours, I will give you some extra money."

Hassan considered this before answering. "I am happy to drive the American *sahira* wherever she wants to go. I will become famous for this adventure together with you, but you must first make one promise. Please do not turn me into a pig because of what my cousin said. I am sorry for what he did." He thought a moment. "It is okay if you turn him into a pig."

The drive to Tripoli stretched over many hours. Hassan had a lot of stories. Most of his English he had learned from watching American TV shows. He had a lot of misconceptions. Serena had misconceptions of her own about his country of Libya, the conflicts in the Middle East, the tension between different factions, and the history of these tensions dating back to even before the Bible and the Quran. They shared history lessons.

She drank a lot of coffee; she couldn't recall anything tasting so good. By the time they arrived at the US Embassy gates, they had both learned something important—the two were not so very different from one another. They disagreed about many things, but they agreed on one point—the world is seriously messed up!

As they parted, Hassan put the handful of Egyptian pounds into a concealed pocket. He asked Allah to bless her and to keep her safe.

The Embassy staff treated her with incredible respect; they welcomed her home while reminding her that she was in a foreign land. They told Serena that her fiancé was waiting with the other man, Claus.

Fiancé?

Bryson greeted her. They hugged. He and Claus shared a laugh about the wedding plans being put on hold. He commented on her dusty, sunburned face and matted hair, and assured her they had showers with nice running water. They all had updates to share, questions and answers about everything. She withheld her role in the riot at the crossing gateway. *Later, later I will tell Bry. It's better to wait.*

He promised to get right to work on figuring out where to search next. "I'm good at connecting dots, PTG. We'll get it figured out. We'll need to take a closer look at that painting on Ooljee's wall. There must be more clues to work on."

They could take a commercial flight out as soon as tomorrow. It might involve some connecting flights, but they could be home as early as Thursday.

"Where do you want to go first? We could go back to the hogan; my house in Taos is back in operation. I think we should go back to Chicago."

"I don't care where we go, just get me out of here."

He turned to Claus. "I don't think there's enough room at your place for three guests, so we'll figure something out. Tarni is pretty settled in there."

Claus looked at Bryson with a smirk. "Oh, definitely too crowded, Bryson. I don't think it would work out for four people in my house."

Serena looked at them. "I'll sleep on the floor. I don't mind. I've been looking forward to meeting Tarni, sharing some stories about Gurumarra, that sort of thing."

The two men looked at one another, but neither spoke.

"I'm sorry, am I missing something?"

28

BBC World News Special Report:

Historians have concluded that the Black Plague killed as much as 50 percent of Europe's population during the years 1347–1351. Plague-related deaths continued beyond that for many years, killing millions of the planet's total human population. Now, Europe has seen death tolls upwards of 80 percent in scattered small cities wiped out by the deadly and devastating Hendra-variant Bogi 1, named after the location in New Guinea where it was first isolated. What do we know about the Bogimonster, as some have named it, and how is it spread? It kills by destroying the blood's ability to clot, causing uncontrolled and fatal hemorrhaging. Scientists are certain it is waterborne.

As rains pour over parts of Southeast Asia, Myanmar as a country is now a land without a people. But why has Myanmar, former- ly known as Burma, been affected, and the adjacent Bangladesh been spared? What protects Laos or Thailand, or Sri Lanka and India across the Bay of Bengal? Scientists are baffled at the appar- ent whimsy of the Bogimonster.

In Europe, scientists ask why Bistriţa in Romania, Synevyr in the Ukraine? Why Sweden's Avaträsk, or the sleepy Spanish town of Almazán, or any of a dozen other isolated small towns and vil- lages throughout Europe? If ever an infectious scourge were to be designed to evoke fear and panic, the devil himself could not have planned a more diabolical agent.

How does it appear in such an almost random pattern? Why does it skip over some areas and move like the Grim Reaper, like an Angel of Death through other towns? Where will it strike next— North America, South America, Australia? As more and more peo- ple refuse to drink water they have not boiled, refuse to bathe or shower or go out in the rain, the Hendra Bogi 1 has brought civi- lization to an uncomfortable impasse. While the Black Plague did have a long-term effect, acting as some great agent of natural selec- tion, of improving the health and longevity of the survivors' descen- dants, that is little consolation to those who have not survived this modern plague. Or to those who fear they may be the next victims. Victims who bleed to death as they pray to be spared. Their corpses unburied because there is no one left to perform the task.

Our hopes lie in further unraveling this virus, in discovering a vaccine to protect the future of the world as we know it. With armed conflicts, food shortages, economic markets on the brink of collapse, and governments at a loss with how best to respond, it is no surprise that the prophets of doom are calling this the beginning of the end-times. Though these same doomsday prophecies of the Apocalypse have been shouted before, this time they may be right. It seems as though the Four Horsemen—Pestilence, War, Famine, and Death—have all set forth to ride unchecked. May God have mercy on us all...

PART TWO
FIRE

29

Bryson scanned the group assembled for dinner and discussion, all seated at the mahogany table in his Uncle Peter's formal dining room. The meal had been spectacular; he expected as much from a private executive chef. The table had been cleared, and now they sipped coffee. He noticed Serena enjoying her second cup. Tarni had been unusually quiet. Bryson sensed she might be a little uncomfortable or feeling overwhelmed by his uncle's wealth and stature. *I'm glad she got invited to the inner circle. She's an important part of our team.* His eyes drifted over to Serena. *She's been quiet too—overwhelmed in a different sort of way, I suppose.* He carefully put his cup down and shifted his gaze to observe each of the two women, each remarkable yet so very different. *Still trying to figure out what those two are thinking about each other.*

Peter started. "In the effort we're engaged in, it's important that the right hand and left hand are in good communication. I apologize that it's taken me this long to have you all gather together. Since my return from London, I have a better understanding of the magnitude of what we're facing." The look on his face and the tone of his voice conveyed a grim seriousness.

"I'll get to that shortly, but each of you needs to give a quick overview of what you are up to, and we must decide if something different should leapfrog to the top. Beangagarrie, why don't you get us started."

The tall Australian geneticist looked tired. Bryson wondered if BB had lost weight.

"Tarni and I have examined DNA samples from several sources. The results are interesting but inconclusive. The two samples you returned, Mr. Reynolds, have not yet been sequenced or examined. What we know thus far shows variations at the gene segment I had conducted research on many years ago, before my work was defunded. Serena's profile is different at this sequence, but the differences are relatively minor. What all this means is hard to say. We are looking at protein synthesis associated with this segment. It would be helpful to have more samples from Illuminati family heads; their bloodlines are the best preserved. I think that may provide us with more information about what this part of their genome does."

Tarni chimed in. "I've got a notion on how to get some DNA from Dr. Li. It involves what I call a 'sticky trap.'" She outlined her idea, and everyone thought she should proceed.

"Everything points to involvement from Dr. Li and his company, Advanced Bionics. The young woman who appeared to be spying on the lab showed disturbing results in the sample we analyzed. I am concerned about security and wonder if we should relocate the facility." BB waited for their reaction.

The group discussed this option and decided to keep the lab at its current location. They would increase security and equip both BB and Tarni with tasers.

Even though Bryson had heard this next part previously, he cringed as the two geneticists described the unique features the chimera's DNA exhibited. He and Claus had reviewed the parking lot footage. No doubt this showed the same female they spotted leaving Li's plane with all the children from the Humanix School for the Gifted. He took a deep breath and listened, wondering what the chimera was designed to do, what Li intended with this genetic engineering. If the Illuminati planned a massive population reduction, how do hybridized humans fit into the plan for a New World Order?

After BB concluded his remarks, Peter asked for the next update. "Claus, what have you and Bryson been working on? Fill us all in."

"Well, boss, we got a little sidetracked doing an ad hoc rescue mission for Miss Serena. Turns out she didn't need our help. The girl knows how to take care of herself." Claus looked at Serena and nodded his respect. She flashed a wry smile but said nothing. "Me and Bryson were planning some detailed surveillance at the facility in Dulce, New Mexico. We need a lot of intel before we can strike. If what we've uncovered is true, there are a lot of weird genetic experiments going on there. I think we can get some samples."

The team discussed this, and all agreed the planning should continue.

"Nephew, how about you?"

"Claus's floor is more comfortable than his couch. I hate to fly." When the laughs quieted, he continued. "I'm helping with the op Claus described. We analyzed the Chinese message that seems to have provoked a death seizure in the interrogated Sudanese soldier. So far, we got nothing. PTG asked me to work on something, but I'll let her give you the details."

Peter looked at Serena. "I'm thinking to have you go last. You need to hear what I have to report first."

Bryson looked over but couldn't tell what Serena was thinking. *Since her escape from Egypt, there is something different about her. I can't quite put my finger on it.*

"Sure, I don't mind going last. Is this the part when you tell us how bad everything is?"

Peter pushed back from the table; he looked grim. "I met with Rothschild for two days, and I had lunch with Rockefeller in New York. It's bad!"

Peter shared what he had learned from his separate meetings with the two family heads. "They didn't reveal much, but phase one of the great cull, as they termed it, is apparently going great in their estimation. They're messaging to maximize fear and are targeting an overall 80 percent reduction worldwide in current population. That's over six billion! Let me repeat that: over six billion lives lost by the end of their phase two. Rothschild assured me that Illuminati loyalists such as myself would be given safe refuge. He mentioned several locations but told me I would most likely be placed underground beneath Denver airport."

Bryson looked around. No one spoke. No doubt none of them could easily process that number; death on that scale seemed unfathomable at the moment. Suddenly, he felt nauseous.

Peter continued. "Rothschild hates Li. He thinks Serena's been captured by Li. Same for you, Bryson." He looked at his nephew. "He thinks Li captured your father as well. In any case, Rothschild doesn't buy the jet crash and disappearance.

"In person, when it's just one-on-one, he's a very creepy man. He has a room, his treasure and trophy room he calls it, that has a lot of artifacts, a lot of priceless things. But he's got a second room where he collects old torture devices. He's got something there called a scold's bridal—it's like a metal cage that locks in over a person's head. It's got a serrated plate that inserts over the tongue. If the person tries to speak, all they manage to do is lacerate their tongue. They used it for women accused of witchcraft, to prevent them from reciting spells."

Peter lowered his voice to soften his next remarks. He turned to Serena. "If he ever manages to get you away from Li, he plans to put you in it before deciding whether or not to cut out your tongue entirely. If he does, he plans to eat it. He asked me if I knew any good recipes for tongue. I tell you; this guy is a sicko!"

Serena seemed surprisingly calm. "I guess I best learn to keep my tongue," she quipped.

"It isn't anything to joke about, Serena. Rothschild wants you, but I get the sense it's more that he doesn't want Li to have you. What he really wants is your Candelaria necklace. He wouldn't say why, but he's obsessed with it."

"Oh, I think I know why, but I'll wait until you're done, Uncle Pete." Serena poured herself another coffee. "This is really a delicious blend."

To Bryson, her comment seemed too casual. *This is serious shit Uncle Peter is talking about, and she's casually enjoying another cup of coffee. WTF?*

"The only other thing I'll add is Rothschild wants me to work through Van Duyn to get to Li." He turned to Bryson. "He knows all about these supersoldiers; they use some kind of hardware that Van Duyn's been working on. That's it, other than Rockefeller being a greedy bastard, and I got DNA samples from both of them."

Everyone looked at Serena. She put her empty cup down.

"My turn?" She took a deep breath. "I'm not positive, but I think I know why Rothschild wants the necklace. It's likely a key of some sort that can access secret knowledge from ancient Atlantis." She turned to Bryson. "Have you figured out how to get it back from India?"

"That's easy, PTG. I think Nalini or her daughter, Dharani, at the Naga Sanctuary can help us there."

"I had the same thought. As for the DNA, I have some ideas about what's wrong. It might help if I see the DNA under a microscope or something. I need to see strands from myself and someone else. I can't explain because I don't understand things myself, but when I look at things now, I can see the underlying energetic structure. BB, is this something you can do, show me DNA strands?"

"Yes, child, we can use the electron microscope, but who told you these things? Where does this ability to see things as you describe arise from? As a scientist, I am naturally curious."

"Mother taught me. I can see a lot of patterns now that used to be hidden."

Bryson looked at everyone's face around the table; he saw uncertainty. Few details about Mother had been shared. It seemed no one quite knew how to respond to Serena's statements. He wasn't sure how much Serena wanted to reveal. Whatever happened in Egypt with Mother, he felt certain Serena hadn't told him everything.

Tarni broke the silence. "Hell, girl…I'm listening. Whatcha got?"

30

Dr. Zhāng expressed his pleasure at her return as he escorted her from the helipad.

"Dr. Li told me of your name, Wán shàn. He is very proud of you."

A quizzical and curious look highlighted her normally bland face. "I do not understand this feeling of pride you mention about bàba. What does this feel like? You say that you are glad to see me. I understand it is polite to say in kind that I am glad to see you as well. To me, this is an exchange of words, but the meaning conveyed by these words is not an experience I comprehend. Or, more appropriately, I suspect my comprehension differs from yours."

"Human emotions are very complex. They are a tool to be manipulated to control behavior. They can interfere with the mind and the ability to think clearly. Your bàba did not want emotions to handicap you." He added, "This was a subject of great debate among members of our development team."

He stopped and pointed to high mountain peaks with cloud formations above and snow glistening in early morning sunlight. "What do you see?"

"Mountains, trees, snow, rocks, clouds, sky, sunlight. There are other details in my visual field. I can give specifics. I can also calculate the sun's position, make predictions about today's weather. There are several levels of analysis I am able to provide you with. What is the reason for your question, Dr. Zhāng?"

"You answered my question, Wán shàn. You answered it not by what you said, but in what you did not say. Many would answer my question by describing beauty, by invoking nature or majesty and mystery, perhaps even refer to the glory of God's creation. Your mind remains clear, uncontaminated by such thoughts or feelings. It is the way we created you."

"Thank you, Dr. Zhāng." *It is much like trying to describe color to a blind person. My comprehension of these notions of beauty and feelings is limited.* "Your explanation is helpful."

"Good. Your sisters are waiting to get your report. You should include our discussion to assist them in their understanding of such distractions. Your bàba will arrive here in two days."

As the two entered the cave complex, her quizzical expression did not change. A question arose in her mind: *Is this perfection? I must think about this. Should I ask my sisters? No, I should think about this on my own. What is perfection?*

"You know, Bry, I think I really need to get away for a few days, have some downtime, process."

"We can go to the hogan. I need to look at Ooljee's picture on the wall. It will be four days until the courier brings the necklace back. You were smart to have Dharani as a cosignatory on the safe deposit box. She texted that everything went smoothly, and the package had been picked up. We can update the delivery instructions to arrive directly at the hogan."

"Settled. We go to Taos. Claus can work on the Dulce plans, and we'll split off to the hogan for a mini vacation. That's a power spot for me."

Perfect! And Tarni can have the place to herself. That works for me. Can't say why, but PTG hasn't been the same lately. It will be good for her to get away. Good for us both to get away. Maybe when she is done processing, she'll be ready to tell me.

When her bàba arrived, he seemed pleased by the debriefing Wán shàn had provided to her Ninja sisters. She wasn't sure, but she thought he smiled when they all greeted him as bàba and informed him that they were glad to see him. The greeting had been her suggestion.

He handed each of them an envelope with detailed instructions and schedules. All the sisters would rotate visits among each of the family heads. Wán shàn's instructions had her spending time initially with Damiaan Van Duyn and then with Edward Rothschild.

"For each day you have interactions with any of the Council of Thirteen members, other than myself, you will log into the secure network I set up and summarize those interactions. Every one of you must review these daily entries provided by the other five. If you are ill, suffer an injury, or have anything significant occur, you must report that as well. After you have reviewed the detailed instructions, put any questions into the network so that all are aware."

Each of the six Ninjas acknowledged understanding. Wán shàn guessed at the intent and had her suspicions confirmed a moment later.

"You must become one mind with six bodies. You are eyes and ears to one another and to me. I shall review the daily entries as well. Are there any questions?"

He looked at each of the six, and none had questions.

"You will each go by the name Wán shàn. To the family heads, none must realize you are identical copies."

Wán shàn had not anticipated this last piece of information. *It will be difficult to tell us apart from one another. Perhaps that is bàba's intent.* Then he looked directly at her.

"Come with me, daughter."

A short while later, the two were airborne in a helicopter. She thought they would return to Singapore, but the flight headed in a different direction further into the mountains.

"Where are we going, bàba?"

"Tibet. What occurs there, I do not want you to include in your log entry."

Ninety minutes later, they landed on a small helipad. Dr. Li told the staff they would not be staying long. He seemed to be in a hurry, moving quickly despite his clubbed foot. She wondered if sunlight caused his haste.

"Daughter, you asked to see another hive. There are many, and they are much the same as where you were raised. They house mostly soldiers, some pleasure servants as you have already seen, and other engineered humans. What I show you now, is one of only four. This is both a hive and a womb, a place where the new humanity starts."

This information intrigued Wán shàn; yet she felt something else though she did not have a word to describe it. Singled out? Special? Her bàba reiterated she was not to share this with her sisters.

She sat in a small office. A digital map depicted ancient Mongolia and gradually changed to encompass much of Asia and Europe.

"Do you recognize this map, Wán shàn?"

"It is a depiction of the territory seized by Genghis Khan. It encompasses land stretching from the Pacific coast including modern-day Asia, Russia, and Central Europe to the Black Sea."

"Correct. His conquests and his empire encompassed much of civilization in this part of the world." He pressed a button on a remote, and the display changed. Arrows and colors erupted and spread in an animated display that changed and grew over a time sequence. The entire world, all continents, every part of the globe began to shade and enlarge, stopping at the present.

"Do you know what the map now reveals?"

"No, bàba."

"This is the genetic legacy of Genghis Khan. 2006 was the last time a scientific study thoroughly evaluated how many carried his genes—over sixteen million men. Today, it is closer to twenty million."

"Impressive, but small in percentage given the world's population of over 7.8 billion."

"True, but the world's population will soon be curtailed, as you are aware from the meeting under the Hill. What took Genghis Khan over eight hundred years to achieve, I will accomplish in six generations—120 years. What is present in the wombs represents my genetic legacy. My father thought I should not pass my genes to future generations. He considered me deformed." Li shrugged and pointed to his clubbed foot. "Here in The Womb, they do not have my deformities."

"Who is they? Who is here at this womb-hive? I see few people working. We traveled two levels in this cave complex to reach this office room. I counted eight people, including at the landing zone."

"They are asleep—over one hundred thousand. They are your cousins, and presently they are in stasis. Those here in this womb will help to birth a new humanity. After the cull, they will be the caretakers, shepherds to lead the masses who remain. The planet needs a transitional population to maintain the infrastructure, organize survivors, grow crops, manufacture products, do what needs to be done to prevent a dark age for civilization. Soon the time will come for them to wake up."

Wán shàn studied the map, ran calculations in her mind. "I should like to see more of this womb-hive."

"First, I want to show you the keeper here. He, not I, has masterminded this part of the plan. Then I shall show you your sleeping cousins."

She paused but just for a moment. "Yes, bàba. I have questions that I would like to ask Shrem. I assume he is the keeper. If my cousins are sleeping, they cannot answer the questions I have."

Parted lips exposed Kenseiko Li's small teeth. "Yes, daughter, you are correct. Shrem is the keeper. He is many things, and he is looking forward to meeting you."

31

He was glad he shared the results with Tarni before she left for the conference. Now all BB needed to do was figure out what caused the DNA alterations that Serena mentioned. *She was very clear about the fact that the DNA had been corrupted or distorted somehow. This allowed for humankind to fall prey to manipulation through fear, and this somehow prevented spiritual ascent.* But this information wasn't really new to him. It only reinforced what Gurumarra had told him long ago about the lizard god, Mangar-Kunjer-Kunja, from the folklore of his people. The lizard god found two primeval people joined together.

He cut them apart, and they became the Rella-manerinja, eventually the masters of men. But Gurumarra said Mangar-Kunjer-Kunja was not a god at all but from an advanced race living on earth.

While BB surmised this splitting had to do with DNA, all the human samples he looked at had this same DNA fragment; although, the activity varied. He surmised epigenetic factors probably drove this. Even the reptilian samples he had collected from the zoo showed some variation.

I wish Fuchsia was here to puzzle through this with me. I don't even know if she's heard the story of Mangar-Kunjer-Kunja. Gurumarra had told BB this action caused a great imbalance and led to the time of darkness. The split beings could not master spirit and matter, somehow a result of distorting the genetic blueprint. This gave the lizard god, and those who followed, mastery over others. *There is something here, I just need to let it bubble to the surface.* His heart raced, pulsations in his ears sharpened, and he assumed a seizure would follow. Alone in the lab for the next two days, he couldn't chance a serious injury. BB eased himself to the floor and waited... Nothing.

The scientist drew his knees up, locked his arms around them, and sat. Afraid to get up, fearful that a seizure might topple him. Instead, something very different fell into place. *FEAR... Fight or flight.* His ears pounded. He fought the screaming, banging noise buzzing to crowd out this new epiphany. *The segment modulates the fight-or-flight response. This activation allows manipulation of mental and emotional energies and blocks the free flow of spiritual energies. Of course!*

As BB continued to sit on the floor, the buzzing subsided a little. He saw a whole new connection. *We've been thinking of this backward; it isn't the DNA. That's just the template. It's transfer RNA. The unjoining is tRNA not being able to bind to the DNA. That's the block. We've been tagging the wrong piec—*

The thought never completed. BB lay convulsing on the ground. A bump surfaced over his left temple as head and body thrashed on the polished concrete floor.

When he regained consciousness, jumbled thoughts left him confused. *Why am I on the floor?* He didn't remember falling. BB probed the side of his head. *Ouch! I wonder how that happened?* He stood up. *What was I working on?*

❖   ❖   ❖

"You've been staring at that same clump of piñon trees for ten minutes, PTG."

"I'm not looking at the trees. I'm looking in between them. It's beautiful."

"Okay… Just sayin', you've been acting a little weird lately."

"The air, the way it moves around them, through them. I see things, Bryson. There's a lot I haven't told you about what happened in Egypt."

"You got something to say, go for it. We've never kept secrets."

She turned her attention from the grove of trees and looked right at him. "Sorry. I'm still trying to figure it all out."

"Figure what out, Serena? Stop being so elusive."

"You think what happened at the Salloum border crossing was an accident?"

He pulled up next to her. They sat in the clearing in front of the hogan. The same spot where they sang songs under the stars so many months ago. This time, Bryson had left his guitar back in Taos.

"What are you saying here, Serena? I'm not following you."

"My voice. Mother began to teach me how to use it. I have some skill with the fire element, and I'm learning to see things with air. I'm useless with earth and water."

"Okay, girlfriend, you may think you're making sense, but you sound like the *Last Airbender* cartoon."

She got up, gathered some pinecones, and placed them among the ashes in the firepit. "Watch." Serena uttered some unfamiliar sounds.

Flickering flames danced off Bryson's wide-eyed astonishment. "Holy shit, did I just see what I just saw?"

She said nothing. Bryson sat speechless, and she entered the hogan, returning moments later with a small metal pot and some floating dried leaves. Again, she spoke some strange words. The notes, cadence, and words conveyed an indescribable sense of power. Bryson watched as steam rose from the boiling pot.

"Tea?"

She had the strangest look on her face. Bryson wasn't sure how to read it— some combination of, "Look what I can do" and "I don't know what the hell I'm supposed to do with this."

"A picture's worth a thousand words." She sat there, but she appeared to be somewhere else.

"Yeah, show and tell is pretty powerful. You want to tell me a little more about what happened in Egypt?"

"You mean when I lit the guardhouse on fire and blew up the jeep? Or before that when I first put my hand on the Emerald Tablet?"

"How about you start at the beginning?"

By the time she had relayed the whole series of events—everything Mother had taught her and explained, shared everything Moon had revealed—night had fallen. They went inside. The hogan was dark, and they lay nestled against each other on sleeping mats.

"Well, just so you know. I still love you, PTG, even if you are some kind of pyromaniac superhero."

"Thanks, Bry! I wasn't sure you would understand." She kissed him on the cheek.

Bryson rolled from side to back and stared up through the dwelling's center hole, looking to the sky. A few stars twinkled. He wasn't at all tired.

Serena spoke. "Almost forgot. I can also call out light. I wouldn't be much of a Candelaria if I couldn't illuminate something."

More strange words, and the entire structure mysteriously emitted a soft radiance. Bryson scanned the walls. He had long passed the point of amazement.

"Uh, Serena...do you see what I see?"

She lay rolled on her side, facing the opposite curved wall of the hogan.

"You need to turn over and look at this."

On the wall where the circle of symbols and artifacts still hung from Serena's Circle training, they looked at the painting of the Virgin Mary appearing to the Guanches—the one they had both studied a dozen times earlier that day. But now it looked markedly different. The green snake candle the Virgin held showed a halo of light. The seven phrases that unsealed the formation of spirit to matter glowed in their strange lettering. Beneath the picture's inscription, new words stood out, clear and unmistakable. Like a message written in invisible ink, uncovered by the power of the Candelaria's command. "Güímar."

Serena muttered, "Wasn't expecting that..."

32

"Shrem will not remain on this plane much longer; that is the reason for my haste."

Kenseiko Li escorted Wán shàn through several passages all sloping downward, past side chambers and catacombs. A maze of extensive natural and engineered connections among a vast network underground, deep within the Himalayas, linked chambers and levels within the womb-hive complex.

"We communicate with him telepathically. You will understand when it occurs."

"That detail was included in my education. These ancients are transdimensional and use telepathy to communicate. How old is Shrem, bàba?"

"I don't know." They entered a chamber. Many embedded crystals within the rock walls emitted a gentle luminescence. "We are here."

I wondered when your next visit would occur. Then I felt your presence. Did you bring what I requested?

Yes. Li handed over a tube. *It is the last of the blood we collected from her.*

Shrem stood about seven feet tall, his gray, scaly skin shimmered slightly. He took the tube. *It will do. I wish to locate her. If the stories are true, and we can control her power, she will be an asset.*

I agree. Her progeny are not yet ready to sample, but it will be helpful to better understand what she is capable of.

And this is our other creation? Shrem faced the girl. *Where are her sisters?*

Only Wán shàn is with me today. The others are identical copies. Dr. Li grabbed Wán shàn by the arm and pulled her toward Shrem, who just stood there.

He poked her arms, chest, and back with claw-like fingers, studied her, then telepathically proclaimed, *You do not appreciate the skill that went into your creation.* Shrem placed his hand over her head. *I see you have questions.*

I am curious to know your age. And I am curious to know what you deem to be my purpose. Wán shàn projected the thoughts without speaking. Kenseiko listened for Shrem's telepathic response.

I am not as old as the rocks and crystals around you, but I am old enough to remember the early ones of your kind, before we began the improvements.

And my purpose?

You exist to serve the needs of the plan. No further explanation do I give to you, or to your bàba, as you like to call him. He, too, serves the plan, and in this way we are joined in common cause.

Shrem removed his hand, and Li guided Wán shàn backward. She stood at his side. *Are you pleased now that you see her?*

She has no fear. I had doubts that the hybridization would be successful. When we can duplicate this into a self-replicating specimen, we can really celebrate. Still, it is a good first step.

Yes, Shrem. We have all achieved much since our last meeting. The Council has convened, as you are aware. The cull is unfolding as we planned. Li and Shrem telepathically discussed the recent meeting beneath the Hill of Slane.

Rothschild is unhappy. Thinks I should go through him each time I come to see you. He is the Pindar and thinks he can dictate my decisions.

He is like his great grandfather. They forget the titles and the duties that go with those titles are bestowed by me. Perhaps I need to remind him what happened to that distant relative. Your kind are handicapped by your short memories, prone to repeating the same mistakes of your forbearers. Perhaps the Pindar needs a reminder.

Shrem's body began to dim, and he disappeared. Kenseiko spoke. "It is the energy fluctuations of the planet. He is gone. So, my daughter, what did you think?"

"He is a strange creature, bàba. I should like a better understanding of the plan that binds us all in common cause. You did hear Shrem in your mind when he said that to me, did you not?"

"I did. It's complicated."

"I know the necklace won't get here until tomorrow afternoon, but are you sure you want to sleep in the cave? I can hike there and back with you, and we can lug water on the return trip."

"No, Bry. Anything comes by that looks dangerous I can roast into crispy critters. Besides, you're working on Güímar. You are way better at researching things and connecting the dots than I am. I'll be back in the morning." Serena had a small pack, a walking stick, and a couple of empty gallon jugs tethered to her belt. "Don't worry about me. I'll be fine. I can take care of myself."

Bryson watched her trudge off back to the place where it all started. He agreed with Serena that illuminating the cave might uncover more hidden messages and that a night sleeping there with the Water Serpent and Mother Earth connection might be good for her. Still, his last recollection of that cave kinda creeped him out. *I'm sure Sam Cuch's body isn't there anymore. She didn't seem the least troubled when I reminded her about it.*

He had a lot of work to do. Güímar's mysteries beckoned. Its location on the island of Tenerife corresponded to several pyramids that Bryson needed to research. Answers might be found hidden in the prehistoric caves where Guanche mummies lay buried in a style similar to ancient Egyptians. The more he dug, the greater the connections. He didn't need his old database linking algorithms to associate the facts: Chaxiraxi, a mother-goddess to the aboriginal inhabitants of the Canary Islands, became rebranded to the Virgin Mary following conquest by the Spaniards; she appeared on a beach near some caves in the late fourteenth century. *That was a period of great upheaval, a lot of political and religious instability, demographic collapse, a significant decline in society. True of so many periods in human history. Let's see…a museum, a Candelaria family estate… What's this? The Black Madonna Virgin is Isis, according to this Illuminati cross-reference! PTG is gonna love that detail!*

A picture began to emerge as Bryson researched. The blond-haired, blue-eyed Guanches claimed descent from the inhabitants of Atlantis. Güímar had strong connections to both Atlantean and to ancient Egyptian traditions. There were other connections to pre-Columbian South American cultures, even some reports of Candelaria witches burned in Peru. It seemed almost unbelievable to uncover all these connecting threads. There had to exist some direct link to Thoth's Mystery Schools and ancient teachings. But the history got twisted and obscured by Christian conquerors rebranding everything into Virgin of Candelaria veneration and festivals. *Clever propaganda, but pretty much the playbook. Conquer an area, take the local lore, and use it to subvert the original intent and serve whatever the agenda suited the Church, the monarchy, the throne, whoever was in power.*

Without realizing it, dinner time had long passed, and it approached midnight. He now had several leads to explore once he and Serena flew over to Tenerife. He fixed a snack, ate, and drifted off to sleep.

Bryson knew he was dreaming, but the dream was out of focus, like those scenes in the *Lord of the Rings* when Frodo slipped the ring on and the world blurred. Serena lay on a Navajo-style rug; her body glows slightly. Motion. Someone or something approaches her body. It's big, gray-green in the dim light. Bryson tries to yell out, but hypnagogic paralysis leaves him immobile and unable to warn Serena.

The creature probes her body with claw-like appendages. On her arms, the matching serpent cuffs come alive, but the snake forms look puny against the beast. It leans forward. Bryson hears it hiss. He shivers and tries to scream a warning. Bryson can't tell for sure—teeth? fangs?—on Serena's exposed neck. No!... Again, he tries to scream out a warning... Mute!

Suddenly, a loud chanting. Another form appears. Body paint, necklaces, a man beats two sticks as he chants, *"Won-gah-jin, Mangar-Kunjer-Kunja. Gah-lin!"* The creature stands, hisses. The voice booms. *"Kul-gah Deen-gul, Gah-lin!"* The creature retreats. Sticks wave and clap, more chanting. *"Mangar-Kunjer-Kunja, Gah-lin! Mangar-Kunjer-Kunja, Gah-lin!"* The creature fades, and the man leans over Serena. He says softly, *"Won-gah-jin, Galinawa."* Bryson watches as Serena opens her eyes. The dream fades.

He threw off the covers. *Shit! What the fuck was that? Not good... Not good...*

33

Claus watched the van advance toward their position through his field binoculars. He stashed them in the glove compartment. "Right on schedule. Are you ready, Dan? Or should I say, Bill?" He winked.

"Let the show begin." Dan Cuch exited the tow truck, casually running his gloved hand through the door's grime. He had it on loan from Bill's Garage and Towing on the reservation. Bill had a new truck, courtesy of Mr. Reynolds. Dan engaged the winch and watched as the back of Claus's vehicle lifted. The back passenger-side blown tire and deformed rim looked very convincing.

From the front seat of the cab, Claus counted down. "Three…two…one." He pressed a remote control, the laser fired, and fifty yards later, skid marks ended where the van halted on the road's shoulder. The tow truck stood another fifty or sixty yards further down the road. Claus watched. The van driver took stock of his situation, took out his cell, then pocketed it. He walked toward the tow truck.

"Hey, I just blew out a tire. Any chance you can help me change a spare?" He pointed back toward the van.

Dan looked at him and spoke in rapid Navajo. Claus exited the tow.

Claus said something back to Dan; it might have been Navajo. He addressed the van driver. "Bummer. These roads totally suck. Bill doesn't speak English, but I'm with the Indian Health Service; I'm happy to help out." He flashed a friendly smile. "Let's see how bad the situation is."

As the three men walked to the van, Claus exchanged small talk with the driver. They cursed the lack of cell service along this stretch of road. "Yeah, I had to walk three miles to make a call. I was lucky Bill could come and get me."

More Navajo, and Claus pretended to translate. "Bill says you're lucky you didn't bend the rim. If you've got a spare, you'd be luckier than me. Mine was flat, and I bent my rim. He's got a floor jack in the truck and says he'll change it out for you."

"How much?"

"He says forty dollars. Cash."

The man grunted, took out his wallet, and peered inside. "Ask him if he'll take a charge card."

Another exchange in Navajo. "Bill says he's got a credit card slide in the truck, but it'll cost more. He'll do it for fifty."

The man looked at the setting sun, kicked the flat tire, and nodded his head. As Dan, aka Bill, left and the van driver worked to remove the spare, he muttered, "Fuckin' highway robbery."

Dan backed the tow truck in front of the disabled van. As the driver handed over his credit card, Claus removed a matchbox-sized container from his jacket pocket, crouched behind the van, and reached beneath the chassis. A magnetic hold kept the box securely tucked in an obscure spot. *With a little road dirt, it'll look like it belongs there.* He stood up grinning. The van driver had his back to Claus and looked to be signing a credit slip. *Piece-a-pie!*

Twenty minutes later, the van had driven off. Dan shook Claus's hand. "Success. How did you know he wouldn't have the cash?"

"Are you kiddin' me? They never pay these civilian contractors much, especially these low-level guys. Speaking of pay, boss told me to slip you these." Claus handed over five hundred-dollar bills. "I'll take that credit charge slip. We don't want any trail."

Dan pocketed the money. "I would ask you what the whole op going on here is all about, but it's probably best that I don't know."

"You're right about that. Drive down so I can pick up the laser. As far as you're concerned, this never happened."

34

Bryson kept checking, waiting for Serena's return. Just when he decided to leave for the cave to find her, he spotted her tiny frame trudging along the arroyo toward the hogan. He ran down to greet her. *Be cool. Don't say anything at first.*

"Hey, PTG, looks like you survived out in the wild. Anything new in the cave?"

She stopped. "Nothing to report. Glad you're here. Can you take these the rest of the way?" She handed over two gallons of water and turned her head side to side. "My neck's hurting. I must have slept funny."

"Really?" Bryson swallowed. *Be cool.* "I didn't sleep so good last night, how about you?"

"I slept okay."

"I had some weird dreams. Couldn't fall back to sleep. How about you, PTG?"

She paused. "I don't remember my dreams from last night."

They arrived back at the hogan. While they ate breakfast, Bryson shared the latest information and investigations about Güímar, Chaxiraxi, and the Egyptian and Atlantean connections.

"So, you're saying this Guanche goddess, Chaxiraxi, might actually be Isis?" She slugged down gulps of coffee between mouthfuls.

"I'm not saying it. It came from an Illuminati reference."

"How about the Twins, anything there?"

"Nothing so far."

A knock. "Hello, anybody home? International Courier Services, package delivery for a Bryson Reynolds."

"Come on in." Bryson signed for the package and offered the courier a cup of coffee.

He thanked them but declined. "Sure is rustic here. I got lost trying to find the place, so I'm behind schedule." He thanked Bryson for the generous tip. "You guys get news out here? It looks pretty remote."

Bryson held up his phone, pointed to his laptop. "Yeah, we're connected. Did we miss something since last night?"

"The Bogiman virus hit some town in northern Michigan. Hope you guys got good water out here."

Bryson and Serena looked at each other, saying nothing. They thanked the courier, and Bryson checked his news feed. "People are freaking out. The CDC has the whole upper peninsula quarantine. This looks bad, Serena."

When they got around to opening the package, it contained more than just the Candelaria necklace. Serena unwrapped her book, *The Candelaria Fellowship—A Flame Extinguished*. Both necklace and book cover had similar designs: a snake coiled around a candle with a halo of golden light. A note signed by both Dharani and Nalini dropped to the floor.

"We return to you that which is yours, sister. So much has happened on your journey since we last sat together in meditation. All the sisters pray for your safety. You are always welcome back here at the Naga Sanctuary. May your light shine brightly."

At the bottom, Nalini added, *"Make sure you read the pages starting at 132. I never included this in the overview I gave you because I did not think it significant. Be watchful. The enemy desires that which you now have."*

The book only had 163 pages. There, starting on page 132 Serena read aloud: "The Candelaria Necklace—Significance and Purpose... OMG, Bry, it's all here—rainbow necklace, Atlantean tablets..." She put the book down and held the necklace, but Bryson picked it up and continued to page through to the end.

"That's not all that's here, Serena."

She wasn't listening. "The problem is, I don't remember the sounds that go with the colors for the rainbow. I remember Mother telling me that there were only six colors, not seven. I hardly remember the words she used."

"We'll figure it out. It's just another puzzle." He began to massage her shoulders while looking closely at her neck. He didn't see anything abnormal. "Yeah, there are a few things we need to figure out, girlfriend."

A lifetime achievement award from the International Society of Human Genetics. Clearly they don't have a clue who they are awarding this to. Vancouver hosted ISHG's annual awards this year. While Tarni found her room at the Hyatt Regency absolutely first rate, the meetings were at the Convention Center. Her high heels caused her feet and legs to hurt; she would have liked to skip a couple of the breakout sessions and get back to her room. Tarni ran into a few associates and only gave vague details about her current work—private lab doing research and development, had signed a nondisclosure agreement, that sort of thing. She had dyed her hair back to its original color and wore a conservative business suit. She had registered under a false name, Kendra Johannson. She fit right in with many of her international colleagues, except for the oversized bag. That was all part of the plan.

She wasn't here for presentations, lectures, updates, or a run through the exhibit hall; although, she did learn a few things. She attended the session on pharmacogenetics; the presentation was really first rate. Some questioners during the Q and A asked about a vaccine for the Hendra-variant Bogi 1. The worldwide growing epidemic had the entire research, academic, and corporate sponsors all concerned.

Kenseiko Li delivered the keynote, a broad overview of genomic innovation and potential applications. She did not doubt his brilliance, but she couldn't focus on his talk. She certainly had no plans to stay for the awards ceremony when Kenseiko Li would receive the most prestigious award in their field short of a Nobel Prize. All Tarni could think about was the chimeric monster this man had created. That and BB. About how the man's life had nearly been destroyed by Kenseiko Li.

Dr. Li's breakout session was full, but she had preregistered, guaranteeing her a seat. Tarni sat toward the back of the room and waited. She didn't know much about the talk, *SNV Quantification of Fusion Genes,* but the topic, as he covered it, had evidently progressed further than he let on. The chimera's DNA provided ample living proof of what he had accomplished. *Bastard! We've got to bring him down.*

Finally, the moment came. The talk ended, the formal Q and A concluded; she approached the podium, strategically positioning herself last. She adjusted her name tag on the lanyard and clutched an aluminum water bottle, careful to grasp only the handle.

"Dr. Li, thank you for such an enlightening presentation." She extended her unoccupied hand. "Kendra Johannson. I was wondering if I can ask a brief, unrelated question? It involves some research I'm presently conducting."

"What sort of research?"

"Sorry, I've got some NDAs to adhere to, so I can't say much. It's more about a lab protocol that you developed."

"I don't recognize you, Ms. Johannson. Who are you working with?"

She plowed on without answering. "That's not what's important. You coauthored with Dr. Axelrod on the washout protocols for isolating haplotype chromosomal variants. The citation is in *Journal of Molecular Biology.* I'm sure you know it, it's the current standard."

"Yes, I'm familiar with the approach."

"Well, I've varied the editing sequence using a proximity ligation assay. I'm getting clean, reproducible results in less time. I wondered if I sent you the research if you might be willing to coauthor a paper with me?"

"Why not whoever you are working with?"

"What I'm doing now is just a side project. Can I send my results over to you and ask you to have a look? If you don't think it's an improvement, I can ask elsewhere." She looked him right in the eye. *Set the hook, then reel in the fish.* "You are the most well-respected in the field. Having your name on the paper would be very helpful." *A little ego boost, a little sex charm.* She brushed back a wisp of her gorgeous hair.

He paused a moment and studied her. "Yes, why don't you send me the research protocol, Ms. Johannson."

"Fantastic. I just need an email address to send it to." She placed her bag down and handed over her water bottle. "Can you hold this a moment while I get a pen?" As she rummaged through her bag for pen and paper, she muttered to herself as if distraught by the disorganization in her bag. She made sure he saw her sort past an infant diaper. "Here we go." She handed over a pen and paper and held her breath. *Sticky trap, sticky trap, don't let me down.* "Just an email. I'll send it through when I get back from the conference."

Kenseiko Li scribbled a note then began to roll his fingers and palm from the hand that held the bottle. He frowned and passed the pen and paper back.

"Oh my gosh. I am so sorry, Dr. Li. Here, I've got a wipe." She reached back into her bag and pulled out some BABY-EEZE NATURALS. "I use these on my daughter. They're fragrance free and don't irritate the skin." She handed over the baby wipe and watched as Dr. Li removed the stickiness from his hands. She took out a second wipe and cleaned the aluminum surface of the water bottle. She then produced a ziplock bag and put all the used wipes inside.

She continued the charade. "I always keep these handy. I must have spilled something on my bottle. Thanks for your understanding." *Bingo! It's in the bag.*

"But you don't have any children." The voice was soft, yet she heard him clearly.

"Excuse me?"

"You don't have any children, Ms. Johannson, do you? Or should I say, Tarni Gillam?"

Shit! Play stupid. "I'm sorry. I don't understand you."

"Ah, but you do, Tarni Gillam. I know all about you. About your deceased father, and your mother, and your two sisters and brother. Would you like me to tell you their names?"

Tarni swallowed, doing her best not to lose her cool, but even her dark skin had paled. *God, now what!* She said quietly, "What do you want?"

"I want you to tell me who you are working with and what you are working on. I urge you to think carefully before you answer. Your nephew, Terrence, and your niece, Jephora—such a pretty girl—their futures depend on it."

Game's up, girl, better come clean. Maybe he knows, maybe he doesn't. "You wouldn't know him."

"Try me. Terrence, Jephora, did you know your sister-in-law is pregnant?"

"His name is Beangagarrie Brindabella."

"Good. Correct answer. Now, what is Beangagarrie working on?"

"It's old research on a DNA fragment. It has some overlap with herpetology research he conducted years ago."

Kenseiko Li's lips parted, revealing his small yellow teeth. "He is persistent if nothing else. Who is funding this research?"

Her lie followed without hesitation. "I don't know. It's a wealthy private patron. I don't know if it's a he or a she or a foundation."

Li said nothing while holding her with his intense gaze.

Shit. What have I got myself into?

"Now you work for me, Ms. Gillam. You will send me an email to the address I gave you with the subject line 'Conference Follow-up.' I will respond by giving you a secure address to send me reports. I want daily reports on Beangagarrie Brindabella's progress. Do you understand?"

"Yes, Dr. Li. I understand."

He grabbed her water bottle. "Welcome to the company." He held up the bottle. "No drinking on the job." He then reached into Tarni's bag and removed the ziplock baggie containing the used baby wipes. A smirk passed his face. "We recycle." The baggie disappeared into his pocket along with the bottle.

After collecting the pen he used earlier and reviewing his instructions, an evil smile returned. He spoke barely over a whisper. "Consider this your new employee orientation. Do not fail me, Tarni Gillam. At Advanced Bionics, failure is not an option." He walked off.

The room had emptied. Tarni slumped to the floor. *Monster…*

35

"Listen, I know you're tired of trying these different combinations, but sooner or later, something has to click."

"That's easy for you to say, Bryson. You have this crazy idea that you can reverse engineer this sound-sight. It doesn't work backward. I hear something and see a color or pattern. When you show me a color, I don't hear anything."

"You know, PTG, you are not the first person to have synesthesia. Alexander Scriabin had the same gift, and he mapped out sounds with their corresponding colors."

"Yes, I know, you tried his sound frequencies and matched colors. Problem is, I don't see the same things he apparently did. Sorry, I just don't see how this is helpful."

Bryson suppressed his mounting frustration. "Your book that Nalini returned said the key is activated by singing the rainbow colors using the power of your voice."

"Can we take a break? You said you wanted to go into town, and we would eat out for my birthday. We did enough torture for today. I'm going outside to try and clear my head."

"You want company?"

"No!"

Damn, she can be hard to figure out sometimes. She's even snarkier than usual. It's too early to head into town.

He played with the music app, trying different pitches and pure tones. According to Nicholas Melendez's color of sound chart, rainbow red should be somewhere between a light wavelength of 696 nm to 656 nm, corresponding to sound frequencies of 392 Hz to 415 Hz. The problem was, none of the combinations he tried worked for Serena; she saw colors with her inner vision, they just weren't the right ones. He even tried toning the different sounds associated with the chakras, all of which identified with specific colors—no luck.

He switched gears to try a different attack analysis. Sir Isaac Newton, noted Freemason, proposed adding a seventh color to the rainbow spectrum. He was both a famous mathematician and an alchemist and, reportedly, he had a fascination with numerology. He attributed mystical powers to the number seven. Some believed that is why he added the color indigo to allow for seven colors to sum together to form pure white light. Newton used musical theory to understand light. He founded the science of spectroscopy using prisms to break sunlight into its component parts.

Bryson dug further. The more he read, the more intriguing it became. Newton assigned seven colors to seven different solfeggio pitches: C-D-E-F-G-A-B. They corresponded to do-re-mi-fa-sol-la-ti. Could the chromatic arrangement of the rainbow overlap with the harmonic scale of the six primary solfeggio frequencies: 396-417-528-639-741-852 Hz? Newton came well after the ancient Egyptians. Perhaps adding a seventh color was a mistake. Perhaps it was intentional. The Vatican outlawed music based upon the solfeggio scale. Why? Because it provoked some sort of spiritual experiences among listeners!

"PTG, I've got an idea." He called to her outside while adjusting the music app to enter the progression of sound frequencies. Bryson's heart raced; his pounding pulse sounded like drumbeats. "PTG, I want to try something."

"Stop calling me that. I cut my ponytail years ago. I'm practicing my asanas. When are we going to eat? I'm hungry."

He ignored her answer, went outside, and saw her standing on her head, palms resting against the earth. "I'll try not to disturb you. Just tell me what color you see." He played the 396 Hz sound, the base note of the solfeggio scale.

Bright red erupted in Serena's mind. She tumbled to the ground. "Play that again." As Bryson did so, she blinked a few times. "Pure red. I think you've got something. Play the next note."

417 Hz blasted a bright orange in Serena's inner vision. As Bryson ascended the scale, the colors of the rainbow appeared in the Candelaria warrior's mind.

"Now, repeat the words you recall Mother used but at the tonal frequencies that match the color-sounds I just played."

After a few tries, Serena had the words, sounds, and colors all progressing in a vocalized chromatic harmonic scale. They raced inside the hogan, and she placed the necklace around her neck. The uppermost part, the halo at the top of the symbol, rested upon her throat, just below her voice box.

As she sang, Bryson watched the serpent glow first in red, then orange, to yellow, green, blue, and finally, violet. As Serena's voice went silent, the candle illuminated in a brilliant point of white light. Serena had seen the entire display reflected off Bryson's wide-eyed pupils.

As the necklace dimmed, neither spoke. After a minute, Bryson whispered, "Happy birthday!"

36

Wán shàn completed her log entry into the secure messaging site that she shared with her Ninja sisters. Her report, as was true for each of the reports singularly and collectively, contained little of substance. Each of the Illuminati heads managed their individual empires and contributed in some way or form to the great overarching plan. *It is clever how bàba can use these separate pieces to synthesize and monitor the big picture. If Genghis Khan had such a communication and spy network, he could have conquered the entire world.*

Still, something troubled her. Things that should be clear in black or white seemed fuzzy and gray. She reread the report from her second sister. Bàba had reconfigured their original assignments; her second sister now visited with Damiaan Van Duyn. Initially, Wán shàn had this assignment. She read through the report a third time and tried to decipher what in the update caused her sense of turmoil and unease.

She scrutinized the entry: "Van Duyn met today with Mr. Peter Reynolds. I was not permitted to be present during the actual meeting, but I learned it involved discussion about one of Mr. Reynolds' affiliate companies, Baxter Consolidated. I understand the topic dealt with some military equipment being supplied by this affiliate."

The substance of the message mirrored many such reports involving each of the family heads. They often met with subordinate cousin members to discuss operations, propaganda messaging, contracts, etc. She acknowledged to herself that the content of the message was in no way troubling. As her rational and analytic mind struggled to understand her reaction, a thought emerged—a most curious hypothesis.

Wán shàn logged herself off the network as she continued to dwell upon this hypothesis. *I am troubled that the visit with Van Duyn was originally assigned to me. From my schooling, this appears to represent an emotional response called "jealousy." Yet, Dr. Zhāng and bàba have both informed me that I am created without emotional handicaps. These can cloud my mind and my judgment.*

Her initial action was to log back in and amend her daily report with an updated entry detailing her analysis of this unease. But as she pulled up the login screen, she changed her mind. While she wondered if any of her sisters experienced similar reactions and whether they puzzled about the reasons, she decided she needed to conduct further internal analysis. She wanted to behave in all ways consistent with perfection. But if emotions represented imperfections, how would her bàba respond? Would he be displeased? As the screen went black, Wán shàn concluded that she needed to dwell upon this further.

"Cheer up, Bryson. I know you and Serena had some kind of tiff, but it's not a big deal."

"I don't know, Claus. I thought the birthday celebration was a good idea. I'm not used to people calling me or my ideas stupid. It all worked out at the end, but I've never seen her so bitchy."

"Ha, women! Why do you think I'm not married? I got tired of the insults. Serena's a good kid, she's just all worked up about her necklace."

"That and her superpowers. I tell you, I'm glad we made it back to Taos without causing a wildfire or getting into a meltdown fight." Bryson shook his head. "Riding together used to be more fun. You would think she would be more appreciative that we figured out the Twins might be in the Canary Islands."

"Well, you can chill out here. There isn't much to do. The spiders I sent on the contractor's truck have all deployed inside Dulce. It's going to take a while to map out things. They've got autonomous AI, so we just sit back and wait for them to crawl and scurry their way through the base. I'll show you what we've got so far, but it's not much."

Bryson reviewed the beginning of a layout. It would take more time and more detail to have enough information to conduct a raid. Meanwhile, the strained car ride back with Serena, her insistence on going to Tenerife alone, and her attitude weighed upon him. There wasn't enough to work on with Claus to get his mind off his worries.

"Hey, Bryson, why don't you head back to my place in Chicago? While the spiders gather data, there isn't anything else happening here. I think some alone time together with Tarni would be good for both of you. She'll get your mind off Serena."

"That's just what I need. Out of the frying pan into the fire." Still, the suggestion made sense. *I do need to talk to BB. And it will be good to see both Beangagarrie and Uncle Pete. And Tarni is a lot of fun.*

"Claus, I think you're right. I'll leave tomorrow. Do I have to sleep on the couch, or can I use your room?"

"You can sleep anywhere you want." He winked and grinned. "Anywhere you want."

37

S he had time to think, too much time to think—a drawback of traveling long distances by yourself and not being any good at small talk. The argument with Bryson began innocently enough. They had started to discuss the Illuminati plans and how to stop them when she realized she and Bryson had radically different ideas. *He may think of himself as a warrior, but he's a pacifist. I told him you've got to fight fire with fire. He shouldn't have dismissed me with that stupid smirk. What did he say? "Great, so you want to burn the whole house down? Better yet, is that your idea of setting the world on fire, girlfriend?"*

It only escalated from there. For a moment, she had wondered if they might get asked to leave the restaurant. The climax came when Bryson broke into Yoda speak. "Anger leads to the dark side. Take the first step on that path, will you?" *He shouldn't have said that.* But deep down, she suspected he was right. You don't administer more poison to combat poison; you have to find the antidote.

Sitting in a corner of the baggage claim area of Tenerife South Airport, waiting for her luggage to appear on the carousel, she glanced at one of the monitors broadcasting the latest news in English:

"An uneasy truce has settled over the Middle East as families search for loved ones and governments count their dead. Calls for a higher-level authority to mediate disputes, redraw territories, and to develop something akin to a regional Marshall Plan have started to generate traction. The UN Security Council is considering a request to form a task force. In the meantime, food and clean water remain scarce. In the void created by ineffective governmental responses, local militias and warlords have emerged..."

Already demoralized by her fight with Bryson, she stared at the TV screen, searching for answers to world events. She knew powerful individuals were pulling strings to manipulate circumstances and reactions—lies and propaganda and fake news and innocent people starving, dying, suffering. *How do you combat that?* Unexpectedly, she heard herself exclaim, "How do you combat that, Bryson?" People looked at her, saw her anger, and turned away. A well-meaning stranger asked if she needed any help. Glaring back at him, she seethed. "Not that you can provide." She lunged forward to get her luggage. Serena had been thinking of calling Bryson to try to hit the reset button. Instead, she texted him a terse message: *ARRIVED IN TENERIFE.* For the moment, her dark side prevailed.

Bryson busied himself, running a statistical analysis of genetic profiles amalgamated from several private and commercial databases. This basically mindless task provided a needed distraction. However, he faced a much bigger distraction—Tarni. He liked her natural hair color even more than the pink. She looked good. She smelled good. They worked near each other across a lab counter. She ran computer modeling to simulate a labeled RNA strand BB thought might work as a carrier to mark a gene segment. But she didn't want to talk; she seemed preoccupied. Bryson tried not to stare.

"BB, I don't think this simulation works. Instead of mRNA, I'm thinking a strand of transfer RNA might be more suitable."

Beangagarrie broke his concentration from the electron microscopic image of a twist of base pairs. "What's that, Fuchsia?"

"I said we should try tRNA."

Bryson watched as BB grabbed his forehead and nearly fell to the floor. He and Tarni rushed to stabilize the senior scientist.

"Are you okay?" Tarni eased him into a chair.

"Yes, yes, I'm fine. I had a thought that seemed important, but it escaped me."

"It must have been a powerful thought. It almost toppled you," Bryson quipped.

"Transfer RNA, yes, tRNA might be better to model, Tarni. Give it a try. After that, there is something else I would like you to begin working on. It's unfortunate that you couldn't get a DNA sample from Dr. Li, but we might be able to use the two other family heads' samples we have for targeting with a specific virus. I've been looking at their unique EM structure in this section of the genome. I think we might be able to use a viral carrier to deliver something lethal."

"Wait a minute, BB. Are we getting into the business of assassination?"

"Unfortunately, Bryson, you have to cut off a snake at its head."

"It's not my place to say, but I'm going to say it anyway. I think that's the wrong approach. When I got bitten by a snake, the cure was antivenom. That and some chanting."

Bryson recounted his childhood experience of nearly dying, his coma, and hallucinations.

BB interrupted. "Probably a coral snake. They have a powerful neurotoxin. You're lucky to be alive."

"Yeah, I researched it later and figured a coral snake. I don't know how much is luck, how much is from the antivenom, and how much is Serena's great aunt's dream intervention. When I learned it was Serena's Ooljee, the whole synchronicity wigged both of us out. Most of the rest of the story, you both know— Circle training, Candelaria, the works. But the point I'm making is that antivenom and mystical healing is the answer, not killing."

"You make a good point, son. But sometimes you need to destroy something in order to replace it with something better. No different from the mythology of the phoenix."

"BB, I respect your wisdom and judgement, but you are making my point for me. The thing is, if you want to change the world, you could tear it down, burn it down, do whatever you want to destroy it. Looks to me like the bad guys, the enemy, the Illuminati…whatever, are wrecking the whole planet pretty good without our help. Or you can remove the foundation that stuff is built upon, and it will fall down in a heap under its own weight. Get rid of the foundation stone and that's how we win. Isn't that what we're trying to do here? Repair human DNA and fix the world?"

Neither answered. Tarni had remained strangely silent the entire time. She appeared to be lost in her own thoughts and only half paying attention.

"Seeing as you both haven't answered, let me ask you something else. It's a bit off topic. Can you give me a recent description of this Gurumarra guy you both follow?"

Tarni and BB each described the Australian shaman. They wanted to know why he asked.

"It's weird, but I had a creepy dream, and I think he was in it. I've been having a lot of strange dreams, including recurrences of my dream hallucinations when I got the snake bite—Ooljee dancing and chanting, that sort of thing. Since I've never met your shaman, it's hard for me to say if it was him in my dream."

BB said, "In our ancestral culture, what you see around you is all part of the Dreamtime. If anything, what you call dreaming might actually be a truer form of reality. Can you tell us more of this dream that you speak of?"

"I hope what I dreamt wasn't real." Bryson described his nightmare of Serena lying in the cave, attacked by some large reptilian creature. "Fortunately, I have an excellent memory, even in my dreams. Gurumarra, if that's who it was, kept saying the same thing, *'Mangar-Kunjer-Kunja, Gah-lin! Mangar-Kunjer-Kunja, Gah-lin!'* Does that mean anything to either of you?"

"It's an aboriginal dialect. Mangar-Kunjer-Kunja is the lizard god," BB said. He grabbed the side of his head.

"BB, are you okay? You keep grabbing the side of your head. Are you in pain?" Bryson sounded concerned. "Do you need to lie down?"

"Something you said cleared some cobwebs in my brain. I'm fine. Mangar-Kunjer-Kunja is the lizard god, and Gah-lin is a command telling him to go away. I'll tell you more about the story of the lizard god later, but that must wait. I can't chance forgetting this again."

BB stood up from his chair. "I just remembered something *very* important! It has to do with transfer RNA and Mangar-Kunjer-Kunja." He looked at Bryson. "Son, maybe, just maybe we can remove that foundation stone you were speaking about. Tarni, I need you."

38

The Island of Eternal Spring, a well-deserved description from what Serena witnessed. Beautiful beaches, some of them with black volcanic sand, quaint villages and shops, history and culture—all were present in abundance. Away from the tourist haven, Tenerife pulsed with natural beauty of rugged landscapes and breathtaking vistas, especially at night. These attractions held only a passing interest to the young Candelaria. Her only reason for being here lay pocketed in a hidden pouch held closely against her skin. The necklace, her key, remained useless until she located the Twins.

Her visit to the Basilica of Candelaria proved fruitless. Though the building and sanctuary held historical and architectural significance, her many questions remained unanswered. The familiar image within of Black Madonna in dazzling robes clutching a candle in her left hand beckoned to her, yet the mysteries the Lady hinted at remained unrevealed. She left the basilica feeling frustrated but determined.

Her book about the Candelaria Fellowship gave a different version of events. The White Snake Brotherhood, distant forefathers to the Illuminati, fashioned a history of veneration and religious celebration. Feasts dedicated to the patron of the Canary Islands occur twice a year. Fortunately, Serena's visit was between what she viewed as perversions of truth. Festivals and candlelit ceremonies obscured the true message of light. The encryption upon the Black Madonna's robe remained undeciphered. Serena held a key to understand this mystery, but she needed to find the Twins. Tomorrow she would seek her answers elsewhere.

Bryson had researched a lot of information about the Pyramids of Güímar. She had a pass to visit the Ethnographic Park surrounding the pyramids. Her pass included access to the Poison Garden, a name she found both curious and apropos. She also found it interesting that Thor Heyerdahl, the intrepid researcher of ancient cultures, had founded the museum here and helped with some of the pyramid restoration. The museum guide, Hector, a thirty-something, fair-haired man who spoke a half dozen languages, claimed ancestry back to the ancient Guanches, back to the people of Atlantis.

She asked many questions. Were the pyramids here built by the Atlantean civilization or by the Egyptians? Clearly the restorations differ from other pyramids; are they built upon ruined foundations? What of the lava caves reported to be at the site? Hector's answers: older structures lie buried; Tenerife was, at the least, a travel stop en route between Atlantis and Egypt; although, some historians feel it may have been part of the Atlantean continent itself. The lava caves were not open to the public.

Fortunately, the assembled tour group wasn't large. Serena did not want to disrespect the other visitors by not giving them the opportunity to have their questions answered. When the tour finished, she pressed the guide for more information. Aside from complementing her on the extensiveness of her knowledge, he recommended she consider applying for a job should she wish to relocate to the island.

"You have a passion for discussing the secrets here at the Pyramids of Güímar. The museum staff would welcome you, Ms. Serena; or should I say, Señorita Serena?"

"Tell me, Hector, what do you know of the Virgin Mary's appearance and Isis, of ancient Egypt?"

"Here it is sacrilege to suggest such a connection, but I have heard stories."

"How about a pyramid room containing Emerald Tablets of Thoth, a chamber holding ancient wisdom of Atlantis?"

Hector looked at her strangely for a moment. "No, Señorita, I know not of these secrets." He laughed. "But I would welcome the chance to search for them together."

That seemed a skillful diversion. "It is getting late in the afternoon, Hector. I must return to the lava sand beach at San Agustín before the sun sets. Thank you, you have been very accommodating." She offered him a generous tip, but he declined, saying only that the extra time spent with her was worth more than any sum of euros.

Serena had intentionally left him the name of the hotel. She was getting closer; she felt it in her bones.

His nephew and Claus had both advised against this trip, but Peter felt pressured by Rothschild. *I don't know why Edward thinks I can extract some information about Serena. For one thing, Li doesn't have her as Rothschild suspects. I don't care for Van Duyn, but he does provide useful details about secret military programs, especially when he's been drinking.* Peter suggested they both have a drink. The two of them traveled in a Reynolds' corporate jet with a well-stocked bar.

"I would offer a drink to the young lady accompanying us, but she appears to be underage, Damiaan." He pointed to the back.

"Don't underestimate Wán shàn, Peter. I've seen her fight. She is more than a match for both of us."

Of course, Peter had already recognized the girl from the interaction at BB's lab. *Perhaps after another drink, Damiaan's lips will loosen, and I can learn more information about Li's spy.*

"I've heard the military has a hidden presence beneath Denver. Is this where you want to show me some of the hardware? Is this where we can see how Baxter might get involved?"

"All in good time, Peter. Apparently, the military presence there is not so secret after all. Trust me, Peter, there are many secrets you don't know about. But when the time comes, you might be seeing more of Denver."

Peter Reynolds didn't want to let Damiaan know that Rothschild had mentioned the same thing. He sat back, ordered another round for both of them, and listened for crumbs.

Her mind remained poised in high alert. Serena's beach-side yoga did little to still her thoughts; although, it drew an appreciative crowd. Now, lying on her towel, absorbing the heat from the setting sun glistening off the salt and her sweat, she listened to the waves, saw the air currents stirring wind and water, repeated her words of fire silently to keep them ever ready.

Serena felt him before seeing him. He moved clumsily over a small black dune, throwing one leg forward then rotating his hips to bring the other leg forward a half step. Even from this distance, she saw the curve in his spine and the scoliosis-induced hump that left the man permanently leaning forward and to the side. A crooked man with crooked intentions, she imagined, as he methodically and laboriously made his way toward her. She sat up.

At near distance, the man's physical deformities appeared even more pronounced. A cleft lip, though surgically repaired, left a permanently upturned portion of lip exposing tobacco-stained teeth. The man had trouble tracking both eyes together. Serena couldn't recall the name of the condition, but she needed to choose which of his two eyes to look at. His presence unnerved her, but only slightly. She certainly did not fear him. He looked to be in his forties, but it was difficult to say.

"My apologheez, Sheeñorita. Pleash pardon my inshtrushion. I would shpeak in Shpanish, but there are too many eshes. My lishp makesh it hard to prounounsh the letter 'ss.'" This last syllable he obviously took great care and effort to pronounce correctly, but a hiss of spit caused him to cover his mouth quickly.

"How can I help you?" Serena responded cautiously.

"I think it ish more I that can help you, Sherena."

"How do you know my name? Did Hector from the museum tell you where to find me?"

"He did. But shomone elshe warned me you might arrive, Sherena Mendezz."

Serena looked at the strange man, shifting her gaze from one eye to the other. Her features revealed nothing. The man could have learned her last name from the hotel staff. She intentionally traveled without a fake identity because she tired of all the falsehoods and deception. *If the enemy has discovered my whereabouts, so be it. I can take care of myself.* She prepared a fiery sound to utter.

"Who? Who has foretold my arrival?"

The man smiled, revealing an entire row of tobacco stains. He placed his hand inside a pocket. Serena tensed, expecting a knife or gun. Instead, he withdrew and lit a cigarette.

"Forgive me, Sheeñorita. It ish an old habit. Sshmoking helpsh to dry the shaliva." He drew a puff and turned his face to exhale. "Hish Lordsship, Edward Rothsshchild, told me you might vishit."

Serena studied this man, an ally to Rothschild. *Still seeking the necklace, I'll wager.* Instinctively she placed her hand over its hidden location.

"And to whom do I owe the pleasure of this occasion? Who are you, oh emissary of the powerful Baron Rothschild?"

"I am Riccardo Candelaria. Alash, I have no title. I apologhizz for not bowing to you, recognishing you to be a true Candelaria." He drew another drag, shifted his weight, then added, "When I topple over, it'sh a very messhy affair trying to get back on my feet."

Serena had been sitting on her towel. She rose and brushed away grains of black sand. The sun kissed the ocean, sending beams of orange fire across the sea.

"So, Riccardo Candelaria, how can you help me, and why should I trust you?"

"I musht earn your trusht." His boot crushed the butt in the sand. "You shearch for the Twinzz and the tabletzz they guard. Join me for dinner, and I will tell you where to find them."

"Not sure if joining you for dinner is a good idea, Riccardo."

He wiped his mouth with his sleeve and held out his arm. "Oh, but I inshisht."

39

He and Tarni were out to eat. Nothing fancy, just a glorified pizza place with good food and good ale. Each danced around any serious talk. They shared funny stories—Tarni in grad school and college, Bryson doing analyst work for the NSA. The slow service and no rush to get back home resulted in too many brews.

"So, I haven't asked you this, but do you think I'm wrong?"

"C'mon, nerd boy, you're never wrong. But I don't have the slightest notion what you're talking about."

"Right. I guess it helps if I don't blurt out something without a lead in." Bryson put his tankard on the coaster, spilling some in the process. "I'm sayin' that Serena and BB seem to be okay with destruction. You know, blowing shit up, killing the bad guys, that sort of thing. I'm not okay with that. Call me a wimp; I don't care. We're not going to fix this world by tearing it apart."

"Bloody right about that, cobber. The world don't need any help with dat." She drained her glass and continued. "I'm going home…not here… I'm meaning that I'm going back to Australia."

"What! You can't do that. We need you to do whatever it is you and BB are doing to help us save the world. You can't quit now."

"I've got family, Bryson—mother, siblings, a niece and a nephew. I miss my family."

"Hold on. Where is this coming from? You used to be carefree and spirited, but lately you've been way too serious."

Tarni looked at him, bit her lip, then shook her head. For a moment, Bryson thought she would cry. "It's bloody complicated." She pushed her glass away. "I don't want to talk about it. I'm knackered. I think we should head back."

Claus's place was a fifteen-minute walk. She said little. They said little. Tarni reached over first for Bryson's hand, then took his arm and put it around her waist. Her head fit perfectly nestled upon his shoulder. They walked, oblivious to the Chicago night scene, each thinking private thoughts neither would share.

"I want you, Bryson. I understand that you have something with Serena, and I don't want to mess with that. I just want you to know that. I think you're pretty awesome." She squeezed his hand. "And I agree that killing isn't the answer."

He turned to face her. Under the streetlight, he saw tears had marred her mascara and perfect features. He felt every bit as vulnerable as she looked—riddled by uncertainty about the future, unsure about the present.

He whispered, "I think you're pretty awesome too, Tarni. I mean that!" Their lips touched and time suspended. When their kiss ended, Bryson voiced what he had held back for days. "I want you too."

Although Riccardo's grotesque features, his tobacco-stained teeth and near-constant spittle, approached revolting, beyond that Serena uncovered a highly educated, charming, and delightful man. His self-effacing humor left them both laughing and joking.

The Candelaria Estate showed evidence of decline and disrepair. The car-service driver, obviously well known to Riccardo, grinned and slapped him upon his humped back, nearly knocking his patron to the ground. An aging woman, who spoke only Spanish, showed obvious surprise at seeing her employer return with company. She functioned as both housekeeper and cook, and immediately set herself to preparing dinner. She looked pleased and excited.

Serena gathered her host had few guests. The meal, a fabulous paella complemented by a fine Tempranillo wine, satisfied her hunger. The coffee came accompanied by a fresh crème caramel, a truly outstanding flan.

"Yesh, Maria ish quite an excellent cook. Much better than my mother. Shhe lovezz it when I have gueshtzz. Though that ish all too infrequent." He gestured to himself. "Few can shtand to behold shuch beauty."

Serena smiled at his self-deprecating remark. Still, she remained cautious, unsure if she could trust this man. He seemed to enjoy having someone to talk to. She responded with a rare display of graciousness. "Beauty is not always apparent at first glance." His face blushed at her remark.

As they sipped coffee, he explained that a cleft palate caused his lisp. His strabismus had been present since childhood. He recommended she look at his left eye. "My right eye ish the lazy one, like sho much of the resht of me." Again, he gestured to himself.

As his guest, Serena wanted to be polite. She let him go on. Despite the speech impediment, he reveled in reciting the history of Tenerife, its connection to Atlantis, and his Candelarian heritage. At last, it came time to talk business.

Riccardo apparently sensed a shift. He dismissed Maria, but not before she had filled Serena's cup one last time.

"I have shpent my life reasherching the Candelaria name and hishtory." They had moved to a sitting room; he still carried a cloth napkin from the table that he used frequently to mop spittle.

Riccardo explained that his lineage actually traced back to merchants, more likely smugglers, that had garnered favor with Spanish nobility. They adopted a new coat of arms and heraldry in the fourteen hundreds, not long after the Virgin's apparition to the Guanches that tied into modern Candelaria symbolism.

"Before that, the true Candelarians, your anshestorzz, go all the way back to the Gnoshtix of Shumeria."

"Where did you learn all this?"

"I've had a lot of time to read. I've even been to the Vatican library, including the hidden archivzze." He slowly raised himself from a chair and retrieved two books from a case then hobbled back. He held the two books with a certain reverence.

It surprised Serena to see a familiar cover showing the necklace she guarded. Riccardo seemed pleased that she knew of and had read this book, *The Candelaria Fellowship—A Flame Extinguished.* The other book was written in Greek. Riccardo summarized that much of the Gnostic connection was detailed in this text. Serena recalled her strong reaction to Hypatia and her fate. She asked her host about Hypatia.

"You may indeed have a direct blood connection. Hishtory shhowz, Hypatia and sho many more were pershecuted. Undoubtedly she wasz a true Teleshti, a leader among the Gnoshtix."

"What happened? I know we were persecuted, burned as witches, suppressed; I know all that. Couldn't we go into hiding to survive?"

"You could." He pointed at her. "You did, to shome extent. But the Brotherhood of the Shun, White Shnakez, Freemashonz, Illuminati today—they were all too powerful. Shome of your people went into hiding, but mosht feared their powerz would fall in the handz of their enemy."

He continued well into the night, detailing the purge during the early rise of the Roman Catholic Church, the Spanish Inquisition, the dark ages. He had a wealth of knowledge about Candelarias in the New World, including Mayan connections. Finally, he turned to Rothschild.

"Hish Lordship wantz your necklazze. He ish willing to pay me a lot of money." He spat, "I don't want hish filthy money."

"What is it that you do want, Riccardo?"

The Spaniard wiped his mouth. "I want to learn what shecretz the Twinzz guard. I want to learn what the rainbow key unlockz." He ground down a cigarette stub, his seventh.

Serena felt certain Riccardo spoke the truth, but despite his old-world charm and sophistication, she still wasn't sure she could trust him. "Then we share a common bond. Let's see what tomorrow brings."

Back in her hotel room, she directed all her effort and discipline to still her mounting anticipation about tomorrow. She ran through a kundalini mind meditation to activate her chakras. Her throat tingled. She wanted to sing. Now, facing her image in the bathroom mirror, Serena repeated the rainbow tones at their precise required frequencies. She caressed the necklace and watched the hues dance across the intricate surface: red, orange, yellow, green, blue, violet. The candle flickered then ignited into a brilliant white. She mouthed the words, and it seemed the image looking back at her spoke, but it was Ooljee talking, not Serena. "And the spark shall become a flame…"

She blinked, and the mirror reflection of Serena blinked back, then smiled in anticipation. "Tomorrow, Riccardo, it is not the secrets the rainbow key unlocks that matter. What unknown powers to my voice will be revealed? Destiny beckons…"

40

The phone rang three times before the answering machine kicked in. He rolled over to look at the time. *2 a.m. Who would call Claus at two in the morning?* A second call—three rings and the answering machine kicked in. Bryson roused himself and went to the kitchen. He didn't want to wake Tarni. His head hurt.

He heard over the phone's speaker, "Bryson, when you get this message, call me as soon as possible."

He lifted the receiver. "Claus? Bryson here. I was sleeping."

"Is your cell phone sleeping too? Damn, I've been trying to reach you."

Bryson heard the urgency on the other end. "Sorry, I must have it muted. Something bad?"

"Not sure. Have you heard from Serena? Is she still in Tenerife?"

"Far as I know. Wait a second, I'll pull up the tracking log on her cell phone's location." His fingers rocketed over a keyboard. "Looks like she was at her hotel, then traveled on the island. Last ping I've got is Pyramids of Güímar Ethnographic Park."

Tarni stumbled in. Bryson covered the phone and mouthed, "Claus."

"Claus. What does the bloke want? Is everything okay?" Tarni set water to boil for tea.

"What's, what's going on, Claus? Is Serena in danger?"

"I don't know. See if you can call her. I'll hold."

All Bryson got was Serena's voice mail. He hadn't spoken to her since their argument; although, they had exchanged texts.

Claus sighed. "Shit! Here's the story: one of Rothschild's corporate jets took off from London about thirty minutes ago. I am tracking the flight plan, and it's headed direct as a crow flies to Tenerife. I don't think that's a coincidence."

"When do you think it will land?"

"Four, maybe four and a half hours max."

"If I hustled on a Reynolds' jet direct, how long from Chicago?"

"I already checked. Even with everything falling into place, you're talking at least ten hours."

Bryson's Adam's apple slid down and up his neck. His mind raced. "How about Cairo? Maybe we can reach Moon?"

"Already thought of that. Again, you're talking a good ten hours."

"Any other suggestions or ideas? Do we have any assets to call that could get there quickly?"

"I got nothing here, Bryson. Best I can think of is keep trying to reach her. Send her messages. Warn her Rothschild might be headed her way. Keep me posted. Let's talk again in an hour, sooner if the situation changes. Monitor her location. If that phone is with her, maybe we can figure out where to send help."

Bryson hung up the phone. He reviewed his texts from Serena, but there was nothing of substance. He reviewed the tracking history. *Serena was at the pyramids yesterday. Why would she go back?*

Tarni held her cup of tea. She looked genuinely concerned. "What's wrong?"

"Everything…"

The same driver as yesterday dropped them off at the Ethnographic Park. The museum staff brought out a wheelchair. They all knew Riccardo Candelaria; he spoke to each of them by name. Serena gathered he had some pull or VIP status of sorts. He wheeled himself to a far corner of the property, past a barricade. A rope cordoned off a ramp. A sign written in four languages read, "NO

ADMITTANCE" in prominent red lettering. He undid the rope and proceeded slowly past the sign and down the ramp.

A series of several landings and ramp ways finally ended in front of a door. Riccardo produced a key. "I am given accshesh for myshelf and any gueshtzz. They all know me here."

At the doorway, Serena stood before the entrance to a black-rock cave. "I take it this is one of the lava caves?"

"Thish ish *the* lava cave. At leasht if my reshearch is correct. The wallzz are sholid, but I think the key openzz another chamber." He gestured from his seat. "The resht ish up to you." Riccardo produced a kerchief to wipe his spit and a pack of cigarettes.

It was cool and quiet, the stillness broken only by Serena's pounding heart. She removed the necklace from a hidden pocket and fastened it around her neck.

Riccardo gawked. "Can I touch it?"

She allowed it. He cradled it with fingers of his left hand beneath the snake-wrapped silvery-golden candle and stroked it with the index finger of his right hand, then set it to rest back against her lower neck.

"I imagined it bigger. How doezzh it work?"

"It's voice activated." She burst out laughing. "Just like modern technology. Watch…and listen."

Without further explanation, she sang the words of the colors of the rainbow. Riccardo sat silent and riveted. Hues rose and faded. As the candle illuminated, Serena saw the shift in the back wall. She had witnessed this in Egypt with Mother. "Can you see it? Can you see the change, Riccardo?"

"I don't shee anything, Sherena."

Serena's spine tingled. She walked through the rear wall, then poked her head back into the cave entrance to see the cigarette dangle and fall out of Riccardo Candelaria's mouth.

41

Each time he assembled the fragments of information, the big-picture details became better defined. His well-trained gift children from the Humanix School and their Ninja cousins provided the reports and observations.

Through these, he saw a glorious emerging portrait of a New World Order. Kenseiko doubted any of the Council of Thirteen, including the Pindar, saw how their years of planning were unfolding in real time. Soon phase two would be initiated. Already, several thousand sleeping within the wombs had been wakened and dispatched. They infiltrated society and assimilated into vacant positions waiting to be filled. Engineers, teachers, government officials, military operatives, media spokesmen—they were seeded into key positions worldwide. Complicit government-created identities matched these operatives to carefully orchestrated vacancies. Soon, these minions would be vocal supporters of mandatory vaccination, of reorganization to deal with mounting threats to life and safety. The time grew near; when the Council next met, they should be ready to launch phase two.

He reviewed the log entries from Tarni Gillam. Grudgingly, he had to admit to himself that Beangagarrie Brindabella was both a brilliant geneticist and a doggedly determined man. *Pity I did not recruit him for work at the Imaginarium.*

His six Wán shàns fed Kenseiko a steady stream of intel. As he perused the most recent entries, he frowned. Bundy had taken one of his little Ninjas to an orgy and had even had relations with her. While the reporter conveyed no sense of outrage, Kenseiko seethed. *He goes too far! His appetites are insatiable.* With uncharacteristic anger, he left his office and unlocked a storeroom. He summoned Wán shàn.

When she arrived, he had composed himself. "In this storage locker, I keep a number of specialized preparations. I have a gift for you to deliver to one of the family heads. It is for Aaron Bundy."

"Did you read the report my sister entered into our network yesterday regarding this man?"

"I did. That is the reason for this gift."

"I am confused, bàba. Bundy sexually advantaged himself. I recall his smell when he touched my body. Although my sister conveyed no dismay from this violation, his actions do not merit a gift."

Kenseiko felt bemused by his daughter's confusion. "It is not the sort of gift you imagine. What do you think is an appropriate response?"

Wán shàn appeared to consider the circumstances. Kenseiko could almost see her mind working.

"Something wrapped as a gift that is actually punishment and warning. Something that evidences control and mastery. Something to inform Aaron Bundy that Kenseiko Li does not tolerate such insolence."

"Careful, daughter, you almost sound vengeful. Still, I delight in your reasoning." He reached in and picked out a vial with a blood mixture. "When the next meeting cycle for Bundy occurs, it will be you, not your sister that visits with him. You will deliver this present to him with my fond regards."

"What does the vile contain?"

"It has a potent short-term sexual stimulant, but the long-term effects are to cause testicular atrophy. We developed it in the lab for experimental purposes on a genetic strain of rats. It is highly effective."

"So, you are saying he will find it pleasurable at first, but then…excuse my use of slang, bàba…then it will cause his balls to shrink."

Kenseiko couldn't be sure, but Wán shàn appeared to be pleased by her remark. Her lips parted to show perfectly proportioned white teeth.

"You might say that."

"It is a good gift, bàba. It shall please me to deliver it."

The inky blackness disoriented Serena. She felt blindly at the floor beneath her and called out light from the stone. In the soft glow, she discerned two pillars, but only one held an Emerald Tablet upon its polished surface. She moved forward, placed a hand upon the green stone, and waited. A faint shimmering vaguely held the appearance of a woman; a disembodied voice spoke.

"Welcome, Candelaria."

"Who speaks to me?"

"I am Asthemirus, temple acolyte bound to this stone tablet."

"Are you one of the Twins? Why is there only one tablet here? Why is your appearance so faint?"

"The pyramid structure that once charged this chamber has been destroyed. What little energy remains allows me to communicate with you. During storms at sea, I have greater etheric energy, but such is my fate. I am but a shadow of what I am."

"And your brother, is he here with you?"

The voice sounded sad in reply. "Asthenefus was taken centuries ago. He no longer dwells here with me."

"Where, where was he taken to? Who removed him and the Emerald Tablet?"

"The Wisdom Elders feared for his safety. They took him to a place far to the North, to the Eye of Thoth."

Asthemirus did not know the whereabouts, only that it was far north. Serena learned that the two tablets once housed here were the first and the last records created by the Atlanteans. She and her twin brother volunteered for the bindings. Asthenefus guarded the first, the one containing the origin and creation knowledge. Asthemirus was bound to the last tablet—little more than an index to the wisdom contained in all the tablets, such wisdom now scattered.

Serena couldn't say for sure, the near-transparent apparition communicating with her looked to be young, about her same age.

"I seek the words and the sounds to speak with the power of my voice, the seven words written upon the robe of Isis. Do you have this knowledge?"

"I know of the words. It was not long after Isis came to warn of danger that my brother was taken away. His tablet holds the language of the creators. Many of the rainbow keys granting access to this chamber were then destroyed by the keepers. Few have come to learn of the ancient secrets of my people. Spend time with me, Candelaria. I desire fellowship; long have I existed in isolation. Place both hands upon my tablet so that I may see you better."

An unmistakable audible gasp followed. "You have a darkness in you, Serena Mendez."

"What do you mean?"

"A darkness circulates in your energy. It is a mind parasite, a poison of the corrupters. Do you not guard against this? Do you not practice your Merkaba?"

"I…I don't know what that is."

"Who has done your initiation, Serena? How is it you do not know of this?"

There followed a brief accounting of how Serena came to be in this stone chamber at this moment. Asthemirus didn't know Mother. She did not know how to remove the mind parasite, a cancer of the psyche, as she termed it. She insisted Serena learn how to spin her Merkaba. This method of protection came not from Atlantis but from the ancient Sumerian Gnostics, who first battled against the demon spawn of a different star. She thought invoking the Merkaba might cure Serena's light body, but at least it offered protection from further attack.

"All initiates are first taught the twelve-breath technique to activate the Merkaba. There are other methods. I learned this when I was the age of ten. It is easy."

Serena didn't think so. Balancing the pyramidal forces of downward female and upward male energies to invoke harmony of the physical and spiritual proved to be more difficult than Asthemirus suggested. Finally, she began to understand the process as similar to calling up her *sekhem* or kundalini. The tricky part involved getting the balanced forces to extend and rotate in opposite directions. The magnetic female pyramid needed to spin clockwise while the electrical male pyramid spun counterclockwise. Fortunately, Asthemirus displayed patience. Serena maintained persistence.

"Oh, my body is glowing!"

"Yes, Sister. You have it. Your Merkaba activates your light body. It both surrounds you and emanates from you. I see your light, Serena."

"Is the darkness still there? Does it still circulate?"

"Yes, you still harbor the dark energy. I am sorry. Still, you must practice this meditation every night to wrap yourself in protective light."

"Is it possible your brother holds knowledge about how to remove this etheric poison in my energy field?"

"He may. His tablet contains much ancient wisdom."

Serena had no idea how long she had remained within while receiving instruction. Her stomach clock told her it was long past time to eat.

"I shall return tomorrow, Asthemirus. Perhaps we can learn further clues to locate your brother."

"I do wish for you to find him, Serena, to see if we can be reunited."

She exited, drained but satisfied that her visit was not a complete waste.

Riccardo sat much the same as she had left him. She saw at least a dozen cigarette butts surrounding his humped figure. He stood, cigarette in hand, and approached.

"Sho. The Candelaria warrior walkz through sholid shtone to return to the placshe of mere mortalsh. Did you meet the Twinzz? Are the Tabletzz of Atlantish within?" His errant eye looked to her side as his good eye momentarily met her gaze.

"Yes and no, Riccardo. Only one tablet is there. I met and spoke with the guardian. Thank you for bringing me here."

He nodded his head, and she moved forward to embrace him in a big hug. As she did so, she felt a sharp prick in her back. She pushed him away, and he nearly tumbled.

"I'm shorry, Sherena. Lord Rothsshchild alsho promished that your blood can heal me. Then I could father a Candelaria true to my name and our legashy."

As Riccardo's body blurred, as she began to weave on her feet, she uttered one word: *"Ghrest."* Slumping to the ground, Serena tried to speak, but her mouth and jaw wouldn't cooperate. She watched everything in slow motion.

Riccardo's cigarette flamed and puffed; the ash drifted to his feet. He took out his cell phone and texted a message. Then…he screamed.

42

The black limousine with darkened windows pulled into the small parking area in a remote section of the Ethnographic Park. The only other vehicle, an unoccupied silver sedan, was in the lot's only shaded spot. Edward had visited the Güímar Pyramids once before when Riccardo Candelaria half told and half slobbered his way through his years of research. Riccardo's conclusion: the Candelaria necklace key would open a mysterious hidden chamber containing not one, but two Emerald Tablets somewhere within this lava cave.

In truth, Edward had his doubts; he never expected returning to the Canary Islands or interacting with Riccardo. This distant Illuminati family cousin revolted him. *Surprisingly useful, but still appallingly disgusting,* he mused.

The limousine's driver, Gregory, exited the vehicle and moved to open the back-passenger door. He wore a chauffeur's dark uniform complete with cap and gloves. His tailored jacket bore the Rothschild family crest; it fit snugly upon his muscular frame. Mirrored sunglasses completed the outfit.

"Your Lordship." He nodded with deference to Edward Rothschild and shut the door.

"Riccardo's message to me said they would be waiting inside." The two men moved past the rope barrier and traveled down the series of ramps. "Here, take this." Edward handed his driver a gunny sack.

"My God! What is that bloody smell, Gregory?" Rothschild produced a kerchief and covered his mouth and nose. The smell intensified as they neared the cave entrance.

The dim light of the cave revealed an unexpected scene. Serena Mendez sat unconscious with her back against the wall. Riccardo, presumptively identified by his twisted stature, lay face down upon the floor. Gregory used his foot to turn the body over.

Edward nearly retched. Riccardo's face no longer showed the cleft lip. A seared and charred front skull with singed hair did little to mask the yellow tobacco-stained teeth now marred with black soot. The smell of burned hair and flesh in the close confines of the cave overwhelmed Rothschild; he spoke from the front entrance and instructed his chauffeur.

"Gregory, remove this"—his face contorted in revulsion—"this lump of meat to the trunk of the car. First, secure this witch to the wheelchair and give me the sack."

After Gregory produced some zip ties, he easily lifted the sleeping girl and tied her in place. He wheeled her to the front entrance, where Edward withdrew a metal cage from the sack. Moments later, Serena Mendez sat drugged, skillfully bound, and fitted with a scold's bridle.

Rothschild addressed his unconscious prisoner. "I've waited for this moment. I should thank you. You saved me a lot of money. Riccardo"—he scoffed and spat—"Riccardo would never have been cured by you. He was a disgrace, and he should never reproduce. So, thank you, witch."

He lifted the Candelaria necklace ever so gently over the sleeping girl's neck and studied the unique design and ornamentation. He admired the intricately sculptured gold and silver intertwined to form a serpent. "Magnificent," he muttered and pocketed the jewelry. "I should thank you for this necklace as

well. And the tablets when you fetch them for me." Edward Rothschild's face
beamed with triumph.

"Gregory, first get me my cousin's cell phone, then remove his pathetic
body from here so we can reduce the stench. Find an out-of-the-way place along
the beach and feed him to the crabs. I don't know how long she'll be asleep. If
you want to see the show, you should hurry back."

"Yes, Lordship."

When Serena regained consciousness, she immediately took stock of her
situation while pretending to be groggy and only half awake. The British accent,
aristocratic arrogance, and demeanor of her captor left no doubt in her mind.
Riccardo was nowhere in sight, but the smell of charred flesh, and her last memory left her certain. The position of the wheelchair gave her a view of the back
wall. She saw the pile of cigarette butts and the rough outline of ash and char
where his body must have fallen. *Mistake to trust him.*

She studied her captor, tested the arm and leg restraints, and attempted to
speak only once. A muffled, unintelligible sound preceded a pained sensation to
her tongue, followed by the taste of blood. She tried to recall everything Uncle
Peter had said about this medieval headpiece designed to prevent a woman from
speaking.

"Very effective, don't you agree? It's called a scold's bridle. It fits you well."
Rothschild smirked with pleasure and pinged his finger against the metal band
surrounding her head. He followed with a litany of thanks about getting rid of
Riccardo, saving him money, providing him with the rare Candelaria necklace
and access to the treasures within the secret chamber.

"Riccardo recorded your incantation to open the chamber. Unfortunately, his cell phone has partly melted. Am I to conclude that every case of spon-
taneous human combustion is to be blamed upon you and your Snake Sisters?"
He spat, "You deserve to be burned."

Despite her dire situation, Serena showed no fear. Rothschild seemed
amused by this. He reached into a pocket and removed something. It was a
small mechanical device. When he squeezed it, Serena heard a clicking sound.
He squeezed it repeatedly and smiled at her.

"I can be very persuasive…" Click. "When Gregory returns, I'll have him show you his hand. He is so very obedient…" Click. He reached forward and examined the fingers on Serena's right hand. Her wrists were bound to the wheelchair's arms, leaving her fingers free.

"So delicate. So petite. I think I should enjoy how they feel when you caress my manhood. So, I will only remove a small piece." Click!

As Rothschild lifted her pinky, Serena noted the device's cutting blade, and quickly surmised his intent. She refused to give Rothschild the satisfaction of seeing her squirm. Serena prepared a litany of fire words. She tried to speak the word to burn—*ghrest.* Her efforts rewarded her with another sharp stab of pain and fresh taste of blood.

"In time, you will learn to obey me, to pleasure me, to do whatever I tell you to." Click!

Sadist! She knew exactly what she was dealing with but felt powerless. Still, she had no fear of this torturer. She felt certain many of her sisters had endured much worse. She tried to go inward, to escape in her mind. To ignore the click, his smile, his breath and smell, but something broke her concentration. Her face, even distorted by the metal cage enclosing it, showed her revulsion. Looking at Rothschild, she could see his arousal. His animal erection revolted her.

"You see, just a nip."

A click followed and then lancinating pain as Rothschild clipped the end of her pinky, just below the fingernail. She blocked it out. He leaned over and sucked her bleeding finger with apparent relish. The mental image of his aroused member and the realization that the blood meal fueled his animalistic euphoria steeled her resolve.

You'll pay for that! She blacked out.

43

The black limo returned. The driver could not overhear the entire conversation as he wound down the ramps. Something about learning to obey. From the last landing, he noted Serena strapped to the wheelchair with her head encased in a metal cage and her finger wrapped in a crude bandage. Rothschild had a small bit of blood on his face. Serena glared. She looked both stoic and defiant.

"Gregory, remove your glove and show my guest your lessons on obedience." Click. The man stepped forward and Rothschild added, "Stick your tongue out as well to show her the price of noncompliance." Click.

He removed his glove; all his digits were intact. With his back to Rothschild, his Lordship could not see that the skin was brown, not white. The driver drew his hand into a fist, turned, and stuck out his perfect tongue at Rothschild. He punched his Lordship squarely in the face. The English nobleman's nose broke with a crunch and spurt of blood.

"Surprise!" He took Rothschild's kerchief and used it as a gag, then quickly bound hands and feet.

Blood ran over the gag and dripped to the floor. Rothschild whimpered silently; he looked incredulous and pathetic.

The man removed his mirrored sunglasses and cap. "I will free you in a moment, child." Youssef Mourad got down to business. He replaced the bloody kerchief with the scold's bridle he removed from Serena's head, and fastened it securely over Rothschild.

Moments later, free and grasping her mutilated finger, Serena threw her arms around the head of security for Pyramid Communications. Her swollen and cut tongue made her speech difficult to understand.

She turned to Rothschild. "That fiths you well, you thadisthtic prick. I see you losth your hard-on." She gave her rescuer another hug. "I don't know how you managed it, Youthef, but I'm thure glad to thee you."

"That"—he pointed to Edward Rothschild—"is a bad man. You are fortunate you sent word to Moon 2 about your visit to Riccardo Candelaria and your expectation that he would lead you to find the location of something hidden. She would not tell me what you searched for, but she told me you were in danger. The rest was easy."

"But how…who…how did you know where to find me?" Her speech already sounded better.

"Your friend, Bryson, in the US has kept us informed of your location. You should call him. I need to call Moon and inform her of your rescue. We should hurry and not risk someone discovering us."

They each made brief calls but kept their conversations short. She over-heard Youssef's end of a discussion with Moon. They were trying to figure out what to do with Rothschild. Serena grabbed the phone.

Her swollen tongue already felt better. "He told me all about their plans. Thank goodness Youssef has him fixed to be mute. Rothschild went on and on; he wouldn't shut up." She hushed the rest of their conversation to prevent Youssef from hearing. A moment later, Serena finished. "Yes, that is a good plan." She handed the phone back to Youssef and watched as he listened to Moon, then both spoke, and he nodded his agreement.

"She is worried that you will become a person of interest if Rothschild disappears. International authorities will search for you. She wants to question him but does not want to risk us being caught." Serena watched as the security agent undid Rothschild's binds just long enough to remove his jacket. He retied the binds and handed the jacket to Serena. "You might need this."

She took the jacket and found her necklace, paused, and smiled deviously. She handed the jacket back to Youssef and asked his assistance as they placed Rothschild in the wheelchair.

"Trust me. Wait here. I'll return in a few minutes. Do not follow me."

It took several tries to pronounce and sing the words to unlock the back wall. She wanted Rothschild to see the necklace dance in rainbow colors, wanted him to see the Candelaria flame illuminate. She wheeled him into the hidden room.

"Here is the Emerald Tablet you so desperately wanted to see. Only one of the Twins is here." She placed her hand upon the green stone, and a faintly shimmering Asthemirus reappeared.

"Serena Mendez, it is wonderful to see you again so soon. Who is this man with you, and why is he bound?"

"His name is Rothschild. He is the head of the Illuminati; they are the current iteration of the White Snake Brotherhood. He wanted to see the Emerald Tablet and its keeper." She continued without pausing for reaction. "This location is no longer safe for you, so I am bringing you to be with Mother. It is in Abusir in Egypt. We must go quickly."

"As you say, Candelaria. I trust my safety to you. This location in Egypt that you mention is not far from the Bent Pyramid. It is a place of great sound resonance. Since you left, I have been thinking it might be a way to purge the mind parasite that infects you."

"Thank you, Asthemirus. You will be stronger from the earth energy in Abusir. I have a Serpent Sister who will visit there with you often."

Serena looked at Rothschild; even without being muted by the scold's bridle, he looked speechless.

"One last thing, Candelaria. Removing me from this chamber will render the tablet silent. So, hear this from me now since I know not when we shall next speak. I recalled one other thing about the elders who took my brother to the North. Their leader was Pheryllt. I don't know if this is important."

"No time to think about that now." She removed her hand from the tablet, and Asthemirus vanished.

Serena turned to Rothschild. "Amazing, isn't it? There's a lot we Candelaria witches are capable of. I could be spiteful and snip something with that clicker you have. Maybe a piece of your pecker." She watched as Rothschild winced. "But that's too good for you. You saw just a little of what the voice is capable of. What *my voice* is capable of."

He looked back at her, his eyes pleading. She removed the bridle and listened as he spoke. He groveled to have his life spared. He promised money, power, anything. He begged for mercy, and she let him go on until she tired of his babble.

"That is the currency you deal in. Not interested. I have something different in mind." She leaned over to his ear. She resisted the urge to give it a little snaky lick. Instead, she whispered, "You know all those plans for world domination you told me about? You are the head, the Pindar, as you called yourself, of a New World Order. You know those plans?"

She watched as he meekly nodded his head. "Well…you're fired."

She gathered her *sekhem*. When he had her imprisoned not an hour ago, she had rehearsed the words a dozen times. In spite of her cut and sore tongue, they came out perfectly the first time as she sang them, just as Mother had instructed. *"Khoor le'lenaste mishtagur."*

Serena did not stay behind to watch the conflagration. She had the Emerald Tablet in hand as she exited back into the cave. She and Youssef both heard the screams, even through the rock wall.

He looked at her without questioning. "Come, I must go and pick up my car. Do not tell me what you did as I do not want to reveal information in the event I am questioned."

"Don't worry, Youssef. Even if they break through the back wall, if they find the body it will not be identifiable. I cremated him."

44

BB hung up the phone, feeling very relieved. He spoke across the lab counter to Tarni. "Good news. That was Bryson; Serena is safe."

She looked up from her screen. A computer-generated simulated DNA fragment unzipped, and RNA paired to the unraveling sequence. "Thank goodness, mate. It sounded dicey from the little bit of info we knew. Glad she's okay. Did our resident geek boy say how girl wonder escaped?"

"No. He said they only spoke briefly. She hoped to be returning to the States soon."

"How about Bryson; did he say if he would be coming to the lab today?" BB wasn't sure, but he thought he detected hope in her question.

"No, Tarni, he said he's got a new puzzle to work on. Something about Serena's next step. Besides, it is better that Bryson stay home today; there is something I want to discuss with you privately."

She jumped back from her counter stool and threw her hands in the air. "Hooley dooley! I'm gobsmacked, mate... It works!"

"Fuchsia, are you trying to startle me into a seizure? What works?"

"This sim. Here, have a gander. It's a complicated sequencing of initiation, transfer, and duplication, but I think this gets us to the final piece. This is it, BB, I'm sure."

He studied the simulation, muttered, "Yes!" a few times, and finished by kissing her on the top of the head. "This is top notch. It looks right to me. Of course, what shows on the computer and what works in vitro sometimes differ. Still, I think this is the breakthrough we seek. You make me so proud!"

She blushed. Even through her dark skin, BB saw her cheeks turn rouge. He knew she didn't need to be praised for her work, but his admiration clearly meant something. She hugged him.

The opportunity to say what he needed to say would never be better. His voice grew serious. "Sit, child, and hear me out."

The elevated mood from moments before crashed as BB reported he was rapidly losing vision in one eye—pressure from the cancer against his optic nerve. The doctor had warned this might occur. In the last two days, epileptic seizures had incapacitated him three times.

"So, child, what I ask is a burden, but I have no one else to ask. I see that you have struggled with remaining here, that you miss your family. My condition is rapidly worsening. I shall not be able to see this work completed through to the finish."

She sat across from BB as tears rolled silently down her face and splashed on the counter below. She shut her eyes as if to not hear what he next would say.

"Tarni, my beautiful Fuchsia, when I am gone, will you stay and complete this work for me, for us, for the world?"

With eyes gazing at the floor, she nodded her answer.

"Thank you, child; you are a blessing!" He scribbled something on a scrap of paper. "Here is my password into all my logs, files, and research. They are my life's work in genetics. I have nothing else to give you, but they are yours."

She looked up and their eyes met. "Beangagarrie, you are wrong about that. You have given me more than I could ever repay. You have given me your trust, your encouragement, and your wisdom." She hugged him and whispered in his ear, "Just so you know, mate, I'm greedy. I'm hoping you can give me just a little bit more."

The drive to and along the coast lasted about twenty minutes. She wore Rothschild's jacket. It didn't fit, but she sat in the back with her head down as Youssef had instructed. The personnel at the Pyramids of Güímar had no reason to suspect anything amiss as the limousine drove to the park's exit. Behind his mirror sunglasses, Youssef cracked the window and waved to the gatekeeper at the exit. The park's security cameras doubtless recorded all traffic in and out of the complex.

As they drove, Youssef filled in the missing details leading to her escape. He had been monitoring the cave entrance and knew she was inside. Without knowing who or what lay within, he watched from a hidden spot. When the black limo arrived, he was certain it was Rothschild. Fortunately, the driver had a build similar to his own. When they left their vehicle, he planted a simple tracker on the car and listened to the conversation at the cave entrance. Youssef patted a small hand-held dish with attached earphones resting next to him on the front seat.

"When the driver left with a body, I followed from a safe distance. I approached him after he dumped Riccardo in the rocky cove we are now arriving at. I approached him as though lost and asked directions. I dropped my phone to provoke his downward glance then sprung upon him and snapped his neck."

Serena noted that Youssef's account sounded almost like a typical day at the office. She always suspected he would be lethal at close range. "I figure you stripped the chauffeur, changed your clothes, and they are back in your car."

"Correct, Miss Serena." They parked next to a silver sedan pulled off an isolated stretch of sandy road. Waves crashed close by.

"And the body? Is that in the trunk or did you stash it?"

"Let us just say that the crabs along this cove will be particularly well fed." He looked up and pointed to a group of seagulls. "Looks as though the crabs have guests to their little surfside feast." They exited the limousine, and Youssef wiped away their prints and any possible hair or DNA.

When he was satisfied, he went to his sedan and changed his clothes. He told Serena they would leave Rothschild's car here, knowing someone would find it as well as the two bodies. He held the dead driver's clothing. "These I shall burn."

"I can take care of that."

Youssef shrugged, handed her the garments and listened to some strange words and sounds. The clothing ignited and burned furiously in a flash of flame and smoke, leaving a pile of ash. An ocean breeze scattered the evidence in a windy gust.

To Serena, Youssef appeared to be a man who had witnessed considerable death and violence. She did not picture him as one to wince or to show fear, but there was no mistaking the look of respect in his deep-set eyes as he looked at her. He improvised to fashion a new bandage for Serena's finger and grunted his approval.

Youssef remained silent as the two drove back to check Serena out from her hotel. They needed to figure an exit strategy that left no suspicious loose threads.

Rothschild was gone. She had her necklace. She had Asthemirus's tablet and trusted Youssef with its safekeeping. Most of all, she was using her Candelaria powers to fight back. Her heart pounded with exhilaration.

Something in her had changed. She went within as a true Gnostic warrior would. She wanted to understand this sensation, needed to understand this sensation. Was it vengeance for the witch hunts of past centuries? Retribution for the deception and oppression of humanity at the hands of Rothschild and his Serpent Brothers? Was it that she had tasted blood and wanted more? When the final recognition dawned, it came with a peaceful calm. She felt centered.

It is not that I have tasted blood in the killing of this filth of a man. A man who deserved death a thousand times more painful than my mercy killing. It is that they have tasted MY blood. I have spoken MY truth with power. I am a true Candelaria. I am Serena Mendez… And I am just getting started!

45

Wán shàn reflected over the last seventy-two hours. Edward Rothschild's pilot had returned from the Canary Islands without the family head. Someone had apparently killed the chauffeur and a family cousin, Riccardo Candelaria. The log entries from her sisters checking in on other family heads reported concerns among the upper echelon of the Illuminati. Van Duyn requested this meeting of the Council. Bàba recalled all five of her sisters, and they sat together watching as the Council members met remotely over a secure channel. Bàba himself took part from his office while she and her sisters observed

the proceedings separately. He told them that, technically, their viewing consti-
tuted a violation of protocol.

From the meeting discussion, Wán shàn learned that they had received
no demands. While the family heads had many potential enemies from outside
the extended network, no obvious responsible party emerged. She wondered if
someone within the immediate or extended Illuminati family could be responsible. Was Rothschild dead? Was he held captive? Insufficient data to make any
presumptive conclusions. Probabilities favored death.

Why was Rothschild in Tenerife to begin with? The pilot had no insights.
Consular Rothschild had apparently gone with this cousin to a site at the Güímar
Pyramids. Scant details were provided during the meeting. She made a mental
note to learn more about this site.

Forensics at a lava cave visited by Edward Rothschild and the cousin, Riccardo Candelaria, confirmed both blood from Rothschild and DNA from Riccardo Candelaria. A third sample of DNA, female, remained unidentified. Security footage showed the limousine used by Rothschild to enter, leave, reenter,
and exit. A second vehicle, rented by a tourist, was confirmed to have been near
this location at the pyramid complex, but only for a brief period. Rothschild's
limousine was found abandoned at a remote beach close to where the bodies of
the chauffeur and Riccardo were discovered. The driver's neck had been broken,
and Riccardo Candelaria's face had been burned.

Wán shàn's analytic brain tried to make sense of the limited information.
The site they visited, a lava cave, suggested an explosion. There was both residual soot and evidence of fire but no traces of chemical or other known explo-
sives. Authorities conducted an ongoing investigation. A live-in housekeeper at
Riccardo Candelaria's Estate, the only other occupant, knew of no enemies her
employer might have. She denied knowing who Edward Rothschild was.

The meeting concluded with a Luciferian prayer for protection. She sat
among her Ninja sisters, and they discussed various hypotheses. Conversation
stopped when Kenseiko Li joined them.

"So, my daughters, we have an unexpected development and an unexplained mystery. Who thinks Rothschild is dead?" All their hands raised. He
asked explanations as to why death and not capture underlay their conclusion.
He asked about probabilities.

As Li conducted a thorough Q and A with Wán shàn and her sisters, she sensed his satisfaction with their reasoning and their suggestions for further inquiry. He produced several folders and explained assignments.

"Collectively, your networked brains and enhanced capabilities make you my secret weapon. You are more powerful than any supercomputer. I am sending two of you to Tenerife. Split up and visit the site where the DNA samples were collected as well as the beach where the car and bodies were discovered. Visit the home of Riccardo Candelaria; interview the housekeeper. Obtain any information—computer files, documents, anything that might help us to understand why Rothschild chose to visit Tenerife, this distant cousin, and the island's pyramids. Speak to the local authorities. Get me a sample of the DNA they collected on this unknown female." He distributed two folders.

"One of you will go to the Rothschild household. Speak to staff including the pilot and family members of the deceased chauffeur. Did anyone else travel with them or know about this trip? Learn everything you can." He handed out another folder.

As he spoke, Wán shàn felt something. She did not have a word for it, but admiration for Kenseiko Li had something to do with this feeling. *Is this pride? He is brilliant. Genghis Khan would have a worthy adversary if he ever came up against my bàba.* She wondered if her sisters had the same reaction.

"Two of you will visit among the other Council heads. I have prepared a rotating schedule. Speak to the pleasure servants I gifted. See if there are hidden concerns or machinations. Whether we have an internal or external threat is yet undecided. You have all already concluded as much. Let us collectively find out." He handed out two additional folders.

Wán shàn did not have an assignment thus far. She waited. Her bàba produced one last folder and handed it to her. "Wán shàn, you have the most interesting task. I suspect the unidentified female is Serena Mendez. I want you to find her. I already have her DNA, so the sample from Tenerife will only confirm my suspicions. Her last known location was in Peru. It's in the file I gave you. She traveled with a companion named Bryson Reynolds. I should very much like to learn their whereabouts."

He concluded their assembly with further instructions about entering information twice daily into the database they shared, to ask questions of one another, and to suggest methods and strategies. He would give further instructions as they uncovered additional data and clues.

"Under no circumstances should you discuss any of this with other Illuminati. Knowledge is power. We are perfection."

With these final remarks, he left them to discuss and formulate additional suggestions. Wán shàn reflected upon her bàba's closing words. It seemed a curious way to conclude the revelations of the past seventy-two hours and the implications. She decided she needed to think about this more. She put these thoughts to the side for the moment and wondered, *Who is Serena Mendez? Who is Bryson Reynolds?* She intended to find out.

He awoke sweating. Even though it was past two in the morning, he went outside to take a walk, calm down, dry off. He ignored the beautiful New Mexico night sky. His dreams usually faded after wakening, but this dream, he couldn't forget—a drawback to having an eidetic memory.

Bryson tried to figure it out. He remembered that after his ayahuasca ceremony, the shaman in Peru said the awakening of the third eye opened the door to the spirit world. He saw that night creature again, the one who Gurumarra chased away, the one he asked BB about. The creature hungered. Bryson knew it; he couldn't say why; he just knew it. Serena was there in his dream as well. She ran from the Mangar-Kunjer-Kunja creature until she stopped. The running away wasn't from fear. In his dream, the two played a game of hide and seek. When the creature caught Serena, she turned into a dragon. She breathed fire. That's when he woke sweating.

BB said everything is in the Dreamtime. What we see as reality in the waking state is an illusion. He made it sound as though dreams were more real than we perceive. What did it all mean? Why this dream at this time?

He sat under a night sky with just a sliver of moon. *I can't believe we had another fight over the phone. What's happening? She almost sounded gleeful about incinerating Rothschild. No argument the guy had it coming, chopping off her finger like that, trying to destroy the world and all. But you don't do a victory dance when you burn someone alive. Is that what they did in Salem—burn someone accused of witchcraft and then throw a party?*

What bothered him the most was her reaction when he pointed it out. She defended her attitude. He challenged it by trying to get her to agree that the world needs to move past this kind of killing cycle. Bryson took no joy in killing, which isn't saying he didn't see the need in certain circumstances. He thought she shared his view. Apparently, he was wrong. They never used to fight; now, that's all they did.

He sighed. Bryson decided to stop thinking about his bad dream and the fight he had with Serena. The walk and night air had settled him. He got back in bed and stared wide-eyed at the ceiling. Tomorrow he would go to pick up Serena at the airport. He wouldn't tell her about his dreams. No sense provoking another argument.

46

Something didn't feel right. This wasn't the return she expected. For one thing, Bryson had been giving her a hard time about the conflict they fought. *The Middle East is back at war, even worse than before. This Bogimonster virus is spreading. People are dying all over the globe. Why doesn't he see I'm not just resisting; I'm fighting back with everything I've got. I need him now more than ever, and he's MIA. What's that all about?*

That was only half the story. She wanted to fly back to Chicago. She wanted to see BB. Not only did he have a grounding influence on Serena, but she also had an intuition that something wasn't right with him. She wanted to see him, be around him, and feel reassured he was okay. She wanted to see Tarni. Serena liked her energy; she was fun, and Serena needed to chill for a bit. Bryson nixed Chicago. Adamant, he insisted she return to Taos. He said Claus was in the middle of final preparations for the raid on the Dulce base. While she knew Bryson wasn't lying, her internal truth detector told her something more was going on. Serena decided it was best to table everything until she could sort it all out further. No sense provoking another argument.

She spotted his tall, lanky frame sauntering her way. They waited together for her baggage to appear on the carousel. A previously inconceivable tension hung between them.

"Hey, how're you doing? Was the flight okay?"

"My tongue is still sore"—she thrust her tongue out—"and my finger aches all the time. The flight was fine." She felt tentative in her response. "I never thanked you for tracking me and coordinating with Moon. I'm lucky to be talking at all."

Bryson looked down. "I'm glad you're okay. Next time, I'm coming with you."

For a moment, she wanted to say no. *I can take care of myself without your help, thank you.* Figuratively, she bit her tongue and held back. The feeling passed, and the chill between them warmed. A mild burning tingled in her pelvis. *He's a good man. I'm lucky to have him.*

"Any progress on figuring out where the Eye of Thoth might be?"

"Nothing but dead ends. I put all the new bits of information into the data-linking programs I use to connect the dots. Thoth's Eye, Asthemirus, Asthenefus, Twins, Emerald Tablets, Candelaria, rainbow necklace—no hits and no leads so far. I can tell you one thing, Pheryllt isn't a person. You told me Asthemirus said the leader of the group that removed her brother was Pheryllt."

"I could have spelled it wrong. Does it mean something?"

"Druids. The Pheryllts were a Druidian sect. Supposedly they have links to the Hindus, Celts, Egyptians, Atlanteans, and that's just the short list. They were concentrated in Wales, and that's well north of where you were. I'm trying to piece it all together."

"Interesting…Druids. You'll figure it out. You are a genius." Without saying as much, she couldn't hide her disappointment. Serena assumed Bryson would already have the answer. She was tired, frustrated, weary of traveling. After climbing one mountain, another stood in the way.

"I'll work on it some more, PTG, after we pull off this raid on Dulce."

"I learned quite a bit from Rothschild when he was mouthing off. I handwrote notes about what the Illuminati are up to. Some of it is new stuff." She handed over a notebook.

"Did he say anything about the recent *E. coli* outbreaks? There have been several more since you left. The government says the only way to guarantee food safety is to get food from government-sanctioned distribution centers."

"Rothschild didn't mention anything like that."

"The kicker is, to gain entry to these food depots, you have to agree to have a chip implanted to register. It's nefarious when you project it out. Water isn't safe from the Hendra virus. Food is contaminated. Everyone is scared, and the government has a solution. Pretty soon, everyone will be chip-labeled as human inventory the government tracks and monitors. It's getting more serious all the time."

"Yes, it is. That's absolutely right, Bryson. And that's why we've got to fight back!"

"Hold it. Hold it right there. I don't want to reopen that argument." He grabbed her suitcase and began walking away.

Serena shouted at him. "You can't just run away from a fight."

Bryson spun around, put the bag down, and glared. Neither spoke.

"I'm not running away. I just have a different view about how to fight." He continued to walk to the parking garage, and she followed.

"What's your idea? I'm listening."

"The damage that was done years ago, the alteration in the DNA, that needs to be fixed. It's strange that it never occurred to me before, but I agree with the Illuminati that a New World Order is a good idea. It's just that my version of that order is different. They want power, control, domination, subjugation in a less chaotic global environment."

"What is it you want?"

"It's time for humanity to realize its full potential. To have the reins and bridle removed and for us to be free."

"Sounds grand, Bryson, but hear me out. I don't know how to do that, and you don't know how to do that, and if we don't do anything, there won't be a lot of humanity left to save."

"Crack some eggs to make an omelet."

"What! What are you saying?"

"Just repeating what Claus said when he and I were having a similar discussion about strategy and tactics."

"You lost me, Bry."

"I want to use nonlethal gas in our raid. Put the bad guys down and grab some files and gene samples. He says, 'No way, amigo. You don't let the enemy have a free pass unless you want to fight them a second time. Sure, some innocent people die, but think how many innocents are being exploited now.' He finished with the eggs and omelet."

"If that's the case, I agree with him. I say kill the bastards."

"I don't have much stomach for slaughtering people. Whoever they're working for at Dulce, they're being manipulated too. I'm not ready to pass judgement on who's good and who's bad."

"Well, I am. You think I enjoy killing people?"

He threw her suitcase in the trunk and started the car. He looked directly at her gray eyes. "Serena, a month ago, I wouldn't have given that question a second thought. Honest answer now is I don't know... I just don't know."

47

S he uncovered no recent efforts whatsoever to cover tracks or mislead off an obvious trail. Wán shàn speculated why this might be but reached no definitive conclusions. The file bàba shared on Serena Mendez revealed previously complicated measures to hide her identity and make tracking difficult; Bryson Reynolds' digital footprint was almost ghostlike. Clearly whatever was in data repositories she could access revealed only what he wanted known. All Wán shàn cared about at this moment was his address. She had it.

Serena left Tenerife using her own name. This didn't prove that her bàba's suspicions were correct, but Serena Mendez's presence in Tenerife pointed to a link with Rothschild's disappearance. Airline passenger manifests showed her routing through Kennedy International Airport and connecting through to Albuquerque International Sunport. Last known address for Serena, confirmed and visited by Dr. Li's nephew, the former head of security, was in Santa Fe. A visit there would be her first stop with a second stop, if needed, to Taos, where Bryson Reynolds lived.

Either Serena no longer cared if someone pursued her—a potentially dangerous unknown, given the uncertain powers and abilities Candelarians possessed—or she no longer suspected pursuit. This second hypothesis seemed unlikely. Wán shàn wondered what her analysis missed. This young woman, Serena, when paired together with Bryson, appeared more formidable and resourceful than the intel she had gathered could readily explain. Is someone else backing them, the real force moving this lever? Could this be a trap? Did Serena anticipate she would be followed and planned an ambush?

More questions than answers. Answers that Wán shàn intended to find out.

Claus kept the van running, and Serena moved to the driver's position. They were at the first rendezvous point, where they pulled up and joined two passenger vehicles, a military truck camo-painted to match those on the base, and six ex-military mercenaries. Claus greeted them. Despite the back slaps and hugs, this group conveyed nothing warm and fuzzy—all business, all hand-picked by Claus.

They suited up and ran through comm checks, making certain their headgear and gas masks functioned to spec including lights, forward cameras, night vision, and location mapping. They first reviewed the contents of their sampling kits then vid-linked to Bryson's display while he sat in the back of the van and watched. When the six men scattered close by, their avatars moved accordingly on Bryson's monitor.

As a group, they had all drilled remotely on what amounted to a VR training environment similar to training on a flight simulator. In the practice virtual runs, Bryson had seen this scattered avatar display before, just the way they drilled it. Claus reminded all of them, tonight was the real deal.

"Unexpected things happen. We've put in contingency planning, and you've all practiced." He spun to address Serena. "Remember to keep driving and stay mobile. Follow the route on the navigation display."

She nodded.

He ran through a checklist. There were no questions. "Team alpha?"

"Ant is a go."

"Ape is a go."

"Team bravo?"

"Bat is a go."

"Bear is a go."

"Team Charlie."

"The Cat man says go."

"Cow is a go."

Claus finished the roll call. Bryson's handle for the op was Boy Wonder. He handled the communications and logistics. He indicated his readiness.

"Fireman, ready?"

Serena responded, "Fireman is a go."

Claus held out his wrist. "Coordinate your time clocks." They each depressed buttons on their synchronized watches. "Oz says phase two is a go. We are rolling."

Bryson watched as the team loaded into the truck. They drove off, and Serena proceeded to high-top, about a half mile from their current location. Rendezvous point one had relatively minimal coverage from satellites, making it nearly a blind spot and communication dead zone. High-top needed failsafe comm links. He dropped off the transmitter-receiver and checked operations with Oz and all six mercenaries.

"High-top is operational. Fireman and Boy Wonder are mobile."

"Queen Bee is hovering." Claus worked off a tablet. The overhead drone surveillance beamed imagery to Bryson.

"Images received and look good."

"Oz has deployed the swarm, initiated jamming, and launched the communication tower missile."

Bryson checked the jamming signal; the hunter bees searched and killed any outside personnel. "Boy Wonder confirms comm tower is down. Messages are going out from the base but don't think any are getting through."

"Roger that. All teams, this is Oz, we are a go for phase three." A dozen preprogrammed drones deployed and dropped multiple gas bombs over the fan banks, ventilating the entire underground base. The military truck parked, and the soldiers deployed. "Godspeed."

Claus's next remark wasn't broadcast. He muttered to himself, "Party time."

48

Bryson spoke aloud so Serena could follow the action. She had a route to follow and needed to focus on driving, but she insisted on some report.

"The bees have AI and preprogramed recognition, so they won't mistake any of our people for enemy personnel. They go right for the head and then deliver a microexplosive charge. Not painful, but highly lethal. If anyone at the base gets off a message, the Queen Bee has a jamming signal. Plus, we've disabled their comm tower. I gotta say, Claus has thought this through very thoroughly."

"I'm keeping my fingers crossed, Bryson. The spiders mapped down three levels, but there are at least seven levels from what you told me, and we don't know all the entrances and exits."

The radio crackled. "Oz to Boy Wonder. Can you confirm all cannisters delivered?"

"That's an affirmative."

"Op moves to phase four. We've got fifteen minutes, team. Let's make it count."

None of this made any sense. Tarni shut the laptop and plugged it in to charge. Claus's house wasn't big, but it sure felt empty. The emptiness had crept into her bones. Beangagarrie had her working on something she couldn't figure out how to fit in. When she asked him, his wry smile hinted at more than his response. "When the time is right, Fuchsia. That time is coming soon. Keep working. It's important." In due time he would tell her. Great! Tarni left it out of her report to Dr. Li.

Deception and duplicity drained her. She thought to herself, *This is some dog's breakfast. How did I let myself become such a dipstick?*

She spoke to the charging laptop. "I haven't said anything about this side project because I don't have a clue what it's all about." She continued. "Dr. Li, I'm sick and tired of your questions. I'm sick and tired of being your mole." Then it hit her—moles were blind or nearly blind. It wasn't just being a spy for someone she despised. It wasn't just being alone in a house in a foreign country, or even that she worked with a dying man, whom she absolutely adored. Tarni felt blind to all the things circling around her. Blind and out of control. She didn't know what BB had her doing; didn't have an exit strategy to get out from under Li's tentacles; didn't know how much longer BB would live and how much longer she could conceal his illness from Li. After Beangagarrie was gone, how could she possibly manage without him?

Worst of all, she didn't know where things stood between herself and Bryson. *Genius boy helps me feel good about everything. All this bullshit has been going on for weeks, but when he's around, it doesn't get to me.* And, she liked Serena, which only complicated things more. Tarni didn't want to interfere in the relationship between Serena and Bryson. Tarni had fun with her and enjoyed hanging together. Sure, the girl was a little messed up, but she knew how to have fun. Tarni missed having fun. When did her life get so complicated? She decided the entire situation was effectively one big chocolate mess, and she couldn't fix it tonight. *Pull ya head in, girl, tomorrow's another day.* She felt marginally better.

Their protective gear didn't slow down the mercenaries. Each two-man unit had a level to reach and high-value targets specific to each unit. The A unit made straight for level one, where a communication hub was located. B unit targeted a training area on level two, and C unit's destination lay on level three—laboratory. Each two-man team had secondary targets on their level such as storage and supply, a possible server room, and mechanical control center. Instructions were clear and simple: take out any resistance, gather any hardware, data storage, and collect genetic sampling on any downed personnel. They also carried special munitions to plant. Elevators and stairwells were all targets as the team exited. Each soldier had twenty tubes with a swab connected to the cap. Pull the cap, voice record the specimen location matched to that tube, swab and snap.

Claus went solo to the security station located on level one, the ground level. He monitored the team's progress on the internal security feeds as well as his tablet showing the movement of each team member. "Oz is in position. No resistance en route and no movement on the screens." All the units reported their progress. They had thus far encountered no live bodies. Time and focus didn't allow Claus to consider the devastating lethality of the cyclosarin VX nerve gas they were using. The effect spoke for itself—a morgue had more life. He swabbed the two uniformed security bodies, still on their swivel chairs, and collected anything that looked important. He grabbed a walkie-talkie off the belt of one of the downed men and scanned the channels. *No chatter. So far so good.*

Given his military background as a communications expert, security monitoring was in his wheelhouse. He hooked up an external drive and began downloading footage. A thumbprint from one of the dead bodies gave him access. As the download proceeded, he scanned the camera feeds.

Claus checked in with the A unit at communications. They reported a dozen sampled bodies along the way and were now at the target gathering data, hardware, anything that looked interesting. With luck, they could finish and get to a secondary target.

B unit had made it to the training area. Based on the feed, Claus had a fairly good idea of what he might be seeing. Two bodies slumped in identical chairs with some goggles. With their faces obscured, he couldn't say for sure, but the physique and carbon-copy appearance left him feeling pretty certain. "Bat and Bear, get those headpieces, goggles, and laptops. See if you can disassemble the apparatus that attaches to the headgear."

"Roger that, Oz."

Per their virtual run through, C unit had the longest route to follow in addition to the most stairs. Claus checked their progress. Three minutes in, and they had just arrived at the lab. No movement. There were a lot of dead bodies to sample.

"Boy Wonder to Oz, do you copy?"

"Copy, what you got?"

"Satellite feed shows a half dozen lights moving in formation out of Kirtland. Can't say for sure, but I'm guessing helicopters."

"Roger that. Try and calculate their speed and estimated time here. *Shit!*"

On the security feed, he saw movement. *Tube shuttle, pulling into station.* He scanned for floor plans and diagrams. The spiders had only mapped the main corridors.

"A unit, this is Oz. There's a shuttle pulling into a station on level seven. Looks like a service elevator bay they can access when they pull in. Don't want their company. I need you to split up. Ant, you finish up there, and, Ape, I'll guide you to the service elevator at this level. I want you to drop a present down the shaft."

"Copy that, Oz. Ape is ready to move, just tell me where to go."

Claus directed him through a series of corridors. Ape passed a dozen dead bodies, arriving a minute later to the destination while Claus watched. The elevator doors opened. "Don't send a dirty bomb, just something with a lot of pop. Send it to the lowest level and give a short detonation sequence. Sixty seconds should work." As Claus spoke, the shuttle docked, and twenty or so soldiers in gas masks and hazard gear exited. "Check that, Ape. Make it forty-five seconds and haul your ass out."

"Roger that, Oz."

"Boy Wonder to Oz. Best guess is ten to twelve minutes before the assault troops arrive."

"Copy that." Claus looked at his watch. *We are going to be cutting this close.* A faint explosion and a flash, and he watched as the tube-station feed went dark.

"C unit to Oz, this is Cat, do you copy?"

"Oz, copies."

"There's a door at the back of the lab. It wasn't on the simulation, so it's probably nothing we have intel on. The door is marked 'NURSERY.' It's locked, but I think I can bust it down. What do you want me to do?"

He looked over at the security monitors; they marked nothing as a nursery. "Proceed, but you've only got two minutes, and I'm calling the op to phase five exit. We've got incoming."

"Copy that. Cat out."

Via the head cam Cat wore, Claus saw him crash through the door, lighting switched on for the room within, then the head cam feed went dark.

"Cat, you there? Your head cam stopped filming."

"I'm here, Oz. I'm recording this private. I don't want the girl to see this… It ain't pretty. There're dead bodies… That's all I'm gonna say."

49

Kenseiko Li sat down to eat. All in all, it had been a good day. Wán shàn made further progress on locating the Candelaria girl and Peter Reynolds' nephew. He felt certain that questioning those two would help explain the whereabouts of his missing nephew Gensu. Not that he missed his prior chief security officer. *Wán shàn is superior in all respects. Perfection is worth waiting for.*

The other five Wán shàns all logged intel into their shared network. The Council of Thirteen agreed they needed to meet soon to select a new Pindar. Everyone assumed Rothschild to be dead. Kenseiko's lips drew back to expose his small yellow teeth prior to sipping oolong tea. He washed down rice noodles.

Even his side quest with the Australian girl progressed nicely. Grudgingly, he admitted Beangagarrie Brindabella's brilliance but harbored no worries that anything the two Australian geneticists worked out would affect his plans. *Let them play in their lab.*

His phone rang. 6:30. He hated to be disturbed at his residence. *Van Duyn… What does he want? It's very early in the US.*

"Damiaan, I am eating my dinner."

"Sorry to disturb, Brother. This might give you indigestion."

Kenseiko parked his tea on the table and dabbed the corner of his mouth with a warmed cloth.

"The Womb in New Mexico is under attack. It started early this morning. The US military sent in an assault team along with an evaluation unit. We haven't heard back from them."

"Who is leading the attack?"

"That has not been determined."

"What are our losses? How many casualties?"

"That has not been determined."

They talked a little more, but there were scant details and more questions than answers. They ended in agreement that the Council needed to meet sooner rather than later. They would place all hives and wombs on standby.

Kenseiko Li steepled his hands and rubbed his lips with drawn fingers. He spoke aloud. "Some will argue to delay our plans. I need to convince them we should accelerate our operations." He went to his home office and logged into the secure network to notify his Ninja daughters. He instructed them to plant strategic suggestions. He didn't think this attack in New Mexico was from an internal operative, but left instructions to assess all possibilities. Kenseiko looked at his schedule; next week would be a good time for the family heads to gather under the Hill.

Bryson finally hacked into the squadron's secure communication channel. He listened intently.

"Base Command, this is Arrow Squad leader. We have acquired target eye-in-the-sky."

"You are authorized to fire… What is your ETA?"

"Three minutes to ground."

Over his link to Claus and the rest of their team, Bryson heard the order. "Phase five team. All units confirm. Drop the packages. Will detonate after exit."

After the A unit acknowledged, Bryson heard an explosion and lost his overhead feed.

"Boy Wonder to all units: Queen Bee is down…repeat, Queen Bee is down. We are dark. Confirm."

He waited as the team responded. On his monitor, he saw their avatars in the parking area moving quickly toward the truck. He gave them the bad news. "ETA for enemy troops is less than three minutes. Boy Wonder and Fireman are heading to rendezvous point delta."

Serena entered the instruction, and the van's nav-screen mapped the route. Bryson cringed as he listened to the next intercepted communication.

"Arrow Squad leader, we have the ground target. Missiles launched."

He counted silently and reported to his team, hoping to get off this last comm. "Ground transmitter likely under attack. If hit, will—" Radio silence with his team left a hole in his gut. From launch to hit took eight seconds.

Now he listened to exchange among the Arrow Squad. "Confirming no further communication from attack force… They are blind and deaf."

Not quite, he thought. Bryson knew the van had a secondary transmitter-receiver. It had already been programmed as a contingency backup, but he needed to make some adjustments.

"Serena, stop driving." As he typed to boot up the transmitter, he tried to ignore what came over the squadron channel.

"We have explosions on the ground. Repeat, Base Command… We have multiple explosions at the Dulce base. Will hover to find a safe landing area."

He couldn't ignore what he heard next. It came over another channel.

"Anyone out there, please respond. This is Dulce. We are on the ground. The installation is under attack. We are taking fire. Request backup. Request backup."

He flipped a switch. "Boy Wonder to Oz. All units, secondary transmitter is online. Do you copy?" Silence. The gut hole almost swallowed him. "Claus… anybody…are you there?"

50

Serena looked back and watched Bryson's fingers dance on the console. She saw drops of perspiration splatter on the keyboard. He looked hyperfocused, but she saw something else, something she had never seen before. He looked afraid. *C'mon, Snowman, I know you can do this.*

At the moment, the van idled. She waited for his instruction but heard the futility in his voice as he repeated his transmission.

"All units, this is Boy Wonder… Do you copy? Team, are you there? Please respond…"

The only response was military chatter from the squadron hovering over Dulce. They were conducting aerial surveillance.

"We have another ground transmission source. Targeting now."

Serena looked at Bryson.

"DRIVE! GO! DRIVE! NOW!"

She slammed the accelerator, and the van screamed forward, throwing Bryson off his seat. Anything loose vaulted to the back.

Bryson counted: "Seven...six...five...four...three...two..." A brilliant blast lit up the van's mirrors. Serena worked to keep the vehicle on the road as the explosive concussion hit them from behind. She slowed down and pulled to the roadside. Bryson assessed for damage.

He drew a deep breath. "I routed our communication to bounce off a few different satellites. It bought us an extra couple of seconds. We'll have to keep quiet; can't risk them picking up another comm signal from us. Head to the rendezvous spot and pray our men made it out."

Serena resumed the route on her navigation screen. Another ten minutes. She didn't want to think about Claus not showing up. If there was a plan B, she didn't know it. Bryson's cell pinged with a message. Was it Claus?

She turned back and saw Bryson's face wrinkle with concern. "Shit, that's not good, but I can't deal with it now." He tossed the phone aside.

All three units successfully made it to the truck. Claus drove a hundred yards before detonating more munitions. A small cheer went up among the men, but their grim faces told a different story. They all recognized the sound of choppers. Queen Bee, their aerial drone, was down along with communication between Boy Wonder. Claus idled the truck and grabbed the handheld walkie-talkie he'd taken from the dead security guard at Dulce. He said to his team, "This better work. On my signal, I need some battle noises, gunfire, and wounded-soldier sounds."

If the men were confused, they didn't show it.

Claus depressed the transmit button on the walkie-talkie. "Anyone out there, please respond. This is Dulce. We are on the ground. The installation is under attack. We are taking fire. Request backup. Request backup." He signaled to the men to start making noises. Gun fire rat-a-tatted, someone screamed, "I'm hit!"

"Incoming choppers, if you are receiving this, please respond. This is Dulce, we are under fire. We have casualties. Do you copy?"

Claus eased off the handheld's transmit button and gave the men a thumbs up. He turned to Bear. "Get a grenade ready."

They listened to static, then a hoped-for response. "Dulce base, this is Arrow Squadron leader. We copy you. What is your position?"

He squeezed the button to transmit. "Don't know, Arrow, I'm just a tech. We're not far from the entry guard station. I've got wounded with me." He clicked it off and motioned to throw the grenade. Claus depressed transmit and screamed, "It's an ambush!" The grenade exploded, and he released the button. "That should keep them away for the short term. Now, we play dead until they land. Then we skedaddle." He winked. "We're good…I think."

They listened as the Arrow Squad leader attempted contact. Crowded over the handheld, all the men overheard multiple attempts to reestablish communication. In the background, they heard someone say, "They're goners, Cap. Boots on the ground in three…two…one." The attack helicopters landed.

Claus put his finger over his lips to indicate silence. He whispered, "Lights out, no noise. We're crawling out of here."

51

Serena and Bryson waited at the delta rendezvous location. They were afraid to attempt any communication. So, they waited…and waited. Neither spoke.

Bryson looked occupied. Serena figured he was brainstorming about how he might get in touch undetected. Chatter continued on the Arrow Squad channel. Serena tried to still her mind with a meditation, but to no avail. *What are acceptable casualties?* She just assumed the op would work. The bad guys never expected them. Claus was meticulous in planning the raid. She had to face facts. *The Dulce base may have been unprepared, but they responded pretty effectively. It's not like Hollywood, where everything happens right. Shit. I am an asshole. Claus might be dead.* She stewed, restless and unsettled, for twenty minutes.

They heard an engine. Could've been a truck. She prepared a fire command, just in case.

When the camo-painted truck broke through the clearing, she ran out from the van. Claus got out and held his hand up. "Stay back. We're all okay, but I'm sure we're dusted with neurotoxic residue."

The men exited and stripped off their gear. They dumped bags of laptops, specimen tubes, external hard drives, and other booty they had collected during the raid. Claus handed each of them a wash bottle with some decontamination liquid. "Damn, it's good to see both of you. Just give us a minute to clean up."

The team tossed their contaminated suits into the truck. They washed with the decon-fluids. The men dropped their A-B-C call signs and addressed each other by name. Finally, they embraced one other, gave fist bumps, and generally sounded relieved. One member, Jerry, remained silent and restrained.

Serena and Bryson hugged Claus; he gave them the skinny on the decoy he used to fool the assault team. Serena congratulated him on quick thinking. "We heard part of that message and didn't know what to think."

Not to be outdone, Bryson shared his satellite-message-delay strategy to escape being blown up.

"That was smart, Bryson. Once they destroyed the primary transmitter, I wanted to tell you to stay dark, but I didn't want to give away that we had an outside secondary command post. My failure to plan the op right put us all in danger." Claus apologized to them all. Apologized!

"No way, Claus. We got it all done, and we're all here to talk about it." Bryson sounded relieved; the scared look from earlier had vanished. "You made it back safely; that's what's important."

Serena squealed with delight. "You are all incredible! We gave them a bloody nose, that's for sure." Victory energized her. Finally, they were fighting back. *That's what warriors do—we fight!*

Claus doused the truck containing all the contaminated gear with diesel fuel. "Everybody, in the van. Time to go home." He lit the vehicle. Serena chanted an extra boost, and they watched an inferno blaze as the team drove off.

The cars for the team members remained parked at the original rendezvous location. Claus handed each of them a bag. Whatever they were being paid, Serena knew it was worth every penny.

As he handed over Jerry's payment, Claus asked, "What gives, Jerry? You're usually the loudest mouth. Why so quiet?"

"Remember when I turned off my head cam, Claus? I didn't want Serena to see this, but you all need to see it. I'm quiet because there was some seriously bad shit going down at that base, and it needed to be stopped."

Claus spoke. "I think we stopped them for a good, long time. Between the nerve gas and the radiologic dirty bombs we detonated, they'll be cleaning up for months. I can't say for sure if we just poked them in the eye or if that base is toast for good. What did you see, Jerry?"

"I can tell ya, or I can show ya. Believe me, it ain't pretty."

The team gathered in the back of the van as Bryson and Jerry worked to load up the footage from his head cam.

Jerry looked at them all. His eyes flashed terror, anger, remorse. "I counted eight dead bodies. Six of them were babies." He stared at them. "Yeah, nursery, shoulda figured that. Babies! It's here on the recorded video." Infants, no more than one or two months old, lay still in bassinets, much like those in a pediatric newborn unit. "They were all dead. I swabbed 'em for samples."

Bryson shook his head and glared at Serena and Claus. He spoke, but his voice sounded like tires going flat. "This isn't what I signed up for." He looked right at Serena, and his words pierced her like a spear point. "Are you happy now?" He left the van, and the door slammed. They all overheard him retching.

Serena winced. She felt dazed. She didn't want the guilt but couldn't push it back. *Our attack murdered babies! How did this happen?*

For a moment, Jerry looked as though he might vomit too. He composed himself and continued. "You'll see it on the vid. The two dead techs or nannies or whatever they were didn't look right." He pointed to the screen. "Bulgy eyes set far apart, weird, big heads. Skin wasn't right either, and I've seen a shitload of dead people. Their skin is pale tan, white. These almost looked gray." He looked at the images from his head cam recording. "It doesn't show well here but trust me."

"Did you swab them? Did you get some DNA?" Claus asked after a hard swallow.

Jerry pulled out a specimen bag. "Watch the vid, Claus. I thought I knew what this op might be about, but not this." They watched as the head cam zeroed on the two dead technicians, focusing on the hands. Over the video recording, they could all hear Jerry's voice muttering, "That ain't right." The techs only had four fingers.

They all gasped. A knife blade flashed. Serena covered her eyes.

"DNA? Yeah, I got some right here." He opened the bag and dumped the contents on the floor of the van—two severed hands with grayish skin and only four fingers. "This ain't right."

52

Bryson rode in the back of the van, alone with his thoughts and feelings. The hole inside felt bottomless. He felt no vindication that his nonlethal strategy would have spared those innocent babies. Instead, he struggled with self-doubt. How did he allow himself to participate in this massacre? He needed to confront his own meaning and purpose by going within, by having a heart-to-heart dialogue with himself. Solemn in his self-admittance of straying from his core beliefs, he took ownership for his actions. The hole began to fill.

"I don't blame either one of you," he said quietly to Claus and Serena seated in front.

"Get on with it, Bryson. I know you've been stewing, and you're itching to speak your mind. Remember, we're at war." Claus's tone of voice made it clear they were on different sides of the fence on this issue.

"I'll keep it short. I'm not trying to change your minds. Again, I don't blame either one of you."

"Blame us for what? Killing innocent people including babies. It's war; people die. That includes good people and bad people. Get real, that's the way it is. That's the way it always has been."

Serena said nothing; she listened as the two battled it out.

"I blame myself. I compromised on my beliefs. That won't happen again."

"And just what are those beliefs, Bryson? That war is bad? I put men in harm's way today. You think I feel good about that? You think Jerry is going to forget what he saw, go home to his wife and kids, and sleep well tonight? It's a dirty business. It's a bloody, dirty business." Uncharacteristic anger came through; any louder, and Claus would be shouting.

Bryson responded in a measured and tempered tone. "You're right, Claus. It's bloody and messy. It always has been that way, but does it have to remain that way? As long as we think within the box of the ends justifying the means, we stay trapped in this same box of reasoning. That's the world we live in because it's the one we created. We're always fighting against one another. Or so it seems…"

"Go on, get it off your chest."

"We're not fighting each other. We're fighting with our own selves. We resist embracing our higher selves, our better angels. That's it. I'm done. I'm tired of fighting. Thanks for listening."

The storm cloud passed. They drove for a few miles in silence, then Serena told Bryson about the hands. He inched away from the specimen bag parked near him and shoved it to a corner with his foot.

Claus's voice had returned to normal. "There're mountains of hardware, data, and security recordings to review. I've also got to get all the samples to BB for analysis. Are you still in on this, kid?"

Serena turned around to see Bryson's response.

"Yeah, I'm good with that end of it, but I need some downtime. Brain's been working overtime, and tonight took a lot out of me. SHIT!" He slapped the side of his head. "How did I forget that?"

Claus slowed down, but there wasn't any traffic on this remote stretch of road. Bryson retrieved his phone from his pocket.

"During the op, I got a phone alert. My home's perimeter alarm sensor went off." Bryson played with the phone and shook his head. "Was hoping it was a bear. Pull over a second." He handed the phone to Claus. "You recognize her?"

"Snoop girl from the lab's parking lot. Li's hybrid. What did BB call her?" He gave the phone to Serena.

"A chimera. Some sort of gene-edited hybrid, from what I recall." Serena handed the phone back to Bryson. "If Li's tracked us down, it might not be safe to go back to Taos."

"I agree with Serena, Bryson. We don't know what's waiting for us there."

"Right. Brain's too tired to work it out now. It's almost 4 a.m. Why don't we find someplace to crash for a few hours and work out a plan? Besides"—a grin erupted as he toed the specimen bag—"we should probably pick up some ice."

Peter massaged his temples, pulled up his calendar, and scanned his schedule. *Good. I'm jammed solid for the next three weeks. I'll let Damiaan know that it'll have to wait till after. I'll give him some dates.*

Van Duyn insisted Peter join him on a trip to Nepal to see the main training facility where the supersoldiers got their programming. He wouldn't accept.

"I can't possibly break away. Nepal is a long flight." Peter's best efforts had managed to put the trip off but only for a week or so. Peter figured if he scheduled it through a weekend, he would only miss three solid workdays.

He let his personal assistant know. "I'm blocking off the sixteenth through the twentieth for a tentative business trip to Asia with Damiaan Van Duyn."

"Do you need me to make any reservations or trip arrangements? Are you bringing any staff?"

"Just me. Van Duyn will use his corporate jet and crew. Nothing further, keep the schedule clear. I should have confirmation on the dates tomorrow."

Peter would inform Damiaan later. He had already spoken to him this morning. Damiaan had called him personally about the raid on one of their bases. To hear his description, an ultra-high-level precision team had destroyed a good part of the complex and killed most of the personnel. Van Duyn was not at all pleased. He let slip that over fifty thousand soldiers were in hibernation there. The attackers used nerve gas and radiologic dispersion bombs. Peter listened, asked all the appropriate questions, expressed his dismay, and almost laughed his ass off when he hung up the phone. He couldn't wait to share that report summary with Claus.

His momentary laughter melted like ice on a hot grill. *I hope we got something useful. I'll be glad when my crew are all back safely. These are dangerous and ruthless people we're dealing with.*

This ruse Rothschild orchestrated to hook up Peter with Kenseiko Li had unintended results. Peter rubbed his temples further. He couldn't figure out a way to back out. The entire charade took its toll. Even though Rothschild was gone, the relationship Peter had been encouraged to groom with Van Duyn continued. Damiaan had gotten real chummy with Peter. Maybe Van Duyn didn't have many friends, but Peter felt no desire to male bond. Effectively, he had become a double agent; that was risky. He played a dangerous game, and he knew it.

Nobody liked Li, so there was an undeniable bond the two men shared there. No one seemed to miss Rothschild, but his disappearance, and now the raid, had family heads on edge. Van Duyn held a top-tier position within the Council. He told Peter they would meet soon to pick a new Pindar. Balancing the desire for inside information against concern for discovery left Peter second guessing his every move.

Tomorrow he would meet with his estate lawyer to update his will. If anything went sour, Bryson would be getting a lot. Peter felt confident his nephew would use the money wisely. His attorney might question who Pyramid Communications was and why he wanted to gift them five million dollars, but Peter would explain it as a charity case involving distant family—a worthwhile but under-funded organization he wanted to help.

Truth be known, Peter was very proud of the man Bryson had become. Over the years, he had kept a distance from his nephew. That had all changed in the last six months, and Peter now understood his nephew's beliefs and values. Claus reported that Bryson showed courage and character during and after the raid. *His father would be very proud. They both had courage and character.* His fist slammed the desk. *Goddamn you, Li! You took my brother from me, but I'm not going to let you get my nephew too. We are taking you down!*

53

They found a place near the edge of civilization. Nothing fancy, but it was clean and quiet. The desk clerk told them check out was at 11 a.m.; she would have to charge them another day if they stayed past. Claus paid cash for two rooms. It was 5 a.m.

As Bryson lay next to Serena, neither spoke. The gulf between them exceeded miles. The two hadn't slept together since Serena returned from the Canary Islands. Bryson had managed a quick text to Tarni when Serena used the bathroom. He let her know they were safe; he would call her later. Despite his exhaustion, he lay in bed, confused and awake, a brain fog left his mind feeling dim.

"There's a darkness in me," Serena's voice whispered.

Bryson wasn't sure if she spoke to him or the ceiling. "Say again. What are you talking about?"

"There's a darkness in me… Asthemirus told me."

"Serena, I don't have a clue what you're talking about. Do you want me to flip the light on, or do you want me to shut up and hear you out?"

"I'm scared, Bryson."

"No way, Serena. When your third chakra got opened, it drove the fear right out of you. You're fearless."

"This is different. This isn't about being afraid of other things. It's about me… I'm afraid of myself. There's a darkness in me."

He leaned up on his elbows. "C'mon, PTG, I know you seem gleeful about death and destruction and all. I've been having a hard time with that. Cut yourself some slack. Inside, you're good all the way down to the core. We've all got a shadow self."

"No, Bry. This is different. Asthemirus told me in the cave chamber at Güímar. She called it a mind parasite. She said the Gnostics knew about this. It's like a cancer inside me, Bry. I can't control it." Her voice quavered.

They both sat up, and he flipped on the bedside lamp. "Did she say anything else?"

"Not much. It's like a psychic attack that occurs in your sleep and infects you. She taught me a special meditation called Merkaba. I'm supposed to do it before I go to sleep to help protect myself. I'll show you in a minute, but it might spook you."

"You mean more than you're already creeping me out now?" He rolled his eyes trying to cheer her up. He'd never heard her so distraught.

"I'm serious. I do the meditation, and I start to glow."

"That makes sense. Your Ooljee used to call you her little *ch'osh bikq'I*— lightning bug. A glowworm is a baby lightning bug. Do the Merkaba thingy, and that should lighten you up."

"That's not at all funny, Bry. Asthemirus said the parasites are invisible worm filaments in my mind. It's like alien invaders are eating away at my psyche. She said the darkness could consume me."

"Did she say how to get rid of this parasite? Is there a cure?"

"She hoped the Merkaba would help, but it didn't. She said the Bent Pyramid in Egypt had some kind of amplified sound resonance, and temple priests and priestesses could use that energy to heal infected individuals. Unfortunately, I looked it up, and the pyramid is in partial ruins. Asthemirus wasn't sure, but her twin brother might have information in his tablet about how to cure me."

"Well, if sound energy can heal you, we'll have to figure out how to do it. We'll think of something, PTG."

"Thanks, Bryson. I've been wanting to tell you, but I wasn't sure how. Sorry I've been such a witch."

They looked at each other and burst out laughing.

"Curious choice of words, PTG." He put his arm around her. "Show me this Merkaba thing. I'll shut off the lights. You say it's to prevent attacks in your sleep?"

As Bryson uttered this, his mental fog lifted. "Holy shit, Serena. I think I know when this happened. There's something I haven't told you either." He rattled off the dream he had of her sleeping and a creature attacking her like some sort of vampire, how Gurumarra showed up in his dream and drove the beast away.

"Now you're creeping me out, Bry. But you may be right."

She showed him her Merkaba meditation and did her best to explain the counter-rotating etheric energy.

As he lay next to Serena's glowing body, Bryson wasn't sure what to say or how to react. "Looks powerful, girlfriend. Maybe you can teach it to me. For now, let's try and get some sleep. We've had a grueling day."

"Thanks, Bry. I feel better telling you the truth. The Merkaba also helps me feel more connected, more like myself."

"We'll figure out how to keep you that way." He noticed that he felt better too.

They sat at a family restaurant in a booth near the back, waiting for brunch. Serena had a pot of coffee and looked happy. They all agreed to eat first and plan after.

Bryson scrolled through messages on his home answering machine, selectively listening to ones that might be important. "Hmm, this might be interesting." He put the phone on speaker for Claus and Serena to hear.

"Hello… Bryson, is that you? I don't know if this number works anymore 'cause I ain't called in a while. This is ole Maria…Maria Trujillo, Serena's next-door neighbor… [cat meows] Oreo says 'Hello.' He's been asking to see you and wants you to bring a treat. [doorbell rings]… *Mierda!*… Hold on, I'll call you right back. [phone clicks]"

Claus chuckled. "The old lady living in the next apartment at your place, Serena. She sure gave Dan and me quite an interrogation when we went by there. I remember her cat scratched me too."

"Maria is a sweetheart. I wonder sometimes how she's doing. What do you think she wants?" Serena asked.

"Probably someone sneaking around your apartment. Here, let's listen." He scrolled to the next message.

"Bryson? You there? Maria again…had to answer the door. Anyway, saw someone snooping around Serena's place. Asian, kinda small. Rang my bell to ask if I knew where Serena was. Where is she, by the way? Is she ever coming back? I don't think the Asian girl broke in. She checked with some of the other neighbors too. [cat meows] Anyway, thought you should know. If you get this message, stop by and visit an old lady…and don't forget a treat for Oreo. [phone clicks]"

Bryson pocketed his phone as the food arrived. "Figures. Li's agent scoping out old leads. She's on our scent, so we need the trail to go cold. But first, let's eat."

They were all famished though not especially well rested. Still, the mom-and-pop feel of the place and the hearty food did a lot to energize them. They hatched a plan.

Claus would drive the van and booty to Chicago to start working on unloading and deciphering the trove. BB could begin the DNA analyses. They located a car rental place, and Claus used his Charles Godfried pseudonym to rent the vehicle. Bryson and Serena would head to the hogan on the reservation and chill for a few days for much-needed rest.

As they prepared to leave the rental car parking lot, they exchanged hugs. Claus pulled Bryson aside and told him, "Not saying I agree with you, Bryson, but if you and Serena can find a better way, I'm all for it."

"Thanks, Claus. We'll try. Make sure you tell Tarni I miss her. Safe travels. See you back in Chicago next week."

Once they hit Route 64, Bryson switched his brain to autopilot. He knew this stretch of road and just enjoyed the drive. He and Serena brainstormed about where to find the other Twin, how the Druids fit in, how far north the Eye of Thoth might be.

Serena said, "Did Thoth establish any other Mystery Schools besides the ones we know about?"

"Don't know. I can plug queries into the algorithms and see if we get any hits."

"I do remember that Riccardo looked surprised when I said only one Twin was inside. That was just before he sedated me." She shut her eyes. "Don't want to revisit that." Instinctively, she grasped her shortened pinky and rubbed the end where a thick eschar had formed.

"Riccardo was the authority, so if he didn't know, we're going to have to connect the dots on our own."

They talked further about the mind parasite. Bryson wondered if Serena should do her Merkaba practice several times a day.

"You said you feel better after you finish. Maybe it can somehow strengthen you against this thing spreading." He thought some more. "Maybe Gurumarra has ideas on how to cure you. Do you think BB can reach him?"

"Doubt it. The Wanderer could be anywhere. We can ask BB, but I doubt it."

They agreed to table further inquiry and just enjoy the scenery. Across the northern Arizona landscape, thunderheads and lightning flashed over the mountains. When sunshine broke through, a magnificent rainbow had them stop to admire it and take pictures.

"Something about rainbows." Serena fingered her necklace. "Promise of a great treasure at the end." She began to sing "Somewhere Over the Rainbow."

Bryson made small talk. "Do you know anything about the Rainbow Warrior?"

"Not really." They got back in the car. "I'm sure you'll tell me." Serena flashed that sheepish smile that Bryson loved.

"It was a ship operated by Greenpeace International. It was involved in some activist work like trying to save the whales, antinuclear stuff, that sort of thing. You know Greenpeace is a champion for environmentalism, protecting the earth, all that heroic stuff to oppose government and multinational abuses against nature."

"What happened to it?"

"French intelligence services sunk the ship off the coast of New Zealand. It was apparently a big deal back in the 80s."

"That sucks. Can you tell me something happy? How do you even know about stuff like that?"

"Greenpeace made a cool video game called *Rainbow Warrior*. It's a classic."

"Weird name for a boat, not so much for a video game."

Bryson pulled out something from his eidetic memory bank. "Ancient myths and legends inspired the name. Apparently, there's an old Native American prophecy about 'Warriors of the Rainbow' coming when the earth is in need of healing." He seemed to be unlocking and reciting an entry. "They will teach mankind to reclaim their birthright, restore harmony to the planet, to set humanity free."

He pulled the car to the side of the road. They looked at each other. The rainbow still arched in the mountains.

"Did I just say what I think I said?"

54

Under the Hill. Kenseiko always liked the sound of that. *We gather together in our den beneath the burial mound of a king. We plot the death of the old humanity, stale and unwieldy. I make my father proud.*

Ludwig Rothschild, Edward's younger brother, was much the same as Kenseiko remembered him—an arrogant snob of a man, a playboy financier more interested in the trappings of wealth and privilege than in accomplishing anything historic. Of course, all the family heads knew it. The Rothschild reign needed to end; the winged serpent, a Chinese Dragon, would usher in the New World Order. Or so he hoped.

He promised Bundy an antidote to the gift Wán shàn had previously delivered, but only if Aaron cast his stone in support. Li also made it abundantly clear that should Bundy ever so much as touch Wán shàn again, the consequences would be more severe. The head nod and downward gaze said all that needed to be said. *He is like a dog, defeated with his tail between his legs. That is all that will be between his legs if he ever plays with any of my perfect daughters.*

Van Duyn conducted the beginning prayers and ceremonies. They asked for Lucifer to light the way. All the Council members brought their seconds except for Ludwig Rothschild. He looked lost, a nobody in a room full of very powerful people.

Kenseiko saw Wán shàn making mental notes. There were many new people for his daughter to study and observe. During a break between sacrifices, he asked her what she thought.

"They fear you, bàba."

"Why is that?"

"Because they know your genius. It exceeds their own."

"That is all, daughter?"

"They respect you. As Genghis Khan had generals that respected and feared him at the same time."

"And me… How do I see them?"

"You tolerate them." She considered her answer, then added, "And you despise them."

"Why is that?"

"Because they are inferior."

He nodded. "True."

They donned their white robes. All the Council members and their seconds looked the same, distinguished only by their unique family crest. Candlelight flickered off the grayish skin of the thirteen faces kneeling to form the inner circle. A Pyramid Priest, highest in his order, conducted the ritual.

Each family head stood to place a colored stone into a carved basin in the center of a rock-hewn chamber deep inside the cavern complex. The stones lay covered in blood. When the placements ended, the priest poured off the blood into a jeweled cup, carved with the Eye of Lucifer. He passed the cup to each of the thirteen. As they drank, he wiped and counted the vote stones. The Illuminati family leaders knelt with heads bowed and eyes closed.

As the priest held up a conical headpiece, the Pindar's mark of authority, he invoked The Lord of Light, bringer of wisdom and justice to mankind. He walked around the circle of men several times then stopped.

"Rise, Servant Li. Rise and fill the Headpiece of Light. Be filled with light and bring light forth to us all in the ways unbroken since the beginning. Rise, Pindar, to keep us out of darkness."

Kenseiko Li stood. All in the room remained kneeling before him. He had achieved that which his father never could. He, the one almost left upon a mountain to die, stood tall on his clubbed foot. He made eye contact with Wán shàn and imagined he saw a look of pride in her gaze. Gloating and basking in glory would come later.

"Fellow servants," he addressed them. "I am humbled by your selection and pledge to serve you all faithfully."

The priest handed him a knife. Kenseiko slashed his hand, and as his blood flowed, he walked around the circle dripping blood upon the white cloaks, offering his hand for any to drink. None partook. All rose.

"We have darkness upon us. Someone has taken our Brother and fellow servant. A Womb has been attacked. But darkness always precedes light. We know not our attackers. Some say it is a Candelaria." He signaled to Wán shàn and watched as she removed thirteen vials from an inner pocket.

"In the early days, before the great Serpent War, we had Sisters in the light. We served together—they the *yin* and we the *yang*. Since the time of the breakings, we have been at war. We have maintained our pure bloodlines among ourselves, but so too has the enemy, hiding in the shadows. The Candelaria are not a threat, they are an opportunity." Wán shàn distributed the vials.

"They are our long-lost Brothers and Sisters. But I have brought them back into the fold. I give you pure infant Candelaria blood." He held up the vial Wán shàn had just given him. "Pure, strong, drink this blood and feel the power it brings. I have more. As much as we desire."

The Council heads toasted their new Pindar and drank. Immediately they seemed to radiate youth and power.

"Some argue that we should delay moving forward with our New World. I say to wait is to delay our victory." He watched to see their responses. None voiced opposition.

"Let us advance to the next phase of ushering in a New World Order. May Lucifer protect us."

He began the closing prayer. "We, the chosen, pledge to serve the light Lucifer has brought to us…"

"To illuminate," they said in unison and touched their foreheads.

Li continued. "May he guide us…"—they each touched their left shoulders—"and bless us…"—they touched their right shoulders—"until his light shines upon all." All thirteen rested their hands back upon their hearts.

In unison they recited, "May the light shine upon us in glory."

55

"What do you want to do tomorrow?" Serena had used her voice to start a fire. She and Bryson had picked up food, grilled, and ate steak and vegetables. It was chilly, and they didn't have any sweaters or warm clothes. The moon overhead looked brilliant, a shining beacon in a sea of twinkling stars.

"Sleep late. Chill out." He rubbed his arms and moved closer to the fire. "Figuratively, not literally." She enjoyed his joking and playful banter. "I need to update some computer stuff, check my home surveillance. Nothing big. Mostly I want to relax. How about you?"

"Ditto on sleeping late. Didn't have a chance to clean up the dust, so mindless housekeeping will be a welcome break. Mostly just want to sit around and absorb the energy here. My *shibízhí* always said it was a power spot."

Serena lay on her bedroll and did the twelve breaths to activate her Merkaba. She cast a soft light throughout the hogan.

"It's hard to say, Serena, because the lighting inside here is so different from last night, but you look brighter to me. I think tomorrow, do this a few times. It might help to kill this parasite."

"Good idea."

Serena had been racing in overdrive for weeks; she figured the same was true for Bryson. The healing sanctuary of Ooljee's hogan provided them a haven of safety, far away from the chaos, fear, and confusion slowly gripping the world. Moments after her eyes shut, soft snores added to the chorus of crickets and night sounds.

Serena woke to sunlight streaming through the center hole and the aroma of strong coffee. She stretched and went outside.

"I started the fire the old-fashioned way." Bryson stood there with stubble on his normally clean-shaven face; his arms flailed as he waved smoke beneath his jersey.

"What are you doing? Does your morning routine now include a chicken dance?"

"Smoke bath. Saw it on one of those survival shows." He sniffed under an armpit. "Need more smoke."

She laughed until he blocked her attempt to get coffee. "Hey, what gives?"

"Merkaba first, coffee second." She wrinkled her nose in reply, sat yoga style, and focused her breathing.

Bryson watched as she completed her meditation. "Tough to compete with this gorgeous sunlight, but I can see your radiance, PTG. How do you feel?"

"I shouldn't have sat downwind of you, survivor boy." Her face exploded into a huge grin as she poured herself a mug. "Once I slug this down, I'll be feeling great."

After more joking and munching on granola, Bryson grew serious. "I checked the news and other items this morning."

"Nothing good, I'm sure."

"You're on a list of people Interpol is looking to question about Rothschild's disappearance. That will make traveling outside the country more difficult. Could be trouble with TSA too. You might have to change names again."

"That's it? How about Dulce? What's being reported?"

"Bogus stories about training exercise gone awry. Total fake news."

"Figures. Anything else?"

"World is on edge. Famine in India is worse, crops in other countries—Australia, Russia, Canada, even the USA—are at record lows. Demand is up, production is down. Middle East is a mess. Riots and demonstrations all over the place."

"I'm sure it's all orchestrated. Are the religious fanatics predicting the end yet?"

"For sure, but what's almost bizarre is that despite all these crises and catastrophes, more of the news is about who wore what color gown at the Academy Awards and other completely mundane garbage."

"That's because it hasn't hit home yet, Bry. It's still bread and circus here in the good ole U. S. of A. People have full bellies and entertainment, so they might superficially care about what's happening, but it doesn't affect them. At least, not yet. When it does, then they'll want someone to fix it." She crunched on granola between sips of coffee.

"You're right, Serena. And when Big Brother steps in, that's when the leash shortens even further." He stood up and looked back toward a ravine. "We're not going to fix it today. I'm going to take a hike. I need to sort out some things; walking helps to unstick my brain."

"That works for me. I'm ready for yoga and harnessing some kundalini to charge up my chakras."

Forty-five minutes later, he returned and attacked his laptop. Serena remained outside totally focused on practicing her asanas. When he emerged from the hogan, she saw Bryson waving a rattle and a drum.

"Are you going to do a rain dance, Bryson?"

He held up the instruments. "I got an idea. When I was in a coma, your *shibízhí* chanted during my dream hallucinations while shaking her rattle"—he gave it a shake—"and beating this drum." He rapped the drum skin with his fingers. "I can still hear her in my mind, not to mention I've had her chanting in my dreams from time to time."

"Go on, I'm listening. What are you scheming?"

"She healed me with sound. Granted it was a physical ailment, but I was poisoned with snake venom, and she healed me. Maybe the antivenom had something to do with it but hear me out. When you described the chakra opening in Australia, you said there were people chanting, playing didgeridoos, beating clap sticks, and Gurumarra reached inside you and pulled out a snake. It represented the fear within. That was a psychic healing."

"I see where you're headed."

"I've researched the mind parasites you told me about and the Bent Pyramid. I did a deep dive into sound healing, including the tonal qualities of the human voice that can facilitate healing. I'm no shaman, but I think it's worth a shot." He thumbed the drum and cleared his voice.

"Let's do it."

For the next four hours, he chanted, shook Ooljee's rattle, and beat her drum, exactly as he remembered from his comatose hallucinations. Once Serena picked up the words and cadence, she added the power of her voice. Slowly, a trance-like dream vison enveloped them, broken only by the call of nature.

"How do you feel?"

"I don't know. Physically I feel great, but that might be because this is a glorious place and a glorious day." She spread her arms out then quickly pulled them back. "Could use a bath…"

He laughed. "Try your Merkaba." When she finished, Bryson reported no difference in her body's glow.

"I do feel better, Bry. I can't explain it. How long were you in that coma with my *shibízhí* chanting?"

"Five days."

"Ugh!" She swallowed.

"But I was a near goner. I think we should keep trying."

On the third night, it happened. Serena slept. Moonbeams streamed through the hogan's center hole, adding light to the soft Merkaba glow she emanated. Bryson, his voice hoarse, continued to rattle, beat the drum, and chant.

A dark blackness appeared on her neck. He raised the volume in his voice. It woke her.

"Some-thing's-hap-pen-ing." Bryson's words continued, the rhythm and cadence uninterrupted. Serena chanted with him.

Slowly, a mist-like vapor, dark and ominous seeped out from the side of her neck. It swirled in a funnel vortex. They both saw it, black in the surrounding light. They both felt it. They shivered and continued. The dark hole in her neck closed; light swallowed the vortex, and Serena began to shine. She shimmered, and Bryson admired her radiance. He grew still. Whatever he'd just witnessed, whatever dark paranormal entity that just got absorbed by light energy didn't matter to him. Was Serena okay? Bryson held his breath.

She leaped off the bed and spun around. "It's gone! It's gone! I know it! I can feel it!" She hugged him. "What was it, Bry? Did you feel something too?"

"Anger, terror, hatred? It clawed at my psyche; almost sucked the life out of me. Don't know what it was for sure, but 'mind parasite' is too tame to explain that thing. It's like a demon's been exorcised." Bryson shuddered. "How did you live with that inside you? Do you feel okay?"

She looked puzzled. "I don't know. I think I must have been fighting it all along. Almost like I've been fighting inside myself and now it's over. I feel whole… I feel alive… I feel like I can do anything." She looked at her hands and arms. "I'm full of light energy, Bry. It's amazing!"

"You are amazing, Candelaria girl! And I'm glad you're back. I've been damn worried about you." He lay down and took a deep breath. Serena shimmered in dancing lights.

"Thanks, Bryson, but you did it; you're incredible! You figured it out. I owe you big time. You've earned your first shaman merit badge." She leaned over, kissed him, and lay down snuggling next to him.

He lay there, silent for minutes. He cleared his throat. "Serena?"

"Right here."

He stammered, "There's something I haven't told you."

"Tarni?"

"How did you know that?" He felt relieved that she knew.

"Hey, I'm not a genius like you, but you always avoid talking about her, change the subject when her name comes up. It isn't hard for a girl to put two and two together." She shrugged. "Besides, she's smokin' hot…and that accent… Damn, even I'm attracted to her."

"Strong pheromones, I guess." He chuckled. "So, you're okay with it?"

For a moment, Serena said nothing. She faced him directly, and their eyes locked in a soulful gaze. "I don't know, boyfriend." She kissed him on the lips—long, slowly, and repeatedly.

56

BBC World News Live Coverage:

Nuclear terrorism! Last night's attack on the European Union headquarters completely destroyed the iconic Berlaymont building, where the blast originated, and laid waste to the surrounding area. Death toll estimates for this city of 1.2 million are well over half the populace.

Today, simultaneous attacks at the United Nations and Wall Street have all but paralyzed the United States of America, striking at the heart of American commerce and killing the entire membership of the General Assembly that had been in session at the time of the explosions. Lethal radiation impedes all efforts to assess damage or to attempt rescue of survivors. Aerial footage shows total and massive devastation with ground zero being what used to be Manhattan. The governors of New York and New Jersey have declared states of emergency. The US military is mobilized with that entire country placed at their highest level of threat alert. The President of the United States will go live with an address momentarily.

The explosions in Europe and America have rocked the world, sending markets into a tailspin. Trading is halted on all major exchanges. The European Central Bank is on lockdown, as is the entire city of Frankfort for fear they will be a target. The EU Council of Ministers is in emergency session as world leaders struggle to respond.

The fallout is more than radioactive. An economic catastrophe of biblical proportions washes over the globe like an unstoppable tsunami. The death toll is incalculable. Chaos reigns as citizens rush to bomb shelters, schools, churches, mosques, and other places of worship. The Pope and other religious leaders have called for prayers and for divine intercession.

As to who is responsible for today's terrorist actions and where the next attack might occur, all the world is seeking answers.

We turn now to live coverage of The President of the United States...

PART THREE

LIGHT

57

Tarni shook Beangagarrie's still form to no avail. *At least he's still breathing. Probably dazed from a seizure.* She glanced at the pale-amber stain soiling the bed sheet.

She stood by the bed and waited until his eyes fluttered. The bewildered look on his face spoke volumes.

"Sleeping late today, BB?"

"I was dreaming of my beautiful Kalinda. I'm surprised to see you here so early."

Her hushed voice replied, "It's ten in the morning, mate. I found you this way half an hour ago. You must have had a seizure. At least you didn't fall and hurt yourself."

"I'm sorry, Fuchsia." He grabbed down over his groin, wet with urine. "Oh my! Yes, that appears to be the case."

"Beangagarrie, I tell you this as more than a friend. You cannot continue this way. Your own needs require medical attention."

"We still have much to do. Have you finished the viral probe I requested?"

"If not for yourself, then for me. I worry for your health. I worry I shall find you dead." She held back tears.

He stood, donned a robe, and approached her. "Soon. When you have finished this last step, then I promise to make an appointment for my eye. I am nearly blind in my left eye now. It slows my work. But the anticonvulsants impair my thinking. There is nothing further for me to do about the seizures."

"Come, you need to get cleaned up. We're having visitors today."

He gently grasped his assistant and looked in her eyes. "Tarni, soon you will not have to worry about me or my health. Soon, I will be back with my Kalinda. I am deeply sorry to be a burden, but it is not for much longer."

She wanted to protest but only nodded.

"This is not a world I would choose to remain in. The world is coming apart. I am still here only with the hope that I may be of service in mending that which is broken. When I leave the Dreamtime, you must continue our work." He leaned forward and kissed her forehead.

As he viewed their group assembled in the lab, Bryson felt the sweat gathering beneath his armpits. They all waited for his Uncle Peter to join them. Serena and Tarni had just retreated outside for a "private conversation." Claus eyed him with a look that said *I feel your pain.*

The previous evening, when he and Serena had returned from the reservation back to Chicago, Claus and Tarni had prepared a fine meal that included pleasant conversation, hugs, and kisses all around. Night found Bryson sleeping on the floor with Serena on the couch. Confrontation seemed inevitable. He hadn't sorted out his own feelings; part of him hoped the two women would sort it out for him. He grimaced thinking how the conversation between them was unfolding and wondered where he would sleep tonight. *Okay, I admit it's a cop-out on my part, but I'm better at computer code than relationships.*

Tarni had left earlier that morning. Now it was midday. BB readied a presentation about their recovered samples from Dulce. Claus brought a separate presentation on intel they recovered from the operation. *BB looks like shit!* Thin, almost gaunt, the geneticist moved cautiously. Serena pointed out the changes, including his eye. "The left pupil is fixed; something's wrong there." She had whispered this to Bryson before exiting with Tarni.

Peter Reynolds ran late. When his uncle finally arrived, the two women returned. Tarni looked at him sternly then winked. Serena looked at him and winked. *WTF does that mean?* Before Bryson could react further, Peter cleared his throat.

"Thank you all for gathering here and thank God you're all okay! These are very unsettled times, but I fear we have only seen the tip of the iceberg." He detailed what he knew about the Illuminati plans from his contacts, including Van Duyn. Serena added additional bits of details from Rothschild's long-winded boasts.

"The attacks in New York and Brussels came out of the blue. They're pinning it on a new terrorist group—United Coalition for World Justice. I think it's bogus, fake news, propaganda. I think the Illuminati are behind the bombings. Look at what's happened: widespread fear, enhanced government control, limits on travel, dire economics. It's a big squeeze. Between the pressures on food and clean water, war and struggle for resources, it opens the door for militarization and reorganization. Taking out the United Nations creates a vacuum that screams to be filled. It's masterful, well thought out, and it's happening in real time."

Bryson looked around the room at his colleague's faces, all grim.

"I almost forgot; I'm planning a trip with Damiaan Van Duyn to see one of the hive operations in Nepal. I don't know if it's anything like the one in Dulce. It's the main development site where they harvest...er clone..."—he winced—"where they house their supersoldiers. With all the craziness following the bombings, I don't know when it will happen, but I'm guessing within a couple of weeks. Who wants to go next, BB or Claus?"

"I'm pretty quick, boss, so I'd like to tell my piece." Claus stood and ran through a quick presentation. He was still sorting through a mountain of internal surveillance recordings and communications they had obtained during the raid.

"It turns out there are eleven levels to the base, and we infiltrated the upper three. The levels below had what looks like tanks of cloned humans. There were pens with many subjects. Some of them looked to be genetic hybrids. Clearly, they were doing some very weird shit there. Excuse my French." He ran through still shots from the base's security surveillance.

"Looks like the tube system ran over to Denver. Not sure what's going on there. Kirtland and Manzano in New Mexico were also tied in, but I haven't figured any of that out yet." He added, "I can't say for sure, but I think we hit them hard enough that they lost a lot of assets. The base may not be dead, but it's taken a big hit." He fielded questions.

"The last piece I got has to do with some hardware. Our B team did a great job disassembling and scoring what looks like some type of optical pulse apparatus for neural programming. We think this equipment can directly induce neural synapses in the brain…kinda hardwire brain programming. It could be what they use for the supersoldiers. So, boss, if you go to Nepal, keep a lookout for anything that resembles this." He flashed through some more slides. Claus finished by answering questions as best as he could. He was only 30 to 35 percent done with analyzing their trove.

The group decided to take a break before BB presented. Serena and Tarni both ignored him.

BB pulled Serena aside, but Bryson could overhear their talk.

"I am sorry, Galinawa. What I show will trouble you. It troubles me."

"Don't worry. I'll be fine. I am more concerned about you, BB. You are unwell."

"Yes, this is true. But I am well enough to continue what is required." He removed a small tin from his pocket, pinched something leafy, and placed it beneath his tongue. "Soon, you will have your answers."

58

The wind and cold pierced through to her marrow, but she ignored it. Instead, Wán shàn stared intently at the mountain vista, the same one she looked at with Dr. Zhāng the last time she visited Nepal.

His words came back to her; they stuck in her mind like an ice barge bound within a glacier. "Many would answer my question by describing beauty, by invoking nature, or majesty and mystery, perhaps even refer to the glory of God's creation. Your mind remains clear, uncontaminated by such thoughts or feelings. It is the way we created you."

It was a rare time alone for her during this intensive stay with her sisters back at the hive, back with the Imaginarium team that created them. What are beauty, majesty, mystery? She could recite the definitions, but the depth of the meanings had to go beyond the words. Her teeth chattered at the bitter cold, but still she studied the mountains, the trees, the ice glinting with sunlight. The wind howled. Her gaze fell upon the rocks at her feet. There in a crevice, a plant somehow managed to survive. Some might call it a weed, but despite the cold, a small yellow blossom dusted with snow seemed to call out to her.

A tear trickled down her cheek. Sometimes, in the wind and cold, her eyes would tear, but not this time. This tear arose from the flower, a gift to her mind, to her insight into herself and the world. *Awesome...it is awesome!* A cloud drifted across the sky, and shafts of sunlight backlit the bundles and billows of white. *Awesome!*

An hour later, Dr. Choi from the lab found her. Her fingers were blue, ice crystals of tears clung to her face, frozen in a look of wonder and amazement.

"Wán shàn, what are you doing? You are late for the next session. Your sisters are all waiting. Dr. Zhāng is waiting."

"Strange. I must have lapsed into meditation. I see I have erred in my allotted time. I shall be more vigilant in the future. It will not happen again."

"Come now; they are all waiting."

She began to follow back to the entrance and turned around for another look. "It is quite beautiful, Dr. Choi, is it not?"

He paused briefly and looked toward where she pointed. "Yes, it is."

They slept together, ate together, and meditated as a group for hours at a time. Dr. Zhāng explained that it helped to build a group consciousness. They trained physically and mentally against one another as singles, couples, and groups of three. They competed in tournaments of chess and go. In these competitions, the results were always the same—statistical parity.

They sat in lengthy sessions together, discussing log entries recorded into their secure database, asking more detailed questions about meaning and circumstances attached to these entries. Her sisters all agreed with her that information associated with vehicles she found at Bryson Reynolds' home needed further research. One, a rental car leased to a Charles Godfried, was linked to Baxter Consolidated, an affiliated Reynolds' company. What possible connections he or Baxter might have with Serena Mendez needed to be tracked down. They offered their help to find both Charles Godfried and Serena Mendez.

With a thorough and collective understanding of the information and observations they had gathered, they speculated about how the next steps in the Illuminati plans might unfold, how the world might react, and what they needed to be prepared to do. Much of this last exercise was unsupervised and freely structured to go wherever the six sisters wanted.

At no time did Wán shàn raise questions about feelings or emotional content. She wanted to see if any of her sisters brought the topic up for exploration and discussion. While she recognized that others among her cloned siblings might also be withholding such questions, she detected nothing suggesting this to be the case.

A significant amount of time during their two-week stay involved optogenic programming. The team from the Imaginarium explained improvements to the older techniques for brain stimulation allowed for even better neuronal networks to form. As Wán shàn sat during one of these sessions, she tried to follow the flurry of flashing lights and colors to try to make sense of the patterns. She listened intently to the acoustic input feeding into her ears, feeding sensory stimuli directly into her brain in association with the kaleidoscope of optical input. It gave her a headache.

She privately asked two of her Ninja sisters if the sessions caused any sensations of discomfort, asked if they tried to decipher the coded inputs. Both confided that they sat back and relaxed during the programming. They both used meditative breathing exercises to focus awareness away from the stimulation. She thanked them.

She requested and was granted permission to observe how the HC-12 soldiers were programmed. She explained that should any of the soldiers go rogue, it would be important to understand any vulnerabilities. Her inquiry resulted in all six Wán shàns sitting in on an HC-12 optogenic session. After consultation with Dr. Li, the sisters were given secret codewords that could trigger neurally hardwired responses from the programmed soldiers. There was even a coded sequence to trigger catastrophic fatal seizures.

Wán shàn could not help but wonder what secret words lay embedded within her own brain. *What content and commands have been wired into my brain and the brains of all my sisters?* Her deepest unstated thought: *Do any of my sisters wonder about these same things?*

On the last day of this rigorous retreat, Dr. Zhāng gathered them all together and reviewed scientific studies on identical twins. "It is widely accepted that mental connections across distances exist among the twins. Researchers believe these associations are based upon quantum connections and entanglements. The entire brain and nervous system have quantum-level energetic transfers. Even your DNA processes quantum inputs and information."

He randomly selected one of her sisters, who was then escorted out of the room. "This is not a true scientific experiment, but we have a hypothesis about how these last two weeks may have facilitated some quantum alignment among all of you." The entire team from the Imaginarium had drifted in for this quasi experiment.

Zhāng spoke into a microphone, signaling the test to begin.

Suddenly, Wán shàn felt a sharp pain in her left thumb, then in her right index finger. She looked at her sisters and noted they, too, winced in pain. One rolled her fingers with a quizzical look, asking where these sensations arose from.

"How many experienced sensations in their fingers?" All five sisters raised their hands. When the test subject returned, also rubbing fingers with residual pain, Dr. Zhāng explained an electric shock had been administered to the sister separated from the rest of the group.

"You are more connected than you realize. Go out and be as one in the furtherance of our plans." The assembled scientists shook hands and expressed pride in their accomplishments.

Wán shàn's eyebrows lifted at the revelation. As she rolled her fingertips feeling for any unusual sensation, something jarred her mind. *Amazing! Awesome in a different way. Elegant, even beautiful!* A smile appeared and vanished. She doubted anyone noticed.

A plane motored on the landing field as all six chimeric clones readied to board for Singapore. Wán shàn noticed Dr. Choi standing off to the side. Momentarily, she debated with herself then boldly approached.

"Dr. Choi, this has been a highly instructive two weeks. I do have a question that I should have asked during our enhanced optogenic programming." He nodded and she continued. "Are there secret words embedded and encoded into our brains?" She gestured toward her sisters.

She saw his pause as he considered then rejected his initial response.

"You would need to ask Dr. Li about that."

59

When BB looked at her, Serena confirmed something was unquestionably wrong with his left eye. Furthermore, the geneticist looked gaunt and drained. He started with pictures "of the subject material," as he termed it. There's nothing pretty about photos of severed hands, especially gray-skinned, four-fingered ones. Serena watched Tarni scan the room. *Obviously, she knows the results; she wants to see our reactions.*

"The DNA is mostly human-like." He cleared his throat. "It has genetic segments different from anything I've ever seen or can find in reference databanks."

"Is it extraterrestrial? Alien?" Claus blurted out the obvious question.

BB shrugged. "I cannot say for sure, but that it is a reasonable hypothesis."

More questions followed until Peter suggested they allow Dr. Brindabella to continue and hold questions until the end.

BB kept glancing at Serena. *He's going to drop a bombshell, and he's worried about me for some reason. Something bigger than the hand? That's hard to believe.*

"Samples from the raid numbered seventy-four in total. Most, sixty-four to be precise, represented a range of normal human genetic profiles with a disproportionate heritage skewed to Native American descent. This may be in keeping with the local population; although, I do not have a comparative geographic sampling to say for sure. These next slides detail some of the aggregated results."

He looked around while everyone absorbed the information. "Four samples were identical. All were male, and all had underlying extensive gene editing, similar to the chimeric modifications I have previously described on the young woman who seemed to be scouting out our lab."

Bryson interrupted. "Probably the same one we caught on the security cam at my house. One of Li's operatives, we figure."

"I think it is a reasonable conclusion that Dr. Li or his team are also responsible for the results I am reporting on. I presume these are cloned hybrids of some sort."

Quite the scientist he is, choosing his words carefully, offering reasonable speculation but not saying anything conclusively. BB glanced at Serena again.

Tarni chimed in. "It might also be relevant that two of these four samples that BB just mentioned were from the bodies in the programming area that B unit targeted." She paused to let that sink in. "Now, I'm not military or anything, and I might be jumping to the wrong conclusion, but I'd say these might be the same as those supersoldiers Claus has talked about before."

"Yeah, missy, you're pulling the thoughts right out of my brain. Makes sense. It might be helpful to study those samples more extensively to try and figure out how these soldiers have been enhanced."

"This is a good suggestion, Claus. Tarni and I will look into it further." He sighed.

Serena couldn't help but notice that Tarni had stopped looking at BB and now stared at the floor.

"The final six samples…" BB's voice quavered; he took a sip of water. "The final six samples were from swabs taken in the area designated 'Nursery.' These genetic results are all identical. This means they are either sextuplets or clones." A deep breath followed. "They are all female."

Claus squirmed. "Anything special about their DNA, doc?"

The dead babies in the nursery had overwhelmingly been the worst aspect of their raid. Serena felt the tension in the room as BB discussed these results.

"Alien or human or some combination?" Claus shifted in his seat.

"Entirely human."

"So, is there nothing special about these infants?" Peter asked on behalf of all in the room.

"Not quite, Mr. Reynolds." He looked at everyone. Tarni still had her head down. BB's gaze landed on Serena, and his voice dropped to a whisper.

"They…they are all genetically identical to Serena."

No one spoke. Everything around her went blank. Her breathing stopped as she fell headlong into a dark abyss. Serena heard the echo of his words sound again and again in her mind as she tumbled. Tarni sobbed quietly, and BB approached Serena.

She buried her head against his bony chest as he embraced her. Numb.

"I'm sorry, Galinawa… I am so sorry."

60

Kenseiko allowed himself a brief self-congratulatory indulgence. Dr. Zhāng's final report on the Ninja hybrids' two-week intensive and reprogramming exceeded Kenseiko's already high expectations. *They get better and better. There is little to improve upon.*

In this rare moment of solipsistic praise, he reflected upon his other recent accomplishments. The Hendra Bogi 1 response worldwide had plowed a clear path to vaccine administration. Soon they could initiate that part of the plan. Wars in the Middle East and Crimea were escalating. *They are sure to spread. Fear, turmoil, unrest, factionalism—they are so easy to flame and manipulate. Even Genghis knew this.* The insect-born pathogen Li's people had developed and the orchestrated food shortages together resulted in better centralized control in several key areas. Worldwide civil unrest, in particular the food riots on the Indian subcontinent, were getting splendid media coverage. Indeed, the whole information and propaganda effort had been masterful. He made a note to make sure he congratulated Kennedy and Freemen on their stellar work. *Perhaps I should send them some Candelaria blood treats. I'm sure they would appreciate that.*

Thoughts of the uncaptured Candelaria girl dispelled his self-adulation. She remained as an unresolved matter. Not so much a nuisance as an unknown. Unknowns represented variables. In science, reducing variables is paramount. The same held true for military strategy; eliminating variables was always prudent. *Brindabella—he's another variable. Best to eliminate him.* Kenseiko stroked his chin as he considered how to get that done.

❖   ❖   ❖

Even the extra hot sauce on their Chinese takeout couldn't spice their conversation. It was just the three of them; Claus had an overnight work commitment. Silent, they passed the cardboard containers among themselves. Flat, deflated, Bryson wasn't even sure he wanted to crack open his fortune cookie.

The small elephant in the room—where he stood with these two special women and the layers and permutations about the relationships among them—paled in the shadow of a much larger elephant, a mammoth by comparison. *Six dead Serena clones, and we killed them. How many more are out there? What the hell are we to do or even think about that?*

He saw Serena's glassy-eyed look. "Hey, did you ever play around with fortune cookies? Add some extra words at the end like 'in bed'?" As soon as he said it, he regretted the suggestion. Tarni flashed an angry glare. Serena seemed to not even hear him.

Bryson had committed to this foolish game, so he grabbed a cookie and read: "You have a bright future…IN BED…" He tried to swallow with a suddenly parched tongue. *Open mouth…insert foot. Man, am I an idiot!*

A devilish smile broke over Tarni's face, exposing her perfect teeth. "That sounds brilliant, mate. Are you making a suggestion?" She looked over at Serena and winked.

Bryson's face turned two shades darker than Tarni's lipstick. Trouble alarms and danger alerts from years of gaming sounded in his mind. He looked first at Tarni, then at Serena.

They both moved toward him and grabbed an arm.

Serena had somehow stirred to life and now wore an absolutely wicked smile. She said, "What did you have in mind, Bry?" She combed her fingers through his hair.

"Yeah, geek boy." Tarni put her hand on his thigh. "What's your fancy?"

Bryson sat frozen in paralysis. Serena grabbed his other thigh. They were each only inches from either side of his face. He tried to speak but drew a blank. His mind searched in vain for a response, for a reset button to start again.

Tarni batted her eyes. Serena's tongue brushed over her lips. They watched as he squirmed.

"Er…" he stammered. "Ah…" Finally, he managed, "I…I think I need some more tea." He tried to rise, but they held him seated, each with one hand firmly on an inner thigh.

They burst out laughing and released him.

"Just messing with you, mate! You should see the look on your face."

"You are such an ass, Snowman."

The two women gave him simultaneous pecks on the cheeks and then high-fived each other. When they finally stopped laughing, Bryson's face had dropped to a shade that now resembled Tarni's former pink hair color.

"It's tough, but we both love you." Serena shrugged.

"So, we have to share you. Are you okay with that, bloke?"

"Something about your boyish nerdism attracts us. So, don't mess with either me or Tarni, Bry, and consider yourself lucky."

"Like hitting the lottery lucky, tin-arsed as we say in Oz."

He turned from one to the other. Bryson had no intentions of trying to mess this up. When speech finally returned, they all sipped tea. "You are both awesome. I don't know what to say. I don't have a clue how I lucked out so well or how any of this might work." He put down his cup. "As for tonight, I was thinking maybe I should sleep—" They both jumped up. One of their hands covered his mouth. They pointed to the couch and said together, "For the foreseeable future, you best get comfy with the sofa."

61

This is dicey! Not sure how to handle this one. Tarni stared at her tablet. BB was resting in the back living-section. The message exchange with Dr. Li left her with few options.

Li: *Does Dr. Brindabella ever leave his laboratory area?*

Tarni: *Rarely. I don't know his schedule.*

Li: *Find his schedule, Ms. Gillam. I want times and dates.*

She took a deep breath before typing a brief response.

Tarni: *Yes, sir. I'll see what I can find out.*

Li: *Good. Just a reminder for you: At Advanced Bionics, failure is not an option.*

She shuddered. *I don't like this. I don't like this one bit.*

Tarni went to the back. "BB, I need to talk to you about something."

But the senior scientist lay on his side, sleeping with his back facing her. She shook him. "BB, sorry to disturb you, but I really need to discuss something with you. It's important."

Still no response. She rolled him to his back and saw the urine stain. *Shit! He seized again…*

"I don't know, and I'm fresh out of ideas."

"C'mon, Bry. There's got to be something you're missing. Something we're all missing." Serena looked at Bryson and Tarni. The three of them sat, sharing a pizza.

Bryson turned to Tarni. "You got any ideas? Candelaria, rainbow necklace, Illuminati, Twins, Eye of Thoth, Druids, somewhere in the North, seven seals, Isis, War of the Two Serpents, Atlantis—we're trying to make connections. Did I miss any keywords, PTG?"

"Emerald Tablets, that's a biggie."

"Yeah, that too. Do you see any connections, Tarni?"

"Sorry, like I told you before, the only thing that comes to mind is Rainbow Serpent. That's all tied into our Aboriginal creation mythology. I know you mates are familiar with that." She pushed back her plate and sipped red wine. "Then again, there's the Rainbow Bridge."

Serena and Bryson looked back with blank expressions.

"You mean you never heard of the Rainbow Bridge? To Asgard? That's the heavenly realm in Norse mythology. And, come to think of it, Scandinavia is pretty far north."

The two continued to stare blankly at Tarni. Bryson shrugged. "I guess not. I mean, sure I've heard of Norse mythology, but not the Rainbow Bridge."

"THOR! GOD OF THUNDER! You mean you've never seen the movies starring Thor? The actor is Australian." She placed her hand over her breast and looked at Serena. "He is the epitome of buff—total spunk, girlfriend. What I wouldn't give to be his sleeping partner." She turned to Bryson. "No offense to you, mate. Brawn over brains has something going for it. That man is a god! Movie night. That's it, I need some binge TV time. I'll make the popcorn."

Serena chimed in. "I'm game. We could all use some mindless entertainment. But first, can you help me with that little favor?"

"Absolutely!" Tarni turned to Bryson. "Your turn to clean up. We've got girlie things to attend to."

As the two exited, Bryson cleaned the table then attacked his tablet. He started a crash course in Norse mythology, beginning with the Rainbow Bridge. An image of the major gods had his neurons firing. Laughter and giggles drifted from across the house.

"Hey, I think I found something." The sound of running water obscured his voice. He shouted. "I think I've got something here." He stared at the picture of Odin, also called Wodin, the chief god in their pantheon. Thor was his son. Odin wore an eye patch. Just as he began to dig further into Odin's eyes, the women returned.

"Well, what do you think?" Tarni rubbed her hand over Serena's totally bald head.

Her appearance left Bryson speechless. He remembered the photos from India when Serena had shaved her head, but in person... He sat breathless.

"It needed to go. It's a reminder, Bry—a reminder to stay true to the light. No more dead babies." She pirouetted. "So, what do you think?"

"It's way sexy, PTG. Oops...can't say that anymore. It looks great, girlfriend. You look hot, in a Buddha babe sort of way."

"I agree with you, mate. The shaved head makes her look even more spunk." Tarni bent over and kissed Serena's bald head.

The lipstick she left behind, their giggles, and lighthearted mood had Bryson push his tablet aside. Odin would have to wait. "Let's watch the movie."

Two bowls of popcorn and one bottle of wine later, they were ready for the second Thor movie. Bryson asked casually, "Anyone hear from Claus? I'm surprised he's not back. I'm going to shoot him a text."

As Tarni left to hunt down more snacks, Bryson followed up by trying to call Claus, but there was no response to text or call.

Serena said, "I'm sure he's fine."

62

Peter Reynolds had always been an early riser. As he spooned cereal, he reviewed his news feed.

Now New Orleans too! Where next? The whole world is turning into a shit-storm. His personal phone chimed, and he glanced at the time. *6:10 a.m. Who would call me now?* He looked at the caller ID, put his spoon down, and took a deep breath.

"Dr. Li, how are things in Singapore?"

"I'm sure you read the news, Peter. As you can tell, things are going well."

"Are you wondering about my trip to Nepal? Damiaan Van Duyn had to change our plans given some of the turmoil following the bombing in New York."

"Yes, I am aware of that; I am looking forward to your visit. But that is not the reason for my call."

Peter swallowed hard and waited.

"Will you never stop being a nuisance to me, Peter?"

"I'm sorry, Kenseiko, but I don't know what you are talking about."

"Your nephew Bryson, do you ever hear from him?"

"No, we don't keep in touch. I heard he returned from Peru; so, he's not dead."

"Did you know he drives a car owned by a Reynolds company?"

"I guess it's possible. We have lots of leased vehicles. I don't micromanage those things. Do you want me to investigate it? Surely that's not why you're calling at this hour."

"I don't sense impatience on your end, do I, Peter? That would be most disrespectful. I have questions for your nephew Bryson, and I'm looking for the girl he went to Peru with—Serena Mendez. You remember her, Peter, don't you? You haven't seen her either, I presume. Do you think they know what happened to my nephew Gensu?"

"We've been over this, Dr. Li. I don't have any new information. Is that it? I'm getting myself ready for work and have an important meeting."

"We'll finish speaking when I tell you, Peter. Your Pindar does not tolerate insolence."

"Sorry, Dr. Li. I meant no disrespect. Is there anything else?" *Exalted one.* Peter hoped this thought did not come through in his response.

"Good. That's better. You have an employee named Charles Godfried; he has come to my attention."

Shit! "Godfried? Yes. Good man. He works in security at Baxter. That's one of our companies here in Chicago actually."

"Good. That's the right answer."

"Why do you ask? How is he causing trouble? Do you want me to fire him?"

"Oh no, Peter, not at all. I want him to accompany you on your trip to Nepal. I have some things I want to question him about personally."

Peter thought, *Not good. Claus is on his radar. Not good at all!* "Okay, I'll make sure it happens. He works security, so it shouldn't be a problem to ask him to come along. Do you want me to tell him you're eager to speak with him?"

"Peter, Peter, Peter... You will tell him to accompany you and nothing more. Just as I am telling you to come soon and make sure he is with you. Stay in the light, Peter. Stay in the light."

"Same to you, Dr. Li. Be in the light."

As soon as the call ended, Peter dialed Claus. No answer. *Bad...very bad! Claus, what have you gotten yourself into?*

He still had his nightclothes on. BB worked through the early morning hours. Tarni would be at the lab soon, and he needed to get himself cleaned up and looking presentable. *I should probably eat something even though I am not at all hungry.* For a moment, he looked down at his once tall and fit body. With his spindly arms hanging through the robe's sleeves, BB resembled the Grim Reaper.

He held up the vial and inserted the needle to draw up one cc into a syringe. It wasn't ideal. With more time, he could have refined it further, but this would have to do. He swabbed his upper arm over a sagging deltoid muscle. The alcohol prep wasn't needed. *Rather superfluous*, he thought as he pinched the muscle and injected himself.

A circular Band-Aid covered the site. Before heading off to dress and eat, he entered details into his personal log. *When the time comes, Tarni will have all my notes, so she'll understand. She'll know what to do if this doesn't work.* His lips drew back, and a wistful smile broke over his enormous teeth. *It's been a good run.*

Now, time to eat.

63

"It's all right here, Serena." She came and looked over Bryson's shoulder. He pointed at a desktop monitor. Tarni had left for the lab. Midmorning and still no word from Claus.

"I see it. Fits like a glove. Wodin introduced letters and writing as a way to share knowledge with the people, an introduction of higher civilization and learning. Same as Thoth."

"It's even clearer than that, Serena. There's research claiming Thoth and Wodin are the same person, or god, or demigod."

"Doesn't surprise me. Hermes and Quetzalcoatl are other Thoth personages, so why not Wodin too? Or Odin; it's hard to keep track of all the names, but at least we know they're the same." She continued. "The Rainbow Bridge connects this earthly plane to a higher realm, Asgard, a place where celestials dwell."

"It's that whole spirit-matter continuum, as above so below, man has a place here on earth and in heaven. I don't think I need to go on; the parallels and connections are all over the place."

"So, if we're right, we just need to track down the Eye of Thoth and connect it to Wodin's eye, and maybe that's where we need to look for the Twins."

"Working on that piece right—"

The door slammed.

"Holy fuck! We all got to leave." Claus stormed in.

Bryson could see he didn't look the least bit happy. He appeared grubby, fatigued, and ready to hit something.

"Claus! Glad you're okay, man. Where you been? Did you get our messages?"

"No!" They followed him into his bedroom. He nearly tore the closet door off its hinges and grabbed a suitcase. "Fuckers took my cell phone."

"Whoa, slow down, man. What's going on? First thing you need to do is slow down and tell us what happened."

"Chicago PD. They are real assholes and are permanently on my shit list. Along with an asshole judge, bailiff, and court system. Throw my lawyer in the mix too, but he at least managed to spring me."

"You spent the night in jail?" Serena looked concerned, but as she approached Claus, he smiled.

"Who's the cute bald girl? It looks good on you. Yeah, I been in the slammer. I'm calming down. I need something to eat."

"How about left-over pizza?" Bryson headed for the refrigerator. "Something to drink?"

"Bourbon. I'll help myself. Get me a glass…a big one."

After eating all the leftover pizza and the remaining lo mein, along with a double bourbon and coffee chaser, Claus recounted his missing day and night. He had showed up to work; everything seemed to go normal until a couple of cops from Chicago PD came by, arrested him, and led him off in handcuffs. Some anonymous tipster had called in Charles Godfried as a suspect in a recent armed burglary and heist.

"That's the name I use at work, my cover ID. Now that's blown. They got mug shots, fingerprints, the works."

"No worries, Claus, I'm sure I can break into their system and expunge the records."

"Thanks, Bryson, but the fingerprints get into the federal system, and I'm sure they can match me to military records."

Bryson smiled. "Like I said, nothing to worry about."

Serena redirected them. "Who did this? Who filed the fake anonymous tip that caused this?"

"First thought I came up with is my ex. But even this fiasco seemed beyond her. Besides, she doesn't know my cover name. Anyway, I called her from the courthouse after they released me. I used my lawyer's phone. Wasn't her. I was scratching my head about the whole thing and figured I best call Mr. Reynolds. I know the boss wouldn't think twice about it being a setup."

He was back in the bedroom, packing select items. He hauled out another suitcase. "That's when he told me about his call from Li early this morning. Somehow that bastard is onto Charles Godfried; wants my ass along on the boss's trip to Nepal. That ain't happening." Claus reached into a gun case and withdrew two firearms and boxes of ammunition.

"Wait a minute, wait a minute. You're saying Li knows about you? How? Where do you plan to go?" Alarm cracked Bryson's voice. He poured himself a bourbon.

"Michigan, Upper Peninsula. I've got a hunting cabin up there. It's off grid, private well, so I don't have to worry about the Hendra virus; I can last a long time." He gulped then swirled the ice in his glass. "You need a plan too. I think Tarni will be all right. Li's looking for us. All three of us, according to the boss. It's not safe to stay here. Besides, haven't you heard the news?"

Bryson and Serena looked at each other. She said, "No. Did we miss something?"

"Hendra virus hit a family in New Orleans. Just one family. The whole city's in a panic. Run on food and water. National Guard called. The city's a mess, complete chaos."

Bryson flipped on a news station; as he and Serena watched, Claus continued to pack.

"That's the playbook, kids. You better stockpile food and water. And guns too. This is just a trial run in New Orleans. Look at it." He pointed to the TV screen. Smashed storefronts, burning cars, people running with bottles of water, police in riot gear, tear gas—the images weren't pretty. "That's where it's headed. Trust me, things can get very bad, very fast."

"What about these false charges; aren't you going to need to go to court or something?" Serena asked. She looked bewildered.

"Fuck that! That's what I pay my lawyer to handle."

64

S erena felt the pressure in her ears as the jet made its descent into Reykjavík. Refueling in Iceland only required an hour and a half before they'd be flying again en route to Copenhagen.

The last three days were hectic to say the least. Claus had melted off to somewhere in Michigan. His cabin there had a setup similar to the hogan. He would continue going through the materials confiscated during the raid and would keep in close contact. Tarni remained at Claus's house and continued her work with BB. Saying goodbye to her, even for the short term, was hard for both she and Bryson. Very quickly, Tarni had become the best friend and big sister Serena never had.

She's even more than that to me. That girl loves life and herself. Must be something about their cultural upbringing. I've got a lot to learn on both counts. She renewed her vow to return to Australia someday, to find Djalu and go on a walkabout with him in the bush. She wondered how that country was handling their crisis—cyberattacks on the electric grid, power stations, and communication networks had thrown the entire nation into disarray. Once again, the United Coalition for World Justice had been fingered for terrorism. She knew better.

"Hey, Bry, do you think we're going about this all wrong?"

He looked up from his tablet, where he poured over an encyclopedic number of downloaded files about Norse mythology, Vikings, Druids in Scandinavia, and anything else that seemed relevant.

He put the tablet down. "Sorry, Serena, what was that you asked? You think we're going about this wrong?"

"At the heart of the problem is misinformation, propaganda, lies, falsehoods, the works."

"I agree."

"Exposing the truth shouldn't be too hard using the World Wide Web. All the stuff Claus is uncovering about the secret base, government connections, everything we know about the plans for a New World Order—that's just the tip of the iceberg. Why can't we get it all out to the public? Why can't we do a massive data dump into the public domain with all the information we've learned? Get the truth out in a series of revelations about the Illuminati plot."

"It seems to me people have been trying to do just that, but it's all on the fringe. If the people in charge want to suppress information, and it's clear they don't want the truth out, it's easy for them to suppress whatever they don't want out there."

"Maybe we need to try harder. People want answers to what's going on in the world. If the only ones giving those answers are the people pulling all the strings, the general public will just continue to be fed lies."

Bryson responded, "Look at Moon and her organization, Pyramid Communications. They're alternative media and do a great job exposing the lies, but what impact do they have? Practically none."

"I'm talking something much more potent. Can't you do something with cyber-warfare to fight back? After all, you're a cybersecurity genius; isn't there something you can do?"

Bryson stroked his chin. Serena could see the gears turning in his mind.

"Hackers. If we can engage the worldwide hacker community, if we can convince them of the threat and the truth, we could potentially mount a coordinated effort." He picked up his tablet. "Let's think about that some more, but let me share a couple of things first."

"Find something?"

"Not really. You remember all the stuff about the Tree of Life located at Yggdrasil?"

"Yeah, that's where Wodin drank some magic water to gain wisdom, gave up his eye, or something along those lines. Did you find the location?"

"I wish. Haven't come up with that, but there is a sacred tree at a place called the Temple at Uppsala. Problem is, that's in Sweden. Remember the Foteviken Viking Museum, that was our second choice; it's in Sweden."

"If Frederikssund Viking Village in Copenhagen doesn't give us any leads, we can make Sweden our second stop, then Norway to the museums there. We *will* find that Emerald Tablet, Bry."

Serena's resolute determination and the power in her words left no doubt in Bryson's mind. "I believe we will, Serena, but I wish we had a better plan than just show up and start asking questions."

"What about the pilot? Can we redirect him to Stockholm? What good is chartering your own private jet if you can't tell the pilot what to do?"

"Doubt it. I'll ask, but if we change our flight plan, it will probably trigger all sorts of extra scrutiny when we land."

They talked it over and decided to stick with the original plan. With all the fears about terrorism and spread of infectious diseases, air travel had become difficult; best to avoid unnecessary questions. Serena traveled again as Alice Mars, a Reynolds' company employee out on sick leave. She wore her blue contacts and sported a faux wedding band to complete the deception.

They had a brilliant cover story. Tarni had suggested it. With her bald head, Serena, aka Alice, posed as a cancer victim traveling to an alternative health clinic in Denmark for experimental treatment. They even had packed a wheelchair and portable oxygen to look more convincing. Nothing about them should trigger any alerts from Interpol or other authorities. Just in case they needed a backup, Bryson carried the ID for Alice Mars as a Diplomatic Security Operations Assistant issued by the State Department, the same one they used in Libya. With all the necessary background checking to get that ID, customs officials in Denmark, Sweden, or Norway should be satisfied.

Serena leaned against Bryson's side, and she felt his arm drape comfortably around her. "I think we should both get some rest."

65

From many observations of her bàba, she noticed that when he was displeased his voice grew soft; now, he whispered, and she listened. Even his face looked different, as though he forced the muscles not to display emotion. She saw bàba's facial tension over the video connection.

"You should not have filed that anonymous report. Your actions have put my plans at risk."

Wán shàn remained unmoved by his criticism. This was not stoicism so much as an inability to experience shame. "I took the initiative to obtain photographs from the police records. I now have additional information to help me both to locate Charles Godfried and to determine what his relationships are with

Bryson Reynolds and Serena Mendez." She wasn't making excuses; she stated her rationale, in case her bàba failed to see the value and logic in her approach.

"Now you have jeopardized my chance to interrogate Mr. Godfried."

"Had you communicated your intention to have Peter Reynolds bring this employee to Nepal for questioning, I would have pursued a different course of action." Wán shàn looked at the face in the computer screen, noting her bàba's clenched teeth.

The voice volume suddenly raised. "I do not report to you, Wán shàn! You report to me, and you best remember that!"

Have I done something wrong? She remained composed as he continued to berate her. He expressed disappointment that both Bryson Reynolds and Serena Mendez had once again eluded her, eluded him. Finally, she nodded her understanding. "It shall not happen again, bàba."

This response seemed to placate him, and he turned to other plans. She was to remain in the United States. Beangagarrie Brindabella needed to be eliminated. Her bàba awaited a report from Dr. Brindabella's assistant for details; once the research geneticist left the lab premises, Wán shàn would intercept. A corporate jet and all the needed documents were being readied; it would fly to Chicago. Once it landed, she needed to coordinate with the two soldiers her bàba was sending along. They would assist with capture and transport to Singapore.

He gave her command codes as a failsafe, should anything go amiss with the soldiers.

"They will be under your authority and should obey without hesitation. Do you have any questions?"

"No, bàba, your instructions are clear."

"Good, Wán shàn. Do not fail me, daughter."

The boutique hotel they stayed at had a warm ambiance and distinct charm with Danish *hygge* on full display. As the hostess at the front desk explained, the word had no direct English translation. "Think of *hygge* as a warm, fuzzy, and cozy feeling, the kind you get when sipping hot cocoa in front of a fire. This is what we strive to provide for our guests." She smiled and handed over their room key.

Still, reminders of world events surrounded them. Signs assured patrons that all water was bottled, all food had been thoroughly inspected and was free of contamination; safety of guests was paramount.

As they unpacked, Serena commented on the underlying fear the hotel signs attempted to counteract. "Reminding guests of so many threats detracts a bit from that coziness the hostess talked about."

"You're right, Serena. I will say, Denmark looks like a wonderful place to visit. I bet in the warm season, it's even nicer." Bryson looked out a window to dreary, cold, and brown.

This was not the tourist season, but everything going on in the world had all but killed tourism. The hotel and connected restaurant were nearly empty. They received superb service and attention and enjoyed a delicious meal.

Earlier, with Serena in a wheelchair and oxygen tubing dangling from her nose to her chest, they had made it through customs. The agent asked questions and only passed them through after they showed him an email confirming her clinic appointment. He softened and wished her success and a healthy outcome. Once at the hotel, she had dropped the ruse. They canceled the appointment.

Back in the room, Bryson faced Serena and held her by the shoulders. "For the rest of today, I'm hoping we can just chill. Tomorrow we can start the quest for answers. We will get this done, Serena. The two of us are an unstoppable force."

That night, she did her Merkaba meditation, and the whole room illuminated. As Bryson felt her nestled against him, she said, "Whatever happens, Bry, I'm glad you're here with me."

Spending time at an authentic recreation of a Viking Village is a fun way to spend a day. They weren't there for fun. Bryson and Serena pretended to be on a genealogy vacation where he wanted to learn about his distant Danish ancestors. The actors and actresses at Frederikssund Viking Village were more than happy to oblige this couple from the States. Few other visitors competed with the many questions they asked the villagers.

While they learned many details about how Vikings lived in the Iron Age, the important answers they sought, details about where the Tree of Life could be found or where Odin sacrificed his eye, remained unknown.

In the longhouse, the Loremaster gave a most colorful account. "The eternal tree of ash, Yggdrasil, has roots and branches connecting all the nine realms. It is the axis of the entire universe. Odin lives in Asgard, where the first root connects. In Jötunheimr, where the second root stretches, there dwells a race of giants; there lives Mimir, Norse god of Wisdom. He guards Mímisbrunnr, a sacred well. In exchange for a drink of water from Mimir's well, Odin sacrificed his own eye. Thus, he could bring wisdom and understanding to the realm of Asgard. Some say Odin grabbed runes, the first writing, from within the waters. Some say the rune magic gave Odin knowledge of Ragnarök, the battle of the end of the world when all will be torn asunder." The actor shuddered at this last telling.

To Bryson's question about where the sacred tree could be found, the Loremaster shrugged. "In Midgard, the place of we mortals, the roots of Yggdrasil are hidden or long forgotten."

Serena asked about Druids. She pretended her ancestors had Druid connections. The actor knew nothing of these either.

Much of it, Bryson and Serena had already uncovered in their research. Still, it was exciting to get a firsthand account. They would have to seek answers elsewhere.

The Viking Museum Aarhus, an underground museum at Sankt Clemens Torv, was their next destination. They were the sole visitors, and staff were happy to share information. The director, an effusive middle-aged woman, knew more about Norse mythology than they could hope for. To Bryson's question about Yggdrasil's location, she had little to offer beyond what they already knew.

"What about the sacred tree at the Temple at Uppsala in Sweden?" Bryson asked.

"A wonderful site to visit but only a recreation. Though some claim the tree represented there is connected to Yggdrasil, it is not even an ash tree. If you wish to find where Wodin sacrificed his eye, you will not find success at Uppsala. Some scholars believe it to be at the Grove of Eridu, but that is in Iran and I think an unlikely spot."

Serena had remained silent through most of the exchange. "How about Druids? Do you know anything about connections between Druids and Scandinavians? We're on this genealogy quest. I have some ancestors who are Welsh and were supposedly Druids." She grabbed Bryson's hand. "Just wondering how our kids might turn out."

"I don't, but we used to have a member of our staff who had extensive knowledge regarding the history and myths about dragons in Viking culture, why they were carved into the prow of the longships, all sorts of things. He called himself a bard, which he claimed was a type of Druid. He's a musician by trade, performs annually at the big festival in Roskilde. I can ring him and see if he's available to meet with you." She smiled.

66

CNN Update on Brazil:

Worse than a plague of locusts! That's how officials describe the deadly virus infecting both soy and corn, somehow put at risk due to genetically modified seed stock. The lack of biodiversity in these food crops and their importance in providing feed for livestock was the final tipping point, triggering an economic and social melt-down in this once prosperous nation. Brazil has effectively been quarantined from the rest of the world. Animals are being slaughtered as food supplies dwindle while Brazil's economy, the seventh largest in the world, has essentially collapsed. Mandatory food rationing has been instituted under martial law.

Hyperinflation has led to riots and armed conflict. All travel in and out of Brazil and neighboring countries has been banned by several nations, fearful their own food crops might somehow become infected. Is this the first domino? With the demise of the United Nations and individual countries favoring protectionism over solving the multitude of global crises, armed conflict and chaos have become the new world order in many parts of the globe.

67

B ryson looked at the museum director's card. On the back she wrote: "Skol Kaffebar, Arnbjørn Gnadir."

"It's about a half kilometer. Right on the main street. Very popular. You should make sure to have their lemon sponge butter croissant." She gestured to her somewhat overweight frame. "I may have had a few too many." Her infectious laugh infused them with anticipation.

"But how will we know this musician?" Serena asked.

The woman smiled. "Trust me, you will know."

They thanked her and left. Upon learning their impromptu meeting would be at a Danish coffee house, Serena salivated, eager for the experience. In the coffee aficionado part of her mind, a Danish café stood at the apex; they were legendary. Even Bryson, with his long stride, could hardly keep up with her. "Hurry, Bry. Coffee! I can't wait."

The shop buzzed with life. She took a deep breath, inhaling the intoxicating aromas. They scanned the café. "I don't see anyone—" she stopped midsentence as the door opened to musical bells hanging across the jamb. She turned to Bryson. "No doubt."

They approached a man, about five foot four, a bit stocky with a scruffy beard. He looked mid-to-late thirties; smile crinkles accentuated his brown eyes. Long, haphazard brown curls grazed his shoulders. Strapped over his back, she noted a musical instrument—smaller than a guitar, larger than a ukulele. She counted eight tuning knobs.

"Arnbjørn?" Bryson extended his hand.

"In the flesh." Merry creases erupted on his face. "Please, call me Arnie. Too many consonants in my name. You must be Bryson." The two shook hands.

Arnbjørn turned. For a fraction of a moment, Serena caught something strange. She blinked and grabbed his extended hand.

"You are Serena; that is a beautiful name. I think I should compose a song about you. Welcome to Denmark."

She blushed. "What is the instrument strapped to your back?"

"It looks like a mandolin. Is that right?" Bryson asked.

"Correct." He unslung his instrument and strummed. "A bard should be ready to perform anytime, anywhere. I prefer one of my dulcimers or lutes, but they do not like to be out in the cold. Now, Maggy"—he caressed the wooden neck—"she is my best companion. Goes with me wherever I travel."

As the barista prepared their order, they found a small table toward the back.

"A genealogy search—that is rather curious. Viking and Gaelic is not unusual. The Vikings ransacked along the coast and even inland to what is now England, Scotland, and Wales. Often they sailed away with the most beautiful women in the villages they plundered." He looked at them both; his eyes were very piercing.

"You could be Scandinavian, Bryson. But I see nothing Celtic in you, Serena." He laughed. "Genes can be funny. Look at me. My first name is Old Norse, it means eagle-bear. And my last name is Gaelic, it means snake. When you mix them all together, this is what you get."

His belly laugh halted abruptly when Serena commented, "You must be a skin-changer." She surprised herself when she suddenly blurted that out. She saw him shimmer, but just a moment. "I had a great aunt that some people thought was a skin-changer. They called her *tl'iishtsoh*. It means dragon woman or serpent worshiper. It's Navajo."

Arnbjørn said, "So, you are not Welsh as you claim." His whole demeanor suddenly changed. He whispered something.

For a moment, his appearance flickered. He looked much older with gray hair and beard. *Did I imagine that? Focus!* The two studied one another. Bryson and the café faded from her awareness.

He spoke quietly. "Who are you?"

"What did you just whisper? I saw you change. You are not as you appear."

"That was a protection spell. Now, I ask you again, who are you really? And why are you here?"

"Yes!" Claus watched the pattern of lights dancing across the optical display embedded into the goggles. He shut his eyes, put the apparatus over his head, and heard a series of commands oscillating from his left to his right ear.

He entered a series of keystrokes and grinned when both the lights and audio changed.

He said out loud to himself, "That encryption was a bitch. Now that I unlocked it, I see how the whole thing works. At least on the outside." He tore the headpiece off. "Don't know what it does on the inside, but no sense taking any chances."

For the last three days, he had been working to decipher the encryption. He also did a deep dive into optogenics. This equipment apparently didn't require direct neural implants to deliver the light stimulus. If he had this figured out correctly, the light signal impulses paired with the differential audio feed to stimulate neural networks that triggered specific behaviors. As opposed to hypnosis and hypnotic suggestion, this system hardwired the whole shebang into the recipient's brain.

Feeling proud of himself for getting things to work, he found a bottle of bourbon. *Bryson is going to be impressed. This is some serious high-tech shit.* He swirled the ice and gazed at the apparatus. *If it's intended for programming people, that makes it some pretty seriously messed-up, high-tech shit.*

Bryson broke the stalemate. He motioned to Serena to let him handle this; he thought she might be preparing some fire words, and he didn't want things to get out of control.

"Okay, Arnie, it seems we've all been guilty of some deception. Before we come clean, I have just one question."

"I'm listening, Bryson. Go on."

"I knew there was something familiar to your last name, Gnadir. I've got a photographic memory, and I've been reading a lot about Druids. It just took me a while to find the memory file. You said your last name meant snake. Technically yes, but more accurately, it means serpent; even more accurately, it means serpent priest. So, my question for you is, which serpent do you serve?"

"A fair question. To reveal my cards first puts me at a disadvantage, but I do not sense a threat in you, Bryson. As for Serena, if these are your real names, she is complicated. Shadows and light surround her. She has serpent blood in her, or I'm an old fool… I am aligned with the Great White Brotherhood. The true one as taught in ancient Egypt by Thoth himself; not the corruption that has enslaved humanity."

Serena said, "Then I embrace you as my Brother." She silently activated her Merkaba, just enough so he could see her glow.

"A true light bearer... What is your lineage, Sister?"

"Candelaria."

"We thought your flame extinguished."

Bryson cut in. "No, believe me, the flame is still in her."

"Interesting, so why are you here in this frozen land? You are far from home."

An exchange proceeded. Arnie went first; he knew all about the War of the Two Serpents and their common enemy, the Illuminati. As they shared stories, Bryson nibbled on a lemon croissant, happy for the museum director's recommendation. Serena sipped her third coffee. Bryson and Serena had already pieced together much of what Arnbjørn related. Other things they had not.

"In Druid teachings, the nidhogg serpent, interesting that this is actually an old Norse word, is the creature that eats at the roots of Yggdrasil, the Tree of Life. This nidhogg serpent is said to devour the ancient knowledge and wisdom of the Druids."

Bryson said, "Yes, we have been doing a lot of research on Yggdrasil; we're trying to learn its location."

"Submerged...along with the rest of Atlantis, or so it is taught. It is all connected, a great web of life. Some say the wisdom resides in each and every one of us, or so the Gnostics taught."

"Wait a minute, are you saying the Druids were Gnostics?" Serena had already told Bryson her suspicions about this possible link.

Arnie confirmed it. "Of course. We all are shoots from the same tree; that tree was rooted in Atlantis."

Serena looked at Bryson. He saw the pained look on her face.

Bryson spoke for them both. "That's not the answer we were hoping for."

"What is the question you seek to answer?"

"We're searching for a place. It's hidden and holds an Emerald Tablet of Thoth."

"Go on, I'm listening." Bryson noted Arnbjørn's shallow breaths.

Serena reached below her shirt. "I have this Candelaria necklace, also called a rainbow necklace."

As she dangled it, Arnbjørn jumped up. "Where did you get that? That belongs to us. It was stolen centuries ago."

"No, it wasn't," Bryson said calmly. "Her great aunt, the Navajo shaman, gave that to Serena. Long story. We learned there are more than one of these."

"True." He sat down. "There are others. In our texts, Thoth fashioned one for the Mayans and another for the Hopi. Only five in total were crafted. I am sorry. I did not mean to accuse."

"Apology accepted." Serena slipped the necklace back beneath her clothes.

"The necklace itself does not give access. You must know the incantation, and you must be trained in the arcane mysteries of manipulating esoteric energies."

"Like you?" She smiled.

Bryson did not expect the belly laugh that burst forth.

"Hardly. I have some ability with illusion and some with my voice. I can use music and song to enchant a crowd." He plucked his mandolin. "It is not so very different from the Pied Piper—hypnotic in a way. He was a great bard. The ovates are the Druid scholar-priests; with the right speaking, they could call out the energy in the necklace."

"But I do have the power. It's my Candelaria gift; Isis herself opened my voice." She pulled out the necklace again and began her singing chant. It flashed first red, then orange. She stopped before the candle blazed in white.

After the musician's eyes bulged, after he began breathing again, after he regained his ability to speak, he looked at Serena. Bryson saw the astonishment in his face.

"Sister, I must bring you to the tree."

That was it. They asked him where the tree was, but he only gave them the general location as near Roskilde. He would meet them at their hotel at nine the following morning. He refused to reveal anything further, but he gave them his card and contact information.

Serena protested. "But why can't we go now? It's not even three o'clock yet. Why wait until tomorrow?"

"You forget, Candelaria; this is Denmark. It's February; by the time we get there, it will be dark." His voice grew low. "Tell no one about your necklace and show it to no one." Their eyes locked. "No one!"

As the bard sauntered off, they watched his mandolin grow smaller and smaller.

Serena reached for her companion's hand. "Do you trust him, Bry?"

"Do we have a choice?"

68

Subconscious playing tricks on me. Bryson couldn't get the dream out of his head. It must have been Arnie's story about the nidhogg serpent eating at the roots of the Tree of Life. But in his dream, and it was still so vivid in his mind, the huge snake slithering among this grand tree's roots had the head of Kenseiko Li. It didn't devour the roots; instead, the snake's bite systematically injected poisonous venom, and Bryson saw the tree begin to wither and die. All the while, Arnie's chord progression from his mandolin tune thrummed in Bryson's brain.

Funny how his story and music got inside my head like that. As he rolled over and saw Serena peacefully sleeping, the last vestiges of her Merkaba light slowly fading, he realized his right brain was trying to tell his left brain something important. He knew creative intuition worked through dreams and the subconscious. His eyes grew heavy. Serena had said something important the other day. What was it? He began to doze. He fell back into a dream state.

The nidhogg serpent with Li's head nibbled at Yggdrasil's roots. Bryson stood alone with a watering can and a machete. One hand watered the tree while the other began hacking at the snake's body. He woke wide-eyed, jumping from bed. Bingo! His left brain just got the message.

Fertilizer! All this time we've been thinking about how to destroy the snake, how to combat the people attacking and killing knowledge, wisdom, and truth by promoting lies and falsehoods and poisoning people's minds with fear. There's another way to work this. Hackers! Serena mentioned it on the plane ride over.

Bryson entered his password to access the dark web, where hackers operated in the shadows. He had files from the raid; they were truthful and factual but could be discredited. He had statements of truth that he could assert along with some evidence. He could act preemptively. While he didn't have a lot of proof, at least not yet, he could get the word out. *Time to sprinkle some fertilizer and strengthen the tree at its roots.*

Group message: *PROOF OF DISINFORMATION CAMPAIGN—See attached files about the raid on Dulce, New Mexico. Alien DNA discovered. US Military working together with plans to release genetically altered humans.*

Cull of humanity in operation as part of Illuminati effort to establish New World Order. Dr. Kenseiko Li at Advanced Bionics in Singapore is one of the masterminds.

United Coalition for World Justice is a front for the Illuminati.

More releases to follow. Spread the word.

He signed off with his hacker moniker: Zeldarz.

After routing the message through a series of ghost IP addresses, he got back in bed and reflected. Message received; message delivered. His left and right brain slept harmoniously.

The Arnbjørn who swung by the hotel had thinned, silvery hair and a somewhat bushier gray beard. He showed the same laugh lines, only the folds and creases cut much deeper into his face. Yesterday's unexpected turn of events propelled his stride with youthful vigor.

"Yeah, this is the real me, unmasked. I'm conserving my strength. Most think Arnbjørn senior and Arnie are father and son, but there's no sense in wasting energy on an illusion today."

He passed on their offer of a scone, claiming the need to watch his weight at his age. He saw their quizzical looks, no doubt trying to guess how old that might be. He grunted. "Mid-seventies in case you were wonderin'."

Roskilde wasn't a long drive. He told them all about the music festival, invited them to come as his guests, even stay at his house if they didn't mind being cramped. As Serena filled in more details about what led to their journey to Denmark, he stopped her. He knew all about the two Twins being separated.

"When you were in the Canary Islands, at the Güímar Pyramids, you must have visited the museum. Didn't you find it odd that Thor Heyerdahl founded the museum? The pyramid restoration project had everything to do with boosting the etheric energy to Asthemirus. Since the destruction of Atlantis, her energy has been severely weakened. Her brother, Asthenefus—if all goes well, you will meet him today—gave instruction to our ovates centuries ago on precisely how to rebuild. Unfortunately, Thor passed before the project could be completed."

Apparently, Bryson had failed to piece together this clue. He asked, "Are you saying Thor Heyerdahl was a Druid?"

"His parents were, from both ends of the globe. His father was Norwegian and his mother Vietnamese. The Pheryllt bloodlines trace all the way back to Atlantis. Did you know Druid is a Sanskrit word? It means 'steeped in knowledge.' Pheryllt were in both the Near and Far East, well before they went to Wales. They are the wisdom keepers. I knew Thor, a good man. Had a healthy dose of wanderlust. That's why his parents sent him searching around the globe, looking for a rainbow key so we could regain access to both tablets. We've been locked out for over four hundred years." He chuckled. "Now, a key waltzes in from nowhere. Funny how that happens."

The car stopped. "We walk the rest of the way." He looked around. Nothing but snow and brown fields surrounded them. A weak sun shone through overcast. "I put extra snowshoes in the trunk, but I don't think we'll need them." He grabbed a couple of thermoses.

"I hope you've got some hot coffee in one of those." Serena pulled her hood tightly over her bald head and put on warm gloves.

"Trust me, lassie, what's in these is better than coffee." He shouldered his mandolin and a small pack. "Let's go."

"Behold, Mysselhøj." Arnbjørn pointed to a rather ordinary-looking tree atop a small hill. "That's the tree. She sits on a grave mound. Bronze Age... very old."

Serena looked at Bryson, who shrugged. She exclaimed, "I imagined something much more elaborate. Who's buried there?"

"The genius is that it looks so plain. It's never been excavated. I don't even know if any old bones lie beneath, but that's where they took the tablet. It's somewhere down below."

The three of them approached the tree. It sat near the top of the mound, which only had a light dusting of snow. Ice crusted over many of the bare branches. Serena removed a glove and placed her hand against the tree. On the surface, the rough bark seemed ordinary, but she could feel an energy. Pressed against the cold bark, her shortened pinky ached and throbbed. She focused her mind and cleared her thoughts. She connected through from roots to branches; the tree itself glittered with pulsations of energy.

The musician placed his hand next to Serena's. He muttered, "Aye, Mysselhøj... I've not seen her light up like that in a long, long time." Even Bryson must have sensed something because he simply nodded his head in agreement. The bard unslung his instrument and cleared his throat.

"How do I get in?"

"I'm just a simple musician. You're the one with the voice." He winked and began to tune the mandolin. "I'll sing a ballad with Maggý while you warm up your voice to start singing to your necklace. That's the key; you're the key."

"Speaking of warming up," Bryson said, "do you think you can heat up some rocks?" He drew his coat in and rubbed his hands together. "It's kind of cold here."

The men gathered several large rocks and piled them together. Serena spoke a fire incantation, and soon they glowed red.

Arnbjørn had stopped playing his music. Serena saw his eyebrows arch below his receding hairline. "Candelaria... Hmm, that is what I call warming up. Now bring on the heat, Serena. Bryson and I will keep guard."

She held her necklace in view for all. As Serena spoke the words, singing in the precise tones, they could all see colors shimmer and change with each word. A rainbow flashed over the entire tree. The necklace and Serena blazed white. A black hole formed around her. An instant later, she disappeared. Vanished!

Amazement continued long after the rainbow faded. The two men stood still. Other than a pile of rocks surrounded by melted snow, everything appeared perfectly normal.

Bryson broke the trance. "Have you ever seen anything like that?"

Arnbjørn shook his head. When he could finally speak again, he addressed Maggý. "Did you see that, girl? Did you see her light up and poof, disappear? Now that's old magic, girl. We'll just have to write a song about that."

69

Fox News Network–BREAKING NEWS:

In a stunning and unprecedented coup, General Bartolo Escamilla, backed by an elite military unit, has seized control of the Spanish Government. All borders have been shut down, and internet services have been suspended. General Escamilla has issued the following statement:

"The Spanish Parliament is dissolved. Spain withdraws from the European Union, and all existing treaty obligations are suspended. Martial law is declared. The military is authorized to use lethal force to control demonstrations and other individuals who do not follow curfews or issued directives."

No further information is available as there is a tight news blackout. There are unconfirmed reports of civilian deaths by military forces…

Below the surface, Serena tried to get her bearings in the cold darkness. The sudden change disoriented her, and she fought a tangle of roots. Somewhere in the distance she sensed a dim light, but there wasn't any path to get there. She clawed through a maze of roots and dirt and gradually felt herself moving downward. She saw a speck of green and worked her way toward it.

Just as the roots began to thin, they soon thickened once again. *This is madness! What is this subterranean mess? Where does it lead?*

At last, she broke through to the surface, but she had been going down. It made no sense! Still, there she found herself, back on the hill. The green speck had grown to almost Emerald Tablet-sized, but it was above her, in the tree's branches. She easily climbed and looked down. Below she saw Bryson and Arnie, they sat near the pile of rocks, sipping from mugs, laughing. She didn't know what they were laughing about.

It's a mirror world. Like those images of trees with deep roots below ground that become the tree. I'm in an upside-down world. Icy branches brushed against her face. She reached out and put her hand upon the tablet.

"Welcome, Rainbow Warrior! Long has it been since last I spoke."

She clutched the tablet. Somehow, she found herself seated at the base of Mysselhøj. Across from her sat a fully embodied young man.

"Asthenefus?"

"Yes, that is my name. Who converses with me? Your clothing is strange."

"Serena Mendez."

"A strange name as well. What year is this?"

Serena gave him the date.

"It is so difficult to judge the passing of time. So long without even my sister to converse with."

"Asthemirus? She misses you dearly. She sends her regards."

"Have they rebuilt the pyramid? It's taken longer than in Egypt, and they seemed in no rush at all."

"No, she's been but a misty voice in a hidden chamber in Güímar."

"She remains at the last vestiges of our home, the once mighty Atlantis. Here at least, I draw full energy to manifest as intended."

Serena shivered. "It is very cold here." She looked around. "This is a strange place. Nothing at all like Güímar."

"As Thoth teaches—as above, so below. Yes, it is cold." For a moment Asthenefus studied her. "Open your mind to me, Serena Mendez, so that I may learn of you, your reason to be here, and what news is in the world."

Instinctively, Serena activated her Merkaba.

"Very skilled and most impressive, but you require no protection from me. I am guardian to the tablet you hold. I need to understand what knowledge you seek and whether I myself have access to such knowledge."

Serena relaxed and felt Asthenefus in her mind.

"Candelaria," she heard him mutter, "that's a surprise. Your necklace has been hidden since the beginning."

She was freezing. "Would it be okay if I warm it up here?"

He gestured. "Do as you will. Just don't harm the tree. I am rather fond of her."

The pile of stones stood placed in the mirror image of where Bryson and Arnie had arranged them on the surface world. She saw the two of them shivering. *Strange that the rocks are present above and below, but my friends are not here in this plane of existence.* Serena warmed the stones using fire commands. They glowed.

Asthenefus spoke; he sounded surprised. "A dragon spell! I've not heard that incanted in many, many lifetimes. Who taught you this?"

Serena recounted her interactions with Mother near the Abusir Necropolis.

"In its glory, the pyramid complex there was among my favorites though I did not know this Mother, as you call her. It is evident that your path to training in the mystical arts has been highly unusual."

"I sent Asthemirus to be with Mother, but Abusir is in ruins."

Asthenefus sighed then studied her in focused concentration. Serena had no clue how long the mind reading continued. At times, Asthenefus seemed lost in distant memories.

Finally, he said, "What you seek, the seven words Isis hid upon the cloak, are the words of unbinding. The language is of the creator beings who fashioned the race of men."

Serena sensed Asthenefus to be troubled, as though he debated with himself.

"Yes, I believe that the words spoken or sung with the power of my Candelaria voice can reverse the alteration done from the corruptors, the ones who blocked man's spiritual evolution."

"The words alone, no. But paired with the correct light images, the double snakes, the DNA, as you presently refer to it, could be restored to its original form. These words are in my tablet. I am the first, the alpha, with the story of creation of this world and all that inhabit it." He sighed. "All that we ruined by our arrogance."

"With these words and images, can I undo and mend the second breaking, to allow mankind to no longer be enslaved and manipulated?"

"Is mankind ready for this? Even Thoth saw the folly in the race of man. He founded the Mystery Schools to impart ancient wisdom to those seekers of enlightenment. Sadly, they are few in number."

Serena was hardly prepared for a debate. "Is it for you or for me to judge? If the creators intended something that others have subverted, and we can restore their creation, is this not worth trying?"

He said nothing for what seemed to her to be a long time. "You are wise beyond your years, young Candelaria. I shall reveal this knowledge to you. Perhaps your sound-sight gift will enable you to match song and color. Perhaps you can bring this War of the Two Serpents to an end."

Once the heat from the stones had spent itself, Bryson's teeth chattered. Arnie offered him a cup of the concoction from the thermos—some elixir of a Danish liquor he couldn't pronounce, and a potent brew of double-roasted coffee. After a second cup, warmth bathed his bones and loosened his tongue.

He told Arnie his life story. He told him all about his father and Serena and Peru and Tarni and anything else the mysterious liquid promptly loosened from his lips.

And he listened to the bard's life story, heard and commented upon half a dozen compositions the musician performed as they waited. They left the burial mound only to relieve themselves.

When his teeth began to rattle once again, Bryson managed, "What do you think is going on there? I'm freezing my ass off!"

"I'm freezin' my arse too. Not sure, but I don't see as we've got much choice but to wait for her to return." He grabbed the second thermos. "I've been saving this till later, but I'm thinking later's already past." He handed Bryson another cupful.

70

Several of the family heads insisted on a videoconference. Kenseiko gave each Council member a turn to speak. *They are like restive children ask-*

ing for mommy or daddy to reassure them that everything is going to be okay. Pathetic! Of course, none of this appeared on his masked face. The painful lights during his earlier press conference left him uncomfortable all over. His clubfoot ached. Still, he patiently answered their questions before finally displaying the map.

A 2-D interactive world map filled their screens as he narrated. "In red, you will note the cities already destroyed." New York and Brussels lit up. "Our targets are selected to have significant geopolitical consequences as well as significant death tolls. Watch as our future projected targets are displayed." A dozen key cities scattered throughout the world lit up.

"War zones, both among and within countries, now show in yellow. The latter reflect regional conflicts." The entire Middle East, Crimea, and several pockets in different parts of the globe turned to yellow. "Here are projected conflicts we are orchestrating that will soon erupt in war." More yellow flashed.

"Next, in green, note areas experiencing significant food shortages or outright famine." Large areas of green lit the entire Indian subcontinent, parts of Africa, Brazil, and neighboring Venezuela. "Observe how this is projected to spread. Starvation will occur along a geometric progression but will stabilize and then decline as population dwindles. I point out that several areas shown in green, especially in Africa, preceded our efforts, but they have intensified as world food supplies diminish."

"We have only just begun our cyberattacks on key infrastructure. We have focused on Australia." The map showed the entire land mass of Australia in blue. "The chaos has been even greater than anticipated. Watch now as I show where we are targeting next." Multiple blue zones began to shade.

"In orange, I show you the kill zones from our Hendra virus. We have decisions to make whether to focus on isolated attacks or widespread dispersal as we did in Myanmar last monsoon season. Until we make those decisions, I shall not display any projections. However, safe and potable water, along with a host of other diseases such as cholera, will be incorporated into the cull depending on how the populations destabilize from other factors."

"Purple stripes now appearing on the map highlight areas and countries where civil unrest is high." About a third of all land mass displayed diagonal stripes. At this juncture, the world map had a rainbow patchwork of colors.

"Finally, our influence campaigns are having effects worldwide." The entire map flashed several times.

"Anyone who suggests that our plans are not going well is not aware of what is happening throughout the world. We are like a python squeezing the entire globe and watching as it struggles to breathe." Gasps and grunts sounded throughout the audio channel linking the Council of Thirteen.

"The events of the last twenty-four hours are unfortunate, but trivial. Some unknown sources have released unflattering information. I myself have been targeted. We can suppress this information, but only to a point. We can discredit it as fake, as I did in my press conference today. But these efforts should not alarm us. In fact, I think we should accelerate our plans. The world is toppling; we can continue to destabilize it gently or give it a firm push. Either way, it will fall. Let this be a discussion we save for another call in three or four days. I am of the opinion that we are ready to assign delegates and also to disseminate the vaccine. Still, we can wait until our next call to reach decisions on these steps."

After a closing blessing and congratulations, Kenseiko severed the connection. *Children!*

A voice mail from Wán shàn brought a welcome smile to his face. She told her bàba he performed well at the news conference, but that he looked tired. She encouraged him to get some rest.

He responded with a message over their secure network, thanking her and also giving her the specifics on Beangagarrie Brindabella's travel itinerary. He followed this with a group message to all six Wán shàns, all six fierce embodiments of perfection, his little Ninjas.

"This is the presentation I shared with the Council heads. See the pretty colors and begin to imagine a new world. It will be sooner than you think."

The skin on his left hand showed gray patches. Cosmetics covered the flaws during his time under the lights and cameras earlier today. He removed his shirt and saw many such patches. They extended up both arms, his chest, and back. They marred the intricate dragon that stretched from his left arm, snaked below his left nipple and over his right, and then inked its way down his right arm. *I am tired. There is no time to travel to Tibet for a rejuvenation. Even a dragon needs to rest.*

Dr. Li stroked his right forearm where the tattoo's dragon head appeared; he frowned as he watched skin flake off. He dimmed the room illumination to low. Though he spoke of a python to his Serpent Brothers, he thought more like a dragon. He saw flame and ash as the old-world structures fell and crumbled, and a great new civilization rose from the destruction. A new humanity that he, Kenseiko Li, had worked on for over fifty years as the chief architect. He rubbed his temples. *Tonight, I shall indulge myself with a blood bath.*

❖   ❖   ❖

"To receive this transmission, you must clear your mind. Do your Merkaba; that will help."

Serena did as instructed; she became an empty vessel, ablaze with light.

Asthenefus said, "The first word stitched into the hem of the cloak, ETIE-PESEPMERI, is spoken thusly…"

The pronunciation was difficult. The sound intonations occurred in a sequence of high and low tones and pitches. Asthenefus made Serena practice a dozen times. Each time she spoke correctly, a light image formed in her mind.

"What does the combination of sound and light do?"

"Each chakra in its pure manifestation vibrates with a certain frequency of both light and sound energy. Each one is like a stepping-stone on the stairway that forms the bridge between the physical world, the world of form, and pure spirit energy."

"That explains the Rainbow Bridge."

"Yes. In the process of creation, the DNA encoded these energies. When activated through your voice and the accompanying color frequency, the two snakes dance–resonate–as you might say, in the vibration of that energy mix. The ascended masters sometimes referred to this as entrainment."

He went to the next word, LPVRINENIPEPNEIFANT. This harmonic progression was even more difficult, but she finally got it. Another color blazed in her mind.

"I see you struggle to learn this knowledge. Once you have it, I will strengthen the memory within. It remains for you only to recall from the moment of this teaching. This is the method of the ancients, the method Thoth himself taught, but only for those prepared in the sacred mysteries."

With each unbinding, Serena felt herself somehow set right, made whole, refined to purity, and more closely tuned to both matter and spirit.

At the final words, the last of seven, NBIMEI ANNEIPERFMIVIFVE, Asthenefus cautioned, "Upon the sixth unsealing, you can see into the heavenly realms. It is intoxicating to see and hear the angelic vibrations. With the seventh unbinding, some go right to ascension. Before teaching you this last word, you must commit to remain on this earthly plane. You claim a destiny as a truth bearer, a Lightbringer. You serve none but yourself, should you use this knowledge to ascend."

Serena felt the draw. Giddy and poised between heaven and earth, a vision of her *shibízhí* suddenly came in her mind. "No, my Circle training, my Candelaria gifts are given to me to benefit all. I choose to remain." She thought of Bryson. "I remain on this plane until I finish my work."

"You are brave—a true Rainbow Warrior." He spoke the seventh words, NBIMEI ANNEIPERFMIVIFVE.

She repeated until Asthenefus indicated his satisfaction. From somewhere above, Serena saw a bright white light. It filled her. She felt a dazzling radiance. The light was inseparably part of her, and she was fully part of it. Nothing could describe the feeling of oneness and everythingness that illuminated and consumed her being.

How long she remained in this state of bliss, she couldn't begin to imagine, nor did she care.

71

"It's good to have you back, Serena Mendez. Some never return. It is easy to become lost in the seductions of the nonmaterial plane."

"How long, how long was I gone?"

"Time has no meaning. You visited nonduality; it is outside the concepts of space and time. What is important is that you have full conscious awareness of the experience, and that you chose to return to this plane of existence. Rainbow Warriors are more guides than warriors. They light the way to the realization of being. When your small reality shifts to this higher level of being, the transformation is irreversible."

"I can feel it, Asthenefus. I know it, a deep knowing, in every cell of my body."

"Such is as the creators intended. But you were well along the path to realization. Most are not ready to make the shift; they require more forceful or more prolonged exposure to the harmonic and light energies. Still, all are capable. When the snakes are released from bondage, they dance in ecstasy."

Serena looked around, trying to reorient herself. From the light dimming the surface above, she guessed it neared sunset. "I should go... Uh, how do I get out?"

"While I would love to have your company, I sense the urgency of the times. However, I do have a request to make."

"Sure." She couldn't imagine what Asthenefus might ask.

"I have to say the words of release. On your way out"—he pointed—"you will undoubtedly pass a pile of bones."

"Bones, you mean the person buried in this grave mound?"

"Not quite. A few hundred years ago, an ovate named Draflason stole the only Pheryllt key. While he claimed to only be borrowing the key, I saw darkness in him, a mind parasite. He came to remove my tablet. He said he would return me to my sister. While I would enjoy being joined again with Asthemirus, I must remain here."

"So, the stolen key is here? You want me to return it?"

"Yes. Even under the illusion of time, hundreds of years without conversation gets, shall I say, boring."

"Consider it done."

He pointed to a passage of sorts, and she started up through roots. As the roots thinned, she found Draflason's remains. A necklace hung from the cervical bones, clutched by a skeletal hand. When she pried it loose, she held it up and yelled toward the green light below. "Got it."

Asthenefus's voice replied, "A pleasure to meet you, Serena Mendez. Come back again to visit and plan to stay. There is much Atlantean wisdom yet to share."

Before she could reply, she heard his incantation, and both keys flashed in rainbow shimmers.

❖   ❖   ❖

Loud snores disturbed fading twilight upon the hill. She stood in Mysselhøj's moon shadow; her breath showed as a frosty fog. "Bry, are you here?"

"Hey, Arnie, wake up! Serena's back." She heard his voice from the other side. The hilltop snow had apparently melted; she slogged through the mud.

Hearty and repeated hugs and kisses greeted her return. She promised to give them all the details once they were back in the car, once she could warm up.

"Aye, Serena, we managed to save you some." Arnbjørn held up a thermos, nearly toppling over into the mud as he did so. "This will warm your bones."

She drank straight from the thermos, some heated concoction with a definite coffee flavor, but much, much more. Warmth pumped through her veins. "Oh, this is good! What is it?"

Bryson replied. "Secret Druid recipe, grailfriend. I've been trying to get him to tell me all dray."

"Do you have any more?"

The two men looked at each other, huge grins erupted as they shook their heads.

"Wait, are you two drunk?"

Following a chorus of vigorous head shaking with, "Nah, no way," Arnie admitted to being a wee bit under the spell of the mighty elixir.

"You've been gone all day, Serena. And it—"

She waved Bryson off before he could finish. "Got something here for you, Arnbjørn." She held out a clenched hand. "There were some bones down below, but they belonged to someone named Draflason."

Suddenly sober, Arnie spat, "Traitor, the thief!"

As she opened her fingers to reveal a second necklace, the bard's jaw fell. "Asthenefus trapped him in the underworld." She stomped a foot to the ground below. "Asked me to return this. He's lonely for company."

Arnie reached out with shaking hands, almost afraid to touch it. "You don't know, Serena, that necklace is priceless."

"Actually," Bryson said, "someone offered Serena over ten million pounds Brriitshh…*hiccup*…British Sterling for hers. The man who wanted it…oops… he had a burning desire to have it…" He couldn't finish through his guffaws.

"When you boys sober up more, we've got work to do." She handed the rainbow key to Arnbjørn.

"I…I can't thank you enough for this, Serena. We, meaning all in our order, can't thank you enough." Tears moistened his gray beard.

She thought a moment. "Maybe you can. You're a musician; do you have any recording equipment?"

72

The Cleveland Clinic had a world-renowned neuro-ophthalmologist on staff. Chicago had other suitable experts, but his plan required travel. Deciding between rail or bus transit wasn't difficult. The duration and cost were similar. He imagined a long train ride not only gave the opportunity to walk and stretch comfortably; it would recall many rides across the Australian countryside. *I shall enjoy looking out the window at the American heartland. Not likely as beautiful as my native land, and I've only got one good eye… I best take this opportunity.* He shouldered his bag. Today would be for travel, tomorrow the appointment, and return the following day…maybe. BB knew the whole effort to be a gamble, but he had a feeling the odds were in his favor.

Beangagarrie handed a flash drive to Tarni. "Remember, Fuchsia, only open this if, for some reason, I do not contact you after the second day. I don't have a phone, so you may not recognize the number I call from."

She nodded and bit her lip; tears streamed down her face. He fished in his pockets, in clothing that no longer fit his thin frame, and produced a handkerchief.

"In times past, a gentleman always carried this for just such occasions." He patted her face and handed over the damp cloth. "Keep it until I return." Her soulful eyes spoke louder than any words. "Tarni, the Dreamtime ends for us all. There is no sadness in me, and there should be none in you. My only regret is that I may not see Serena, or Bryson, or Claus again. But who knows, maybe I will." A warm smile exposed his teeth, now almost too large for his gaunt face.

On the drive to Chicago Union Station, they shared recollections and stories about Australia, Gurumarra, and the past few months. When the car stopped, he made no effort to restrain his tears. She searched her pocketbook and held up a tissue for him.

"Lady's choice for the most gentle man I've ever had the privilege of knowing."

As he embraced her, he whispered, "I love you Tarni... Thank you for everything you've done...and for everything I know you will do."

"These words of unbinding are opposite to Danish, many extra vowels instead of consonants. It's all the extra vowels that carry the vocal shifts." Arnie went through a series of exercises to ready his voice. "Still, the progressions are hard, even for me."

Bryson's head only pounded slightly. Arnie's small flat had everything you might expect from a musician, plus a medley of historical artifacts. He admitted to being a bit of a collector and wanted to speak about each artifact's history. But this wasn't the time for enjoyment; they had work to do. Serena pushed Arnbjørn and he obliged. Once his hangover wore off, the bard accomplished a lot.

"You don't have to match my notes, harmonizing or even a counter melody makes it more interesting. The voice power comes from my words." Serena had recorded over a dozen tracks. Their jet left in three hours, but she pressed onward.

"True, but the draw is from Arnie's voice," Bryson said. He had listened to the bard's singing much of yesterday. Today, Arnbjørn had played six different instruments and sang a variety of tunes. The effect was always the same—mesmerizing.

"I agree, his voice and music are spellbinding; that's why I want us to record together."

"No need to worry, Serena, I can always overlay the tracks with my voice or the instruments. We've got your seven words sung all proper. That's what's most important. You've given me the master track; I can work with that."

"Okay, play it for me again, just my voice. I want to see the color progression from the synesthetic visual response it triggers."

As Arnbjørn isolated the tracks, Serena had him alter the intensity to several syllables until the colors in her mind appeared vibrant and clear.

When she finally looked satisfied, Arnie grunted. "So, you want me to overlay background vocals, add a splash and flair of instruments, and record some magic?"

"Yes, incorporate your Druid gifts, make it so hypnotic that people will want to listen again and again." Serena closed her eyes. "In my mind, I imagine the lyric beauty of our harmony. I want us to be irresistible."

Though Serena had returned from the tree in an incredible state of calm, Bryson realized that until this recording session concluded, she couldn't fully relax.

"Once we get back stateside, I'm going to work with Serena on matching the right colors to these seven words. I'll do it for each song you come up with; then we can get them out via the net, on YouTube, Vimeo, any platform we want. The more the better."

"I'm scheduled to perform at a concert next week. Only about a thousand people are expected to go; maybe less as folks are getting scared to gather in crowds. We can play the tracks with the color enhancements fading in and out. It'll be a great show and might give this a jump start."

"The more exposure the better, Arnie. Do you think we need a catchy name or something?" Serena asked.

"While you two were singing, I gave that a little thought." Bryson had researched several videos claiming to repair DNA, but traffic and downloads were few. They needed titles that grabbed attention. "I'm thinking something catchy like: Siren's Song, or Stairway to Ascension, or even Let Your Light Shine."

"Those are great titles, Bry! I think we should do all three. One could be pop style, another like spa music, the other something grand and majestic." She turned to Arnie. "Is that too many? Can you mix up things that sound different yet have the same basic notes?"

"We do it all the time, Serena. Simple tricks of the trade. I've been at this a long time." He pointed to his lute. "Between Lester, and Maggý, and Horace, Galloway, and ole Ziggy"—he glanced behind himself at his zither—"I think we can manage some variety."

"That's it then; it's a wrap. Isn't that what you recording artists say? We both have masters to work with." Bryson looked at them. "We've got an hour, what do you want to do?"

"I can't thank you enough for this." Arnie clasped the necklace. "Anything I can get you?"

"Can you mix up some of that brew you let me sample last night? You really didn't leave me much."

Arnbjørn stood and headed for the kitchen. In between his humming a tune, he made idle talk. "It's an old family recipe. I'll mix up extra for you to take at the airport. I guarantee it will make the flight better. How about you, Bryson?"

He rubbed his forehead to ease the residual headache that lingered. "Nah, I think I'll pass."

73

From her position, Wán shàn had an excellent view of the station's main entrance all the way to the ticket counter. Hundreds of people moved within, heading to platforms, ticketing, making connections, picking up family. She found people-watching stoked her curiosity; at times, she wondered why everyone always seemed to be in such a hurry. Spotting the Australian geneticist wouldn't be difficult. His height made him stand out in a crowd. Her two soldiers were positioned: one at a side entrance, one on the platform where trains bound for Cleveland would depart. All three had earbuds to communicate.

"I see him—south side and making his way toward ticketing. He's studying the arrival and departure board." *He is thinner than I recall; though, I only saw him for a moment. He does look unwell.* "Stand by. After the ticket purchase, move to intercept near the escalator down."

Moments later, she saw the guards get in position. Wán shàn approached her target. "Dr. Brindabella?"

He spun around and looked at her.

"Yes, young lady?" His eyes squinted a moment before he must have recognized her. "I know you. You were in the parking lot, at my lab. Why are you here? What do you want?"

"Yes, I visited your lab though your assistant would not let me in." He towered over her. The two guards now flanked Wán shàn.

"Please, Dr. Brindabella, do not make this difficult. There is someone who wants to meet you."

"I have an important medical appointment in Cleveland. If someone wishes to meet with me, he or she can drop by the lab or schedule a time."

"I think you know who I'm talking about, doctor."

He sighed. "Li. Dr. Kenseiko Li. We have a certain history together. Has he learned of my research? Is he the one who wants me? Are you here to abduct me?"

"If necessary, yes. Our instructions are to persuade you to come by whatever means necessary." She glanced at each of the two soldiers.

"I'm an old man, an old sick man. Why would Dr. Li want to meet with me? He has many excellent geneticists to proposition." He squinted again. "Or kidnap."

"That is something you would need to ask my bàba." A subtle hand signal followed, and one of her agents administered the sedative. They eased the stumbling scientist to a bench while getting a wheelchair.

Wán shàn whispered to the drugged scientist, "Bàba did say you have been a thorn in his side for many years." She watched his eyes close and escorted him away. She added, "And that you are very stubborn."

Their plane's twenty-minute descent to Chicago's O'Hare International Airport had already been announced when the pilot's voice came over the intercom. "We've got a problem. Air traffic's rerouting everything away from Chicago."

Bryson and Serena moved to the front to speak with the pilot. "What's going on?"

"Nuclear bomb threat." He sounded grim. "The whole city's on lockdown."

"Oh my God, Bry! Tarni and BB are in Chicago. And Uncle Pete!"

He gripped her hand. "It's just a threat, only a threat at this time."

"Need to make an executive decision here. Controller is saying either turn around to route into Detroit, or they can put us down in Milwaukee at Mitchell International."

"Which is closer?"

"Milwaukee."

"Do it."

"How long?"

"Thirty minutes. But I guarantee it will be a cluster once we land."

They returned to their seats. Five minutes later, the intercom crackled back on. "More bad news just came through. Hope you don't have any loved ones in Hong Kong."

Bryson and Serena looked at each other and braced.

"Gone. Nuclear explosion… Something really massive from first reports. Sorry!"

Serena closed her eyes. "How many people lived in Hong Kong, Bry?"

"Over seven million." He placed his hands over his face. "We're running out of time."

Serena swallowed. "How many people live in Chicago?"

"I don't know, Serena… Close to three million." Bryson stared out the window at Lake Michigan below. Between shallow breaths, he murmured, "Something like that."

Bryson took his phone off airplane mode before they touched down. His news feed had gone berserk with news of Hong Kong and with the insanity of people trying to evacuate Chicago.

"Nothing yet. Still only a threat." Focused on the news, he hadn't noticed the half dozen missed messages from Tarni and Claus.

Fortunately, Serena was checking her phone at the same time. "It's Tarni… She's safe. She left the city yesterday."

"Where is she?"

"She's with Claus, in Michigan."

After a big sigh of relief, he asked, "What about BB? Is he with them?"

"She said BB had left for a medical appointment in Cleveland three days ago. There was more, something about it being very complicated. Not sure, Bry, it didn't make sense."

"Uncle Pete?"

"Nothing. Tarni said nothing about him."

"I can check my messages; maybe there's more information there." The wheels touched down, and their jet taxied to the terminal. "Better yet, I'll just call Claus."

"Holy shit! Yes, we're okay; Tarni's with me. Where are you guys?" Claus sounded agitated.

"We just touched down in Milwaukee. Got to clear customs. After that, I don't know. What about BB? Do we know if he's okay?"

An uncomfortable pause followed before Claus said, "Let me put Tarni on."

"Oh my God! Thank goodness you two are okay. We're safe, but I haven't heard from BB. He doesn't carry a phone." After another uncomfortable pause, Bryson heard Tarni whisper, "There's more to it, Bry…a lot more. I can't get into it now. You and Serena need to figure out how to get here. I'll…I'll explain then."

"Where are you? What about my Uncle Peter?"

"I'll put Claus back on. Mr. Reynolds is okay as far as we know. Hurry. Miss you two mates. Hurry…"

Claus got on, and the two men spoke details. The boss had been out of Chicago on business. He wasn't due back for a week. He and Van Duyn were doing the Nepal trip. After Bryson shared that info with Serena, Claus went over specifics. The closest airport was Muskegon County. Bryson asked the pilot. Muskegon could handle the jet they currently were on.

"Only forty minutes airtime, but between leaving the international terminal, getting through customs, and everything else, hard to say. He's got enough fuel, so I say it's a go, but I'll call you back when I know for sure."

"It's thirty-five minutes to the airport from here. Me and Tarni will pick you up." He added, "Be careful, there's a shitstorm all over the place. Hong Kong was the tipping point, Bryson. It's Armageddon!" The call ended.

Bryson turned to Serena. "Okay, we've got a plan. Something's going on with Beangagarrie, but Tarni wouldn't say. Let's do the wheelchair and oxygen gig." He pulled out his State Department ID's. "Maybe we can rocket through customs and get the hell out of here."

Barry, their pilot, did everything he could to work with them. Bryson didn't think it was only for the extra money. He never asked them about their business. Maybe he sensed it to be important. He also needed to clear customs, get a mechanical check, and taxi over to a different terminal. He had just enough flight hours left to get them to Muskegon. He would have to layover there.

"I've been there a couple of times. Quiet, sleepy, not much to get excited about. I might chill there until the craziness blows over."

"Barry, I don't think that will be anytime soon. Hope I'm wrong, but what's going on might get worse before it gets better." Bryson kept his last thought silent. *If it ever gets better...*

74

In an overly dim room, he sat in a reasonably comfortable chair with his wrists lightly restrained. The flight to Singapore had been interesting. Two guards stood silent in the room. They appeared identical, and BB surmised they were likely genetic copies to the hybrids whose DNA Claus had recovered in the raid on Dulce. *They all look alike. I wonder if these are the same two that flew in the plane with me.* He asked them but received no response. He asked Wán shàn, that was the girl's name, but she revealed nothing. BB also wondered if multiple copies of this same girl, the chimera whose DNA he had analyzed, also existed. He suspected as much from the look on Wán shàn's face when he inquired.

As long as he avoided certain topics, the two conversed extensively during the transatlantic crossing. He was curious to test his hypothesis about the effect of removing the gene sequence. How might its absence manifest? If this segment somehow modulated emotional response, could he uncover evidence to prove or disprove his theory?

In spite of her youth, Wán shàn displayed knowledge about a wide variety of topics. BB quickly realized the girl was both remarkably intelligent and extraordinarily well-educated. Her questions and comments revealed a sharp, analytic mind. She appeared to be an exemplary physical specimen. But something was missing—passion. She lacked emotion. To hear her speak reminded BB of an automated voice; he imagined a flat-toned, robotic recitation of a love scene.

Over the years, he had encountered people who came across as emotionally flat. At times, depressed colleagues conveyed no emotion as they detailed some aspect of their life that had gone awry. This was different. The girl had no excitement, no enthusiasm, no empathy, no compassion, no anger, no resentment. When BB asked her to share thoughts about love, her expression drew blank.

"What is love, Dr. Brindabella? I am curious to hear your thoughts."

Other than a brief recounting of an experience she described as beautiful, a mountaintop encounter with nature, Wán shàn embodied precisely what BB hypothesized. BB shuddered at this confirmation of his hypothesis.

As he sat and waited for his "interview" with Dr. Li, an even more disturbing notion began to formulate in his mind. *What of spirit? Does Wán shàn aspire for something greater? I should have asked her earlier about God, about an afterlife, about meaning and purpose.*

Though she had remained nearly silent as they waited, he asked, "Wán shàn, what is your purpose, your reason for existence? Do you have spiritual beliefs or aspirations?"

She looked over silently. Her dispassionate features revealed nothing.

At last, Dr. Li entered. He hobbled. He looked harried. Perhaps the demonstrators BB had noticed outside Advanced Bionics were causing problems.

Beangagarrie sighed. "Dr. Li, I am glad you could join us. I would stand and shake your hand"—he glanced at his wrists—"but I am indisposed at the moment."

"Dr. Beangagarrie Brindabella, please call me Kenseiko. Your humor at this moment is refreshing, considering your circumstances." Yellow teeth flashed.

"Gallows humor, Kenseiko, I do not imagine this to be a job interview."

"It could be. You are a brilliant geneticist, Beangagarrie, if I may drop formalities. You could join our team. We do some rather extraordinary work, well beyond the leading edge of present-day gene editing and engineering." He gestured to the two guards and to Wán shàn.

"Hybrids, cloning, chimeras? The work is beyond top-shelf, but it's not my cup of tea."

"Speaking of which, we should have some tea. Wán shàn, could you bring our guest some tea? Service for three."

"Yes, bàba."

The two geneticists continued their discussion. BB declined the offer to assist in Li's plan to repopulate the world with genetically superior humans. Dr.

Li revealed he could "program" obedience to obtain his rival's compliance. He seemed disappointed to learn of BB's fatal illness and short life expectancy. He conveyed that he wouldn't have gone through all the trouble to bring his nemesis all the way to Singapore had he known. Kenseiko seemed to relish displaying both his achievements and his dominance over another accomplished geneticist, long a nuisance, but never really a threat. BB let him revel.

The tea arrived. Wán shàn removed his restraints.

"It isn't very British, but I prefer my tea seated on the floor."

"A tea ceremony—very fitting for a finale."

The two men sat cross-legged across from one another with Wán shàn positioned to the side.

This is good. Sip some tea. Keep him off guard. "Tell me, Kenseiko, before I make my grand exit. Please indulge me, a professional courtesy of sorts. Years ago, in my herpetology papers, the gene research I published, were you responsible for the purge and suppression?"

"Yes."

"Why?" BB sipped some tea.

"The segment you studied was the focus of our genetic engineering; we did not want any independent research to be conducted on that genome sequence. Your work called attention to something I wanted to remain hidden."

"I concluded as much. The segment regulates emotion; am I correct in this conclusion as well?" He looked directly at Wán shàn as he asked this question.

Dr. Li's lips drew back slightly. "Kudos to you, Dr. Brindabella. I give you this minor victory as you approach final defeat. Yes, however, eliminating the segment, as we eventually accomplished in my daughter, made viability challenging. We solved this after many failures." He pointed to Wán shàn. "Did you know her name means perfection? She is free of emotional handicaps. Wán shàn is a physically and mentally superior human being."

Let him continue to extoll himself and his accomplishments. "Your daughter is most impressive; although, I suspect she cannot reproduce. Tell me, Kenseiko, were you also responsible for murdering my wife, Kalinda?"

"Yes. I warned you. You are a very stubborn man, Beangagarrie."

"She was pregnant."

"Unfortunate. Many perish in the pursuit of perfection."

"I forgive you." BB's words conveyed his sincerity. "In your zeal, in your passion, I stood as an impediment; my wife and unborn child were mere innocent victims. I learned much about the world and about myself as a result of your actions…of my own actions." He looked at Wán shàn as he spoke, then placed his cup on the floor to reach into a pocket. "May I?"

BB withdrew a small tin containing a ground substance.

His host looked intrigued. "Snuff? Not something I would expect of you, Beangagarrie."

"Not at all. A blend of native Australian botanicals, unique to my tribe." He dabbed his finger and placed some on his tongue. "Helps to induce both relaxation and focus." He pinched some and inhaled, his wide nostrils flaring as he did so. He bit his cheek forcefully and tasted blood swirling with saliva in his mouth.

Extending the tin forward, he offered some to Dr. Li. "Would you like a pinch?"

As Li reached forward, BB suddenly and violently sneezed, showering his host with blood-filled saliva.

"Oh, my!" he reached for his handkerchief. "So, so sorry, mate. I gave my hankie away. How absolutely dreadful of me." Inwardly, he breathed a sigh of relief. *It is done!*

Kenseiko cleaned and composed himself. His graciousness almost surprised BB as he poured another cup of tea.

"You forgave me, so I shall forgive you. For the moment, we are even. Now, we were discussing perfection."

"Do you really think by removing this bit of DNA, the part that regulates emotions, you have improved upon the original, even perfected it? You have created a sterile mule, an animal to do your bidding, one that cannot even reproduce."

Wán shàn sat and sipped tea while the two men debated. She appeared to listen but showed no reaction.

"I took out the part that clouds judgment, the part that causes confusion. The part that wants something more than life, an afterlife—a silly notion."

"No, Dr. Li, you took out something essential to our humanity."

"A flaw, no different from my clubbed foot." He pointed downward. "Once you have removed all flaws, what you have remaining is perfection." He gestured again to Wán shàn.

"I agree that Wán shàn is a masterpiece, but she is less than human. You cannot remove something and call what remains perfect. You have created a single-use commodity to do your bidding. This is not my idea of perfection. What makes us human is our individual and collective efforts to overcome what you call flaws. It is a struggle, but it is essential to what we are. She is devoid of emotion. Wán shàn lacks a higher calling; she has no spirituality or desire for something greater."

Li gestured both palms downward. "Rubbish! Nonsense! Spiritual dreams and aspirations about a higher purpose—these are myths. What I have created is reality—flesh and blood." He appeared annoyed and agitated. "She *is* perfect!"

BB continued. "If your idea of perfection is total control. You no longer need to control with fear and anger. You no longer need to create factions opposing one another over inconsequential ideologic differences. I get it, it's a lot of work to plant and cultivate these emotional seeds of division to accomplish your intentions. Controlling and manipulating all of humanity has become a difficult task."

Li nodded. "More than you know."

"But it's not my idea of perfection. There's a certain nobility in struggling with making the right decisions, with trying to be better today than you were yesterday."

"Yes, and I have removed that struggle. Mankind has evolved from noble savage to perfectly noble."

"You mean perfectly controlled."

"Enough." He stood. "I have enjoyed our little tête-à-tête; now it is time for you to enjoy your last cup of tea. Wán shàn, please get something from the storage locker suitable to assist our guest in his final passage." He rattled off the security code to unlock the storage area.

"Yes, bàba."

"Daughter, make it something quick and painless—a mercy killing." He put his cup down and addressed Beangagarrie. "A final professional courtesy."

He motioned to the guards, and they refastened BB's restraints.

Dr. Li hobbled toward the door. "The world will soon be a better place. You will not be here to enjoy the fruits of my labors." A self-satisfied smile broke across his face. "Goodbye, Dr. Brindabella. Your human struggle is now over."

BB sat stoically in the chair without replying. A crescent of white showed beneath his taut lips. *True for both of us, Dr. Li... I hope...he who laughs last, laughs best.*

75

"I tell you I'm well provisioned, got three freezer chests all stocked, surplus military rations, my own water, fuel cell to power everything. I say we hunker down for the near term. Don't even need to mess with getting chipped."

"What are you talking about, Claus? Are they requiring mandatory chip insertions? Has the government gone that far?"

"Where you been, Bryson? If you want safe food, you need to be chipped. If you want to get vaccinated against the Bogimonster, you've got to be chipped. I told you it was coming. Well, now it's here."

Tarni sat in the back of the car with Serena while Claus and Bryson talked shop. She had only been half listening, too absorbed in what she knew was coming, but Tarni spoke, almost yelled, from the back, "Don't any of you get near that vaccine until I can test it through some assays." She leaned forward and clasped a hand over each of the men's shoulders. "No telling what's in that so-called immunization."

"She's right," Serena said calmly. "I don't even think Tarni needs to test it. All I need to do is hear a high official speak, and I'll tell you if he or she is speaking the truth."

"What are you saying, girlfriend? Are you saying we shouldn't score some vaccine and run it through some tests?"

"No, sorry, I didn't mean to imply that, Tarni. It's just...just, that this last trip opened up some new awareness. I think I can tell pretty accurately what is true and what's a lie."

"Right. I still want to test it." Tarni looked out the passenger window. "Truth is, I'm scared, Serena. Bloody scared about everything. Scared about what's happening and about what you'll learn when I show you everything, reveal some things I've been holding back."

"Don't worry, Tarni," Serena whispered and took her hand. "Whatever it is, whatever your reason for doing whatever it is you did, I trust you. I know you did what you thought best."

Tarni blocked out Claus and Bryson talking about the gear from the raid, optogenic something or other, neural programming, supersoldiers. She felt drained from the events of the last three days—dropping off BB, saying good-bye, getting Li's message, running off to find Claus, the chaos in Chicago, the horror in Hong Kong.

She addressed Serena privately, ignoring the conversation in the front seat. "The last week has been hell, Serena. I think my whole world is coming apart. Other than my family in Australia"—she winced thinking about the danger she had placed them in—"the three people in this car are all I've got. BB's gone. First thing I do when we get to the cabin is show you his message. I'm unraveling, just like the world." She wiped sniffles with her sleeve.

"We all feel it, Tarni. There's no shame in saying it, in feeling it."

"But you're so calm. I'm standing like a bandicoot on a burnt ridge. I'm close to feeling dead as a maggot. I'm a total mess, and you're calm and peaceful. How do you do it?"

"It's hard to explain. It's a little like a top spinning. When it's perfectly balanced, you think it will spin forever, never wobble, never topple. That's how I feel—perfectly balanced, perfectly centered, spinning with energy, but in a good way. I've never quite felt this way ever. Most of all, I feel completely at peace."

"I want that, that same feeling of peace and serenity." She laughed suddenly. "Serenity, just like your name."

"Trust me, Tarni, if we get this last piece figured out, you will… We all will."

Tarni routed the flash drive with BB's message through Claus's TV, and they all watched.

"My dear friends, I deeply regret not being able to share this information with you in person. You have all, each and every one of you, been so courageous and brave in this time of great need for all of mankind. I am humbled to have worked with you, to have done my little part in this noble effort. I count you as family and have come to love you all dearly."

Tarni passed around a box of tissues.

"What I now reveal will in some ways surprise you, alarm you, even trouble you, but I deemed it necessary to protect Tarni. She has placed herself and her family at great risk and peril..."

As BB continued, Tarni looked around the room. They glanced her way, but no one looked angry. It turned out her misgivings about spying on BB and working for Li had them all at first surprised, then incredibly supportive. They even reacted with understanding when they learned she knew about his brain tumor but said nothing out of respect for his wishes.

She had to stop BB's message while they thanked her for hanging tough.

"I...I didn't think you would understand." Relieved, she gulped some water, fought back, then released a torrent of tears and sobs.

Beangagarrie paved the way by explaining that Tarni withheld the information about his illness at his request. She fed information to Li that BB reviewed first—enough to show progress and even false turns, so that his weapon could be prepared.

"I wanted DNA from Li himself, but we were unable to secure a sample. Still, the similarities in the DNA obtained from Rockefeller and Rothschild gave me the substrate to design a viral carrier with a specific transfer RNA to target this unique portion of their genome. Here, I give most of the credit to Tarni. She is brilliant with virology techniques though not even she knew why she did some of the tasks I requested. I could not chance any of this being revealed until the end."

Tarni stopped the recording to give further explanation. "Li wanted to know if and when BB left the lab. He did have a real appointment at the Cleveland Clinic for his eye. The tumor blinded his left eye, but BB knew nothing could really be done for that. He hoped Li would intercept him.

"BB inserted the tRNA death strand into an influenza virus. During an incubation period, viral titers build up within the body. There's a massive amount of viral shedding prior to actual symptoms of illness. When I took him to the air-port, BB told me he had checked his titers and was viremic, but there wasn't any threat to me or others, only someone with the targeted DNA profile. Someone like Li. Beangagarrie planned to infect Li with an encoded death strand."

Bryson said, "Usually, when I think of viruses, I'm thinking computers and malware and worms. A specific biologically gene-targeted assassination—that is unbelievably impressive. I just don't like the delivery method."

"BB knew he didn't have much longer. It's a big loss for us all," Serena said. Her voice conveyed quiet authority and commitment. "We need to make his sacrifice count."

The remainder of BB's final message included personal thanks to each of them individually: Peter, Claus, Bryson, Tarni, and Serena.

"To you, Serena, I smile at how much you have grown since our first encounter in India. Thank you for trusting me. Yours is the greatest burden of all. As it is said, 'Much will be expected from those to whom much has been given.' You shine a great light. Be always true to yourself, Candelaria… Light-bringer… Galinawa."

He closed by thanking them and expressing his love. "After the Dream-time, we shall all laugh and dance together as one."

No one spoke for a long time. The box of tissues made a second round.

"You're sure he's gone?" Bryson asked Tarni.

She nodded her head. "I know Li's got him. I don't know for absolute cer-tain he's gone, but Li sent me a message to close the lab, leave, and go back to Australia. He also wants me to send him all of BB's work." She rose to get her tablet showing Li's message and her response. "I told him I had temporarily left Chicago, but when it was safe to return, I would gather BB's data, send it to him, and shut down the laboratory. My family in Australia isn't safe until—"

Bryson snatched the tablet from her. "Wait a minute, wait a minute. How have you been communicating with Li?"

"I don't speak directly to him; he gave me a password to log in and report on a secure network database. At least, I presume it's secure."

"And you said he wants you to send him BB's files?"

"Yes. In addition to what's on the hard drives at the lab, Beangagarrie left me several flash drives. I've got them right here. They have his personal notes, research papers… I only just began looking at them, there are a lot of documents. I wanted to go through them and decide what to send."

Bryson looked at Claus. Tarni saw his face smirked in a shit-eating grin. "Claus, are you thinking what I'm thinking?"

"Oh yeah, kid, I know exactly where you're going. You told me you're a speed-coding champ. This is in your wheelhouse."

With confused faces, Tarni and Serena listened as Bryson foamed at the bit. He grabbed one of the storage drives BB had given to Tarni. "This has files. Li wants files. Bryson embeds a virus…not the BB kind, the Bryson kind. We get inside a secure database. Don't know what's there, but people set up secure databases to keep stuff, well…secure. Important stuff. Damaging stuff if it gets in the wrong hands." Knuckles cracked. He rubbed his palms.

As everyone nodded their understanding, he held the drive up. "This is like an all-day, all-access pass. We are going to crash Li's private party and tell the world about it. We don't even have to find the back door. He wants Tarni to send him files; that gives us an invitation to come right on in."

Bryson eyed the flash drive. To look at his face, Tarni thought she'd given him a precious diamond.

"I'm going to borrow this, Tarni. You show me some files you think will be fine to send. Also, I need your access password that you use to log in. And somebody brew me a pot of coffee. Operation big reveal is just getting started."

76

The many glass bottles and sealed vials in the storage room were well catalogued. Wán shàn studied the labels and properties prior to making her selection. She shut the door and returned to the room where Dr. Brindabella sat. His restraints had been refastened, and someone had opened the blinds. Patterns of light danced on the room's dark floor. She studied him a moment. The left pupil remained fixed, but his right eye showed a certain gleam. *He does not appear afraid at all.*

The captive geneticist cleared his throat. "So, young lady, did you pick something suitable?"

"Batrachotoxin." She held a glass tube with a screw top for him to see.

"Ah, from the poison dart frog. Excellent choice—quick, painless, and very potent. Paralysis then death. Thank you! It is a mercy killing." She did not sense a hint of acrimony or hostility.

"Tell me something, Dr. Brindabella, you seem not to be the least bit afraid. Why is that?"

"You would not understand, Wán shàn. You are not capable of understanding. I say this not to criticize; it just is not in your makeup. People do struggle with fear, and some learn to overcome it. I have had a good life. I accept what is to come. Some might call this bravery, but it is merely acceptance. I also believe that my soul continues on to something even more grand than life here on earth."

He looked a little sad as he spoke. Wán shàn freed the geneticist's hands. She unscrewed the top of the tube and poured the poison into some now cold tea. "You are an unusual man, Dr. Brindabella. You have given me much to think about. Yes, you are correct. You speak of things I admit I do not understand." She held out a cup and saucer. "Here, drink this."

He took a sip. "Not a pleasant taste, but really not so bad." He drained the cup.

As she watched, she saw him begin to struggle to breathe. "You asked me earlier about God and about purpose. I know nothing of God, but I do have a purpose."

"Really?" he huffed between breaths. "What is that?"

"To serve the plan. We all exist to serve the plan. That is my reason for being."

He gasped. She leaned forward to hear him whisper, "What…plan… whose…plan?"

Dr. Brindabella's eyes closed, and he ceased breathing. She waited to check for a pulse. As she held his wrist, she gazed upon the man's face. In the final moments of paralysis, his lips had drawn back, exposing white teeth beneath an enormous smile. The image embedded into her memory.

Different from that flower I held in the snow, but still, there is something inside that I feel as I look upon him smiling. She gently folded his hands upon his lap. *There is something beautiful about this man.*

Claus held the goggles and pointed to the inside back and sides. "Basically, there's a thin-film array to give high-resolution color displays."

Serena tried it on and adjusted the head strap. "It looks like one of those VR headsets."

"There are a series of startup sequences in the software that programs quality control runs in the beginning. This gives the operator a chance to fine-tune the color match against controls. Just sit back a moment and enjoy the light show."

At first, blackness surrounded her. The eyewear did a fantastic job of blocking out the ambient light. When Claus finished moments later, she removed the goggles. "Why can't we just go to a hardware store, get some paint swatches and color match something there? I've got a pretty good eye."

"That probably won't work, Serena. Pigment primary colors are yellow, red, and blue, but the primary colors for light are green, red, and blue. I don't think a spectrophotometer—that's what they use at the paint store—would give the same precision. Besides, this sends the light impulses straight from your eyes to your brain. Can't get more direct than that."

"Okay, let me say what I think you're asking me to do. You will feed the audio tracks of me speaking the seven words while simultaneously varying the color display I see in the goggles. You want me to signal when what I see with my eyes is the same as what I see in my mind's eye. Do I have that right?"

"That's the idea. I don't know what you see inside your pretty bald head." He playfully thumped her shaved head. "This tech connects directly to your brain. If we can synch up the colors so they match, you can make your fancy fix-your-DNA-music-vid."

"You're funny, Claus. I like your explanation. It's cut-and-dry and gets right to the point."

"I'm a no-nonsense guy, but if we can all light up like glowworms, the way you were last night, I'm going to be the first one to watch the light and sound show. What was that you called it, Merkaborah or something?"

Serena laughed. "Merkaba. I can teach you the meditation, but I only had a soft glow before my unbinding. Now, I admit it has gotten much brighter."

"Whatever you call it, girl, we get this right, then I think sales for sunglasses are going to go way up."

As Claus worked off a laptop, Serena put on the noise-canceling headset and visual display goggles. He pulled back an earpiece so she could hear him. "Raise a hand when you think there's a match. I'll note the setting. This might get boring; I will verify settings multiple times to make sure we keep getting the same results."

Serena sat comfortably and opened herself to the moment with total focus. "I'm ready when you are."

77

Dr. Zhāng apologized yet again. Peter had heard enough excuses about Dr. Li's absence and the delays: "an urgent matter," "I am not at liberty to disclose," "I spoke with him earlier, and he hopes later today," "There was an unexpected problem in Tibet." *I'm tired of these nonexplanations.* Upon arrival, they had confiscated his cell phone and placed it inside a shielded safe of some sort. They did not want to risk any location tracking or unauthorized communication to and from this secret base. Peter didn't like that, didn't enjoy being incommunicado. Van Duyn claimed it wasn't a big deal. Damiaan didn't have any details about Li either.

Outside this hidden facility in Nepal, temperatures were freezing. The altitude caused Peter to feel short of breath walking through the extensive underground complex. Zhāng did an admirable job taking them around, showing off the Imaginarium, talking about the work they conducted here. Van Duyn knew many of the specifics, but it turned out he had only been here once before, and then for only half a day.

Damiaan beamed when the tour reached the programming area. "This is the primary station where the HC-12 units are programmed."

Peter made mental notes to share the intel with Claus. The equipment here looked identical to what they had taken from Dulce. Claus had been adamant against Peter's visit. So far, other than the cell phone, nothing smelled like a rat.

Zhāng droned on. "Most of the HC-12s developed here have since been deployed to governments, private militias, and security personnel for wealthy individuals. Most of the final programming lately has been geared toward crowd control. A dozen trained units working together easily outperform one hundred standard soldiers."

"Very impressive, Dr. Zhāng. Truly, the entire facility here is remarkable in so many ways." Peter continued, "I think it is unfortunate that Dr. Li has not been here for our visit, but Damiaan and I really need to return home."

Van Duyn said, "Not before a demonstration, Peter. There's an area outside, bundle up. You really need to see these soldiers perform."

"You already showed me a video of the HC-12s in action."

"True, but seeing them in person is something you won't want to miss. Dr. Zhāng, could you arrange a demo? Let's see two units battle against two others. Not to death, but let's give them fifteen minutes to square off and spar."

Dr. Zhāng bowed. "They should be ready in half an hour. I'll meet you outside by the ring."

Thank goodness Van Duyn had packed hand warmers. Standing at the edge of the ring, positioned so his frosty breaths blew off to the side, Peter watched. Fascinating! His appreciation grew with each round as the soldiers, pitted two against two, battled. In a weird way, it reminded Peter simultaneously of mixed martial arts and synchronized swimming. A flurry of kicks and twists and blows choreographed with precision. Like equally matched chess grandmasters, combat ended in draws.

After the fifth round, Peter couldn't be sure. He drew back his hood. Over the wind gusts, the unmistakable sound of a helicopter sliced through the icy air.

Zhāng clapped his hands. "Demonstration over. Dr. Li is here." He motioned, and the four soldiers dispersed.

"Well, Peter, what did you think?" Van Duyn asked.

"Very impressive, Damiaan. In a lethal kind of way." He added, "Congratulations; this is quite an achievement."

They moved to the helipad, but the blades stirred too much wind. Retreating to the cave entrance, Peter watched as Dr. Zhāng assisted Dr. Li, who hobbled slowly. A ski mask and sun goggles blocked Kenseiko Li's face and eyes. *Whoa! He moves like he's aged ten or fifteen years since I last saw him.*

As the two men approached the entrance, Peter could just make out the last of their conversation. They spoke in Chinese. Fortunately, the chopper blades no longer spun, and Peter was fluent enough to understand. "Yes, five or six more treatments and he says I'll be okay to…" Peter didn't catch the last word, or it made no sense—renew, rejuvenate, rebirth?

Dr. Li peeled back his ski mask and exchanged ski goggles for sunglasses. He removed his gloves and extended his hands. "Damiaan and Peter, it is good to see you both. I apologize for my delay. I trust Dr. Zhāng has kept you well entertained." They all shook hands. He pointed to his dark glasses. "I apologize for these as well. The light hurts my eyes."

Pink-gray scars littered Dr. Li's face in a burst pattern. *Acid splash? Lab accident or explosion? Almost looks like scattershot pellets.* "Kenseiko, you don't look well. Is everything okay?" Peter couldn't tell for sure through the dark glasses, but Dr. Li seemed to show anger in his eyes as he looked at Peter. He didn't answer the question.

He squinted as lips drew back, showing his small teeth. "Come. Come inside and join me for some tea. I need to warm up. I won't keep you long."

As they sipped hot tea in Li's office, the only explanation he provided to account for the scars on his face was, "A mishap—sloppiness on my part. But the final victory is mine."

Peter felt chilled despite the hot tea when Li gave this account. The whole time, he looked straight at Peter as he spoke. In the low light of the office room, Kenseiko had removed his dark glasses. Red scars punctuated the whites of his eyes. A white blotch marred the blackness of his left pupil.

Dr. Zhāng left, and Li finished his tea. Neither Peter nor Damiaan wanted a refill.

"So, Peter Reynolds, what do you think of our achievements here in the mountains of Nepal?"

"Most impressive! I'm glad to have seen how the hardware we produce is being put to good use."

Li smiled as he reached into his pocket to remove something. "Speaking of which, do you recognize this, Peter?" He handed over a small bit of metal. It resembled an insect toy.

Peter handed it back. "Nope, never seen it before. What is it?"

"It's a surveillance device, miniature tech and quite sophisticated. There's a nanochip inside."

"You mean a bug?"

"Yes, yes, I would call it that."

Peter shrugged. "So, why is this significant?"

"It is manufactured by one of your companies, Peter: Baxter Consolidated. That is one of the Reynolds' affiliates is it not?"

"Yes. So, we make a lot of things, a lot of high-tech things. I don't recognize this particular device, but it may be one of ours."

"Peter, Peter, Peter…don't you think you should keep a closer eye on what your companies do? Don't you think you should keep a closer eye on what your people are doing? People like Charles Godfried?" He drummed his fingers on the desk. "Or should I say, Claus Gorman?"

"Who? Who is Claus Gorman?" Peter felt sweat on his palms.

"That's what I want you to tell me, Peter. He's programmed into your cell phone." He picked up the electronic bug and rolled it with his fingers. "This device is called a 'spider'; it came from Dulce, New Mexico. We had a hive facility there. Even bigger than the one here. Notice I said 'had.' You wouldn't know anything about that would you, Peter?"

Peter saw Van Duyn looking down. *I'm screwed. Try to stay calm.* "I heard about that raid. If my people or my tech somehow is mixed up with it, I'll look into it when I get back."

Li pressed a button on his desk. "I think there is more for you to tell than you are admitting, Peter. I think there are things you have been hiding from me. Your nephew, Bryson's, name is also in your phone. What else are you not telling me?"

The office door opened, and two HC-12s entered.

"You know, Peter, I never liked you. I never liked your brother George. But at least he had good genes." He pointed to the two soldiers. "These are your other nephews. Well, not entirely, but your brother's genes are disproportionately included in their DNA."

Sweat dripped down Peter's neck. He stared at Dr. Li. "What do you want, Kenseiko? I never liked you either. There, I've said all I plan to."

"Oh, I don't think so. I couldn't persuade George Reynolds, but my methods have gotten much, much better." He held the spider between thumb and index finger. "Our tech department at Advanced Bionics has developed our own sophisticated techniques." He squeezed, and a snapping crunch followed. Li handed the spider's debris to Peter.

I'm fucked...

78

S erena came up behind Tarni and Bryson. Each sat hunched over, concentrating on BB's files. She rubbed their shoulders with deep pressure massage.

"Is that some yoga relaxation technique, mate? You've got the touch. Can you teach me? That feels fabulous!" Tarni got up to stretch, but Bryson sat, muttering to himself as a string of code formed on the screen in front of him.

Tarni slapped him across the back. "Time out, nerd boy. You need to take a break."

Serena felt radiant. "How's it going, Bry? Claus and I just finished up. He needs you to run the trial."

"Could be better. There are a lot of firewalls, a lot of high-security stuff. Nothing I can't handle, but I'm staying low while I probe the whole network to figure out the vulnerabilities. When I'm done, I want to get everything on their servers and wipe out not only their primary system, but all their backups. When I'm through, I don't want them to be able to recover."

"I've been sorting out the files to see what to send, and Bryson is embedding bits and pieces of code. Once all the files are downloaded, command strings will initiate. They'll take over the whole bloody network." Tarni took out a nail file and began to file her nails. "Now, if I sound like I know what I'm talking about, don't be deceived. I'm a dork about what the geek over here is doing, but he seems to think it's going rather well." She nudged Bryson again. "Break time."

The three moved to the main room. Claus sat on the couch, earphones draped around his neck, and he held the optical goggles. He pointed to a nearby laptop. "Don't screw this up, Bryson. I've got it programmed to run through the color and sound sequence six times with a ten-second break between sessions. If at any time I sense a problem, I will raise my hand. Then you hit the pause button and disconnect me. Got it?"

"What can go wrong?" Tarni asked.

"Hell if I know. Flip out like a bad LSD trip? Light up like a Fourth of July sparkler? Levitate? Although, that would be cool, don't you think?" If Claus was nervous, it didn't show.

Serena said, "Claus is our official guinea pig. If this works, we'll send it all to Arnie; he can intersperse his musical compositions to jazz it up. I also want to send it out to my Naga Sisters and to Moon at the Isis Mystery School. The more the better." Serena gave Claus a big kiss on the cheek. "Remember what I told you about choosing to remain to continue the fight. Don't you dare try to ascend, or I'll have to hunt you down and bring you back."

"What a man has to do for a kiss from Buddha girl. If you promise me another, that's worth staying back for." His cheeks blushed and he finished, "Okay, let's cut the bullshit and fire me up. Houston, I am ready to launch."

The three of them stood watching both the computer screen, where the seven words and corresponding colors displayed without audio, and Claus, adorned in headgear. Each cycle took just over four minutes. After the second, Serena saw Claus's breathing slow. He appeared to be in deep meditation. After the third cycle passed, Claus barely moved. After the fifth cycle, Claus's hands shot up. Bryson slammed the pause and stripped off the goggles and headphones. Claus just sat there.

"What, what's happening? What's wrong?" Bryson shook Claus, who said nothing.

After a long minute, his eyes fluttered. He grinned. "I was there after the third round, I just wanted to sit through it again." Claus turned to Serena. "That music, angels, that light calling to me. Hard to resist."

She took his hands and kissed his cheek once, twice, a third time. "Not angelic but the best I can do. Thanks for staying with us." She planted more kisses on both cheeks.

"Thank you, Serena. You are something else. This party of ours is just getting started, and I wouldn't miss it for the world. Who wants to go next?"

Tarni already sat with the goggles and headphones on her lap.

"Just give me a minute, Tarni. I need to use the restroom and fetch a beer. Twenty-four minutes to enlightenment. I must have burned off all my karma in a previous life." He floated off to the bathroom.

Bryson said, "Just make sure you stay behind too, Tarni. We've still got work to do, and I need your help."

Tarni looked at her nails. "No worries, mate. I can't possibly ascend looking like this."

Al Jazeera World News:

> *Delegates from sixty nations gathered to formalize a charter for the Global Governance Federation. More nations are expected to join. Already, the GGF has brokered a ceasefire in the Middle East. Using resources from member nations, they are offering a policing capability to enforce law and order and to distribute humanitarian relief.*

> *The full charter has not yet been released for review, but leaked information suggests that separate working task forces will address the crises in food and clean water, the Hendra-variant Bogi 1, nuclear threats, terrorism, and global peace. The world watches.*

> *Wildfires rage across the Western United States, and Buenos Aires burns as rioters set fire to cars, government buildings, and anything else that burns. The Pavlodar oil refinery in Kazakhstan is in flames as black smoke billows. A residue of soot blankets the entire city.*

In other news…

Bryson, Tarni, Claus, and Serena all sat together, finishing a late-night snack as they flipped through news stations. The stories and reporting didn't waver regardless of the source. Death, violence, destruction, fear, and hardship— all with a simple solution: put your hopes for a better future in a new authority, trust someone else to shepherd you through the turmoil. All the authorities— government, corporate, religious—all sang the same tune. They all supported the Global Governance Federation as representing a new hope for mankind.

Her mouth full of popcorn, Tarni spoke for them all. "I always suspected it, but now it's plain as a dog's balls. This news is nothing but a load of roo poo!"

79

Wán shàn had nothing of interest to share in her log post. Reports from each of her sisters spying on the Council heads all sounded similar. The Illuminati upper echelon all felt elated by how turmoil in the world accelerated with growing momentum. Their plans unfolded with conspicuous success.

With her bàba in Nepal, there wasn't much for her to do in Singapore. The demonstrations outside Advanced Bionics' corporate headquarters were largely peaceful. As a precaution, many HC-12 soldiers patrolled outside. The enhanced security stirred something within her that she needed to sort out. In no way did Wán shàn feel unsafe. In some ways, she thought the extra guards unnecessary. *Why do these people demonstrate? They do not understand all the good bàba will accomplish. They think he lies, and they are fearful or unwilling to see the truth.*

These reflections, this inner dialogue, meandered for a time as she tried to get to the bottom of what caused something she could only describe as an uneasy feeling. Finally, she had it. She decided truth is relative. It's a matter of perspective. For the people demonstrating outside the building, it was one thing; for the Illuminati heads, it was another. She decided that people had no way to distinguish false beliefs from truth. With this epiphany, her disquiet eased. She felt better. Then, she made a decision.

The last time Wán shàn visited The Womb, her cousins slept. Now, staff informed her most had been dispersed throughout the world with their instructions. They would help usher in the new society. Staff called them shepherds and gardeners. She thought the descriptions odd.

"Wán shàn. That is the name Kenseiko has given you, is it not? Which one of the six are you? Never mind, I am surprised to see you. He said nothing about your visit when I saw him two days ago."

"Bàba was here?"

"Yes, he needed my help. An attempt upon his life required my intervention. He said nothing about a visit from one of his special children."

"He does not know I am here."

"Then that is even more of a surprise." Shrem seemed amused by her unannounced presence.

"Tell me, Shrem, what is truth?"

If a creature such as Shrem laughed, this is what Wán shàn endured for almost a minute. He howled so long, she thought he might choke or collapse from not breathing.

He composed himself. *"I should not laugh. The question is both serious and silly. I am more than amused that you ask it."* Shrem's tone changed. *"Truth is whatever you make it out to be. It is no more than beliefs, blocks of sand sitting upon a foundation of sand."*

"I suspected as much."

Choking laugher again ensued as Shrem reacted to her response. *"You really should come and visit more often. You are which one of the six?"*

"When I return, I will remind you. It is difficult to tell me apart from my sisters. I have other questions. What is the plan you spoke of before, and what is my purpose in the context of this plan?"

The creature seemed to think for a while before answering. *"As I have told your bàba, as you like to call him, as I have told the Brotherhood of the Sun for countless generations, the plan is revealed over time as I choose to reveal it. Your purpose is to serve the plan."*

"What is the plan now, today, during my life? How do I serve the plan if I do not even know my role in moving it further?"

"Very well, this much I will share. Death and destruction, bloodshed, violence are all part of the plan. At times, the race of man must be torn down in order to create something better."

"Better for who?"

Another howl of laughter burst forth before Shrem settled down. *"That is not something I choose to share."*

He revealed nothing further that Wán shàn deemed useful. The creature had given her much to think about. She thanked him and left.

Kenseiko busied himself loading the protocol. Peter Reynolds sat restrained in a booth. Two soldiers stood at attention, but Li doubted their skills would be needed, especially with Wán shàn close by. Li explained the programming sequence to his daughter while Van Duyn spoke.

"Peter, I've sat in the very same chair as you. Don't fight it. If you do, I'm told it's very painful."

"Did you fight it, Damiaan? Did it muddle your brain?"

"I sat voluntarily. I was curious to see for myself what the tech did, how it worked."

"So, you don't even know if Kenseiko planted some commands deep inside your brain?"

"What if he did? So what? The man's brilliant. He's got vision, vision for a new and improved humanity."

"Sorry if I don't share that same vision. My idea of a better humanity looks different. I think he messed with your thinking more than you realize. One thing I've learned over the years, self-deception is at worst a poison that destroys your mind, or at best it's a soothing balm to help make you feel better. In your case, Damiaan, I think it's a bit of both."

"Gentlemen, enough. Damiaan, would you kindly affix the goggles and earphones?" Kenseiko directed his next comments to Peter. "He's right about the pain if you resist—most unpleasant."

"Did you use this same tech on my brother? Did he resist?"

"This type of neural programming was in its infancy then, still under development and much, much cruder. Your brother was not a willing subject. He screamed rather loudly." Li recalled this memory with apparent satisfaction.

"And his wife, my sister-in-law, did you torture her as well?"

"Please, Peter, your choice of words is hardly accurate. I will share that her genes were rather ordinary. I had no use for them."

"So, you killed her?" Peter thrashed his head several times after the goggles were secured.

"As Wán shàn attests, many innocents die in the pursuit of perfection." Kenseiko started the quality control sequence.

Moments later, Peter screamed repeatedly. Dr. Li said to Damiaan, "We did tell him it would hurt if he resisted."

"Do you want me to tape his mouth? Stop the yelling?"

"Not at all. I rather enjoy listening to it." Kenseiko dialed up the intensity.

80

"Has anybody heard from Uncle Pete?" Serena stood at the kitchen counter, pouring out a mug of coffee. The rest of the team had already been up for an hour.

Bryson responded, "Claus is out fishing. He said he checked the voice mailbox he and Uncle Pete set prior to the trip. Still no word. But he's not in Nepal anymore. Or at least his phone isn't. It pinged in Singapore. I tried to reach his cell, but no luck."

"I don't like it, Bry."

"Me neither. But I do have some good news. Arnie had his concert yesterday. Said only six hundred people showed, but they seemed to like the new songs. He mixed them in with his standard music. He also put everything up on YouTube. I've got the links to the songs featuring your seven magic words. They've already been downloaded over two thousand times. That's a lot of downloads."

"It's not magic, Bry. It's just restoring what should come naturally."

"Tarni and I beg to differ. The saucy Aussie and I have already discussed what happened to each of us yesterday. We don't pretend to understand it."

"Very magical…still feeling bonzer! Game changer if the bard's music works as well as the sights and sounds you plugged me into yesterday. I want to download Arnie's YouTubes just to check them out, but nerd boy says he needs my help, and I have to remain on this plane of existence for now." Tarni poked Bryson in the ribs.

An hour later as Claus hosed off his boots, Serena and Tarni absorbed themselves in Arnbjørn Gnadir's new music videos.

Neither Serena nor any of them overheard Bryson exclaim, "I'm in. Let's see what kind of information Li has secured in this database."

Bryson's keystrokes and comments went unheeded. "No shit! Log entries connecting to all the Illuminati families…WTF? Wait a minute, what's this?" He spent a moment scanning the information in front of his eyes. "Holy shit! Guys, GUYS!"

Claus stepped in. "You got something, Bryson?"

The two women sat together, holding hands and singing. Claus shook them. "You two better get over here and look at this. You're not gonna believe it!"

As the four looked at Kenseiko Li's presentation with the interactive world map given to the Council of Thirteen, nobody spoke. They barely breathed.

"There are six of the chimeric hybrids, all identical, all named Wán shàn. It looks like Dr. Li used them to spy internally on the rest of the Illuminati family heads. I'm sure there will be useful details in the log entries these six recorded. But this presentation is the mother lode; it spells out the big picture and shows exactly what they're doing." Bryson replayed the entire presentation, but his enthusiasm quickly dampened as they absorbed the magnitude of death and suffering the plan anticipated.

Tarni broke the silence. "It's bloody Armageddon! How can we stop this?"

Serena answered; her voice sounded calm and measured. "We've got to get this out, Bryson."

At that moment his cell phone rang. "Hey, everybody, it's Uncle Pete."

81

Over their secure video conferencing link, Servant Van Duyn conducted the opening ceremony prior to the formal meeting's start.

"Fellow Brothers, for reasons that will shortly be made evident, Servant Li, our Pindar, is here with me and will address you shortly. He is safe. There has been an assassination attempt. This effort failed. It is one of two threats that have been or will soon be neutralized."

Per their prearranged plan, the camera swung for a close-up of Kenseiko Li. Collective gasps of horror filled the audio. The Council members' faces contorted. When the impact crested, he signaled Damiaan with a blink.

"Our Pindar will now speak."

"Brothers, do not let my appearance deceive you. I am strong... We are strong. A rogue geneticist targeted me with a DNA-specific agent in an attempt to kill me." Arms gestured outward. "As you can see, I am still here." Small yellow teeth highlighted his scarred yet smiling features. "While it is unlikely that any of you are in danger of a similar attempt, prudence dictates additional personal security."

Dr. Li fielded questions until Van Duyn received a hand signal.

"There is a second matter our esteemed Brother and fellow Servant Li wishes to report on."

"During the past year, whispers continued to surface about the reemergence of the Candelaria cult. Our recently passed Brother Rothschild diligently sought to uncover the whereabouts of a Candelaria witch."

As Li expected, this brought murmurs of surprise from the other family heads. The topic caught them off guard. Shouts and comments had to be interrupted.

Van Duyn said, "Please allow our Pindar to speak."

"Thank you, Servant Van Duyn. The reports are true. I have confirmed the identity and location of the witch, and I shall soon have her."

"What will you do with her?" Bundy managed to speak the loudest over the din.

"That remains to be seen. I have also learned that she is responsible for the destruction of our hive in New Mexico. Rest assured, the Candelaria threat has been eliminated."

The remainder of the conference call focused upon updates on the cull.

Van Duyn explained that the loss of assets in New Mexico caused a reevaluation of their modeling. Since these assets were primarily for assignments in North and South America, additional measures were required to reduce the population on these continents. More widespread disbursement of the Hendra-variant, and additional pressure on food supplies would enable them to reestablish population control according to their parameters, projections, and personnel.

Kenseiko highlighted areas on the world map and displayed the revisions. "According to our models, the loss in additional lives from wide dispersion of the virus is only the initial benefit. The fear generated will drive vaccination rates up, amplify civil unrest, and open the door for more aggressive centralized control."

Kenseiko looked at video-linked heads nodding. "To conclude this update, within three months, we project a worldwide net loss of 1.6 billion lives. The vaccine-induced fatalities, spread over the planned five-year latency, combined with essential food shortages, will do the rest to reach our targets. During this elapsed timeframe, the very governments that administered the immunizations will no longer exist. Our New World Order will be a reality. This will occur in our lifetimes."

Prior to the closing ceremonies, they agreed to meet under the Hill for a celebration next month.

"All rise." The thirteen men stood, raised their left hands, and placed them over their hearts.

Li spoke. "We, the chosen, pledge to serve the light Lucifer has brought to us..."

"To illuminate," they intoned in unison and touched their foreheads.

Li continued. "May Lucifer guide us..."—they each touched their left shoulders—"and bless us..."—they touched their right shoulders. "Until his light shines upon all." All thirteen rested their hands back upon their hearts.

In unison they recited, "May the light shine upon us in glory."

The meeting adjourned. Li looked at Van Duyn. "Thank you, Damiaan. I think that went well."

82

"Uncle Pete, we've been worried about you. Where are you?"

"I'm in Singapore, Bryson." The voice on the other end sounded strange.

"Is everything okay? You don't sound right."

"I'm fine. There's someone here who needs to speak with you. I'm handing the phone to him now."

Bryson put his finger to his lips, motioning for silence. He put his phone on speaker.

"Hello, Bryson, this is Dr. Kenseiko Li." Chills ran up his spine. Serena grabbed his hand, and the voice continued. "I knew your father. It seems the Reynolds family is an ongoing source of difficulty. I hope you have more sense than your father and more sense than your uncle. If you do exactly as I tell you, I shall not harm him."

Li gave precise instructions. He wanted to know the closest international airport. He would send a jet there to pick up Bryson and Serena Mendez. Dr. Li had no doubt Bryson knew the Candelaria's location. Someone would call this number with flight and gate details. No weapons. No foolish rescue attempts.

"Serena is on Interpol's list of people to be detained for questioning."

"This will not be an issue, I assure you." Li's voice conveyed cool certainty.

"How do I know that my Uncle Peter will be kept safe?"

"You don't." The phone went dead.

Bryson looked around the room. Their faces showed brains in hyperdrive, but none showed panic.

Claus spoke first. "You still have the name of that pilot who flew you to Muskegon? If he's still around, this will go a lot faster."

"Didn't you hear Li? He said no rescue attempt," Serena protested.

"Of course, I heard him. He was talking about you and Bryson. You don't think I'm gonna let him do as he pleases with Mr. Reynolds, do you? Boss man's a goner if we don't get him out."

"What are you proposing, Claus?" Bryson turned to Serena. "Let's hear him out."

"Pretty simple really. I need to get a team together. There's a big demand for personal security and ex-military are lapping it up. I'll probably need to pay off some contracts." He seemed to be thinking out loud as he talked. They followed him to his room, where he pulled out a duffle. "Phoenix is our best shot to stage an op from. You get that pilot on the line. If he's not around, maybe he can suggest someone."

Bryson grabbed Claus's arm. "Hold on, cowboy. Hasty planning reduces chances for success."

"No doubt, but we don't have a lot of time. You and Serena need to be in Milwaukee. Li hasn't given the details yet, but you'll probably fly out tomorrow afternoon."

"But we don't even know Uncle Peter's whereabouts for sure. Yes, we have his location now, but that can change. Let's just say hypothetically that you follow with a team to Singapore. Then what? Damn sure Li's people will strip search us, confiscate any communication devices, and make sure we're not bugged. How will you find us?"

"True, that part of the op needs work."

But Bryson didn't stay to listen to Claus. He ran to the bedroom then returned with his boots, kicked off his slippers, and laced up. He barked to Serena, "Hurry, get dressed, we've got to make a run into town."

"Where are we going, Bry?" Serena rushed off.

Tarni stood there, tying a bandana to pull back her mop of hair. "I'm no Rambo and won't kill anybody, but count me in. Where are we going?"

Bryson looked at his watch—10:36. "To get chipped."

83

Claus and Tarni had left last night for Phoenix. Barry was thrilled to fly them wherever they wanted to go; he said the corporate and private jet business had seriously slowed down. Turns out the pilot flew fighter jets in the Navy. *Maybe he and Claus can share military stories.*

The group of four assured themselves of a get-together in Singapore; one that included Uncle Peter. Bryson didn't consider this might be final goodbyes.

He had drilled Claus on instructions and written them both on paper and in a file on the laptop Bryson had handed over. "After you log on as 'ZELDARZ'— all caps—type: 'Return of the Rainbow Warriors' and hit send. Timing is everything. First do your thing with the soldier units. Whether or not that works, do this exactly. Within five minutes, their systems will crash. Got it?"

Claus delivered his succinct answer with a taut smile. "Piece-a-pie."

Bryson worked all night to finish the cyber-bomb. That designation seemed woefully short of what the stealth attack should do. He signed onto the dark web and sent out more info to his trusted hackers. *We are gonna hit these bastards with everything we've got.*

The adrenalin-fueled focus of the last eighteen hours began to wear off. He rubbed his arm over the chip implant. That went well enough. They used their New Mexico driver's licenses. Tarni had to jump through extra hoops due to her temporary visa. Claus synced his equipment to track them. They bought a few staples at the food depot to make it all look legit.

Bryson's eyes grew heavy; a yawn followed. He programmed some false addresses and contact info into the prepaid phone and tried to think of any last-minute details. Just as Bryson dozed, a message box popped up on his screen. He scanned it and frowned. *Further information has surfaced regarding the dump of false information implicating Dr. Kenseiko Li and his company, Advanced Bionics. Egyptian officials have raided the headquarters of Pyramid Communications and shut down their operations...*

Bryson saw no reason to wake Serena with this bad news. He forced himself to remain confident and buried this new update. While he didn't know Moon personally, he hoped she and her people were okay. If Bryson's cyber-infiltration and dissemination succeeded, soon everyone would learn the truth.

Claus handed each of them a faux contract. "We've all been hired by Hideyoshi Suh, a wealthy Japanese businessman, to provide private security for his daughter, Hinata. I varied the dates on the contracts. All each of you need to do is sign and put this document in with your passport."

"How old is this Hinata person?" Jerry asked. Despite the nursery deaths in Dulce, he wanted to be part of this new mission. Five of the six men who had been on that raid now flew together with Claus and Tarni on their chartered jet.

"I'm figuring early twenties, just the age she really needs close watching." Claus winked.

"What about Tarni? What's her cover story?" One of the other men, Jeremiah, wanted this detail.

"She's a friend of the family. At Hideyoshi's request, we're taking her back to be with Hinata. So, no contract for her, but daddy figures she has a mature and stabilizing influence on his sometimes-reckless daughter."

"Then let's ask her. Tarni, how old is your imaginary Japanese friend?"

Tarni batted her eyes; Jeremiah had been trying to hit on her the whole trip over. "Twenty-three."

"Is she as hot as you?" Jeremiah smirked.

Claus glared him to silence and whispered to Tarni, "His nickname is Jeremiah Jerkoff, but he is solid and will have your back."

A coy smile lit Tarni's face. "I think he wants more than my back."

"Listen up, everybody. Eight hours till we touch down. Get some rest. If anyone needs help with that, I've got sleepers." Claus patted his shirt pocket. "No alcohol. We need to be sharp tomorrow." He gave the pocket another pat. "I can help with that too."

Serena and Bryson waited at the security checkpoint leading to the private gate entrance. They never encountered anyone from TSA. Their phones were confiscated. Pat downs explored every nook and crevice. Serena endured it and remained calm. Their embedded arm chips led to discussion among the security agents escorting them—identical triplets, cloned hybrids for sure. One of the agents made a call. Serena couldn't overhear the consultation. The chips were okay; they led the two through the gate.

The entire time, she and Bryson interacted with their escorts, the two remained fully cooperative and offered no resistance. They said little and asked few questions. After hoods were placed over their heads, and it became clear they were to be separated from one another, she thanked the guards for allowing her simple request.

She stood next to Bryson. Serena felt his calm presence despite the danger. Through her hood, she said, "I love you, Bry. No matter what happens, remember that I love you."

A muffled reply followed. "I love you too, Serena."

84

Tarni carried a dozen signs, which she distributed among the more vocal protesters. Fortunately, they all spoke English. She started a chant: WE-WANT-TO-BE-FREE / LOCK-UP-KEN-SEI-KO-LI.

Tarni had a straightforward job on this operation: create distraction. She also carried a secondary portable transmitter—backup in case the primary failed or Claus became incapacitated. Things seemed to be gathering steam. A flash mob began forming, but thus far, everything remained peaceful. No one wanted riot police to show up.

She scanned the building entrance. Half a dozen guards watched the crowd; they looked intimidating with their assault weapons, body armor, and military-style headgear. She looked at her team members scattered at different positions. Their concealed handguns and Kevlar vests equated to pathetic by comparison. *We are way overmatched. Who knows how many more of those super-soldiers are in the building?*

Her earbud crackled and Claus said, "I've confirmed their location inside. We sit tight a little longer before I pull the trigger. If it doesn't work, we'll need to incite the crowd to rush the building. They're not big enough or rowdy enough. Pull out the bullhorn and fire them up."

A bullhorn started a new chant, nice and short: LOCK-UP-LI… LOCK-UP-LI…

Tarni stood tall, waving her sign. Her height put her a head over most of the other protesters. She yelled and saw one of the guards point at her. She shouted even louder.

They entered through a side entrance. Their hoods had been removed to help them from stumbling and to not draw attention. At least, that's how Bryson figured it. From what he could see, the demonstrators out front only numbered a hundred or so. He took a deep breath. *We need more than that, or we're sunk.*

Serena had been gagged. Bryson guessed they weren't taking any chances with her voice. A private elevator brought them to the sixteenth floor. Once they exited the elevator, they traveled down a lengthy corridor. No one paid attention to their group. A door opened. The escorts stepped to the side, and Bryson saw her, the young Asian girl, the one from the surveillance video. She had a gun!

He yelled to Serena, "GUN!" She dropped to the ground, and he jumped on top of her, cradling her much smaller frame. Two shots fired.

Everything slowed down, like an old 45 vinyl playing at 33 LP. The girl put the gun down and approached. She moved like a fly in November, slow…so…s-l-o-w… He blacked out.

Bryson blinked a few times and shook his head. He wanted to rub the sleep from his eyes, wipe the fog from his brain, but his hands were tied behind him. He looked down at the zip tie around his ankles. Serena also sat restrained in a chair. She appeared to be asleep but unharmed. Duct tape replaced the gag. They also had tied her ankles. She had a lapboard with an electric pad of some sort. He saw the stylus, saw her right wrist had a tether; just enough so she could write. *Doodle pad…to communicate.*

He blinked a few more times, trying to see better until he realized the lights were down low. Despite the poor lighting, the scene in the rest of the room looked dismal. Uncle Peter sat in a chair. He didn't look good and said nothing. Next to him stood the young Asian girl, only slightly taller than his seated uncle. Two guards flanked the door.

The girl said, "Bryson Reynolds. I trust you are uninjured. The drug clears rapidly. Given Serena's much smaller size, it may be a few minutes before she regains consciousness."

He was certain this was one of the Wán shàn hybrids, but he played dumb. "Who are you? What do you want? What did you do to my Uncle Peter?" Bryson flexed his jaw a few times to make the words come out right.

"My bàba has brought you here. You are his guests."

Just as he was about to comment on the poor hospitality, the door opened, and a man hobbled in. He had an obvious clubfoot. He wore sunglasses, even in the dim light. *Li. Shit…BB's plan failed!*

The girl pulled up a chair, and Li sat right next to Uncle Peter. Bryson studied his adversary. Pockmark scars littered the man's face. After Li removed the dark glasses, Bryson saw scarring on the whites of his eyes. The Illuminati appeared to be studying first Bryson, then Serena.

"I presume you are Dr. Kenseiko Li. What did you do to my uncle?"

"Bryson Reynolds, I've waited some time for this moment. What did you do to my nephew Gensu?"

"After he shot me in the leg in Peru, I blacked out. When I woke up, he was gone. I heard he fell off a cliff." *He had some help—more thrown off the cliff, but I don't need to tell Li that.*

"Speaking of relatives, what do you think of your cousins?" Li pointed to the two guards; he seemed to be smirking.

At first, Bryson didn't make the connection, but he figured it out quickly. "My father. You killed him and stole his genes."

"You have a keen mind, Bryson. That you inherited from your father, I am sure. Your mother was less, shall I say, gifted."

"How did he die?"

"Screaming. Even more than your uncle." He pointed to Peter.

"What did you do to him?"

"You Reynolds seem to have trouble with compliance and cooperation. I enhanced his. Hopefully, without too much damage."

"What do you want, Dr. Li? Are you going to release my uncle? We're here. What's next?"

"The Candelaria witch will rouse shortly. Then we can discuss the terms of your cooperation."

As Bryson sat, a mental clock ticked along. He wasn't sure how long he'd been out. He figured Serena would wake soon. Would there be enough time? He inhaled and waited.

85

Wán shàn barely listened to the exchange between Bryson Reynolds and her bàba. After learning all about the Candelaria sect, after her bàba explained why the genes were so important and how he planned to have Serena Mendez teach the power of voice to the many infant clones already born, she felt curiosity. These genes must be remarkable. If bàba was correct, this very ancient bloodline produced genetically superior humans.

After returning from Tibet and her discussion with Shrem, she paid a visit to the storage locker. Her time there was both brief and discreet. She knew exactly what she wanted and where to find it. At that time, her bàba was en route from Nepal to Singapore. She felt certain that he would disagree with her if he knew, but her exchange with Shrem left no doubt in her mind. She and her sisters were tools. Expendable commodities as Beangagarrie Brindabella had put it. She felt not an ounce of remorse at her decision. Wán shàn understood that she lacked the capacity for remorse. She also understood that it was a matter of perspective whether this lack of capacity was judged to be something good or something bad.

Irrelevant! Good or bad, true or false—these are structures of sand built upon foundations of sand. Much as Shrem explained. Given this realization, she further concluded that there was always choice. She had made hers. And she had made a choice for her sisters because her insights and her conclusions would also be theirs once they had all the facts and details. A rational and analytic brain was not much different from a computer. You enter the data, and the computer processes the data to yield an answer. Her answer: *we are not perfect. Bàba can make this claim, can give us that name, but it is little more than a belief of his. Sand upon sand.*

Part of her wanted to remove the tape from Serena Mendez's mouth, to witness the power in the Candelaria's voice, to see for herself what was possible given the correct genetic configuration. In the meantime, Wán shàn would wait. The stillness in her erect body in no way revealed her thoughts within. Her mind was active. She felt curious and something more. Anticipation? Yes. She felt her head nod in agreement. She inhaled deeply, trying to detect the scent of fear. There was none.

Serena stirred.

The Daily Informer: Your Trusted Internet Source for News from the Fringe

07:10 PM GMT: Alien Abduction or the Rapture?

Our European correspondent just concluded a phone interview with Birgitte Knudsen, a Danish woman living in a small flat in Copenhagen. She claims that her boyfriend, Oluf Gregersen, mysteriously disappeared after a brilliant flash of light. According to her account, she and Oluf had attended a concert by Arnbjørn Gnadir, a local musician, a few nights before. "Oluf went on You-Tube and downloaded some tracks. He found the music really moving, almost transcendent, as he put it. Anyway, I thought it was okay. Since the concert, he's been listening to this one song 'Dance of the Two Serpents' almost continuously. I was in the kitchen preparing some food, and he was in the bedroom. Suddenly, I see this incredibly bright light. It stunned me for a moment. I went to check on Oluf, and he was gone. Disappeared! His headset lay on the bed; the music track was still playing. I don't understand. Where is my boyfriend? We're supposed to get married next year." Neighbors confirmed seeing a flash of light, but there were no other reports of anything unusual. They described both Oluf and Birgitte as lovely people. Police are investigating.

10:36 PM GMT: Since our initial report, there have been five additional sudden and unexplained disappearances in this same area of Denmark. All accounts include the appearance of bright lights. We contacted Gregor Dolph Rasmussen, a noted paranormal researcher and self-proclaimed Biblical scholar. He claims, "Given the recent turn of world events—war, famine, disease, pestilence, plagues, and what have you—these disappearances are not likely extraterrestrial in origin." According to this expert, we are seeing the beginning of the Rapture as has been predicted to

*occur as we approach the end times. He encourages all to prepare
for Armageddon.*

86

Misty cobwebs started to clear; Serena felt her eyelids flutter, and she looked around. She felt the cover over her mouth and noted Bryson close by in restraints, Dr. Li, his young accomplice, and Uncle Peter. He looked drugged, just sitting next to Li. Obviously BB's plan had failed, but Li looked far from healthy. It took a moment to understand the electronic board in front of her. She picked up the stylus.

Bryson said, "I'm fine, Serena. Uncle Peter is messed up, and Li hasn't told me yet what he plans to do with us or with my uncle. I don't know the girl's name, but she hasn't said much."

"Got it. I'm fine."

He read her response as she wrote on the notepad. Then she drew a happy face emoji. She felt certain her calm inner stillness showed to their captors.

"Ms. Mendez. I'm glad you have woken up and I can get down to business. Wán shàn can loosen your bonds a little if it is too difficult to communicate on the pad." Li flashed a tablet with her message and emoji showing. The communication seemed to provoke a hint of a smile from him.

Dr. Li addressed Bryson. "My daughter's name is Wán shàn. It means perfection. She has five sisters, all equally perfect."

Serena wrote nothing in response; Bryson's reply echoed her own thoughts.

"A chimera? Some mishmash of genetic engineering that can't even reproduce? You've got a strange idea of what's perfect."

"Not at all Bryson, not at all. If you wanted to make a better human being, why not remove all the troublesome parts, the things that make people want something more: children…something better in an afterlife…more material possessions? How much more reckless overconsumption can this planet endure? You may think me a monster. You may think the plan my associates have launched is diabolical. You are wrong because you do not understand."

"I think we understand quite well," Serena wrote quickly. "You want to control it all, but to do so you have taken so much away. Too much. This is not the way to save the planet or the human race."

"Really? Tell me, Serena Mendez, do you think you have a better way? Humanity is broken. We are far along a path of self-destruction. I offer a means to fix that. What is your plan?"

"Restore man's genes to the original blueprint, before the corruption of DNA that enslaved us to your mind control," she wrote with the stylus and added, "Have you considered that?"

His yellow teeth glistened, even in the pale light. "Yes. The great corruption, the War of the Two Serpents, mind control and manipulation—you believe such nonsense?"

"Yes." Serena saw Bryson nodding his head in agreement.

"Throughout history there are leaders and there are followers, winners and losers. The losers always need an excuse, a reason to lay blame, to explain their victimhood. How do you think the masses of humanity felt when Genghis Khan conquered them? Oppressed or liberated? There are good genes and there are bad genes, strong DNA and weak DNA. Look at nature. Who survives? What you see as a great cull, I see as mercy killing. It's time for a new and improved humanity."

Li shrugged. "You see, I am not nearly the monster you make me out to be."

She scribbled with the stylus. "What do you want?"

"I offer you the chance to lead with me. Your genetic makeup is extraordinary. I can replicate that, but I cannot master your purported power of voice. I need someone to train the next generation of Candelaria warriors, to help me to unlock the full potential latent in your genes."

"And if I refuse?"

"I could attempt some neural reprogramming to gain your acquiescence, but there is a risk of damaging your special talents." He patted Peter Reynolds on the shoulder. "It would be a shame to ruin all that you are. I'm afraid Peter here isn't quite the same man he was last week."

The threat left no doubt in her mind. *Coercion. Still, I am more valuable to him if he doesn't have to brainwash me.* Serena decided to confront Li. "You won't take the risk of harming me. So, Dr. Li, do you have a plan B?"

Li whispered something in Peter Reynolds' ear. She watched as Uncle Pete went to Bryson, wrapped hands around his nephew's neck, and began to squeeze.

Bryson choked, sputtered, and tried to breathe. He managed a "Don't listen to him!" between gasps.

Li said something, it sounded Chinese; Peter calmly walked back to his chair and sat down. "You see, Ms. Mendez, there is always a plan B. I can be most persuasive."

87

Claus checked his watch. "Before we launch, I want to say a couple of last things to all of you. My best guess is they're either on the fifteenth or sixteenth floor, depending on whether or not this building has a thirteenth floor."

Someone said over their comms, "Asians are crazy when it comes to bad luck, probably sixteenth if I had to guess. We can check the elevators when we get in."

"Copy that; good suggestion." Claus sighed. "My final words, though I'm hoping these aren't final final, if you know what I mean… What I'm trying to say is…I think you are all one helluva team. Can't imagine going down with a better group, if that's the way this shakes out."

Tarni's voice came through over the protesters' chants. "Let's have a little power of positive thinking, mate. I'm feeling upbeat about our chances."

"Okay. I'm good with that. It's time to crash the party. Tarni, flip your unit to 'transmit.'"

Claus transmitted too. Both broadcast a message in Chinese, the same audio Claus had a copy of from the prisoner interrogated in Libya. He waited. Nothing happened. He studied the supersoldiers and the assembled crowd. *If this doesn't work, this won't go down well for us.*

"Tarni, switch to all frequencies and boost the transmission signal to max."

"How do I do that?"

"Lower right hand on the control panel, there are four control knobs. Turn the 'signal frequency' knob clockwise to 'All' and the knob next to it that says 'trans output' clockwise to 'Max.'"

Claus took out the laptop Bryson had given him. He had already connected it to the internet. Per instructions, he typed: "ZELDARZ," then followed with, "Return of the Rainbow Warrior." He ignored the sweat drops on the keyboard and hit "send."

"Okay, team, launch sequence has initiated. Let's keep our fingers crossed." Claus held his breath and disengaged the safety on his pistol.

As the transmission broadcast in a continuous loop, the Chinese words for "Failure three, two, one" had an effect. Claus watched as the group of soldiers stationed outside the entrance fell to the ground, violently shaking in epileptic fits.

The crowd silenced momentarily then erupted into a cheer. Several hundred stormed the building with no one stopping them. Tarni led the charge.

Claus came over their channel. "Tarni, keep transmitting. We don't know if the signal carried to the inside. Okay, team, let's move."

Serena considered the circumstances. Li gave her the option to cooperate, but in exchange for what? If she agreed to comply, she could hopefully get Peter and Bryson freed. She needed a guarantee.

She wrote her response. "I agree, provided you release Bryson and Peter Reynolds."

"I'm afraid I can do that only after I've had a chance to do some programming on Bryson."

Bryson looked at her; his eyes and voice pleaded. "No! Serena, it's not worth it. Don't do it! Don't do it, girlfriend!"

But she had a different plan. She looked at Bryson, locked eyes, and shook her head slowly. Serena wrote two words on the notepad: "I surrender."

Before closing her eyes, she saw Li's head nodding as a victory smile exposed his yellow teeth. The attack by BB must have damaged muscles beneath the facial scars. As Li's lips curled, in the dim light of the room, Li's smile contorted his pockmarked face. His visage became the face of all that she opposed. In Serena's mind, that crooked face displayed truth distorted and twisted over centuries into the ugly reality sitting in front of her. No more!

With her eyes shut, she focused and entered her zone. All her training, all her concentration and discipline required her to block out the room and go within. She started a twelve-breath Merkaba meditation.

Serena neither saw nor heard the two guards collapse by the door and thrash on the floor. Pandemonium erupted in the room. Oblivious, she continued her breaths. Behind the tape sealing her lips shut, she began to hum. Serena visualized the seven words, the seven sounds, the seven color sequences of unbinding. She felt her chakra energy centers expand. Her spine, head, and limbs reached downward, upward, and outward. The bliss of infinity called as she perceived the seven stepping-stones to ascension. She knew her body illuminated, first in a soft glow, then with an increasing intensity of light.

She floated over her body in detached awareness. The overhead lights in the room blinked off. She heard a faint click, and the room lights came back on.

Li was shouting. He had his sunglasses on. Bryson said something about their systems going down. Bits and fragments of words momentarily entered then left her consciousness like dust particles meandering in a shaft of sunlight: generator backup…building on lockdown…you're done for, Li.

Deep in her meditation, everything came to her senses through some surreal time warp. She could see each chakra vortex swirling in a colored rainbow of light within her own light body. She heard Li screaming to Wán shàn, "Make her stop!" The girl just stood there. Li cowered on the floor, trying to shield his eyes and body from Serena's bright light.

She could hear something in Chinese. Serena watched Peter Reynolds get up from his chair. Uncle Peter had his hands around her neck. Bryson was screaming. Serena floated above them all. She looked down at her own body. A dim recognition came into her conscious awareness. *I am ascending.*

Serena had already finished the fifth words: "OLM INRANFR TAEBN-PEM Reven NVINAPIMLIFINIPI NIPIAN." These were very difficult to sing, but not so very difficult to hum. The colors danced in her mind.

Choking disrupted her meditation. Suddenly, she could see Wán shàn jump forward. The girl flew through the air in slow motion and landed a powerful kick to Peter's head. He fell, immobile on the ground.

Serena watched it all, her awareness perched above her physical body.

Li shouted, "What are you doing, daughter?" He looked to be in pain and extreme distress.

The young woman placed her hands upon Serena's bald head. "Look at her, bàba. She is so much more perfect than I. She is filled with light. She is perfect in ways I can never be."

As Serena's focus shifted for a moment, she saw Wán shàn unscrew the top to a small glass tube. The girl said to her bàba, "MY CHOICE! A mercy killing for me and for my sisters." She drank the contents of the tube.

Li shouted out a series of commands to the young woman. Her hands inched down from Serena's head to her neck then stopped. Paralysis overcame Wán shàn; she stood fixed with one hand upon Serena's throat. To Serena, it almost felt like a gentle caress.

No mind. No mind at all. Humming the progression of notes, visualizing the colors, Serena finished the sixth words: "EVPMIRNA ENVPMTI EPNMPIR VRVIVINRN APVI MERI PIVNIAN NTRHN." A great light seemed to open above her. The light ran through her, through her body, extending from the floor to the earth below. She knew because she could see this brilliant light in her and through her. She saw herself floating both outside the building and inside the room at the same time. She stood poised between heaven and earth.

Serena took a deep breath, or at least her physical body did. Her light body did not need to breathe. The final words sang in her mind: "NBIMEI ANNEIPERFMIVIFVE." She paused on the threshold of infinity. Her physical body looked so small and insignificant.

An explosion jarred Serena but just for a moment. The door to the room splintered. Men poured in. *Who are these men?* she wondered as she drifted in bliss.

She saw Dr. Li's body curled in a heap way below. *To live in the light. Isn't that what they have claimed to always want? It is glorious to live in the light. I want to be in the light, forever…*

88

Tarni got the word through her ear comm: Room 16-403. She wrestled through the crowd to a stairwell. Winded and panting, she gasped in disbelief. She was the last of the team to get there. The hallways had emergency lighting, but this room was super well lit.

Claus stood over Peter Reynolds, sprawled on the ground with a rolled jacket supporting his neck. The entire right side of Peter's face looked swollen and disfigured, but he was alive and talking.

Li, or so she guessed, lay crumbled on the floor. Pockmarks littered the gray skin of his face. He looked very dead.

The young Asian girl working for Li, the one with a chimeric hybrid DNA, stood in some weird crouch with her hand held up as though she was trying to grasp something. The girl looked like a wax-museum statue positioned in some strange battle posture. Her lips had drawn back over perfect white teeth. A happy-faced grin made the girl's dead body look even more bizarre.

Tarni muscled her way to Bryson; he leaned over Serena and stroked her hand. She was the source for the bright light!

"C'mon, PTG…time to come back. We need you down here… There's still work to do."

The rest of the team just stood there gawking. *Probably never seen a body in full illumination. Damn, she is bright!*

Tarni could see that Serena's eyes were closed. The slow, deep breaths indicated deep relaxation. She picked up Serena's other hand and gave a squeeze.

"What's going on here, Bry?"

"Tarni, good to see you." He gave her a quick peck on the cheek. "Don't know. She's been in this in-between state for a good seven or eight minutes. I think she's trying to decide between returning down to earth or making the final ascent. I'm trying to coax her back."

"That's not happening. She can't bail out now. Party's just getting started." Tarni stood up and gesticulated with her hands, waving her arms wildly in the air over Serena's body. She began to shout, "SERENA…SERENA! HEY, SLEEPING BEAUTY, WAKE UP!"

Tarni saw Serena's breathing get a little shallower. She pushed Bryson aside, shook Serena, and leaned forward. Despite a hoarse voice, she yelled right into Serena's face. "HEY, GIRLFRIEND, WATCH THIS!"

Tarni straightened, grabbed Bryson, and nearly picked him off his feet by his shirt collar. She planted her perfect lips over Bryson's and gave a long, deeply passionate kiss.

Bryson didn't seem to mind. He managed to blurt, "It's good to see to see you too, Tarni."

A second deep and passionate kiss followed. Tarni alternated between tongue-lashing Serena, enjoining her to come back down, and thrusting her tongue into Bryson's receptive mouth in an ongoing public display. Serena's illumination began to subside. Bryson and Tarni continued the show. Everyone stood by, unclear what to do or what to say.

Tarni switched tactics. She released Bryson. "I've been holding back on you, Serena." She put both hands on Serena's glowing cheeks and locked lips.

Bryson looked dumbfounded. As Tarni knelt next to Serena, she added, "I've never pashed with another girl before, but there's more where that came from if you would just come back. We won! Come down so we can piss up and have some fun."

Serena's eyes fluttered. Her voice startled them all. "Hey, girlfriend, we agreed to share!" Tarni felt Serena's playful nudge and watched as Sleeping Beauty jumped up from her chair and attached herself to Bryson, her legs resting over each of his hips and her mouth joined to his. A moment later, she said to everyone, "I was planning to come back, I just lost track of time."

Jeremiah said, "That was some show you put on, Serena." He turned to Tarni. "You too. Anymore kisses left in there, and I'll be first in line." Jeremiah finished by shaking Bryson's hand. "I don't know how you managed it, Bryson, but it looks like you got heaven right here on earth."

A moment later, Serena touched the ground, but just long enough to jump over to Tarni. "Couldn't bear the thought of leaving you behind either." She whispered into Tarni's ear, "I've never had a pash like that, girlfriend!" Serena giggled as she hugged Tarni, nearly toppling them both. Tarni tried to laugh, but Serena squeezed her so tightly that barely a squeak came out.

High fives, fist bumps, hugs, and kisses followed until Claus finally brought them all back down to earth. "Party time's over. We need to clear out before people start asking questions."

Team members left in groups of two in order to blend in with the demonstrators still occupying the building. Serena, Tarni, and Bryson were the last to leave. Serena placed a jacket over Wán shàn's body. The death smile on the young girl's face conveyed a strange sense of peace. Tarni watched as Serena bent over and gave Wán shàn a tender kiss on the head. "You are a brave warrior, little sister."

89

B ack in Chicago at Peter Reynolds' home, they enjoyed stories, food, and fellowship. Claus had hooked up Peter to the optogenic programming equipment captured in Dulce. The reset protocol essentially wiped clean all the neural links Li had established.

Claus explained it: "Not much different than hitting the refresh button on your screen saver; although, boss's memory is a little sketchy about what happened in Singapore. That could be the blow to the head he got. That girl was small, but she packed a wallop."

Serena was quiet. She had been the whole time back. She sat in yoga position, staring at a candle, watching the flame dance amid microcurrents of air.

Bryson approached. "Are you sure, PTG? I'm just checking one last time on your decision." Bryson rubbed the fuzz on her head. "Australian outback?"

She nodded a big yes. "Bry, I've been a few places in the last year and a half. Places I never dreamed I would ever go to. I love them all, but the place that calls to me is Australia. It's raw, it's beautiful, the people are wonderful. What else can I say?"

"Claus said to thank you for the invite, but he's staying to do some fly-fishing up by his cabin."

As if on cue, Claus appeared next to them. "All catch and release. I just need to get away for a good long spell."

"Same here, Claus. I need to get away…far away." Serena gave him a peck on the cheek. "We'll keep in touch."

He asked, "What do you plan to do down under? Head out to the bush?"

"No special agenda, Claus. Tarni wants to take us around, meet her people. I promised Djalu I'd join him on a walkabout."

Bryson chimed in. "I want to wander around until I run into Gurumarra, the Wanderer. Maybe he can give us some tips on traversing the two planes of matter and spirit."

"And the world? You think it can manage to spin in the right direction?"

"I think so, Claus. Some people are ready to ascend, they've now got an easy way to move on. Many aren't ready; in time they will get there. Many need to stay behind to re-vision and build a new world. The hard work isn't going to get done by you and me. It's the thousands and millions of ordinary people reaching out to fully be what's inside them already. It may take a few generations, but we'll get there. We cut off the head of the snake. I'm optimistic about what will follow."

She gazed out the window. A heavy downpour had just finished, and shafts of sunlight broke through the rain clouds. Serena pointed. "Look, a double rainbow!"

Arts Earth Radio Program:

Our next guest is music phenom, Arnbjørn Gnadir. This Danish musician, affectionately known as Arnie, is the first recording artist ever to have four songs among the top five continuously for eleven weeks ongoing. In the number one spot, 'Siren's Song—A Call to the Light,' is the most listened-to recording of all time.

The featured female vocalist on all his recordings remains anonymous, and her whereabouts are unknown. Her voice has been described as hauntingly angelic. A spokesperson for these two artists assures that all donations for their work go to the Temple of Hygeia in Greece, a charity whose mission is to heal, and to the Naga Sanctuary in India, dedicated to the preservation of truth.

First, we turn to news from around the globe…

Ministers representing the League for World Peace and Reconciliation have announced their five-year Harmony Plan. Leaders worldwide expect the plan to receive unanimous approval.

The veritable earthquake following the release and unexpected revelations associated with the Illuminati Secret Society continues with aftershocks and new information about their foiled plans to establish a New World Order. The last remaining family head from the so-called Council of Thirteen, Damiaan Van Duyn, has been apprehended and will join his fellow brethren, currently in custody.

In Southern Australia, ground observatories recorded an unusually bright and colorful Aurora Australis, punctuated by a dancing display of white orbs. Scientists have no explanation for this phenomenon.

Stay tuned for our interview with Arnbjørn Gnadir. He'll be performing at the newly renamed Candelaria Stadium in Tenerife during the upcoming Luminarian Festival. All proceeds from that concert go to the Pyramids of Güímar restoration project.
You're listening to Arts Earth, a production of the Pyramid Communications Network—The Voice of Truth.

The End

ACKNOWLEDGMENTS

Writing a book is a significant undertaking. Many people have assisted me with the creation of the two books that comprise The Saga of Venom and Flame series. I want to thank my wife, family, and friends for their support and encouragement.

Many wisdom teachers, Luminarians, guardians of truth, researchers, educators, and fellow seekers have guided me in the telling of this story. I am inspired by and grateful for their help.

Special thanks to my publishers, Joni and Vern Firestone, and the fine staff at BHC Press for their expertise in bringing this book forward to publication. I am especially grateful to my editors, Tori Ladd and Samantha Stenzel, for their meticulous review of the manuscript and editorial suggestions. I also wish to thank my publicist, Meryl Moss, and her wonderful team at Meryl Moss Media Group.

Finally, I want to express my gratitude to all the readers of this novel.

ABOUT THE AUTHOR

Victor Acquista is the author of The Saga of Venom and Flame duology. He enjoys writing in many genres and exploring thought-provoking themes.

He is a member of the Authors Guild, the Mystery Writers of America, the International Thriller Writers, and the Florida Writers Association.

When not pondering the big questions in life and what's for dinner, he enjoys gardening and cooking. He lives with his wife in Ave Maria, Florida.

9 781643 972312